'I have never held a Norman maid till now.'

'And I was never in any man's arms till now.' The telltale words slipped out before Beatrice had time to snatch them back. She could have groaned aloud.

An insistent tug on her plait drew her face round, and forced her to meet those searching blue eyes.

'Never been in any man's arms? A pretty maid like you. Now I know for certain that the Normans are mad,' Edmund declared.

Beatrice tried to toss her head, but the captured braid had her anchored fast. 'I have lived a cloistered life. I have no knowledge of Saxon convents, but in Normandy there are not too many men in them. At least none who would...' She struggled in vain to free her hair. 'Oh, Edmund, please release me!'

Her plea was ignored. 'Tell me, Mistress Beatrice who-has-never-been-held-by-a-man, have you ever been kissed?'

Beatrice made a choking sound and managed at last to look away. She burned all over.

Edmund had not finished tormenting her. 'Because if you have not, I would like to remedy that omission,' he announced coolly.

Carol Townend is a Yorkshire woman whose nineteenth-century forebears were friendly with the Brontë sisters. Perhaps this fact had something to do with the passion for the past that led her to a history degree at London University, and on, eventually, to writing historical novels.

Widely travelled, Carol Townend has explored places as diverse as North America and Sri Lanka, Mexico and the Mediterranean. When not taking refuge from the modern world by reading historical novels or writing her own, she loves to escape to the deep countryside.

Born in 1953, Carol Townend lives with her copywriter husand and young daughter near Kew Gardens.

Previous Title

SHATTERED VOWS

SAPPHIRE
IN THE SNOW

Carol Townend

MILLS & BOON LIMITED
ETON HOUSE   18-24 PARADISE ROAD
RICHMOND   SURREY   TW9 1SR

First published in Great Britain 1989 by Mills & Boon Limited

© Carol Townend 1989

Australian copyright 1989 Philippine copyright 1989 This edition 1989

ISBN 0 263 76667 5

Masquerade is a trademark published by Mills & Boon Limited, Eton House, 18–24 Paradise Road, Richmond, Surrey TW9 1SR

Set in Times Roman 10 on 10 pt. 04-8912-87474 C

Made and printed in Great Britain

CHAPTER ONE

Caen, Normandy. The Year of Our Lord 1066

'NAY, Mother Adèle! I beg of you, do not do this! Do not send me away!' A suggestion of a tear hovered for a moment in the corner of one of Beatrice's hazel eyes.

'Now, my dear, no tears,' admonished the elderly Prioress gently, but a suspicious brightness in her own eyes matched that in the young girl's.

It was December. The small, sparsely furnished cell was icy. A narrow pallet with a straw mattress was covered by a neatly folded grey blanket of the coarsest wool. The only concession to Mother Adèle's high status was the painted crucifix which hung on the cracked plaster over her bed.

Someone was chopping logs outside. The sound floated in through an unglazed window slit. The women's breath made little smoky clouds in the air which hovered for an instant, and then vanished, snuffed out almost as soon as they were formed by the invasive cold.

A blistering chill came up from the stone floor and penetrated the women's thin leather shoes. But, standing there in the chamber, they were both too distressed to pay any heed to this discomfort.

'But I don't want to go. I'd much rather stay. Who will help Sister Agnes in the new infirmary?' Beatrice protested, her usually melodious voice a shade higher than usual, and threatening to crack. She did not want to leave the convent at La Trinité and go to England— all the way to England—with her cousin. She loved the Abbaye aux Dames, it was the only home she could remember. Her cousin was a stranger and she had no desire to leave on the whim of a stranger.

'Nonsense!' Mother Adèle replied briskly, but warmly, for she had grown very fond of Beatrice in the years the girl had sheltered at the convent. 'Your cousin, Lady Anne, has need of you, and Sister Agnes will have to learn to manage without you. One of the new novices will soon learn to help her.'

Beatrice Giffard was gently bred, and God had blessed her with the gift of healing. Even as a child her skill had manifested itself. The Prioress recalled with a shudder the legions of small, sick creatures that Beatrice had packed into the cloisters. Not that she'd confined her nursing activities to the walkway—she'd even been known to use the chapel.

There had been that spring evening when the child decided to bring into that sacred place the convent's entire flock of motherless lambs. To the small auburn-haired girl the phrase 'Lamb of God' had meant that these lambs would be best cared for where God lived. Interrupted in full voice in the middle of the evening office of Compline, the nuns were struck dumb with astonishment as the lambs were shepherded in.

Discordant bleating had filled the space where the sisters' serene chanting had been. The flock had ignored Beatrice and her frantic, inexpert shepherding. Refusing to be corralled at the west end, the lambs had indulged in vigorous head-butting. And the nuns' well-ordered service had disintegrated into a scene which bore more resemblance to chaos than evening worship.

Other, similar incidents sprang to mind. There was the toad in the refectory that had hopped with such disastrous consequences into Sister Maud's pottage; the piglet Beatrice had kept hidden in the scriptorium, who had eaten his way through the Old Testament because she had forgotten to go and feed him...

But now young Beatrice was sixteen. She had been trained to direct her nurturing instincts into more acceptable channels, and Sister Agnes had indeed come to rely on her, not that the Prioress would dream of swelling the child's head by telling her this. Beatrice had spent the greater part of her life within the convent walls and had tried hard to fit into the unrelenting regime. She had even announced her intention of becoming a nun, saying that her mother had wished this for her. Mother Adèle was doubtful if Beatrice was suited to a life of contemplation, but she would miss the girl. And though the convent would be more peaceful without her, she doubted if it would be as happy.

Beatrice sniffed loudly. 'I'll be back, Mother. As soon as Anne is settled, I'll be back. And then you'll permit me to enter the noviciate, won't you?'

'My dear, you need to experience the world outside our convent gates,' the Prioress replied tactfully. 'You cannot decide to withdraw from the world until you've spent some time in that world.'

Beatrice's mouth set in stubborn lines. 'I know I'll hate it. My cousin is so grand in all her fine clothes. She frightens me. She's unlike anyone I've ever known. I hardly know her. I've only spoken to her once, and then for only half an hour. We have nothing in common. What will we talk about?'

'Anne is only a year older than you,' the Prioress pointed out. 'And as for her clothes, you know as well as I, Beatrice, that they are but worldly vanities. They are of no consequence.'

'But she's been married, and widowed and...oh, Mother, you know what I'm trying to say. Her life has been so different from mine. How can I possibly ever help *her*?'

The Prioress's soft sigh was almost inaudible. 'Nevertheless,' she spoke in rallying tones, 'your cousin is the Lady Anne de Vidâmes. She has requested that you accompany her to England. The good Lord knows she has money enough to pay for whomsoever she likes as a companion. But she has chosen you. She wants your company because you are one of her family. You cannot let her down.

'Consider it from her standpoint, Beatrice. The poor girl has been commanded to marry a Saxon Thegn she has never met, in a country she has never even set foot in. You cannot deny her the solace of your company.'

The calm voice took on an authoritative edge. 'If the Lady Anne can do her duty and obey Duke William's wishes in this, then you will do your duty too and bear your cousin company. Lady Anne's father, Comte Geoffrey de Vidâmes, is with Duke William in England.

He has given his approval to the plan. He is your uncle and your remaining male relative. You must obey him.'

'Aye, Mother.' Beatrice capitulated, her auburn head bowed in submission.

'Good girl. I have decided you may take one of the mares from the stable. You will need a mount of your own. Which one will you choose?' asked the Prioress, permitting a half-smile to soften her austere features.

The bright head lifted. 'Oh!' Beatrice gazed wide-eyed at the older woman. 'May I take Betony? May I? My thanks, Mother. I will take care of her and bring her back safely, I promise.' Impulsively she flung her arms about the Prioress and hugged her.

'Enough, Beatrice! Pray, try for some decorum!' Mother Adèle objected, blinking rather hard. 'You will need another overdress. I have nothing as fine as your cousin's, but please take this. 'Tis a simple gown, but the cloth is good, and 'tis almost new. It belonged to one of the novices who joined us on St Stephen's Day, and as she's now wearing the habit of a novice she won't need it again.'

Beatrice fingered the red cloth. It felt like silk by comparison with the coarse homespun she had worn at the convent. She was aware that its colour would clash dreadfully with her hair, but she pushed the ungrateful thought aside. ''Tis soft as thistledown,' she acknowledged. 'My thanks. I only hope I don't tear it.'

She met the nun's calm grey eyes and noticed to her surprise that they were swimming with unshed tears. This, more than anything, brought home to Beatrice how close she was to leaving the nunnery. Her throat closed up. 'Oh, Mother, I shall miss everything so much,' she got out, the tears welling over.

'Nay, Beatrice. You'll be far too busy, you'll see. You'd best hurry now, and pack that gown with your things. Betony is already saddled up for you.'

'You knew I'd choose her, then?' Beatrice sniffed, rubbing her moist eyes with the back of her hand and swallowing hard.

'Aye. I'd have to have been blind not to know.' Mother Adèle smiled. 'I never had any doubts which mare you'd choose, and I've decided Walter is to go with you, too.

So you see, my dear, you won't be completely alone among new faces. Besides, it really is not right that Walter should stay in our convent now he is fully recovered.'

Beatrice opened her mouth, an objection hovering on her tongue.

'Nay, Beatrice,' Mother Adèle overruled her firmly. 'I'd far rather Walter was in your care than anyone else's. I know you won't take advantage of his...simple nature. I want you to take care of him, as much as I want him to protect you. I know you won't mock him for his disability. He is devoted to you, my dear, and I couldn't send you away completely unprotected. Your mother's bones would rise up from their grave.'

Blinking back tears, and squaring her shoulders, Beatrice managed a nod. She knew the Prioress disliked emotional scenes. 'Farewell, Mother Adèle. M-my thanks for everything. I'll be back, just you see,' she promised with a watery smile.

'And I bid you Godspeed, my child. Now begone, before you have me weeping in earnest.'

Clumsily, Beatrice embraced the nun. Then she turned and stumbled from the chamber.

Mother Adèle stared blindly at the door for a moment after the girl had gone. She shivered. The wintry blast from the window gnawed at every bone in her body. She hugged herself, and rubbed her arms vigorously with her hands. They were blue with cold, the joints stiff and gnarled. The winters grew harsher every year, and Mother Adèle had lived through many cold winters.

Suddenly she felt very old.

Beatrice gazed out across the thriving Norman seaport, conscious of a nervous excitement welling up within her like the rising tide. Water had always frightened her; she had never learnt to swim. But, God willing, she would never have to. She thrust this fear and her other misgivings to the back of her mind—she would not let her worries sour the day. From her vantage point, in the bows of the ship that was to take her to England, she could see it all.

Vessels of every conceivable shape and size thronged the quays, jostling each other as their cargoes were shifted. Crates and coffers passed from hand to hand. Endless lines of porters stretched out in every direction like tangled ribbons. Dark-skinned men from the east haggled with ships' captains. Idle mercenaries waited for troop ships, gambling away imaginary fortunes—fortunes they had yet to earn. Porters bawled. Horses clopped up wooden gangplanks and neighed ear-splitting protestations. The wheeling, shrieking gulls echoed them.

For Beatrice, with the smell of the sea in her nostrils and the sea breezes playing in her veil, the convent was suddenly a lifetime away. She lifted her head and glanced briefly at the sky. It was as grey as the foam-flecked waves.

Her hazel eyes dropped back to the hustle and bustle on the quayside below. They widened. A strange procession was bearing down on the ship. Beatrice recognised her cousin, Lady Anne, at once, though they had met but briefly. Her stomach tightened with nervousness.

Lady Anne sat proudly on a gleaming Spanish mare, leading the cavalcade. She looked every inch the noble-woman. Tongues stilled. All work ceased. The waterfront fell silent. And every eye upon it turned to watch Lady Anne's procession as it cut a swathe through the crowd.

The lady's glossy brown hair was neatly coiled and confined beneath a pale pink silk veil which floated out gracefully behind her on the onshore breeze. She wore a fur-lined cloak. Its rich wine-coloured fabric was clasped at the throat with what looked like a solid gold brooch, though, from her still distant standpoint, Beatrice could not be certain.

Apparently oblivious of the sensation she was causing, Lady Anne spurred on smilingly towards her ship. Beatrice saw Anne's cloak fall open. It revealed a mag-nificent gown, one or two shades lighter than the cloak. Even the leather of her riding boots had been dyed to match the cloak. Beatrice goggled. Lady Anne looked delightful on her prancing black mare, and she knew it. The varying and subtle shades of pink shrieked as loudly of Lady Anne's wealth and standing as did her haughty mien.

Beatrice smoothed down the simple robe which fought so disastrously with her auburn hair and grimaced ruefully. It had seemed so fine at the convent. And now...now it seemed hardly worth making it into dish clouts.

Lady Anne's jennet picked its way delicately through the debris of rotting fish and rubbish on the quayside. The lady's nostrils wrinkled. A fleeting expression of disgust marred the perfection of her proud features as the stench of decay assailed her. Beatrice bit her lip to stifle a giggle.

Behind Lady Anne, another woman of lofty demeanour struggled less successfully to hide her disgust. The woman's hand was pressed hard to her upturned nose, and she sat very stiffly on her mount. From the cut of her clothes, Beatrice judged the woman to be of lesser rank than Lady Anne. Probably her maid, and from the way her nose tilted skywards she had a high opinion of herself.

Behind the two women in the train were four mounted guards and several baggage mules. Could all those chests really belong to her cousin? Beatrice could not believe her eyes. Lady Anne had brought at least half a dozen mules—all heavily laden.

Lady Anne dismounted and ascended the gangplank. She paused halfway up to supervise the unloading of her belongings.

An unfortunate porter slipped on a fishhead and clutched wildly at his burden to save it. The Lady Anne's dark eyes closed, her face expressed such horror that Beatrice expected her to cross herself. Instead Lady Anne shook her head.

'Careful with that coffer, man!' she said in a carrying voice. 'I don't want months of embroidery spread all over the quayside.'

Lady Anne picked up her skirts and went aboard. Beatrice came forward and greeted her with a curtsy.

'Oh, Beatrice! Thank heavens you're here! You cannot imagine the trouble we've had getting here,' Lady Anne said at once. 'I would not have believed so short a journey could be so beset with disasters. Beset, I tell you. First of all, as you can see, there weren't enough mules...'

Beatrice was enfolded in a perfumed embrace.

'Not enough mules!' Beatrice protested. 'But, cousin, I saw six of them.'

'Exactly. When I specifically asked for nine! Still, one can't expect serfs to be able to count. I suppose I should be grateful we got here at all.' Lady Anne shrugged delicately and began to peel off her kid gloves. They, too, Beatrice noted, were dyed to match Lady Anne's ensemble.

'You do have rather a lot of baggage, my lady,' Beatrice commented.

'Oh, you must call me Anne, for heaven's sake. You're to be my friend,' her cousin insisted. 'Now, where was I? Ah, the baggage. Well, naturally I have a lot of it. One can't be expected to travel out to a wilderness without one's chattels. 'Twill serve to mark my real estate to the Saxons. I cannot have them thinking I am of little account.'

'I'm sure there's no danger of that, Anne.' Beatrice suppressed a grin.

'I should hope not!' Anne declared coolly. 'I don't want to bore you with the details, Beatrice, but my serfs are worse than useless. Did you see the way that one almost tossed my trunk into the sea?'

Correctly sensing that no answer was necessary, Beatrice held her tongue. Her cousin was still shaking her head with horror at the thought of her finery lying amid the fishscales. Then Anne brightened and her lustrous brown eyes grew thoughtful.

'Do you think that the serfs might be better trained in England? Nay. 'Tis not likely. They're a pack of barbarians. Maybe barbarians make better serfs, but I doubt it. That would be too much to expect. However, there are some blessings in life: you're here. 'Tis my dearest wish that we shall be friends.' Anne smiled.

'I hope so too,' Beatrice replied, truthfully. But she saw the critical way her cousin's eyes ran up and down her gown, and she knew what Anne was thinking.

Beatrice wanted to tell her cousin that she had not chosen the gown, that she knew it was awful, that it warred with her colouring, but she remembered how generous the Prioress had been. Pride and loyalty stilled her tongue.

Despite her hope that she and Anne could be friends, Beatrice was becoming very much aware that their different backgrounds had placed a barrier between them. She wondered if it could ever be surmounted.

The barrier was breached, however, almost as soon as the ship weighed anchor. For as soon as their vessel started to rise and fall on the heaving waves...

'Beatrice,' Anne moaned, 'I think I'm dying.'

And she did look ill. The Lady Anne hung over the ship's handrail, her fingers white on the coarse timber. Her flawless olive complexion had taken on an alarming pallor. Little pearls of sweat broke out on her brow and she hugged her stomach.

Before Beatrice could respond, a sharp elbow dug in her ribs, shoving her aside. It was the woman companion who had accompanied Anne on board ship.

'My lady, what is it?' the woman asked solicitously. She cocked a jealous eye at Beatrice.

She was Anne's personal maidservant, there was no doubt of it. Her dark eyes flashed malevolently, warning Beatrice off her charge.

'Oh, Ella,' Anne groaned. 'I'm going to be ill.'

Ella's honeyed smile slipped. Sickness always defeated her. Her antagonism fell away, she blenched, and relinquished her position by her ailing mistress.

'Oh, my lady. You know I'm not trained to cope with the sick,' the maid excused herself, her voice becoming a whine. This time, the glance the maidservant shot at Beatrice was tempered with pleading.

Beatrice did not hesitate. ''Tis all right, Ella. I know what to do. You may go. Would you please make sure that your lady's horse is safely stowed next to mine? If you have any problems, ask my man, Walter, to help you.'

Deftly, Beatrice removed Anne's veil and golden circlet. She held back her cousin's thick brown hair and

murmured soothing words. Then, when the paroxysms
of seasickness had abated, she sat her cousin down under
the leather awning that was to be their only protection
against the salt sea-spray and the cutting wind, and supported her, gently mopping her brow.

Suddenly her grand cousin was not so very unlike
herself. The Lady Anne de Vidâmes was but a girl, a
girl being sent to a strange land as she herself was, a
pawn in someone else's game.

When Anne turned dull brown eyes gratefully to
Beatrice and forced a weak smile, Beatrice realised that
the barriers had begun to come down. Though the
cousins had come from very different backgrounds, there
were similarities. They needed each other. She now knew
that they would be friends.

'My thanks, cousin. Already you are becoming indis-
pensable to me,' Anne murmured, uncannily echoing
Beatrice's thoughts. 'I don't know what I would have
done without you.'

The tenuous bond deepened as their vessel forged its
way across the Channel under the pressure of a slashing
wind on the great square sail. Beatrice's sophisticated
cousin had proved to be human. The naïve convent girl
found herself laughing and talking to her aristocratic
cousin with a degree of ease she would never have
dreamed possible.

The ship creaked and groaned across the rolling sea—
a beast running a race with the winds. The awning above
their heads flapped like the wings of a great bird beating
time for the beast. The grey leagues flowed past them,
the wind held. And their native country became, first,
a thin charcoal line dividing grey skies from grey sea—
then there was no line at all.

Pevensey! England! They had arrived. Beatrice had not
once worried about her fear of water. Anne took one
look at the solid, unmoving land and was reborn. Her
brown eyes sparkled. Her colour returned, her cheeks
were tinted with a soft flush.

'Thank God there's no rain,' Anne commented.

'Aye. Look, Anne, the sun will break through that
cloudbank at any moment.' Beatrice pointed.

'Oh, we must hurry!' Anne cried, putting her hand to her uncovered head. 'My veil!' she wailed. 'I cannot let our escort see me looking like a peasant. Where's Ella got to? Oh, never mind. Beatrice, you can help me. Where did you put my circlet?'

Somewhat bemused by her cousin's feverish haste, Beatrice gestured at the back of the shelter. 'It must have rolled to the back,' she told her.

Anne dived under the awning, and scrabbled about like a mad thing. 'Can you see our escort yet?' Anne's voice came out muffled.

Beatrice smoothed down her gown, uncomfortably aware that no amount of preening would improve *her* appearance. 'I'm not sure,' she answered, peering across the beach. The sun poked round a cloud the colour of pewter. 'There's a group of horsemen galloping this way from the fort. They look as though they might be soldiers. Aye. 'Tis our escort. I can see mailcoats reflecting the light.'

Anne emerged from behind the leather curtain, and came to stand at her side. Breathless, but immaculate. 'There! How do I look?' she demanded.

Beatrice saw Anne's gaze wander casually over to the Norman horse-soldiers. Her cousin stiffened, stared. And, unexpectedly, Anne gave a dazzling smile.

'You look completely recovered,' Beatrice reassured her. 'In fact, I've never seen you looking so radiant. Your Saxon Thegn will be delighted when he sees his beautiful wife.'

Anne's face closed up and Beatrice realised that she had blundered. But how? Of course, that must be it—Anne was nervous. After all, Anne had not even met the man she was being sent to marry—to *marry*.

Duke William of Normandy had now become King of England. Mother Adèle had told Beatrice that he had been crowned on Christmas Day. It was January now, and King William was determined to tighten his grip on his new domain. By marriage, if possible, wedding loyal Normans to the local nobility. But if resistance to his rule was strong, then King William would resort to force of arms. Already he had shown the Saxon people that any resistance to Norman rule would be mercilessly put down. The King had proved himself a strong, able man, who was intolerant of any opposition.

Aiden, Saxon Thegn of Lindsey, Anne's betrothed, had soon realised that his interests, and the interests of his people, would be best served by an alliance with the new Norman overlord. Beatrice knew very little about Anne's future husband, except that his name was Aiden and that he was a Saxon lord. Even Anne admitted that she had not been told whether her betrothed was nineteen or ninety.

'I pray that he's not old and stooped like Charles, my first husband,' Anne confessed as the ship glided into the shallows.

'He might be young and strong, and handsome, and you might fall in love with him at once,' Beatrice replied lightly.

'I doubt it. In one sense it might be better if he is old,' Anne said.

Beatrice frowned. 'What?'

'At least there's a chance he'd ... leave me alone then. 'Twas bad enough being pawed by Charles, but at least he was a Norman. Sweet Jesu! I never thought the day would dawn when I'd regard my mockery of a marriage with that hideous old man as a pleasant interlude. But now I'm to let some ... some Saxon clod touch me with his filthy hands and——' Anne noticed the dawning horror on her cousin's face and stopped abruptly.

Beatrice swallowed. She put her hand on her cousin's arm. 'Oh, Anne, I never thought you felt like that,' she said.

'Don't let's talk about it now,' Anne begged. Her brown eyes turned once more towards their Norman escort and came to rest on their leader. He had dismounted and waited for them at the foot of the gangway. 'Thank God there's no sign of the Saxons yet. We can worry about them when we see them. When we get to...' Anne frowned. 'Beatrice, what's the name of the place?'

'Lindsey. 'Tis a long way north,' Beatrice informed her.

'Aye, aye, Lindsey. Come along, Beatrice, we mustn't keep our escort waiting,' Anne said impatiently. She smiled brightly, pretty and vivacious.

Shrugging her shoulders at her cousin's unpredictable changes of mood, Beatrice hurried after her.

Anne walked too quickly down the wooden boards, and her foot must have caught on one of the slats, for she suddenly tripped and went flying.

Beatrice caught her breath, certain her cousin was in for a soaking. She herself was too far behind Anne to break her fall. She need not have worried. The Norman officer was there in a flash and caught her cousin almost before she had tripped.

'My lady, permit me to assist you,' he said, Anne already fast in his arms.

Beatrice gaped at the way the officer held her cousin and carried her close to his chest to dry land.

Anne appeared unperturbed by the familiar manner in which the Norman officer was handling her. She had even put an arm about the man's neck. Beatrice felt shocked, but whether she was more shocked at the Norman's presumption or her cousin's response, she could not tell.

The officer set Anne down at last and stared at her, openly admiring.

Anne gave a shaky laugh. 'So we meet again, Baron,' she said. She sounded shy, almost uncertain.

'The pleasure is all mine, Lady Anne,' the soldier drawled, kissing her hand.

While this exchange was taking place, Beatrice was able to take stock of the Baron. He was big and powerful. Built like a bull, he gave an impression of unstoppable strength. This was emphasised by the heavy mailcoat that he wore. He had flung back his mail hood, and Beatrice saw his hair was dark, closely cropped above his ears in the Norman fashion. His skin was swarthy. He had coal-dark eyes which were riveted on her cousin.

Belatedly, Anne remembered Beatrice. 'Baron, this is my cousin, Beatrice Giffard, who has kindly agreed to accompany me to...to...'

'Lindsey,' hissed Beatrice, rolling her eyes at her cousin's obtuseness.

'Of course. Lindsey. Thank you, cousin. Beatrice, this is an old acquaintance of mine, the Baron Philip de Brionne. I trust, Baron, that you are to be our escort.'

'I am, my lady,' the Baron confirmed in a curt voice. Anne smiled, and the Baron turned to acknowledge Beatrice.

His dark eyes were cold now. Beatrice shuddered as they flickered over her. He bowed slightly, so slightly that the gesture was almost an insult. 'My lady.'

Beatrice did not like him. His harsh features wore the weary cynicism of the professional soldier, and for some reason he frightened her. His mouth was thin-lipped. She could not imagine him smiling. Nor did she like the way he looked her up and down. No one had ever looked at her like that. She felt as though his glance was enough to contaminate her. She shifted uncomfortably and flushed, and her skin crawled.

The Baron saw her redden and he smiled. So he could smile. But it was not a pleasant sight. It was more of a sneer than a smile. A ruthless man. Beatrice could not say how she knew this, but she was positive she had read him aright.

'I'm glad you'll be here to protect us, Baron,' Anne was saying.

Philip de Brionne's harsh gaze was centred once more on Anne, and Beatrice could breathe again. She fancied that those tight lips softened fractionally.

'I am delighted to be able to serve you, my lady, in whatever way I can,' the Norman replied with polished courtesy.

The Baron had not struck Beatrice as a man given to flattery, but Anne accepted his glib words as though they were her due. Probably that was how people spoke in polite society, 'worldly people' as Mother Adèle would have phrased it. Beatrice felt very ignorant. She knew herself to be out of her depth, and suddenly she felt very alone.

'The wind is chill,' de Brionne announced. 'You'd be best advised to wait in this house while my men unload your horses and baggage. This way, my lady.'

The two girls could see a ruined stone fort atop the rise which dominated the shoreline. It was quite obviously an ancient and much neglected building, but attempts had been made—and recently—to fortify it. The new earthworks, a bank and a ditch, scarred the landscape, and a lonely sentry stood at his post, guarding the refurbished barracks for his Norman compatriots.

De Brionne had forgotten Beatrice, and she was conscious of a vague feeling of relief that her cousin should command all of his attention.

'You call this a house,' Anne said scathingly, eyeing the simple wooden dwelling that was set in the lee of the fort. The thatch had recently been burned and was in dire need of repair.

'I grant you it's seen better days,' the Baron agreed, 'but 'tis the best I can offer. I'm afraid it suffered when our troops first landed. However, the walls are still standing, and they will protect you from the wind. We won't be long unloading and then we can start our journey,' he said.

'I see you're eager to thrust me into Saxon hands, Baron,' Anne said sharply.

Affecting to adjust her cloak, Beatrice frowned. There were undercurrents here which she could not fathom.

'Not at all, my lady,' the Baron denied swiftly. 'These winter days are short, and we have some miles to cover before we can make camp for the night. And in any case, my orders are to see you wed, and then to oversee the running of the Saxon's lands.'

Anne's voice took on an eager note. 'You'll stay on at Lindsey, then, after the wedding?'

'Aye, my lady.'

Anne sighed and relaxed. Then, seeing Beatrice's curious glance, she explained. 'I'll be glad of another Norman face. I don't relish the idea of being left alone with a bunch of Saxon savages! Especially if you persist in your idea of retiring to the convent.'

'I'm certain they won't be savages, Anne. Mother Adèle told me they have a strong and ancient culture. And your betrothed is a Thegn,' Beatrice said, diplomatically.

She was aware that the Baron shot her a strange glance, but his thin lips only pursed.

'Oh, ignore Beatrice, Baron! She's lived in a convent all her life. She is practically a nun! She has all these strange ideas about loving one's neighbour. Forgive her. She'll soon learn.'

Philip de Brionne's eyes raked Beatrice from head to toe. Beatrice bristled. The sun hid behind the cloudbank.

'I wonder who'll have the pleasure of teaching her,' de Brionne drawled.

Beatrice bit her lip, knowing he was not referring to her ignorance of the Saxon culture. She hoped she was not blushing again. She did not like Baron Philip de Brionne at all. She never would. But her feelings were unimportant; it was Lady Anne who mattered now. It was her cousin who was to marry the Saxon Thegn, and Anne was clearly delighted with the Norman escort she had been allocated.

Watching Anne's reanimated face, Beatrice decided the Baron could not be all bad to have had such a startling effect on her cousin. If Anne was pleased to have his company on the journey to Lindsey, that was good enough for her. She might not like him, but he was strong. More than strong enough to protect them should the need arise.

Beatrice looked out along the cold grey beach to the rough, unfriendly country beyond. The Baron made her protector, Walter, seem a puny runt. The Norman was clearly a highly capable and efficient soldier. And who was Beatrice to complain, when the King himself had chosen their escort?

CHAPTER TWO

THE ride from Pevensey to Lindsey seemed interminable. If it had not been for Anne's vivacity and obvious happiness, Beatrice would have objected to the snail's pace imposed on her. Their speed was fixed by Anne's baggage mules, and these overladen beasts lumbered wearily along rutted roads beneath the numerous trunks and chests Anne had piled on them. At the rate they were going, it would take a year to reach Lindsey.

It irked Beatrice to ride so slowly. She could see it irked the Baron's black war-horse, too. The brute was so restless it snapped and bit at any other horse which strayed within reach of its champing jaws. Even the Baron was having difficulty holding him back.

Beatrice chafed her chapped hands. Perhaps the Baron had his reasons for delaying. Perhaps he was giving Anne time to adjust to her future role. Beatrice could think of no other explanation. She, too, hoped her cousin was coming to terms with what lay ahead, for if she was not, then heaven help them all!

The harsh weather made things worse. Her hands went red, then blue. She found it difficult to hold Betony's reins. They did not possess such things as gloves at the convent—she simply had to manage without. She knew that Anne had gloves to match every gown, but Anne was too taken up with her escort, and had not thought to offer them. Beatrice did not like to ask.

If only she could have a good gallop along the track. That would set her circulation going again. Her blood felt as though it had frozen into a solid lump in her veins. She could hardly move her fingers.

But the gallop Beatrice longed for was denied her. She had to plod on, freezing mile after freezing and unbearable mile. Days passed in this manner, until Beatrice had given up all hope of their ever reaching their destination. It seemed they were doomed to ride forever. And none but she showed the slightest concern about the length of time their journey was taking.

She roused herself to take stock of the land they rode through. The land King William had conquered.

Their path wound now through a frosted fenland world. There were pools of water whose depths were hidden by layers of ice. Reeds stood tall as sentries, encrusted with tiny water crystals. They guarded frozen lakelets, ice armour glinting in the sunlight like the Norman soldiers' chain-mail. Wispy swirls of morning mist curled about the horse's hooves. In places it was difficult to distinguish between track and marsh. Their pace slowed almost to a halt. Wildfowl shrieked in alarm, warning the inhabitants of this watery world that their territory was being invaded. A queer place this, unearthly and eerie.

A shout floated back from the scout ahead of them. To Beatrice it meant nothing. Another icy ford to cross? A camp site for the night? Her numbed brain had not registered that it was barely past noon, and they would scarcely be stopping to set up camp at that hour.

Suddenly, Beatrice perceived a new tension in the air. Perhaps at last they had reached their destination? Pleased, she turned to Anne, but one look at her cousin's expression wiped the smile from her lips.

Anne's pretty face was taut and white as snow. The vivacity and charm she had demonstrated throughout the tedious journey had vanished as though it had never been.

Their party now skirted the eastern edge of a small lake, and ahead of them Beatrice could see the ground rising gently away from the sedge-filled lowland. Confronting the riders was a small copse. The path divided. De Brionne urged his horse along the steeper westbound path.

'Raoul!' he bawled.

'Baron?'

'Ride ahead to the settlement and announce the arrival of the Lady Anne de Vidâmes, future wife of the Thegn of Lindsey.'

Anne guided her mare closer to Beatrice.

'We...we've arrived.' Anne's voice was flat and dead. She sat stiffly on her mare, staring straight ahead at the tall wooden palisade which loomed up before them.

Beatrice felt her heart lurch. No one was smiling now. The atmosphere was charged, expectant. Their horse-soldiers no longer smiled and joked. Hands moved, and hovered over sword hilts. She did not need anyone to tell her that they were anticipating trouble.

Slowly, the Norman contingent approached the gate. It was open. As they clopped into the crowded compound the silence seemed to grow heavier, and Beatrice felt the oppressive weight of scores of eyes on them. It was a tangible thing now, that heavy silence, broken only by the horses' hooves and Beatrice's pounding heart.

Anne still stared straight in front of her. She looked every inch the proud Norman lady. She had not glanced at the watching Saxon crowd once.

Beatrice did not have such pride bred into her. The oppressive tension frightened her, but she was determined to look right into the heart of it. She could sense resentment lurking not so far beneath the apparently calm surface. None the less, she forced her nervous lips into a smile and gazed around, curious about her cousin's new home and people.

The compound was larger and more substantial than Beatrice had expected. Anne had told her that Saxon lords still built their houses of wood, not stone like their Norman counterparts. And indeed the buildings were for the most part wooden, but they were not the humble dwellings Beatrice had imagined. The most impressive building, presumably the Saxon hall, dominated the courtyard. It was large enough to hold an army. There was a stable, a barn or two, and Beatrice had time to glimpse several other wooden outbuildings within the palisade, as well as one made of stone. A carved cross above the lintel of this building proclaimed it to be the chapel.

It was no longer possible to ignore the strange and wild-looking crowd that stared at them with such hostility. Beatrice forced her gaze down to the Saxon people, seeking for a friendly face among them.

Some of the men boasted long, shaggy beards which turned their human faces into fierce unsmiling masks. Her eyes met curious ones, hostile ones, angry ones, but nowhere could she see a face which contained any hint of friendliness. Her heart plummeted.

In the centre of the yard the Baron and Anne sat firmly on their horses. De Brionne dismounted and faced the entrance to the hall where a reception committee was waiting.

Beatrice received a brief impression of wealth and splendour, for these men were better clad than their fellows. Gold and silver buckles gleamed. Tunics were bright, and richly decorated. Their cloaks were edged with fur.

A Saxon stepped forward to hold Anne's mare, and a finely clad figure moved to help her dismount. This must be Aiden of Lindsey. The Thegn was young. No old man for her cousin, then. He looked much the same age as Anne herself. He was tall and fair. His thick beard hid his expression like a visor, but Beatrice sensed he was nervous.

The Thegn bowed his head to Anne and murmured something to her which Beatrice could not catch.

'What did he say, Baron?' Anne queried in her most imperious manner, barely sparing the Saxon a glance.

Beatrice felt her spirits sink. The blond Thegn could not have missed her deliberate slight.

'My lady, this is your future husband, Aiden, Thegn of Lindsey. He is introducing himself and welcoming you,' de Brionne said.

'Oh.' Anne turned back to the young man and looked at him down her nose, as though he were something unpleasant she had just trodden on. She was not making the slightest effort to be pleasant. Beatrice felt very much like slapping her. Could she not see the sense of making an effort to be polite? She had managed well enough on the hellish journey they had just completed. What had got into her? She was shaming the Saxon Thegn before his own people. Smile, Anne, oh please, at least *smile* at him.

The Thegn of Lindsey met Anne's haughty gaze calmly, and held out his hand to help her from her horse.

'Baron?' Deliberately, Anne looked at the Norman, but de Brionne did not move. His hands were clenched white on his reins, and he watched Anne through cold, ever-calculating eyes.

Anne scowled and tossed her head. Insultingly reluctant, she allowed herself to be helped down by her betrothed. She shook herself free of the Thegn with indecent haste, and rubbed her hand on her skirts.

Close to Beatrice, someone sighed heavily. She glanced down, expecting to see Walter waiting to help her dismount. But Walter was nowhere in sight.

A dark-haired Saxon was standing next to Betony. She found herself staring into the bluest eyes that she had ever seen. For several heartbeats the universe stood still.

'A disdainful Norman lady.' The blue-eyed Saxon addressed her in Latin, and although his accent was strange, Beatrice had no difficulty understanding him. He had a deep and pleasant voice.

She nodded shyly and smiled, grateful for his attention.

'M-my cousin is nervous.' She found herself excusing Anne's behaviour. She was held by that gaze and could not look away.

'Will you accept my help more willingly?' he enquired, holding out his hand to her, eyes warm, his raven hair flung back from a clean-shaven face.

Beatrice nodded.

His hand was well-shaped and took hers firmly, an aristocratic hand. Rings glinted, silver armbands jingled as he moved, and Beatrice wondered who he was. Judging from his apparel, he was of some standing here. She thought she'd seen him standing with his Thegn by the hall.

He wore a woollen tunic, dyed a rich midnight blue. It was gathered at his waist with a silver-buckled swordbelt. Swinging from the belt was a sword, and a beautifully crafted dagger set with lapis lazuli and other semi-precious stones. The Saxon's blue tunic was slit at the sides and bordered with silver braid. His long legs were sheathed in trousers bound to the knee with leather thongs.

To her surprise, the Saxon dropped her hand and reached up to lift her bodily from Betony's back. Beatrice could feel his fingers warm round her waist and she blushed, dropping her eyes before the amusement which sprang into his. She had only ever been this close to a man with Sister Agnes in the infirmary. And this man was far from sick. It was a long moment before he released her. She wondered why it had become so difficult to breathe, and her heart was pounding as though she had just run all the way from Normandy.

He set her down gently and released her. Her limbs were numbed and slow to respond to her will. She staggered, and the Saxon was steadying her. He linked one of her cold hands casually through his arm.

'You will be stiff and cold from your long ride,' he commented.

Beatrice nodded again, grateful for his understanding. She wished she could find her tongue, but could think of nothing to say. He would count her as rude as her cousin if she did not reply quickly. The one sympathetic face she'd yet seen, she did not want to alienate him.

'M-my thanks,' she managed, inwardly cursing her nervous stammer.

He led her towards the large wooden building, and the gawping crowd parted to let them through.

Anne was there before them, standing in the doorway with an expression which put Beatrice in mind of a spoilt princess being asked to step into a hovel.

Simple the Saxon hall might have been, but hovel it clearly was not. The wooden building was a large one, and from the outside looked as though it might contain two storeys. The roof was steep, well thatched, and blue smoke seeped out from the top. There were intricate carvings on the doorposts, a regular geometric design with flowers and animals interspersed throughout the pattern.

Beatrice could see, by the way the long planks fitted together so neatly, that a master carpenter had been at work. She managed to pick out the details of a water serpent. It rose gracefully from a wave which curved along the length of one of the wall plates.

Anne had given neither the hall nor the carvings a second glance. Her usually pretty lips were twisted into an ugly sneer.

Beatrice darted a glance at her Saxon escort, wondering if Anne's blinkered attitude had been noticed. The vivid blue eyes were on her, not Anne. Her cheeks grew warm. She became aware of the feel of his strong arm through the fine cloth of his tunic, of him standing tall and straight and lithe beside her. Beatrice was aware of him as she had been aware of no one else in her young life.

She forced herself to walk casually at his side in the hall, hoping she did not appear as self-conscious as she felt. Every nerve was alive and tingling. She pretended to gaze around the hall and struggled for composure.

Inside, the hall was large and airy. There was a planked wooden floor with a clay hearth and a blazing central fire piled high with logs. Two wooden stairways led upwards, one at each end of the hall, and Beatrice could see a small gallery with a curtained doorway at the top of each stair. So this hall *did* have two storeys, with extra chambers constructed in the gable ends of the building. The wattle walls were black with the soot of generations of fires.

Several awesome Saxon warriors had gathered in the hall ready to greet Lady Anne de Vidâmes. Beatrice had thought to have felt nervous at the sight of their alien and warlike garb, but she did not. She was quite safe on the arm of this blue-eyed Saxon. Even the masked, bearded stares of the warriors now greeting Anne could not frighten her. The man whose arm supported her was far more disturbing, but in a different way. He was watching Anne now, assessing her stiff acknowledgements of the greetings offered her, with his eyes narrowed and frowning.

Covertly, Beatrice examined his features. He was young, like the Thegn of Lindsey, though maybe a year or two older. The Thegn's beard gave him an older appearance, but Beatrice divined this was deceptive. The Saxon at her side had an assurance that the young lord clearly lacked.

Her escort was still watching the newly betrothed couple. The Thegn looked across at them. It was an unmistakable appeal for help. Beatrice's companion smiled back reassuringly. A strong bond must exist between the two men. She knew that her companion was willing Anne to relax her frozen face, to give the Saxon Thegn even the tiniest of smiles. Beatrice added a prayer of her own, and at that moment, as if aware of her silent entreaty, her companion's hand came up to cover the one that Beatrice rested on his arm. She allowed herself to be drawn nearer to the warming fire.

'Mistress.' The hard voice of Baron Philip de Brionne made her start. She had forgotten him.

'Baron?' she enquired. Unknown to her, her hand no longer rested lightly on her escort's arm, but clung to his tunic. The Saxon's eyes flickered quickly to her clinging fingers, before settling warily on the Baron's hard face.

Philip de Brionne's black eyes bored maliciously into those of Beatrice. She shivered. The heat of the fire no longer reached her.

'Shouldn't you be attending to your cousin, instead of consorting with Saxon scum, my dear?' the Baron asked in French, managing to make the simple endearment sound like a threat.

Beatrice caught her breath and glanced at her escort, but his handsome face was impassive.

The Baron raised his voice. 'I doubt he speaks our tongue, my dear, at best they're an uncultured rabble,' he sneered.

'Do *you* speak English?' Beatrice challenged softly in Latin, so her escort could understand. She thought she saw the glimmer of a smile on the Saxon's lips, but could not be sure.

Philip de Brionne's lips grew thinner. He did not speak English, then. His dark eyes went hard as jet.

'Don't be insolent. Allow me to escort you to your cousin. You may supervise your servant in unloading the packhorses. And remember, you are to share Lady Anne's chamber till the wedding day.' The Baron proffered his arm, and Beatrice discovered her fingers were still holding fast on to the Saxon's tunic. Clear hazel eyes raised briefly to warm blue ones.

'I trust I will see you this evening at the betrothal feast?' the Saxon asked, smiling.

Beatrice nodded. 'Who are you?' she asked, aware of the Baron shifting impatiently beside her.

'My name is Edmund. I am half-brother to our Thegn.'

The Baron's derisive snort turned two pairs of eyes on to him. He had urgently taken Beatrice's hand to link through his own arm and was already stalking away. The mailcoat he wore was cold and hard after the warmth of Edmund's cloth-clad one.

'You won't be talking to *him* again, not a convent girl like you,' the Norman drawled.

'What do you mean?' Beatrice demanded, aware that Edmund had stiffened angrily behind her.

The Baron let out a mirthless laugh. 'Oh, not only is he of mixed ancestry, for I believe his mother had Danish blood in her,' de Brionne sneered, 'but I hear the man's a bastard!'

Beatrice gasped, amazed by the Baron's tactlessness.

The Norman's poisonous smile grew broad. He affected to misunderstand the cause of her dismay, and stirred his evil brew anew. 'Aye, shocking, isn't it? Edmund is illegitimate, the bastard son of the old Thegn. I'm sure that the good nuns at La Trinité would not wish you to demean yourself by talking to persons of such low breeding and standing.' As he spoke the Baron pulled Beatrice away from the Saxon, Edmund.

Beatrice hung back, trying to resist the relentless pressure on her arm. 'Nay! I did not mean that! 'Twas *you* I was shocked at for——'

'The man's a mongrel half-breed, a bastard,' gibed the Baron, not listening.

'Nay! You're deliberately trying to provoke a confrontation. You want to cause a scene—I can see it on your face. We are meant to be here to conciliate, not to provoke,' Beatrice cried.

She twisted her head round to smile at Edmund. It suddenly seemed very important that he should understand her.

Edmund was standing staring after them, one hand clenched white on his sword hilt. His finely shaped mouth had become a thin, angry line, his patrician nose was held high, defiance and pride in every line of his tall, straight form.

When his eyes moved from the Baron's back to meet hers, they were filled with such dreadful loathing that Beatrice recoiled. She could not believe they belonged to the same person who had welcomed her with smiling courtesy only a few minutes ago.

He did not understand. He believed his bastardy had repulsed and shocked her.

Beatrice gazed hopelessly at him as the Norman jerked her towards Anne. The sight of the bitterness clouding those clear blue eyes froze her heart.

She had known loneliness. And had thought that loneliness was a terrible curse. But this felt worse. This felt like desolation.

It was as though she had lost a pearl of great price before she had even possessed it.

Yells! Screams! Moaning! The clash of steel on steel!

Beatrice stumbled into the Saxon chapel and slammed the swinging oak door shut. She must shield herself from the bloody scene outside.

Trembling as though she had the marsh fever, she propped her head against the door and took some steadying breaths. Perspiration beaded her brow, she wiped at it with her sleeve and scrubbed clammy palms on her skirt. She felt sick, she thought her heart was going to burst, and a dull roaring sound filled her ears. Surely the air would be tainted with the smell of blood forever...

Her mind was so full of the carnage that she had witnessed that Beatrice did not hear the rustling, shuffling noise deep within the shadows of the chapel.

She shook her head, but the ghastly images so recently imprinted on her brain were not easily dislodged. Her knees gave way and she slumped down on to the stone flags, thick auburn braids trailing in the dust. She brought up a hand that was the colour of wax and covered her eyes. That worked no better. However tightly she shut her eyes, she could not obliterate those hellish pictures; they'd been branded on her mind for all eternity.

Beatrice bit down on her forefinger. Some physical pain of her own would be welcome, but she scarcely felt it. This was no nightmare. She could not escape this by waking. This was reality.

It had all happened so quickly, so unexpectedly. Yet, had she but thought, she might have guessed that de Brionne was planning trouble. Why had those extra Norman soldiers arrived so unexpectedly—just before the betrothal feast? They had not been a part of Anne's escort. And why had the Baron looked at her so angrily when she had come upon him conferring with the new Norman captain in this very chapel?

De Brionne had been behind the flaring violence, of that she was certain. Not only had the Norman made no secret of his loathing for the Saxons, he had even appeared keen to foment discord between the two camps. Utter folly, when any half-wit could have seen that the peace between them was so fragile.

One minute she and her cousin Anne had been watching an apparently friendly wrestling contest between a Saxon and a Norman warrior, and the next . . .

Beatrice took another gulping breath.

The match had been intended as an entertainment, but the seething undercurrents had been there all the time. King William must be hoping for a miracle if he ever thought the two races would unite.

Without warning the bubbling resentment had erupted into horrific and bloody violence. Beatrice frowned, wondering at the suddenness of it. She remembered only that the Saxon wrestler had been losing. Philip de Brionne had cast a sneering comment at his Norman captain, delivering his remark in such a tone that no interpreter was needed for the resentful Saxons to understand it. It was hard to believe that one little phrase had been enough to shatter the fragile peace.

A Norman sword had been drawn. A moment's oppressive silence had followed—and then—the devil incarnate had been loosed among them.

Beatrice shuddered.

The sounds that had followed still rang in her ears; the shouts and shrieks of fighting men, the clash of steel on steel, the sickening tearing of sword through flesh. So much blood. So much pain.

The Norman force must have been prepared. They had ploughed into the Saxons as though de Brionne's drawn sword had been the signal they had been waiting for. It must have been. De Brionne had literally scores of men at his disposal, men enough to cut a fearful swathe through the Saxon ranks.

The Englishmen had been hampered by their need to protect their women and children. Many of their warriors had been cut down in so doing.

Beatrice had never experienced such violence before. She prayed she never would again. Her years with the gentle nuns at La Trinité had not taught her how to cope with such horrors. It was one thing to help Sister Agnes stitch up a peasant lad who had cut his foot on a reaping hook, and quite another to be faced with dozens of groaning men, all desperate for help.

Staring in shock at the bloody aftermath, and conscious of a void where her insides should have been, Beatrice had not known where to start. But start she had, helping both Saxon and Norman alike with an impartiality that would have gladdened the heart of Mother Adèle. Not so that of Baron Philip de Brionne.

The Baron had stalked up to Beatrice as she was tending a young native lad. 'No quarter for this one!' he had snarled, pointing his sword and thrusting it through the helpless boy before Beatrice had known what he was about. No emotion had shown on that swarthy visage. No penitence. Nothing at all. Beatrice burned with shame that she should be a Norman too.

'Can't have you wasting your skills on those who are already dead, can we?' The Baron spat on the boy's still body. 'Tend to our Normans, girl. The rest are carrion.'

With every nerve screaming, Beatrice had held the lad's hand until the light had gone from his eyes. Then she'd staggered up on legs that were as wooden as a tumbler's stilts, and had run straight to the chapel.

She sighed. So quiet in here. So peaceful. She crossed herself, just as the silence in the chapel was broken by a sharp cry from outside, quickly stifled. Another shudder ran through her.

She lifted her head from the door, rose jerkily and moved further inside God's house. The more distance she put between herself and the blood-spattered yard outside, the better. Facing the simple wooden cross, Beatrice put her hands together.

'Sweet Jesus, why?' Her voice rang out loudly in the stillness of the chapel. 'Why? Dear Lord,' she prayed in her native French, 'have mercy on the souls of those who have died today. Especially on the soul of Aiden, Thegn of Lindsey, murdered so foully by Philip de Brionne. Please grant that my cousin bear patiently with these trials, and if her marriage is not to help unite our two races and bring peace, grant that another route be found.'

The rustling sound came from behind the altar. This time Beatrice was nearer its source and she heard it. She shivered. There must be rats in here. She hated rats. She would finish her prayers quickly and be gone. The chapel was a sanctuary no longer.

She must return to tend the wounded. 'Lord, give me strength to help the sick——'

Another furtive scuffling reached her ears and she gabbled to a close. 'And Thy will be done. Amen.'

Beatrice was halfway to the door when a second moan and more shufflings raised the hairs on her neck. That first groan had come from within the chapel, she realised. Not from the yard as she had presumed.

Spine prickling, Beatrice whirled around. She could see only the simple church furnishings and bare stone floor. There was no screen in this chapel. Nowhere anyone could hide. The midday sun streamed through the small windows; it left shadows, but no corner was completely unlit.

A sudden flash of instinct widened her hazel eyes and they were drawn irresistibly towards the altar. The stone table was covered by an embroidered cloth. It moved. She heard another groan. It was quickly suppressed.

Beatrice knelt down. This time to lift one corner of the altar cloth. Her hand shook. The breath froze in her lungs. Suddenly another hand shot out and seized her wrist. She cried out, struggling against a grip of steel.

He was a Saxon. His blue eyes were filled with hatred, his patrician features contorted with pain. Edmund!

Beatrice thought her pounding heart would burst.

The grip on her wrist shifted a fraction as the wounded man moved to bring his jewel-encrusted dagger to her throat. The movement clearly tortured him.

'I...shall...have...to...kill...you.' Though Edmund spoke haltingly in Latin, Beatrice did not understand him at first, his voice clipped with suffering.

Ignoring the dagger, and the hatred blazing in his eyes, Beatrice slowly put out her free hand towards his tunic. It was covered in blood.

'You are hurt.' She strove to keep her voice steady. 'Let me help you.'

The warrior did not relax his bone-crushing grip. 'A Norman—help a Saxon!' Edmund hissed scornfully through set teeth. 'It would appear that your people show no mercy to the helpless. Why should I with you?' He took a shuddering breath. He was very white about the lips. 'You would betray my presence...so I have no choice. I must kill you...or be killed myself. I've seen what your Baron does to wounded Saxons!'

'Nay, nay! I won't betray you,' she swore, her voice breaking on a sob. 'There's been more than enough killing already. Please...release me.' As Beatrice pleaded she tried surreptitiously to free her wrist. Looking into the contorted, sweat-streaked face that glared at her, she realised that the Saxon, Edmund, did indeed mean to kill her. She could read it in his eyes. Any compassion that he was capable of feeling was being ruthlessly suppressed. He, too, must have seen the Baron kill that defenceless boy. And Aiden, his Thegn? Dear God, did this man know his half-brother had been killed too? Her guts turned to water. There was no hope for her.

She fixed her eyes on his bloody tunic. 'Edmund,' she used his name deliberately, 'permit me to help you. I have the skill.'

'There's no need for you to dissemble,' he growled. 'You would never help me. We Saxons were fools indeed to welcome such vipers in our midst. Your wedding gifts are deceit and treachery. I saw you at the betrothal feast. You did not seem to hate us then, though 'tis true your pretty cousin paid us scant attention. She at least was no hypocrite. She was too busy flirting with that Norman dog.' Edmund paused for breath. His breathing was harsh and flurried. He coughed.

'Philip de Brionne,' Beatrice supplied, her revulsion of the Norman evident in her tone. Hazel eyes met blue in sudden concord.

'I see you know him by my description.' The wounded man's lips twisted. 'But I insult all dogs by so naming him.'

'I had hoped to talk with you, my lord, at the feast, to explain...' Beatrice hesitated.

'Aye,' Edmund gasped bitterly. 'It may be that I am lord indeed, now my brother is dead. Go on, girl, what had you hoped at the feast?' His expression was not encouraging.

At Anne's betrothal celebration, Beatrice had sat at the head of the trestle table, close to her cousin. She had hoped that Edmund would chose to sit near his brother. But he had not done so. Instead he had seated himself next to a willowy blonde. He had returned *her* smiles easily enough. Conscious of a baffling and most un-Christian desire to wound as she was being wounded, Beatrice had devoted herself to charming the fair-haired Saxon next to her. And when it had become evident that Anne was not going to attempt to speak with her be-trothed, Beatrice had included the young Thegn in her conversation. She had not wanted these Saxons to think all Normans ill-bred and discourteous.

And now Edmund was waiting for her reply, his hold as unyielding as ever. Beatrice found her heart was too full to speak. She wanted to explain that she did not share de Brionne's scorn for his illegitimacy. But she had read a fierce pride in Edmund's eyes, and that recog-nition left a constriction in her throat, and the words she had ready were never uttered.

Edmund coughed again, he winced and closed his eyes. For a moment his grip on her wrist loosened. Beatrice kept quite still. When he opened his eyes and fastened them on her face, they were cool as ice. His fingers tightened, and slowly but surely he hauled her nearer to the winking blade, watching her like a hawk. He sighed.

'Beatrice. Beatrice,' he muttered. 'To think at first I thought you worthy. I thought...'

She was pulled closer and closer. She tensed as the blade wavered in front of her, noting, in a remote part of her mind that was not frozen with fear, that the blade had not been blooded. She had to shut her eyes, she could not watch her own execution. A few moments passed. No cold blade struck into her flesh.

Possessed with a wild, impossible hope, Beatrice risked a glance. He had troubled to find out her name. She had not told him it. Surely he would not kill her? And the way he had said it...

Edmund was looking past her towards the door. His hold relaxed. Breathing a prayer of thanks, Beatrice snatched her wrist free. The Saxon's face was white as chalk, his breathing alarmingly shallow.

'Someone comes,' he announced, his voice slurring the words like a drunkard. Clouding blue eyes lifted to anxious hazel ones. His lips attempted a smile, it wrung her heart. 'So I shall not have to kill you after all, my pretty Norman maid. Dead men cannot kill.' His breath came out in a long sigh, his eyes glazed over, and his head fell back with a crack on to the cold stone flags.

'Beatrice! Beatrice!' Philip de Brionne's grating voice broke in, growing louder. The Baron was approaching the chapel. 'Hell fry that girl! This is no time for praying! She's got work to do.'

Someone mumbled a reply. The door-latch rattled.

Beatrice moved like the wind. She twitched the altar cloth back into place, flung herself into an attitude of prayer, and gazed up at the cross on the altar.

There were footsteps behind her. A mailed hand landed on her shoulder.

'Here you are,' de Brionne said. 'I thought you'd be helping with the wounded. I did not expect your cousin to help. Nay, Lady Anne is far too squeamish for such work. But I did not expect you to be so delicate. On your feet.'

Beatrice hated his smile. It made her flesh crawl.

She rose and faced the Norman, schooling her face to cloak the loathing she'd felt for this beast of a man ever since she'd seen for herself what a callous, vicious killer he was. She must not show fear, for if he suspected she was hiding someone . . . if he suspected what lay beneath the altar . . .

Beatrice would do all in her power to prevent another mindless murder.

'I will come back now, Baron,' she said, managing to invest her voice with a lightness she did not feel. She moved forwards and her foot caught on something. There was a metallic scrape and the Saxon's dagger skidded across the floor. Immobile with horror, Beatrice could only watch as the Baron bent to retrieve it.

'What have we here?' asked the Baron.

He turned the dagger over in his hand, examining the jewelled shaft with greedy eyes. How large and brutish his hand seemed, holding the delicately wrought instrument. Edmund's hand had not looked so ugly, even though he'd threatened her. De Brionne's hand was made to murder. Hastily Beatrice suppressed that last thought, lest the revulsion she felt show on her face. De Brionne advanced on Beatrice and loomed over her.

'Not, I think, the dagger of a Norman,' he commented.

With an effort Beatrice met his hard gaze. She stretched her lips into a smile. 'Oh, Baron, forgive me.' She looked at the dagger, and made her voice deliberately innocent. ''Tis so pretty with the coloured glass and inlay. I thought no one would miss it if I took it . . .' She paused and, with a coquetry that would have scandalised the good nuns in France, turned the full charm of her hazel eyes on de Brionne. She almost recoiled at the answering flare which lit up his cold eyes, but managed to hold her ground.

The Baron stepped closer, the dagger still resting on his palm. His nails were dirty. 'The Saxon lad?' he persisted, reaching for her shoulder. His hand bit into her, and he scrutinised her as though he had never set eyes on her before.

Her innards churning, Beatrice nodded. Far better that the Baron should think her a thief than he find the Saxon, Edmund, helpless under the altar.

De Brionne lifted his lips from his teeth and sneered, 'So you came here to gloat on your newly acquired loot. Not to pray for my blackened soul. Mistress, you disappoint me, truly you do.' He leered at her, grinning, and as Beatrice caught sight of the gleam lurking at the back of his eyes she knew that he lied. He was pleased to find her apparently without morals. Her mind balked from continuing up the road where *that* thought led her.

A wave of hatred swept through her. She longed to drag the leer off his face with her nails. But instead she kept the bright smile pinned on her lips and lifted the dagger from his callused palm. 'So I may keep it, Baron?' she asked.

'Aye. But guard it well. 'Tis more than coloured glass. Those are jewels, my pretty. They're worth a small fortune.' The Baron employed his skin-shrivelling smile. 'But I'll warrant you know that already.'

His smile faded and he scowled.

'Baron?' Beatrice prompted, feeling suffocated.

''Tis strange. I did not judge that boy to be a noble. Such pretty toys are far from common.'

'Would you have stayed your hand, Baron, had he been noble?' Beatrice wondered.

De Brionne shrugged carelessly. 'He might have been worth something alive. It seems my judgement is awry this day, for I'd not marked you for a magpie, either.'

Jet-dark eyes narrowed to scan the little chapel.

'Baron!' Her voice came out too high. She moderated it. 'Perhaps the lad stole the dagger from his lord,' she suggested, desperately seeking to distract him.

De Brionne ceased his perusal of the chapel. 'Mmm? Oh, aye. Thieving scum, the lot of them. Loyalty? Means nothing to 'em.' His eyes made another circuit of the chapel. ''Tis small, this sanctuary, is it not?' he commented.

Beatrice caught her breath. She prayed his choice of the word 'sanctuary' was accidental. 'Aye, my lord,' she gabbled, snatching wildly at the first words that entered her head. ''Tis small, but its purpose is the same as our

larger churches in Normandy. We should love our
enemies, not——'

'Pious sentiments, my dear, but you won't fool me
again,' the Baron snorted derisively, and looked
pointedly at the dagger. He shifted and seized an auburn
plait. 'I know you won't be ungrateful now I've let you
keep the pretty dagger, eh? *You* know how to give your
betters the respect they deserve, eh, Beatrice? Especially
someone who has turned a blind eye to your
more...er...acquisitive tendencies.'

Beatrice felt the colour drain from her face. Her tongue
twisted into a dry knot that stopped her voice. She tried
to swallow.

De Brionne stripped her with his eyes, and barked a
laugh at the rafters. 'And to think I'd marked you for
the convent! Nay, I've better ideas now. Coloured glass
indeed!' he hooted. 'Come, Beatrice, 'tis time you earned
your booty. There are wounded fighters to attend to.
Among other things...'

Flinging a glance behind her, Beatrice freed a trembling breath. She tucked the jewelled dagger firmly into
her girdle. Dizzy with relief, and meek as a lamb, she
suffered the Norman to lead her out into the pale winter
sunlight.

The altar cloth was fluttering in the draught blown in
from the yard. Beatrice turned back and latched the door,
sealing the unconscious Saxon within.

Her fingers felt dirty where they'd made contact with
de Brionne's palm. She wiped them hard on the stuff of
her gown. Her brow wrinkled. Anne had made the same
gesture after Aiden, Thegn of Lindsey, had handed her
from her horse. Bracing her shoulders, Beatrice followed the Baron out into the bone-chilling afternoon.

On entering the hall, Beatrice saw at once that it had
been cleared of its original Saxon inhabitants. She wondered where they'd gone. Surely even de Brionne could
not have murdered them all?

Wounded Norman soldiers clothed the floorboards.
That morning they'd been strong, whole men. Now they
resembled untidy bundles of flesh and rags—a sad tes-
timony to the bitterness of the conflict. Now and then
a groan rose up above the crackling of the fire, and the

buzz of conversation stilled. It was not the moaning men that Beatrice turned to first. Those who lay voiceless and unmoving had first call on her skills, for their hurts were worst.

Lady Anne de Vidâmes, as the Baron had said, was nowhere to be seen, but her maid was there. She did not look so haughty now. Walter appeared and hovered at Beatrice's side.

'Mistress Beatrice!' the maid wailed, half hysterical. 'Thank heaven you're back! I don't know why *I'm* expected to help. 'Tis not for me, this work. There's so much mess and blood...so many of them hurt. I...I don't know where to start.'

An angry response rose to Beatrice's lips, but she choked it back. The girl was close to tears.

'Where's your mistress?' she asked gently.

'In the upper chamber. She will not help. I don't know what to do,' the girl whined, her voice growing shriller by the minute. 'So many of them——'

'We cannot worry about Lady Anne now,' Beatrice broke in sharply. 'We need to make bandages. Ella, see if you can dig out some cloths, anything will do. Try behind the high table—I think they keep the table linen in that iron-bound chest.'

''Twill be locked, Mistress,' Ella objected.

Beatrice gritted her teeth. 'Ask the Baron to smash the lock. He won't want his men to bleed to death.'

'Aye, Mistress,' replied Ella, with dawning respect. Mistress Beatrice might be young, but she seemed to have a good head on her shoulders.

'And Ella?'

'Mistress?'

'Make sure the linen's clean. Tear it into strips, and bring it to me.'

Ella sniffed, but she nodded.

Beatrice observed that the maidservant's features had relaxed and were no longer pinched with dread. She smiled at the girl. 'Do you understand?' Beatrice asked, kindly.

'Aye,' Ella replied, and suddenly she burst into speech. 'Oh, I'm so glad you're here, Mistress Beatrice. 'Twas terrible when the Baron set me to work. Lady Anne wouldn't give me any instructions, and there was only this——' the girl waved at Walter '—simpleton who seemed to want to help...'

Walter sent Beatrice one of his rare, shy smiles.

'And you know how he is,' Ella finished on a note of scorn.

'I know,' Beatrice answered softly. The note of panic had been eliminated from the girl's voice. No matter if that panic had been replaced by scorn. A scornful girl was of more use to Beatrice than a girl whose wits had been paralysed by fear.

'The bandages, Ella,' Beatrice prompted. 'Walter, you must help Ella. Do exactly as she says.'

This brought a glower from Ella, and she flounced off, shaking her skirts. Walter trailed in her wake.

Beatrice set to work. Most of the soldiers bore superficial wounds. For that mercy she sent up a swift prayer of thanks.

The knowledge that it was the unprepared Saxons who had born the brunt of the pain needled away at the back of her mind. She tried not to think about the Saxon lodged untended in the chapel. She could not help him yet. But she would find a way. In the meantime, her own countrymen demanded all of her attention. Her training at the infirmary would stand her in good stead. Despite the numbers needing her skills she would remain as cool and efficient as Sister Agnes.

'Come on, Walter,' Ella ordered her man as though she had been born to command. 'We need more bandages. Tear these up.'

Beatrice saw Ella send the silent man a puzzled glance, and a small smile crossed her lips. Beatrice had read Ella aright. Once calm, the girl was a stalwart helper. All Ella had needed was clear instructions.

'Walter's not really simple, is he, Mistress?' Ella asked. 'He never speaks, but he understands. Look at him. He's bandaged that man's leg neater than I could. I was afraid of him, because he never speaks. He's not dangerous, is he?'

'Dangerous? Walter? Certainly not. I've always found him a most gentle man,' Beatrice replied.

'Was he always like that?' Ella's curiosity was roused. Vigorously the maid ripped more fabric and handed the strips to Beatrice.

'My thanks. Nay, Ella. I don't think he can have been. He was brought to Sister Agnes' infirmary one day with a terrible head wound.'

'Aye. You can't miss that scar on his temple. The rest of his face is quite handsome. Such a pity.' Ella cast a sideways look at Walter.

Beatrice helped herself to another bandage. 'A young woman came with him to the hospital. We did our best for him. But when the girl learned he could no longer speak, she vanished. They had been betrothed, but she...' Beatrice hesitated. 'I suppose she wanted him as he had been before the accident.'

Ella scrubbed her sleeve furtively across her face. 'And now he stays with you,' she said.

Beatrice took this as a question. 'For the moment. When my cousin said she needed me for a companion, the Prioress thought he should accompany me. Mother Adèle would not permit me to leave the convent on my own. Walter is strong, and Mother thought he could protect me until Anne no longer needed me. Then I shall return to the convent.'

'He smiles at you,' Ella noticed. 'No one else but you.'

'I'm the only person from home, Ella. And I think he's grateful for the care we took of him at the convent. For myself, I'm very glad he came.'

Ella nodded. 'Another bandage, Mistress?'

'Thank you. Ella, I need fresh water in this bowl.'

Her spine was prickling. Beatrice twisted her head round. The Baron was watching her. He perched on the edge of the trestle at the far end of the hall, a horn of wine set square in his clutch. She did not like the way his eyes gleamed across at her.

Beatrice bent over the soldier she was tending, and tried willing the Baron to take himself away. The Baron did not oblige. Although she did not look his way again, she could still feel his eyes making the hairs rise on the nape of her neck. Her flesh shrank. As if he's a snake and I'm his next meal, she thought.

''Tis not that bad, is it?' her patient croaked. A white moon of a face stared up at her, tense with alarm.

'I...I beg your pardon?' Beatrice stuttered.

The soldier indicated the crimson gash on his arm. 'I won't lose it, will I, Mistress?'

'Nay. 'Tis a good, clean wound,' Beatrice assured him.

The man let out his breath. 'Praise the Saints. I saw you shudder, and thought the worst,' he admitted.

'Nay, your arm is quite safe.' She smiled. ''Twill be stiff and sore for a while—you won't be able to wield your sword for at least a month. But if you keep it clean 'twill heal beautifully.'

The Norman soldier had blue eyes. They reminded Beatrice of someone else. Someone who had no one to tend his hurt, and who was lying unconscious on a cold stone floor, with his life-blood draining away with every second that passed. Maybe he was dead already. Gripped by a surge of panic, Beatrice battled with an urge to get up and run to the chapel. She reminded herself that Edmund would not be helped if she were to lead de Brionne and his men there. She *must* be cautious.

Beatrice had never faced panic like this, and she did not like it. A few minutes earlier, she'd been exasperated with Ella for panicking. And now she was doing the same. How many times had Sister Agnes told her never to judge others?

But what of the Saxon encoffined in the chapel? What could Beatrice do for him? It was not safe to go to his aid. Yet she must do something—and soon...

Mother Adèle would put her trust in God. Aye, that was what she must do. Have faith in the Lord. He would find a way.

Beatrice tightened the bandage on the soldier's arm. But worry still gnawed holes in her mind. The comfort of her faith did not seem to be enough. Her stomach remained twisted in a hundred knots. She still wanted to run to the chapel...

'Mistress,' her patient gasped.

She dragged her attention back to him. 'Aye?'

'That bandage is too tight. It hurts,' the man protested.

'I'm sorry.' Beatrice looked askance at her handi-work. The man was right. The bandage was bound round his arm so ill you'd think she was a green novice who'd never treated so much as a sore throat. Murmuring apologies, Beatrice unbound the wrappings and started again. She forced her mind to work on the sick man before her and not on the one in the chapel.

'Is that better?' she asked, the job done at last.

The Norman nodded. Beatrice stood up, and stretched her legs. He had been the last one. But, even so, she could not go to the chapel. Not yet.

De Brionne was still sitting at the board at the end of the hall, impaling her with his devil's eyes. He tossed wine down his throat as though it were water. And all the while he stared...

If only the dagger had stayed out of sight. De Brionne would never have noticed her. She would have remained an insignificant girl from a convent. But the dagger had brought her to his notice, and it did not look as though he was likely to forget. How on earth could she get to the chapel with his gaze boring into her?

'That's all for now, Ella.' Beatrice dismissed Anne's maid. 'Thank you for your help. And you too, Walter. I shall go and wash now. You do the same. We've all earned a rest.'

As Beatrice climbed the single flight of stairs, her attitude was deliberately one of weariness. She made her movements slow and pained as though she could barely haul herself up the wooden steps. She hoped her face appeared drawn and exhausted. In truth, she did feel tired. But her mind was still busy, searching frantically for a route that could take her unobserved to the chapel, to tend to the Saxon, Edmund.

Baron Philip de Brionne's head turned to follow her halting progress up the stairs. His eyes were narrowed, and the suspicious gleam lighting them was thus concealed from view.

CHAPTER THREE

'BEATRICE!' Anne exclaimed pettishly as her cousin entered the chamber. 'I thought you would never finish. I have missed your company.'

'The time would have passed more quickly, Anne, if you had been down there helping.' Beatrice was unable to keep the reproof from her voice.

Anne avoided her cousin's eyes. 'Oh, dear,' she said. 'Your gown is filthy. 'Tis drenched in blood, 'twill have to go. Here, you may have one of mine.'

Suppressing a sigh, Beatrice plumped down on the bed. Anne flung back the lid of one of her travelling chests and began to scrabble through the contents. If Anne felt guilty at not offering to help, and wanted to atone, that was up to her. All Beatrice wanted was peace so she could work out how she was going to get to the chapel. She might be too late even now.

'Here, this green one will suit you,' Anne was saying. 'The dear nuns meant well when they provided you with clothes, but they are all a bit *too* practical, aren't they? Now this one is much better.'

The gown was soft as a dream, and a far cry from the coarser garments the nuns had provided her with. Beatrice buried her face in the folds of delicate green wool. She smiled. Her cousin might not be the most practical of women but she did have a generous nature.

'Oh, Anne,' Beatrice breathed, fingering the cloth with awe, and conscious she had to speak up for the nuns. 'The convent provided me with the best they had.'

Anne grinned at her. 'I'm sure they did. I'm not decrying their generosity. But this is better for you ... you do like it, don't you?'

'I love it,' Beatrice confessed.

'What's that?' Anne asked, pointing curiously at the jewelled dagger.

'A Saxon blade,' Beatrice said warily.

'I can see that. How beautiful it is. I'd no idea the Saxon were capable of such craftsmanship. They all seemed so...so...wild and barbaric. Where did you get it?'

Beatrice picked her words with care. 'From Aiden's...er...from one of Aiden's family. 'Twas dropped.'

'Aiden's dead.' Anne's statement was devoid of feeling. Her face was blank.

'Aye. He is,' Beatrice confirmed, sympathetically. 'I'm sorry, Anne.'

'Sorry! I'm not!' Anne burst out.

'Anne!' Beatrice stared. She was shocked at Anne's seeming callousness, but she recognised the torment in her cousin's eyes and understood Anne to be taking refuge behind a hard façade.

'To think my own people would see me wed with the leader of such...such heathens. Why, I'll wager they're not even Christian!'

Beatrice's brow furrowed. Anne's last remark had not sprung from piety. It was aimed at her. The convent-bred companion was to bear the brunt of Anne's guilt and anger.

'They are Christian,' Beatrice said, mildly. 'Have you not seen their chapel? And apparently there's a monastery nearby——'

Anne gave a little grunt. She was not to be mollified and had more to say. 'Saxon clothes are outlandish. They don't think to trim either hair or beard. They eat like swine. And as for their language—why, I can't understand a word of it.'

'You could learn,' Beatrice pointed out softly. She had already picked up one or two phrases during the short truce that had existed between the two camps.

Anne scowled and began to stalk up and down the chamber. 'I don't think so. There's no logic in their tongue. Besides, Beatrice, remember how violent they are. That fight, for example. You saw it.'

Beatrice shook her head. She loosened her braids and retrieved her bone comb from a willow basket on the chest by the bed. 'That fight was the Baron's work. I'm certain those other Normans arrived on his command to stir up trouble. He has no more interest in King William's plans for peace than you have. Anne, stop pacing up and down like that. Try to relax,' Beatrice advised. 'Here, you can help me with my hair, 'tis tangled beyond my unravelling. I'd be grateful if you could explain to me why you were so happy about coming here if you despise the Saxons so. You knew all along you were to wed one. You had not been deceived. On the way here you seemed so happy. I don't understand it.'

Anne snatched the bone comb from her cousin's hand. 'Sit up properly,' she said, gathering up Beatrice's long tresses. Almost at once the comb caught.

'Ow! Anne, do be careful,' Beatrice laughed and rubbed her smarting scalp. 'I can see you've not had much practice at playing the lady's maid.'

'Nay, why should I? I have Ella to help me. I'm sorry, Beatrice. I'll try to be more gentle,' Anne promised. She bent diligently over her cousin's bright hair. 'I was wrong to rant at you,' she admitted. 'I was upset.'

'I know,' Beatrice smiled.

'And——' Anne gave a rueful grin '—sometimes you are most provoking. I want to shake you.'

Beatrice's heart sank. 'I'm sorry. Why?'

Anne hesitated. 'You're so...so...righteous. Always so Christian.'

'Anne!'

Anne shrugged. 'You are, you know. You accept things so meekly, without a murmur. 'Tis infuriating. Why, when I dragged you away from the convent——'

Beatrice remembered her confrontation with the Prioress, but held her tongue on that matter. 'You didn't drag me. I came willingly enough in the end.'

'Did you? Maybe so. But if I hadn't asked for you to accompany me to England, you have stayed on at the convent willingly enough, too. You'd have let them make a nun of you.'

'I still have plans for——'

'Oh, aye, I know about your plans for taking up the veil,' Anne interrupted irritably, jerking the comb so hard on a knot that tears pricked in Beatrice's eyes. Silently Beatrice peered round to survey the damage Anne was wreaking in her hair. The knot was now twisted so tight it would take an age to remove.

Anne had not noticed. 'But I dare say if your precious Mother Adèle asked you to marry a Saxon, you'd do so just as willingly,' she said.

Beatrice felt her colour rise. 'M-marry a Saxon?' she murmured. 'I don't know.'

'I do,' Anne declared. 'You'd sacrifice yourself quite happily in the cause of unity or peace, or some such high-minded drivel. You're a dreamer, Beatrice. Let me give you a piece of advice. One day you'll wake up to find you actually have a mind of your own. With thoughts and feelings of your own. Not just the ones the nuns have lent you. Their ideas suit you as badly as their clothes. Life is not so starkly simple outside the convent gates. There's more than right and wrong. There are shades in between. Your good sisters do not have all the answers. Sometimes faith is not enough.'

Remembering how prayer had seemed to have failed her for the first time that very day, Beatrice bit her lip. Her faith had never been tested till then. She did not want to think about it.

'Anne, don't.' Beatrice pulled the comb from her cousin's clumsy hands. Whether she was referring to Anne's rough ministrations or her cynicism, she could not have said.

'I'm glad there's no Saxon groom for me!' Anne said defiantly, her eyes challenging Beatrice. When no re-action was forthcoming, she spread her hands in a gesture of self-deprecation. 'See what a monster you have for a cousin, Beatrice. Will you still be my friend?'

'Don't be silly, Anne. You've been unnerved by all this. We all have. Of course I'll be your friend.'

Anne cracked out a bitter laugh which scored deep lines around her mouth and made her voice harsh. 'Oh, Beatrice, Beatrice. You always see the best in people. You're hopeless.'

Anne's mood could change as unexpectedly as April weather. It did so now. Her face relaxed. Her voice lightened. 'Ooh, I know,' she announced. 'I've just the belt for that gown. Your old one is all wrong with it. Come to think of it, yours would be all wrong with

almost anything. Did it do duty tying up sacks before
you laid hands on it? Here, Beatrice, I've a veil you can
have as well. Do you like it? I bought it from a pedlar
in Normandy before we left, and 'tis not a colour I
favour. I must have had you in mind.'

Smiling, Beatrice accepted the gifts, realising these
gestures were her cousin's way of making amends for
her cutting tongue. For all Lady Anne's surface sophis-
tication, she was oddly transparent. Beatrice warmed to
her.

She hung the Saxon dagger at her waist and adjusted
her new veil and circlet.

'Every inch the beautiful Norman lady,' Anne
approved.

'Oh,' Beatrice muttered doubtfully.

'Aren't you pleased?' asked Anne sharply.

'How could I not be?' Beatrice replied. 'My thanks,
Anne. These clothes are much finer than my old ones.'

''Twas nothing. We can't have you walking around
in rags. You'd be indistinguishable from the Saxons.'

Beatrice drew her brows together.

Anne laughed. 'If you're going to look as sour as a
nun on a fast, cousin, you can stay here on your own.
I'll find more entertaining company. Have you seen the
Baron?'

'He was in the hall when I last saw him.'

'You're not coming down?' Anne wondered, straight-
ening her veil.

'Not yet. I'm rather tired. I'll see you at supper.
Always supposing that someone has had the fore-
thought to leave a Saxon alive to cook it,' she said with
a touch of dryness.

Anne grinned back from the door. 'So you do have
a sense of humour, after all. I'd begun to wonder.'
Waving airily, she floated out of the chamber in a swirl
of scented skirts.

Beatrice could hardly believe her luck. With Anne dis-
tracting the Baron, she might have long enough to get
across to the chapel and see to the Saxon's wounds. She
could not have planned it better if she'd tried.

It took a few minutes to comb out the bird's nest Anne
had made of her hair. She did not hurry. It might take

a while for Anne to engage the Baron's attention. When she'd finished with her hair, she rose and fastened her thick cloak about her shoulders. She intended to hide the roll of medicines beneath it.

She prayed that the Baron would not see her. But if he did he would not think it strange to see her venture abroad in her heaviest cloak. It was an exceptionally bitter January. And, if anyone should chance to catch a glimpse of her and accost her, she'd simply say she needed to clear her head after working all afternoon tending the sick.

Notwithstanding all these assurances, cold perspiration trickled down her back as she made her way down the stairs. Neither Anne nor the Baron were in sight. The men on the pallets mumbled and shuffled, but they were as comfortable as could be expected. Her shoes were of soft leather so they made no sound to draw curious eyes her way. She headed for the door.

'Mistress,' a voice croaked up at her, and she started.

'Aye, what is it?' Her heart was hammering like a drum.

'Some ale, Mistress. Please,' the wounded man pleaded.

The pitcher was back there on the trestle. Beatrice cursed the delay. The longer she remained in the hall, the more likely it was that Philip de Brionne would return. Her fingers closed over the vessel. It was heavy in her hands. Someone snatched it from her and her startled eyes met Walter's.

'Walter!' Relief flooded through her. 'You gave me such a fright.'

Walter bent over the man on the pallet, offering him a draught.

'My thanks, Walter,' Beatrice said. 'Please give the others some if they need it. I'll be back soon.'

Patting Walter on the arm, Beatrice gathered her roll of medicines and fled from the hall, pausing on the threshold only long enough to check that her route to the chapel was clear.

There was no sound in the chapel. It was as quiet and as cold as a tomb. Shivering, Beatrice fastened the door.

She drew her cloak closer about her slender body. Outside the sun was low in the sky, and ghostly shadows stretched out across the stone flags.

Had he died here, then, that it was so silent? Please, please, don't let him be dead. Beatrice ran round the altar to the chancel where the last shreds of sunlight shone brightest on the grey floor. She flung back the richly embroidered cloth.

'I've come back to help you,' she whispered. She tensed herself, half expecting a hand to shoot out and grasp her. But Edmund did not move. The Saxon lay where she had left him, inert. All pain and hatred had gone from his face, there was only a breath-stopping, unnatural stillness about the chalk-white features.

Her lips moved in supplication. Edmund's skin felt clammy, but it was warm. Gently, Beatrice shifted the dark head to search for the pulse at his throat. For one horrible moment she could not find it, and thought she had returned too late. Then she felt it. Faint, but steady enough. She breathed again and set to work.

A stained pad covered the wound on his shoulder. Quickly she peeled it away, noting absently that the fabric, which was a richly decorated silk, had certainly not been intended for anything as humble as a bandage. The gold threadwork was dyed with blood. Beatrice shuddered, and forced her attention back to the wound. It was easier to deal with the injury itself. The gore on the silk finery was a poignant reminder of the futility of violence.

Edmund's wound had stopped bleeding, but it was going to be difficult to clean. The clotting blood had caused the Saxon's tunic to stick to the wound and it would all have to be eased gently away. She sighed; no doubt the wound would reopen, but it had to be done lest suppuration set in. He'd lain neglected long enough.

With expert hands, Beatrice ran her hands down his quiescent body, feeling for broken bones or any other sign of damage as Sister Agnes had taught her. The convent was a world away, but Beatrice was grateful for the long hours she had spent with Sister Agnes. She found a small gash on one well-muscled thigh, but it could wait.

Unclasping her cloak, she flung it over Edmund,
leaving only the damaged shoulder uncovered.

'Water, I need water,' she mumbled to herself. Taking
the bowl from her pack, she rose and filled it with holy
water from the piscina. God would not object to her
using His water for healing. Sister Agnes had told her
often enough that her healing skills were to be available
to all men, irrespective of race, creed or birth. It would
never have occurred to Beatrice to dispute this. Baron
de Brionne's iniquitous behaviour made her blush to be
a Norman too. It weighed heavily on her soul. If she
saved this Saxon warrior, she would have redressed the
balance a little, at least. She could not let him die.

Cleansing the wound took much time and patience.
First she must soak and then gently peel back the ruined
tunic. At last she had finished, and the wound was
bleeding as she had expected, but sluggishly. It had to
be bound at once. She drew the Saxon's dagger from
her belt, intending to cut off the remains of his damaged
tunic in order to bind him securely. The fabric had started
to part under the blade when Beatrice noticed the Saxon's
breathing pattern had altered subtly.

He was watching her, a confused expression in his
dazed blue eyes. Weakly he raised a hand to clutch at
her forearm as though he would fend her off.

'Am I to die then?' he rasped. 'Do Norman maids kill
helpless men?' His eyes dropped to the dagger. 'And
with my own blade, too.' He winced.

Firmly Beatrice removed his hand and smiled at him,
shaking her head. She could not read his expression
clearly in the gloomy chancel, nor could she tell if he
could read hers.

'Shh!' she admonished. 'You must be quiet. If de
Brionne discovers you're here, I cannot say what he may
do.'

'My shoulder...' His quiet groan was like the wind
sighing through leafless trees.

'Nay. Don't touch it,' Beatrice reproved gently. 'I've
just cleaned it, and you would undo all my good work.
Let me finish and bind it for you.'

'You must be a rare jewel among your people,' he
said, hoarsely. 'Gentle of touch *and* voice.'

He spoke so low that Beatrice had to bend to hear him. She touched his lips with her forefinger. 'Shh.' She finished cutting the tunic and eased it away, conscious of the puzzled eyes watching her every movement. She was glad when she had finished, for her normally deft fingers were suddenly clumsy under that unwavering stare. 'There! Now all you have to do is keep still, and quiet.'

Edmund made a movement as if to sit up. Beatrice put her hand to his chest and pushed him back as firmly as she dared.

'I cannot stay here,' he protested, subsiding weakly under the pressure of her hand. His voice was dry as dust.

'You are too weak to go anywhere,' Beatrice insisted. 'And the mood out there is distinctly anti-Saxon. You must regain your strength before you move.'

'I'm thirsty.'

'Wait a moment. I'll fetch some water.'

As she rinsed and refilled the bowl at the piscina by the door, the squeak of unoiled hinges set an alarm bell clamouring through Beatrice's mind. The door was swinging wide. She had shut it fast...

Heart pounding, Beatrice peered through the crack in the door. But no danger lurked in the twilit compound. There was only Walter, lounging in the hall doorway, and a lone pig rooting ever-hopeful in barren ground. There was no trace of either her cousin or the Baron.

Frowning, Beatrice closed the door. She rattled it to test the catch. The latch held fast. It was strong enough to withstand a winter gale. It could not have swung open on its own. Anxiety stirred within her.

'Your water.' She eased Edmund's head on to her lap to enable him to drink. Dark lashes, unusually long for a man, stood out against the pallor of his face. His features were strong and finely drawn—Roman nose, well-shaped lips. Not the brutish barbarian of Anne's imaginings, though his long hair did give him a pagan look, at least to convent-bred eyes.

He was helpless now, weak from loss of blood. His lean limbs sprawled out across the floor, all strength drained from them with his blood. He was dependent on her. His life was in her hands. With a pang in her breast, she remembered the strong, upstanding warrior who had greeted her when they had arrived. Now she cradled that proud head in her arms. He was as white as bleached linen.

How greedily he drank. She cleared her throat and chided, 'Not too much, Edmund.'

'Mmm?'

'You mustn't drink too much.' She attempted to remove the bowl, but slender fingers tightened on hers with a hint of their former strength and he continued gulping down the liquid as though it were the very stuff of life.

'Stop it. You'll be sick.' Beatrice wrenched the bowl from his grasp and the water slopped out across the stone slabs.

'You're very fierce,' Edmund grinned. His eyes were alight with mockery.

Beatrice smiled, suddenly shy.

'I wish I could see you properly,' he announced. ''Tis too dark. Your hair shines, but I can't see your eyes. I seem to recall they're green...'

Caught off guard, Beatrice felt her cheeks flood with warmth. 'I'm told they're hazel,' she mumbled, glad that the twilight hid her confusion.

A silence fell, during which time Beatrice realised that Edmund's head still rested comfortably in her arms. He had made no attempt to move away, and was studying her with as much attention as she had earlier studied him. A dark lock of hair fell across one eye. Unthinking, Beatrice smoothed the errant lock from his face. A dark brow arched upwards. Hastily Beatrice snatched her hand from his hair.

She must speak to cover her confusion. 'Edmund?' she blurted.

'Mistress Beatrice?' mockingly.

'You... you don't look like a barbarian to me.' She'd stammered the first thing that entered her head, and no sooner had she said it than she cursed her tactless tongue.

'Do I not? And who told you that I was? De Brionne, I suppose,' he said, mildly enough.

She relaxed. He had not taken it amiss. 'Nay. 'Twas my cousin Anne. She fears all your race as unholy barbarians. The Baron said that Saxons have no sense of loyalty. No honour.'

Edmund's face darkened. 'I'd expect such a comment from that faithless scavenger, but I'd hoped for better from my brother's betrothed.' He gave a choking cough and flinched, screwing up his eyes in pain.

'Forgive me,' Beatrice said. 'I shouldn't be speaking to you like this. You should be resting, not getting angry.'

'Nay,' Edmund disagreed, still with his eyes closed. There was a white line about his lips. 'Talk. It takes my mind off my shoulder. Tell me, Mistress Beatrice, what do *you* think? Am I a . . . what was it . . . a barbarian?'

'Nay. Your clothes are styled somewhat differently from ours, but that's not to say they're barbaric. They're different, that's all. The cloth is good, the embroideries are pretty and neatly done.'

Beatrice chattered nonsense, knowing Edmund was too busy fighting the pain to be listening. If it helped him to have her babble she would not deny him. There was little enough she could do for him. This day he had seen his brother killed. His home had been torn apart, and his people scattered to the four winds. Gradually the lines of pain on Edmund's face eased.

He opened his eyes and looked at her. Beatrice floundered.

'Go on. Don't stop,' he attempted a smile.

''Twas only idle talk. I was saying how you wear your hair longer than a Norman would. I dare say when it's clean it could be quite attractive.' She risked an impish grin.

'My thanks, fair maid,' he said drily. And then he shut his eyes again with a sharp intake of breath. His hands were clenched into fists.

'M-more water?' she offered.

He shook his head and grimaced. 'Talk to me. Just talk,' he managed.

Beatrice nodded. 'When I found you earlier, you terrified me. I thought maybe all the tales we were told about Saxons were true. I'd never believed it till then.

But you seemed so desperate, I was sure you would kill me.'

'And now?' Edmund asked softly.

'Now I . . . I know you won't hurt me. I know you are not barbaric. My cousin and the Baron are both wrong.'

Edmund unclenched his fist and reached for a dangling braid. Slowly he wound it round his fingers.

'What of the Baron?' he asked, casually.

'Oh, he's hateful, I——' She broke off as pain flickered across his drawn features. His fingers were very white on her braid and she put her hand on his in a spontaneous gesture of comfort.

'Is . . . is it very bad?' she heard herself ask, stupidly. Of course it was bad, it must be agony. He had a tear in his shoulder the size of her fist, and she asked him if it hurt.

'Aye,' he admitted. 'But my leg's paining me now, too.' He grinned apologetically.

'Your leg! Oh, sweet Mother, I had forgot. My apologies. I was so concerned about your shoulder that it slipped my mind. 'Tis only a scratch, but I'll dress it for you.'

Beatrice folded the now tattered tunic into a pad and placed it on the stone flags for a pillow.

'The floor is very uneven here. You chose a funny place to hide,' she remarked, easing his long length to a smoother stone. His eyes were screwed shut, and perspiration beaded his brow. His fingers still clutched at her braid. She prised it free, guessing he was near fainting.

'When I've finished bandaging this, I shall have to leave you,' she told him.

A groan of protest slid from his lips.

'I'll leave you with water. And I'll try and return tonight. 'Tis not easy, for the Baron hovers around me like a hawk. I can't risk him finding out you're here. I shall leave you your dagger, so you won't be unarmed in case . . . in case . . .' She left the sentence unfinished.

'No!' he burst out, so loudly that Beatrice started. He was struggling to rise. 'You must keep the dagger,' he insisted. 'De Brionne expects you to have it. He will notice its absence if you leave it with me. I can look after myself.'

'Very well,' Beatrice agreed. 'I'll keep your dagger, but only if you will be still, and rest.'

He subsided with a sigh.

The door-latch rattled.

Beatrice jerked her head up and stared wide-eyed with horror at the door. Her limbs froze along with her wits.

Not so Edmund's. 'Get in here! Quickly!' he hissed, and before she had time to protest she found herself lying in Edmund's arms, held close in the small space. The altar cloth was pulled into place. It veiled them both from sight.

It was very dark in the confined space. Beatrice found her face pressed to the Saxon's bandaged chest. Her heart thumped at her ribs. She was afraid. But she was not afraid of him—not the Saxon. She was afraid for him. Afraid that if it was the Baron outside . . . She shuddered and pressed herself closer to Edmund's side, taking care to avoid his injury.

The man she feared most was Norman, not Saxon. Edmund did not fill her with revulsion. He felt very cold. She burrowed closer, wanting to warm him. She could feel his heart beneath her cheek, fast and uncertain. She was aware of a pleasant masculine scent. She ached to help him, to comfort him. Then a flush scorched across her cheekbones. If he had been well, she would never have let him hold her thus . . .

Quick footsteps sounded in the chapel, coming nearer to the altar.

'You think she's in here, do you, Walter?'

At the sound of that detested voice, every muscle in Beatrice's body went rigid. She could barely draw breath. She felt Edmund's hand move to rest on her head, holding her secure.

'Idiot!' De Brionne's rough tones again. 'She's not in here. Come on, you dribbling half-wit.'

Beatrice heard a heavy sigh.

'God only knows why you were brought along with us,' the Baron declared, speaking slowly as one would to a child. 'I want you to find Beatrice for me. Move, oaf! Find Beatrice! Christ! Someone should have put you out of your misery years ago!'

There was a soft thud, and Beatrice visualised Walter being kicked by the Norman as clearly as though her eyes had pierced through the fabric of the altar cloth. The door slammed, and all went quiet.

Edmund let out his breath and his hold on Beatrice relaxed.

'You're cold,' she whispered, not moving away.

'You could stay and warm me, then,' he suggested huskily.

With a jerk Beatrice pulled herself away. Edmund gave a scornful snort.

'A Norman lady docile in a Saxon's arms. A rare moment. I shall have to treasure it.'

Beatrice tore her gaze from him and shakily began to gather up her medicines. They'd been strewn all over in their haste to hide.

'I have never held a Norman maid till now,' Edmund told her, watching her expression, his own guarded.

Beatrice stuffed a jar of ointment back into her bundle. 'And I was never in any man's arms till now.' The telltale words slipped out before she had time to snatch them back. She could have groaned aloud.

An insistent tug of her plait drew her face round, and forced her to meet those searching blue eyes.

'Never been in any man's arms? A pretty maid like you. Now I know for certain that the Normans are mad,' Edmund declared.

Goaded by what she took for mocking disbelief, Beatrice tried to toss her head, but the captured braid had her anchored fast. 'I have lived a cloistered life. I have no knowledge of Saxon convents, but in Normandy there are not too many men in them. At least none who would...' She struggled in vain to free her hair.

'Brought up by nuns,' Edmund said thoughtfully. 'I thought de Brionne was jesting. Were you?'

'Aye. After my mother died, I stayed on. There was nowhere else for me to go. Oh, Edmund, please release me!'

Her plea was ignored. 'Tell me, Mistress Beatrice who-has-never-been-held-by-a-man, have you ever been kissed?'

Beatrice made a choking sound and managed at last to look away. She burned all over.

Edmund had not finished tormenting her. 'Because if you have not, I would like to remedy that omission,' he announced coolly.

She shot him a swift glance at that.

'Why?' she whispered.

'If I'm not mistaken, that lout de Brionne is hot on your trail, and if I do not kiss you he certainly will. I find that that thought does not please me. I do not think him a man to consider an innocent maid's feelings over-much. You go pale at the merest mention of his name. Do you want him to be the first to kiss you?'

Beatrice shook her head. 'But that doesn't mean...'

Edmund smiled. He had a beautiful mouth.

'I remember when you first arrived. You did not like him then. Your slender fingers have a powerful grip. You clung to me, a stranger, in preference to him. And re-member, Beatrice, I heard your conversation with him earlier this afternoon.'

'You understand Norman French?' she exclaimed, seizing on this as a diversion to distract Edmund from his intention. Oddly, his knowledge of her tongue did not come as a surprise.

'What, a barbarian like me? Surely not?' he mocked.

'I never said you were,' Beatrice mumbled.

'Nevertheless, barbarian or not, I think you dislike him,' Edmund said, refusing to be side-tracked.

'Aye,' she admitted. ''Tis the way he looks at me. All hot, and yet with such cold eyes. 'Tis strange, I've never seen anyone who can watch you like that. It makes me squirm inside. And after this morning...' Her voice wavered.

'So you don't want him to be the first to kiss you, either?'

Beatrice shuddered.

'Does that thought please you?' he prompted.

Beatrice shook her head slowly, wishing she could see more of his face through the gloom. Her heart was racing.

The pull on her braid increased and Beatrice found her head being brought down to meet his. Edmund's eyes dropped to her mouth, went back to search her eyes again, and then, as if satisfied with what he saw there, he slowly pulled her head down the rest of the way, and his lips made contact with hers in a swift, tentative caress.

He released his hold on her braid. Wide-eyed, Beatrice drew back. He was looking deep into her eyes. He smiled, and then she was being drawn gently down again, and this time his kiss was not so tentative. And this time when he released her braids Beatrice did not pull back. She was out of breath. Edmund's hand rose briefly and fluttered a caress across her cheek. Then it dropped back with a jerk.

Beatrice struggled to bring some order back to her senses. His kiss had disorientated her. She saw that he was in pain again, and could not have marked the effect his kiss had had on her. Her lips tingled still, and the place on her cheek burned where he had touched her. She had no idea so simple a thing as a kiss could have such a devastating effect. Was it always like this?

Her mother had told her that ladies did not enjoy such things. That was for common women, for sluts. And the nuns did not speak of kisses, either. They referred to them disparagingly as carnal matters, never to be discussed. She wondered if another kiss would have the same effect on her as his first had done.

She had been taught that lovemaking was a duty that married women had to put up with, and a rather unpleasant one at that. Until this moment nothing had happened to disabuse her of that idea. But Edmund, with one kiss, had filled her with delight. She wondered angrily why she had been lied to, why no one had seen fit to tell her how wonderful kissing could be.

Edmund was covering his face with his hand. His brow was deeply scored with lines.

'Edmund. You've hurt yourself.' Her voice shook.

''Twas worth it.' He removed his hand and gave a lopsided grin.

'Don't be foolish. You're all out of breath. Rest. I'll leave the water here and try and bring you food and clothing later. You *must* rest.'

Edmund held out his hand to her. 'Did you enjoy your first kiss?' he enquired.

Beatrice imagined a hint of uncertainty in his tone.

'Or are you so furious that a Saxon has dared to touch you that you must run away?'

'You are impertinent to ask such questions. I shall not answer.' Beatrice felt the hot blood flooding her cheeks, and knew she was crimson.

'So prim!' he mocked.

'I...I must go. They are looking for me. God keep you till I return.' She smiled and made to leave.

'One thing further,' Edmund's voice hailed her back. 'Hard by there must be a young Saxon girl, Hilda. I worry for her safety, if your Baron lays his filthy paws on her. Please watch out for her. Try and prevent your people from harming her.'

Beatrice went cold to the core. The way he had sneered when he'd said 'your people'. It was as though he considered her in league with the Devil himself.

'She is all I have left,' Edmund was saying.

His voice was husky with emotion, and that betrayed more about his feelings for this Hilda than words ever could. He loved her. Beatrice stiffened her spine, and fought to keep her features in order.

'Hilda,' she repeated stonily. The knots were back, twisting her stomach.

'Aye, Hilda. She's very young. Please try and help her.' Edmund held out his hand towards her. Beatrice ignored the gesture. A puzzled frown crossed his white face and chased away his smile. She ignored that, too. His hand dropped back on to the cloak, his fingers closed on the thick folds.

'There's no need to pretend any more,' Beatrice said coldly, and wrenched the altar cloth down so it screened his face from hers. Her voice was unrecognisable.

As she groped blindly towards the great door, Beatrice fought hard to push back the impression that Edmund's face had watched her go with a strange vulnerability stamped across it.

It's only because he's ailing, she told herself, ruth-lessly squelching the hope that there was another reason for the expression she'd glimpsed. It had been too dark to see him properly, anyway.

'Hilda indeed!' she muttered angrily. She agreed with de Brionne about one thing. The Saxons had no sense of honour. And to think she'd actually enjoyed his kisses. The man was nothing but a barbarian.

CHAPTER FOUR

IN THE hall the smell of tallow lanterns mingled with the aroma of roasted meats. More of the trestle tables had been set up, and those Normans who were still able-bodied were eating in the fitful flare of the light cascading from half a dozen tall iron lampstands.

'Beatrice! Meat is on the board,' Anne called as soon as Beatrice appeared in the entrance. Anne was already ensconced like a Queen in state. At her right hand, her King, and Consort, the Baron Philip de Brionne.

As casually as she could, Beatrice kicked the damning roll of remedies out of sight behind an upturned barrel.

'Where the hell have you been?' the Baron demanded gracelessly.

Beatrice assumed a calm face and stepped into the splash of light. 'Outside.'

'Without your cloak?' he pressed. His eyes gleamed black as sin.

'I went for a short walk,' Beatrice said airily. 'I needed to clear my head.' With a graceful wave of her arm she indicated the invalids.

'Your patients have been tended and fed. So there's no need for you to worry about *them*.' The Baron's voice was dry, his emphasis on the last word alarming.

Beatrice kept a bright smile pinned on her face and took her place on the bench, at her cousin's other side. She peered at the Baron from under her lashes, hoping his suspicions had not been aroused. He must not find out who lay hidden in the chapel. Though the Saxon had used her shamefully, she could not betray him.

'Did you notice the moon is nearly full, Baron?' Anne smiled flirtatiously at the Norman and he laughed. His saturnine face was almost human when lit by genuine laughter. Beatrice found herself giving thanks to the

63

Saints yet again that King William had commanded the Baron to attend to her cousin's every whim.

'Can't say I noticed the moon,' he answered drily. The Baron and Anne exchanged smiles. Marvelling at her cousin's ability to deal with men, Beatrice reached for a hunk of bread and some salt beef. If Anne could soften the Baron's hard heart, she could surely bend the most rigid of minds to her will. Such a talent might have many uses...

'Nay, Beatrice. You mustn't eat tonight.' Anne laughed and pulled the serving platter away.

'Why ever not? I'm hungry,' Beatrice protested, reaching out for her share.

'I never thought *you'd* be asking that. Not with your convent education.' Teasingly Anne edged the platter further from Beatrice. The Baron choked on his wine.

'Anne, don't be so provoking. I'm hungry and I will eat.' A half-eaten heel of a loaf sat within reach and Beatrice beat Anne to it by spearing it with her knife.

'Oh, Beatrice!' Anne pouted.

Deliberately Beatrice bit into the wheaten crust.

'You fool! You shouldn't have done that. You'll have to wait a whole year now before you find out.' Anne glanced coyly at the Baron and added pointedly, '*I* haven't eaten a thing.'

From behind Beatrice a different voice broke into the conversation. 'I don't think the nuns will have told Beatrice about the superstition connected with St Agnes' Eve.'

'Save you, Father Ralph!' Beatrice greeted the Norman priest. 'I didn't see you there. Please sit down.' She shifted towards Anne to make room for the cleric and caught the Baron's cold eyes on her. She jerked her gaze away, afraid lest he should read her secret.

The priest muttered a hasty grace and carved into a side of pork. Noting Beatrice had no meat, he offered her a slice.

Beatrice grinned at Anne and took the food. 'Thank you, Father. Will you tell me about St Agnes' Eve? I've never heard of St Agnes? Who was she?'

Father Ralph's eyes twinkled. 'St Agnes was a young girl who was being forced against her will to marry a pagan officer in Roman times.' He cut a small piece of meat and threw it into his mouth.

'That at least sounds familiar,' Anne drawled, her voice laden with sarcasm.

'Aye, well, ha-hmm.' Father Ralph spluttered, red-faced, and reached for a drinking horn. He was unused to outspoken ladies, and had found the best way to cope with infelicitous remarks was to ignore them. 'Mmm. This is good. Now, where was I? Oh, aye, the young Agnes. She was martyred. She refused to marry the pagan and a superstition has grown up about the eve of her Feast. 'Tis tonight, you know. Feast day tomorrow.

''Tis said that if a young—er—virgin wants to know the identity of the man she will marry, she should retire to bed having fasted since midday. Certain—ah—charms or prayers should be chanted, a specially prepared egg should be eaten, some mulled wine; and the maiden will apparently wake at midnight with a vision of her future husband before her eyes. Some claim 'tis possible the future husband will actually manifest himself in the flesh. Of course, there's no truth in any of this,' Father Ralph stressed, looking hard at both Beatrice and Anne.

There was a little pause, while the tip of the priest's drinking horn pointed up to the tie beam, and he gulped the contents down. He wiped his mouth with his habit and went on. ''Tis a superstition that has pagan origins and as such is not to be heeded. St Agnes is chiefly honoured by the Church as being the patroness of young girls, and of bodily chastity.'

Philip de Brionne threw back his head and roared. 'Come, Father! You can't tell me anyone would really believe such a yarn!'

'Sad to say, there are many who profess to believe in it,' the priest assured him, shaking his head.

'Nay, Father, that cannot be. Even you must see 'tis just an excuse to explain away a sin of the flesh. Tonight at least, those who profess to believe in the divinations can escape the conventions of everyday life.' The Baron aimed a quick smile at Anne. 'Lovers could meet, and claim 'twas merely the prophecy brought them together.'

Beatrice frowned.

'I must say that hadn't occurred to me,' the priest admitted.

'It wouldn't,' de Brionne said curtly. 'In your state of grace.' His thin lips curled. In his jaundiced eyes, innocence was reckoned a sin.

Beatrice sprang to the priest's defence. 'It all sounds utter nonsense to me,' she declared. 'I can see why I was never told of that superstition.'

Father Ralph smiled at her. De Brionne's scornful shaft had left him quite undented. 'Aye, my child. As "Brides of Christ", the nuns would naturally take no interest in more earthly husbands.'

Beatrice proffered the jug of mead.

'Thank you, Beatrice, I *will* have more. 'Tis just the thing to wash this excellent cheese down with.'

'I'll say this for our absent hosts, they keep a good store,' the Baron commented, draining his own vessel, and encompassing the laden board with a wide sweep of his arm.

Anne took the hint and filled the Norman's horn to its silver rim with the wine he favoured. ''Tis the one thing these barbarians know how to do. I've seen the storeroom. There's row after row of salted meat, stacks of dried fruit, ale by the barrel——'

'Ale!' the Baron sneered.

Anne smiled. 'Aye, Baron, but you must allow this wine is good.'

'Aye, Saxons might make good stewards. They're fit for naught else. At least we won't starve in this benighted hole,' de Brionne allowed.

The talk became general. Beatrice ate mechanically, tasting nothing. Her cousin was indeed not eating and this surprised her. She had not judged Anne to be superstitious. Covertly she watched her cousin flirting skilfully with the Baron. That was nothing new, but there was something about Anne's manner that Beatrice had not seen before. She could not put her finger on it. She shrugged and wished that she possessed even an ounce of Anne's sang-froid. She always felt so gawky with men. Anne would never be gawky with anyone.

Father Ralph was complimenting Beatrice on her healing skills, discussing the herbs she used. Inevitably, the conversation worked its way round to the culinary rather than the healing arts, for Father Ralph was all too fond of his stomach. Beatrice found her mind wandering and replied somewhat absently to the priest's queries. The sooner the meal was over, the better.

'...the chapel, Beatrice?' Father Ralph asked, suddenly winning her full attention.

The food curdled in her stomach.

'I shall visit it later to pray for peace. An end to the violence.' Father Ralph announced, his eyes shifting towards the Norman Baron.

Beatrice knew she'd gone pale. She swallowed and groped for her voice. 'Oh, F-father, 'twill be black as pitch in the chapel now. You wouldn't be able to see a thing. I'd go in the morning.'

'You don't need light to pray, my child,' Father Ralph reproved gently.

'N-no, Father, I know that. B-but...' She stuttered to a halt and turned to gauge how much the Baron had gleaned from her stammerings. De Brionne's eyes were narrowed, but when her eyes reached his he diverted his brooding gaze instead to the brimming pitcher of mead.

'More mead, Father?' the Baron offered smoothly. 'Anne, your fasting does not include liquids, I hope.' He was most polished, most charming. And a little voice inside Beatrice began to chant over and over, like a litany, 'He knows, he knows, he knows.'

Beatrice kept a firm check on her tongue, too fearful to speak, almost too fearful to move, lest she betray the Saxon hiding in the chapel. Every time de Brionne's black regard rested on her, she forced herself to smile. She tried to eat, could not face the meat, and bit on her bread. It tasted stale, and stuck in her throat.

'Beatrice! You've moved so far down the board I can't reach your cup.' De Brionne loosed a predatory grin. 'Father, please replenish Beatrice's goblet; methinks she has bitten off more than she can chew. We'll have to keep an eye on her down there at the other end of the trestle.'

'Thank you, Father.' Beatrice clung on grimly to her air of unconcern. 'Will you be celebrating Mass tomorrow, Father?' she smiled brightly.

A valiant attempt at conversation, but not enough. For the rest of the meal the dark, sin-black eyes remained fixed on her.

At last the dreadful meal was over.

The boards were being cleared and set back against the walls of the hall. Beatrice retrieved her bundle from its secret hiding place by the door, and shoved bread and meat inside. A pile of discarded bandages must serve to hide it until later.

The guards were bedding down in the cleared space in the centre of the hall, and the nightly battle had begun. Pillows and blankets flew across the floor as men elbowed and jostled for space. The successful combatants managed to win a place by the fire. The smoke billowing off it hung in the lungs, but it was either breathe fumes or freeze. Most preferred the fumes. The unlucky ones, those slower off the mark, and the wounded who had no comrade to see they were warmly stowed, had to make do with the draughtier sleeping quarters by the door.

They fought and squabbled to their places. On a night when the frost nipped even in the sooty warmth of the hall, most thought it better to suffer the fumes from the fire than the vicious English air as it blasted in through the cracks and stabbed at fingers and toes.

Beatrice glanced at Anne, still conversing with the Baron under the overhanging first-floor gallery. She was grateful that she and Anne had been accorded the privilege of sharing the upper chamber. She bade her dinner companions goodnight and climbed the stairs, a rush light in her hand. She pulled back the wall-hanging that served as a door to the upper chamber. Ella had let the candles blow out. She groped for the candle-clock she knew to be on her coffer, lit it, and sat on the edge of the bed, deep in thought.

When Anne came up some minutes later, a steaming goblet of mulled wine in either hand, Beatrice was already curled up in bed. The auburn head was half-hidden by the coverlet. She was quite still. Anne clunked a goblet down on the floorboards on her cousin's side of the bed. A fragrant aroma of spices and herbs spiralled upwards in the steam and reached the girl in the bed. Anne saw her nostrils quiver.

'Beatrice?' Anne whispered loudly.

No answer.

'Beatrice?' Anne persisted.

Silence.

Anne sighed softly and pinched the candle out. There was a rustle of material as Anne moved round the bed and removed her outer gown. The bed sagged. The covers shifted.

Beatrice smiled into the darkness. Unbudging, she waited until she knew from Anne's breathing that her cousin slept. Then she waited some more. And when she was quite certain she slid soundlessly from the bed. The rush matting felt hard on her feet. She shivered and fumbled for her shoes. It was bitterly cold.

Reaching under the bed-frame, she caught up her outer clothes and, pausing only to snatch up one of Anne's woollen cloaks, crept out of the room.

A dull glow from the fire lit up the hall. The only other source of light was a pinprick of light from a shuttered lantern atop a barrel. Sleeping bodies clustered round the fire. A hound whined in its sleep, legs twitching. Someone snored. A log spat and hissed.

Cautiously, Beatrice picked her way to the door where her pack lay waiting. She fumbled in the uncertain light, and thought she'd mistaken the place. Her heartbeat quickened. She grasped the lantern, opened the shutter a crack and groped again in the mean sliver of light. Her fingers stumbled on a familiar shape and she let her breath out in a slow sigh of relief. Thank God! She must go now. She could not be caught scrabbling about by the door when she should be abed.

Someone moaned and tossed restlessly in his sleep. The sound nudged her out into the night. She shut the hall door, and scurried across the frost-silvered yard, like a mouse with the owl's screech ringing a death-knell in its ears.

''Tis only me,' she spoke into the dark and silent chapel. 'I've brought food and blankets.'

Opening the shutter of the lantern, Beatrice took her bundle round to the back of the altar and hooked up the cloth.

Edmund gazed up at her. His set face looked past her to peer into the darkness beyond the small pool of light.

'What is it?' Beatrice asked.

'You're alone?' he questioned, tightly.

'I would not betray you!' Beatrice said indignantly.

'Would you not?' His question came softly at her through the gloom.

'Nay, I would not. Even though as a Saxon you'd probably kill me, given half the chance!'

'I, kill *you*?' He smiled and held out a hand for hers.

Beatrice ignored his hand and fiddled with the lantern-catch.

'No,' she conceded, 'you probably won't bother to kill me. You consider me a—a harlot. People don't generally kill such women. You think you have bought my help for you and this Hilda with your sweetest kisses. I am not deceived.'

'Were they sweet?' he teased.

'What?' Beatrice glared at him.

'My kisses, were they truly sweet?' Beatrice did not reply, and Edmund continued with a hint of laughter in his voice. 'Is that why you are angry, Mistress Beatrice? Because they *were* sweet?'

His hand covered hers and he stilled her restless fingers with his. She felt her hand grow warm. It tingled. She felt every small, caressing movement his fingers made and nothing else.

'When you left in such haste, I thought that maybe you did not find my kisses so pleasing,' he told her, and pulled her gently towards him. 'Let's find out, shall we?'

Beatrice found herself actually bending her head to his. Not resisting at all. A small voice inside her insisted that she should not be doing this, but she turned a deaf ear to it and allowed Edmund to bring her close.

This kiss was as gentle and searching as his other kisses had been. Beatrice felt a fierce longing sweep through her. Her loins melted. She raised a trembling hand and touched Edmund's cheek. Her lips softened, she kissed him back, and slid her arms around his neck. And all the while the little voice nagged in her brain—condemned her for responding. She was wrong. She was a fool. She would regret this. She held him closer.

Edmund groaned. At once Beatrice pulled free.

'There's no need to cripple yourself to get me to help you. I've already promised my assistance,' she said sharply, and turned to delve in her pack for the tunic she'd found him. 'Here, take this.' Edmund made as if to speak, but Beatrice swept on. 'Here's a sword I picked up for you. It won't be missed. 'Tis from one of your Saxon men.' She avoided his eyes. 'He won't be needing it any more.'

Edmund scowled at her from under dark brows. Probably it was her tactless mention of his bondman. She rattled on, regardless. 'And here's some food. 'Tis all I could smuggle out without raising suspicions——'

'Why are you babbling like this? Beatrice, look at me!' Edmund broke in roughly.

But Beatrice found she could not look at him. Instead she thrust the loaf in his hands.

'Eat. 'Tis good *Saxon* bread, you should find it to your taste,' she muttered.

Beatrice fussed and bustled around him, determined to ignore his air of perplexity. It was easier than she had thought, despite the fact that his air of bemused injury was so convincing. It was almost as if he really cared. But Beatrice knew this was not so. He cared for another, and she would not give him a chance to speak. She did not want him to have to lie to her. Best that he say nothing, best that he did not have to use deceit on her. That way she could at least pretend...

She caught herself wondering what it would be like to be loved by such a man. Then she pulled herself up sharply. She must not allow her thoughts to run away with her. He was a cunning, clever man, and all he wanted from Beatrice was her help for this Hilda of his. He was wounded, and the only road open to him was the one she had unwittingly offered him. He had to try and charm her to his will. Her eyes ran over his pale features, the bandaged shoulder. He was in no position to force her to help.

The loaf that Edmund was chewing looked small, not large enough to satisfy that long warrior's body of his.

She bit her lip. 'I'll return at dawn with more. That was all I could lay my hands on,' she explained. She edged away and sat back on her heels. She felt safer watching him from a distance.

'My appetite is small today. There's no need for you to worry about me,' Edmund said coolly.

'I won't,' she lied.

His face was thrown into relief by the light from the lantern. It could have been carved from chalk. An ugly spasm contorted the clean lines of his features and Beatrice winced in sympathy. A small grunt dropped from his lips. He shifted on the floor.

Beatrice was at his side in an instant. Her fingers gently touched his brow, but there was no trace of rising fever. 'Is the pain no better?' she worried. 'It should be easing by now. I could brew up an infusion of herbs to help speed the healing. 'Tis chancy, I might be seen entering the cookhouse...but 'tis worth the risk if your need is great.'

'Why, Mistress Beatrice, you *do* care.' Edmund grinned up at her, his tone light and bantering.

'You...monster! You did that on purpose, to trick me. You're not hurting at all.'

Angrily, Beatrice made as if to retreat, but long fingers clamped round her wrist, and she dared not struggle for fear of causing him further pain.

'In truth, I am in some discomfort,' he said, 'but honesty compels me to admit I exaggerated it to bring you close again.' His shameless smile reached out to her through the dim light.

'Pig! Saxon pig! Let me go!'

'I'm not holding you tightly, Mistress Beatrice. You can free yourself at any time you wish,' he pointed out.

To her shame, Beatrice discovered he was speaking the truth. His fingers still curled around her wrist, but gently, and his thumb had slipped to caress her palm. Little shafts of delicious sensation went rushing up her arm. She fought to ignore them. She glared at him, and snatched her hand away, her lips preparing an angry retort.

It was never uttered. Just then the chapel door-latch rattled. Someone was coming...

When Baron Philip de Brionne sauntered into the chapel moments later, he found Lady Anne's companion prostrate before the altar. A small lantern glowed feebly at her side.

'Well now, pretty one,' said the Baron. 'What have we here? Doing penance for your thievery, or rather I should say for your recent acquisition?'

Beatrice scrambled to her knees, swallowing down a curse that would have stripped Mother Adèle's face of all colour. The Baron, of all people! It would have been better if it had been Father Ralph, come to say his evening office. He would have been easier to deal with, but the Baron...

'Do get up,' de Brionne drawled unpleasantly. 'Much as I enjoy the sight of a woman on her knees at my feet, that floor must be damnably cold, and hard.' He grabbed her upper arms with fingers that felt like iron hooks, and forced her to her feet.

'Thank you, Baron,' she murmured, not liking the gleam in his eyes. She tried to back away. The hooks sank deeper into her flesh.

'I can think of a penance that's more suitable for you than spending the night alone in a cold chapel.' With sick horror Beatrice realised he intended her to kiss him. As he bent his head, Beatrice averted her face. Her stomach turned.

She could feel cold lips on her neck and ruthlessly repressed a shudder. The Baron grasped her so tightly there was no hope of escaping. Though her brain urged flight, she did not struggle. It took a tremendous effort of will, but she knew she must not anger him.

A single thought whirled in her brain. Fighting revulsion, she clung on to it. She must distract him. Get de Brionne out of here. She must use cunning.

'Please, my lord, I beg you, do not.' Her voice wobbled, despite her brave intentions. There was no time to wonder whether she was more terrified for herself, or for the hidden Saxon. But if he should be discovered...

''Tis no use whining, my pretty. 'Tis time you paid, in full, for the dagger I let you keep.'

The Baron shifted his hold and brought Beatrice closer.
His mailcoat bruised her from breast to knee. He twisted
her chin round to meet him. His kiss was brutal, and
very thorough. The Norman made no attempt to read
the signals given out by the unresponsive body in his
arms. He made no concessions to her youth or
inexperience.

Beatrice had resolved that passive submission was her
best move. But she had not been armed for such a vicious
onslaught. She jerked back, but try as she might, she
could not escape.

Intent only on satisfying his own desires, the Baron
ground her lips under his. When at last he lifted his head,
Beatrice succeeded in tearing herself from his talons. She
backed away, until she felt the altar stone chill against
the small of her back. Glaring at her persecutor, she
scrubbed her hand frantically across her mouth. She felt
sick, and dirty. Soiled by his loathsome touch.

Edmund's kisses had been beautiful. They had warmed
her to her soul's core. The Baron's made her shrivel up
inside. Like slow death.

'You, you . . .' She struggled for a word strong enough
to express her revulsion.

The Norman's cruel laugh vibrated round the stone
walls. He took a pace towards her.

'Don't touch me! Go and find someone who is
willing!' Beatrice cried.

She could not bear him pawing her again, but she knew
this could have only one ending. The Baron had the
strength of ten devils, and she was powerless against him.

Relentless as the incoming tide, the Baron advanced
on her. He was taking his time, playing with her as a
fisherman plays with a fish hooked on his line, enjoying
her discomfort, even prolonging it . . .

'You're not meant to take pleasure in a penance, you
know,' he said. 'It wouldn't be a penance if you did.
Besides, I like women with a bit of fight in them. It adds
spice to the proceedings.' His teeth gleamed yellow like
a wolf's.

'Keep away!' Beatrice put up her hands to ward him
off.

'I think not.' He was breathing heavily. 'Come here, my sweet.'

Beatrice closed her eyes and shook her head. 'You'll have to force me. I'll never kiss you willingly. Never!' Her voice cracked.

With narrowed eyes the Baron closed the space between them. He dug his fingers into her scalp and forced her head round.

Tears of impotent rage shone in her hazel eyes. The cold altar bit into her back and de Brionne's hard mailshirt worried at her chest. She was trapped. Again the Norman lowered his hard mouth down on hers. A sour stench filled her nostrils, and she gagged.

Suddenly, she was released. She gripped the edge of the stone table for support and blinked rapidly to clear away the tears that fogged her sight.

Impossibly, Edmund stood there, confronting the Baron, ashen-faced and swaying on his feet.

'Nay!' she burst out on a note of despair. The sword she had given the Saxon hung limply in his right hand. It was obvious he was in no condition to wield it, and equally obvious he was determined to try.

De Brionne looked from Edmund to Beatrice and back to Edmund, a half-smile twisting his face. 'So,' he breathed softly, 'the noble bastard. How can we serve you, my lord?' De Brionne sketched a bow, his eyes never leaving Edmund's face. His scornful tone belied his courteous words, for his hand was already at the hilt of his sword, easing it from its scabbard.

'This is a place of sanctuary!' Beatrice got out. She took a tentative step towards the Saxon, intending to steady him, but the black and furious look that Edmund threw at her stopped her in her tracks.

'Aye, this is a place of God,' sneered de Brionne. 'A trysting place for thieves and skulking bastards!' His face was ugly. 'I think I shall act as His instrument and send you to meet Him a little early——'

'Nay!' Beatrice cried defiantly, flinging herself between the two men, and boldly facing de Brionne.

'You dare to defy me?' queried the Baron, a dangerous edge to his voice. 'Out of my way, wench!'

'No! This is sanctified ground!' Beatrice cried.

'I'm quite willing to kill him outside if that would please you better, my pretty. I can be accommodating at times,' de Brionne said coldly.

'Nay, my lord. Be merciful. Please. Don't,' Beatrice begged. She searched in vain for pity in the Norman's implacable eyes and, seeing only a grisly blood-lust, groaned aloud. 'There must be something that will persuade you not to... not to...' she stammered. Her innards had turned to water.

'Nay, my pretty, there's nothing will sway me. I would rid the land once and for all of these Saxon leeches, who would steal back what we have won from them in battle.' The Baron let his eyes run down her body and back to her face. His expression changed, and lust of a different sort distorted the hateful visage. 'But perhaps, my pretty, you might try to persuade me...'

Beatrice gulped, his meaning was perfectly clear. She could not meet his eyes, but she heard herself agree. 'Aye, anything.'

'I need no Norman bitch to intercede on my behalf,' Edmund sneered, thrusting her roughly aside. He lurched towards the Norman.

Beatrice gasped. Edmund's words cut her like a dagger thrust in her heart. In the fitful lantern light she saw Edmund's colour had risen, his warrior's instincts thoroughly roused. By rights, he should be lying defenceless on his sickbed, but he looked far from helpless. The sword was firm in his grasp, his legs braced slightly apart.

De Brionne's sword, too, was up. The two men eyed each other balefully, their faces masks of pure hatred.

'My sons!' The calm voice of Father Ralph took them all by surprise.

In other circumstances Beatrice might have laughed at the way the two protagonists jerked round to see the priest standing in the doorway. Guilt and disappointment were stamped across both their faces in equal measure. Instinct told her that both were eager to settle old scores and neither was pleased the priest had interrupted them.

'Father! Thank heaven, you're here!' Beatrice scrambled to pull the priest further into the chapel.

'Make them see sense. They should not fight! This is no place for quarrels.'

'Quarrels!', Edmund burst out bitterly. 'This treacherous knave slew my brother in cold blood, and you call it a quarrel!' He spat on the floor by the Baron's feet.

'You see, Father,' de Brionne said silkily, 'what a difficult task we have persuading these Saxons to live in peace with their neighbours.'

'Not neighbours—invaders!' Edmund ground out through clenched teeth.

'Did you mean to kill his brother?' Beatrice whirled on the Norman.

'Oh, self-defence only. Rest assured, my pretty,' came the glib response.

'You lie!' Edmund accused. 'You butchered him in cold blood!' His sword moved.

'Come, come, come. We are all brothers in the eyes of God,' Father Ralph intervened hastily. He looked at Edmund. 'You, put up your sword.' The Saxon glowered back at him and did not move. 'And you, Baron,' Father Ralph caught the Norman's eye, 'give us your oath that you will grant this man sanctuary.'

'De Brionne has no right here in the first place!' Edmund declared. 'How can he have the right to grant me sanctuary? I do not recognise his authority here. These are Saxon lands!' He gripped his sword.

'But I do have the right. By force of arms. You must agree my men are in control here. Where now are yours?' de Brionne drawled with studied insolence.

A muscle twitched in Edmund's cheek. 'You Normans are so civilised,' he sneered. 'You must excuse my imperfect barbarian understanding. I had forgotten how your society operates. Might is right. And the Devil take the weak and the innocent——' He glanced at Beatrice. 'Brute force wins the day.'

De Brionne leaped forwards, sword poised to strike, but Father Ralph darted between them with astonishing agility.

'Baron, you *will* swear to abide by the conventions of sanctuary,' the priest declared firmly.

De Brionne sighed. 'Aye. Very well, Priest. I swear it.'

'Swear on the cross of Our Saviour,' the priest insisted.

'What?' De Brionne's hesitation was momentary, but Beatrice saw it.

'Well?' pressed Father Ralph.

De Brionne strode to the wooden altar, picked up the cross and swung it aloft. 'I swear on the cross of Our Lord to respect the sanctity of this place.' With careless irreverence, he dropped the cross back on to the altar.

Father Ralph flinched, but he was satisfied with the Baron's words. He nodded and repositioned the cross, genuflecting deeply.

Beatrice perceived the loophole. She opened her mouth to insist de Brionne should swear not to harm Edmund wherever he was, sanctuary or not.

The Baron forestalled her. 'Father, 'tis late for ladies to be abroad.' De Brionne smiled blandly. 'Mistress Beatrice should be safe abed.'

'I agree, my son. Please escort her to her chamber. I will remain here and keep our Saxon friend company.'

The Baron's iron hand crushed her elbow and he towed her towards the door.

Edmund had dropped his guard, his sword pointed at the floor. Blue eyes followed her progress. His face was impassive, his lips tightly compressed. He didn't even have a smile for her. The lamp cast strange shadows across his pallid features and she could detect no warmth at all in that unwavering stare. He looked on her as one would look on an enemy.

The Baron escorted Beatrice every step of the way to the upper chamber. He threw a parting shot through the doorway. 'I will collect my dues from you at some later date. Sleep well, my pretty.'

Beatrice wrenched the tapestry curtain almost off the rod in her haste to blot out his face. 'Don't call me that,' she hissed at him through the fabric. 'I am *not* your pretty.'

'I wonder whose you are, then?' The jeering voice floated back to her. 'The Saxon upstart's?'

Beatrice did not deign to reply. Marching to the bed, she stripped off her overdress with hands that shook. She placed her candle by the bed, and crawled in gingerly next to Anne so as not to disturb her. As she reached out to extinguish the flame her eyes lit on the wine-cup Anne had placed by the bed earlier.

No doubt this was the St Agnes' Eve magic brew. Beatrice had not fasted, and did not believe a word about the vision of her future husband appearing if she drank the potion. But she was thirsty, and tense, and the wine would help her to relax. She looked at the dark liquid swirling in the goblet and sighed. Trusting the drink to calm her disordered nerves, she drained it in one draught.

The spiced wine was no longer warm, its heat had long since evaporated into the cold night air. It tasted pleasantly sweet. Beatrice closed her eyes and sighed again.

When Beatrice awoke, she knew instinctively that much time had passed. The candle she had forgotten to extinguish had gone out and the chamber was pitch-black. Her first thought was that the potion had calmed her nerves, for she had fallen asleep at once. A freezing draught blew across her shoulders and she shivered. Anne must have pulled the covers away from her again. Anne always managed to end up with more than her fair share of blankets. Beatrice gently eased them back in her direction. But how had it got so cold? The bed was freezing. She shivered again and tried to snuggle deeper into the covers.

A horrid suspicion entered her mind and she reached to touch her cousin's warm body. Her hand encountered—nothing. She gasped, the air hung icy in her lungs. Anne had gone; her half of the bed was empty! And, to judge by the cold bedding, her cousin had been gone some time. Still half-drugged with sleep, Beatrice struggled to sit up.

Her eyes were slow adjusting to the darkness. The window shutter had come unfastened, hence the icy blasts. A full moon shone palely through the aperture, silhouetting, as it did so, a shape. It was a man! A man who was seated beneath the window on Anne's travelling chest, silently watching her. Her heart skipped a beat.

'Who is it?' she whispered, and shrank back into the blankets, realising the futility of her action as she did so. If the man intended to harm her the bed was no place of safety. 'Where is Lady Anne? What have you done with her?' she demanded.

The man-shape did not move. 'Do you not know me?' it said.

'Edmund!' she cried and bounced upright, her loosened hair falling forwards. 'How did you get in here?'

She saw him shrug and heard his sharply indrawn breath. The wound troubled him. He could not move comfortably even to shrug his shoulders.

''Twas easily done. The priest set himself to sit with me in the chapel, and de Brionne posted a guard outside. The guard found our northern winters too harsh for his liking and, knowing the priest was with me, asked if he could go and warm himself by the fire. They thought I slept. Your priest agreed to shout the alarm if necessary and the guard departed to toast himself.'

'You've not harmed Father Ralph?' Beatrice worried, chewing on her lower lip.

'Nay,' Edmund reassured her. 'He's trussed up tight, but there's not a mark on him. I even gave him my word I'd be back. I thought to see that you were safe tonight.'

A warm glow ran along her veins. 'Safe? Oh, from de Brionne. Aye, I am safe.' She would not tell him that the Norman had threatened her. She did not want to jeopardise the shaky truce that had been re-established between the two men.

'What would you have done if I had not been...safe?' she asked curiously. 'You could not have killed him. His men would have been on you in an instant. And they would not have hesitated to kill you. They still might if they find you here. 'Twas folly to have come.'

Edmund rose and came to sit on the edge of the bed. He grinned down at her, his face a pale blur in the moonlight.

'I'm glad you're safe,' he whispered, moving closer. 'I own I don't feel like killing tonight.' His hand came out and touched her unravelled hair. The fragrant scent of lavender lingered in the long tresses. His fingers threaded themselves into its rich softness. 'Beautiful, like silk,' he murmured.

The feel of his hands in her hair made her cheeks grow hot. She looked away. He was too close. She felt shy of him, and hoped he would not see her discomfiture in the poor light.

'Where is Anne? Did you send her away?' she blurted, squirming out of reach.

'Anne obviously has some assignment of her own. Damn it, woman, come here. You're not afraid of *me*, are you?'

He put a long finger under her chin and gently turned her face up to examine it.

She shook her head and swallowed. 'N-no. That is no, n-not really,' she stammered, unable to meet that searching gaze of his. She lowered her head and kept her eyes fixed on her hands.

'Tell me,' Edmund prompted gently.

''Tis...oh, I'm confused,' she admitted, glowing like a beacon. 'Nothing is clear any more. But I do know I'm not afraid of you. Even though you are Saxon. I think I... *like* you.' She lifted her eyes to his.

'Then kiss me,' he commanded huskily, 'or do you only kiss wounded warriors who are close to death?'

'I'd never kissed anyone until today, and now I've been kissed by two men,' she reminded him, and then wished she hadn't for his face grew cold.

'He shall not have you,' Beatrice heard him mutter, and she was pulled firmly into his embrace.

Edmund intended the kiss to be simply a light and reassuring caress as before. But Beatrice slipped her arms around his neck and held him to her with irresistible eagerness. He groaned, and this time it was not pain that caused him to do so. He found himself pressing her back into her pillow. She did not protest, and Edmund covered her face with light, butterfly kisses. Her lips met his, and clung.

When he finally pulled away, both were breathless. Eyes still closed, Beatrice murmured a soft protest and tried to pull him back to her. She thought the hand that stroked her cheek trembled slightly, but could not be sure. She opened her eyes and gazed up at him dreamily.

'Nay, I don't think you do fear me,' he agreed lightly, and smiled. 'But this must stop. Don't look at me like that, it doesn't make it easy.'

Abruptly, Edmund sat up. Beatrice's arms fell away from him. She wondered how his mood could change so fast. He made her feel ashamed that she had responded to him with such shameless abandon.

Edmund glanced at her expression and sighed. He covered her hands with his.

Already he thought her a nuisance. His face had grown quite hard.

'I have to go back to the chapel. Your cousin will be returning soon,' he announced, crisply.

All the warmth had gone from his voice. Beatrice stared at him, unable to believe he could change so swiftly from considerate lover to…to…what? Wide eyes watched the man who had kissed her so tenderly and she wondered if she had touched him at all.

'I need you to do something for me—to hide this.' Edmund indicated a small iron-bound box on the floor next to Anne's wooden trunk. 'Is this your travelling chest?' he asked.

'Nay, that's one of Anne's. Mine's this plain one by the bed.'

'Give me the key,' he ordered.

The key hung with her cross on a chain round her neck. Silently she handed it to him, and in a moment he'd unlocked the coffer and buried the casket under her clothes.

'What's in it?' she asked.

His eyes met hers. Cold as ice.

'Try and forget you ever saw that casket,' he said, tossing her the key. 'I hate to leave it with you, but I have no choice.'

'You can trust me.'

'I hope so. I certainly hope so,' he replied coolly.

Beatrice stiffened. He implied he could not trust her. After what they had just shared? How could he spoil something so beautiful with ugly suspicions? Maybe he had not felt the magic in the kisses they shared. Maybe she had not reached him at all.

Edmund stood looking down at her, tall and dark. His long hair was a potent reminder of his Saxon heritage and of the unbridgeable gulf which yawned between them. She was Norman. And he was using her.

'Edmund.' A pleading hand reached out through the darkness.

'What is it?' he demanded curtly. He was listening to something else, turned towards the doorway. She could not reach him. The chasm gaped wider. 'I must go now, before your friend de Brionne finds I've left the chapel,' Edmund announced.

'He's not my friend!'

'Farewell.' Edmund frowned back at her. He caressed her cheek absently with his fingertips, smiled all too briefly, and was gone, leaving Beatrice to stare, bereft and dismayed, at the swinging tapestry in the doorway.

She strained her ears to catch any sounds of commotion or alarm and, hearing none, she rose to peer through the tiny unglazed window. The moonlight illuminated a shadowy shape flitting into the safety of the chapel. She let her breath out in a sigh of relief, and slowly latched the shutter. She fingered the key, still warm from his hand, and looked at her travelling chest. She was sorely tempted. What was in that casket? One little peep could not hurt anyone...surely?

'No!' She found she had spoken aloud. She would not look. She would prove worthy of his trust.

Back under the freezing bedcovers, Beatrice hugged the blankets and wolf pelts close about her neck.

Sleep did not come easily the second time. She shivered. She tossed and turned for hours. Try as she might, she could not get the Saxon warrior, Edmund of Lindsey, out of her mind.

He was an enigma—capable of kindness, for he'd been gentle to her. And yet there was a ruthless streak in him... Was he as calculating as the Baron? Most likely he'd only come to her chamber to persuade her to hide that box. He'd said that he was concerned for her safety. Nay. He'd set himself to flatter her, to charm her. He was probably very adept at charming Saxon maidens. He was certainly handsome enough with that raven hair and those haunting blue eyes. And she had fallen for it without a murmur.

Beatrice tried to pull her thoughts in another direction. But it was no good. They ran stubbornly round and round in circles. Sleep retreated even further away.

Hilda. She'd forgotten Hilda. No doubt this Hilda thought him charming. Did Hilda enjoy Edmund's caresses as much as she did? An unwelcome vision of the unknown rival lying cooing in Edmund's arms pushed itself to the forefront of her mind. Beatrice sat up and pummelled viciously at a lump in the mattress. Then she lay down again. She dismissed her faceless rival from Edmund's embrace. Much better to imagine herself in Edmund's arms. She began to relax.

Finally sleep came back to claim her, and she did not stir even when Anne returned to bed near dawn.

CHAPTER FIVE

BEATRICE yawned and stretched. Ella's clattering as she clumped into the chamber with a steaming ewer of water had woken her. 'You look happy this morning, Anne,' she observed shrewdly, watching her cousin dress for the day.

Anne's smile was smug. It told of secrets that were better left unspoken. Beatrice shrugged, and looked at the plain, unpainted trunk where her own secret lay. She flung back the heavy bedcovers and her skin shrank, chilled. Lord, what she wouldn't give for a fur cloak like Anne's this day.

Fishing down in her coffer for the warm robe her cousin had given her, Beatrice wondered if she'd imagined the Saxon casket. In the bright light of day, Edmund of Lindsey's presence in their chamber seemed like a dream—a St Agnes' Eve visitation. But her groping hand encountered the hard edges of an oblong box. Solid proof that the midnight meeting *had* taken place after all.

Beatrice drew out her new green robe, and donned it. Clasping her belt about her slender waist, she was fumbling for her shoes when her fingers struck another unfamiliar object. She drew it out, puzzled. It was neatly wrapped in a silken cloth.

Beatrice glanced furtively over her shoulder at Anne, but her cousin was too engrossed in her *toilette* to be paying her any heed. Ella had gone. Careful to keep her hands out of Anne's sight, Beatrice unwrapped the package.

She stifled a gasp. It was a jewelled sheath to partner Edmund's dagger, and it was exquisite. There was no doubt that the two objects belonged together. The garnets had been cut by the same craftsman; the intricate design into which the stones were set echoed the pattern on the dagger.

Beatrice slid the dagger from a notch in her belt. She had been wearing it unsheathed, despite Anne's warning that she might cut herself on the blade.

'What's that?' Anne demanded, suddenly standing at her elbow. She was bright-eyed with curiosity.

'You've seen the dagger before,' Beatrice answered warily.

'Aye, but I hadn't seen the whole of it.' Anne plucked both dagger and sheath from her cousin's hand and examined them minutely. 'Very pretty,' Anne pronounced and, instead of plying Beatrice with questions, she handed the sheathed dagger back to her and then returned to brushing out her hair.

Beatrice buckled the small weapon at her waist, conscious that the warm glow of pleasure was spreading through her again. It was meant as a gift. He would not have wrapped it so carefully if he had not intended it to be a gift.

She forgot that a girl in her position should not receive gifts from a Saxon nobleman, or any other man. She forgot that she intended to return to La Trinité. She smiled. She re-covered Edmund's casket with her old grey robe, locked her travelling chest, and returned the key to the chain at her neck.

She perched on the edge of her coffer and shook out the folds of the soft green gown. Anne muttered under her breath.

'What is it?' Beatrice asked.

''Tis nought. I was foolish enough to dismiss Ella, and now I can't do my hair. Beatrice, will you...?'

'My pleasure,' Beatrice said, and removed the comb from her cousin's unpractised fingers.

'Oh, cousin, I am happy,' Anne revealed. 'It seems there is some truth in the St Agnes superstition after all.'

'What do you mean?' Beatrice asked cautiously, hands pausing over her cousin's dark tresses.

'Oh, 'tis nought. I should not speak of it. Not yet,' Anne answered vaguely. 'Beatrice, do you think that Father Ralph would hear my confession this morning?'

Beatrice resumed her ordering of Anne's hair. '*Your* confession?' she asked.

'Aye. I want more than a miserly crust this morn. I could eat a boar, and I'd like to make my confession before I break my fast.'

Beatrice widened her eyes. This sudden show of penitence was a strange thing in her cousin. 'I'm sure Father Ralph will be most pleased to hear your confession,' she replied slowly. 'He'll be in the chapel now, I think.'

Anne smiled. ''Tis well! I'll go straight there. The sooner I confess, the sooner I can fill my belly.'

'There,' Beatrice said. 'Your hair is done. I'd make a good lady's maid, don't you think?'

Anne ran her fingers over Beatrice's handiwork, and grinned. 'That you would. Far better than I ever would.' Anne snatched up her veil, her full skirts swished, and she flung her cloak about her shoulders in a flurry of cold air.

'Anne, there's something *I* would confess to *you*. I——' Beatrice began. But her words hung in the empty air, unheeded. Anne had left the chamber.

Downstairs, the bedding lay piled at one end of the hall and the trestle tables were already up. The wreckage of a light meal of bread and ale littered the tables. Loaves had been torn to shreds, ale-pots emptied and left upended by ravenous Norman soldiers, for whom the scant early meal was never enough.

Hardly a crumb remained.

A solitary loaf and jug of ale sat, out of bounds and safe from marauding hands, on the top table. Beatrice wondered which thoughtful soul had salvaged them and placed them there. She took her place at the board and reached for the ale-jug. Her nose wrinkled. She was unused to the bitter brew, but supposed she must accustom herself to it. Wine seemed to be a rarity reserved for nobles in these northern parts.

'Walter! Shift your carcass over here!'

De Brionne's harsh bawl made her hand jerk and she almost spilled her ale. She had not noticed the Baron hovering in the gloom. Walter shuffled on the edge of her vision. His eyes were wide and staring, and he was sweating despite the cold.

A glance at the Baron revealed him to be in a grim humour. His narrow lips were pursed together, he was scowling, and the eyes that stared out from under his brows were black as death.

'Come hither, clod! Don't think you can escape by cringing into the plaster! I've some questions for you, and you will heed me. You are *not* to take food from the stores in the middle of the night, or any other time. That's theft.' De Brionne's voice softened dangerously. 'Do you know the penalty for theft, half-wit?'

Beatrice scrambled to her feet, her bench scraping on the floor. 'Baron, I beg you not to shout at Walter like that. You're frightening him. He wouldn't take anything,' she asserted.

De Brionne's large hands hooked on to Walter's tunic. He hauled him in. 'I saw him myself,' the Baron mouthed viciously, shaking her manservant so hard that his head snapped back and forth.

'Baron!' Beatrice put out her hand, afraid for more than Walter's neck.

A triumphant gleam lit the dark eyes. 'I know why you're defending him. You're just as much a thief as he is.'

Beatrice had opened her mouth to deny this accusation when she saw the Baron look pointedly at the weapon which hung at her waist. She clamped her teeth firmly together. De Brionne must realise that it was Edmund's dagger and not the dagger of the Saxon lad he had dispatched to Heaven. He knew she'd picked it up from the chapel floor where Edmund had hidden. The Baron's soul was corroded by sin, but not his brain—stupidity was not one of his faults.

'Well, churl, will you admit to taking that food?' the Baron demanded.

Walter licked his lips, eyes darting nervously from Beatrice to the Baron. De Brionne's impatient hands closed round Walter's throat. Walter made a choking sound.

'Baron!' Beatrice cried, pulling frantically at the mailed sleeve.

The thin lips lifted, baring yellow teeth. 'I will have an answer. Did you eat that food I saw you taking?'

Walter gulped. His lips moved but no sound came out. His body hung limp as a corpse from the Baron's large fists. His eyes flashed his mistress a plea more eloquent than words.

'Baron,' Beatrice said, struggling for calm. She forced her hand to rest lightly on the mail-clad arm. 'Please let me ask him. You've struck the wit from his mind with your strength.' She achieved a passable smile. 'If you would have an answer, let me try. He will answer me. Release him.'

Her insides crawled as the Norman Baron looked down at the small hand she had laid on his sleeve. His eyes slid up and lingered on her lips. He smiled. The brutish hands uncurled themselves from around Walter's neck.

A heady fury shook Beatrice. Without a shadow of a doubt the Baron had engineered the whole in order to wring a reaction from her. She loathed every fibre of his being.

'Walter, please answer me,' she commanded, her voice taut with the effort it took to cloak her anger. 'Did you take some food last night?'

There was a grisly silence.

'Walter?' she prompted, more gently.

Walter assented, his frightened eyes clinging to Beatrice's as though they were a lifeline. He rubbed the red marks on his neck.

'Why?' Beatrice probed. 'Were you hungry, Walter? Did you eat the food yourself?' she pressed.

Her manservant shook his head.

'Guilty!' crowed the Baron. 'Your dumb half-wit didn't even need the food for himself. I told you he was a thief. I'll wager he sold it for profit.'

'You would think that,' Beatrice murmured.

'Eh?'

'Nothing, Baron. I but thought aloud.' She faced Walter. 'Did you sell the food, Walter?'

Walter shook his head emphatically.

'Liar! I'll have your right hand off for this,' the Baron threatened, face engorged.

Walter snatched his hands from his neck and hid them behind his back. De Brionne let out a short laugh and moved like lightning, wrenching Walter's right arm out and pinning it to the table. Walter whimpered.

'Nay! Baron, you cannot maim him for so minor a transgression. Even you could not be so cruel!' Beatrice shrieked, wondering at the twisted mind that would devise so cruel a game merely for amusement.

Black eyes narrowed. 'Even I? Mistress, you honour me.' He edged his sword part way from the scabbard.

'He did not sell the food. You heard him.' Beatrice said desperately. The blood was roaring in her ears. Walter's face looked like that of an old man.

Walter had seen the way his mistress had reacted when the Baron had smiled at her. Mistress Beatrice did not like this Norman. Mistress Beatrice was afraid of him. And Mistress Beatrice was defending him, Walter, against this Norman lord.

Walter judged the Baron to be an evil man. Whenever the Baron looked his way, Walter broke out in a cold sweat. This evil man enjoyed baiting his mistress. He took pleasure in it. Walter did not like that. Neither did he like the way the devil leered at his mistress. Walter was not sure whether the Baron really intended to carry out his threat to maim him. But he did know that the monster was upsetting Mistress Beatrice. And Walter did not like that at all.

Beatrice still pleaded. 'Please, my lord, do not take his hand. Walter has suffered enough. You cannot do this.'

'We-ell. If it means so much to you, my pretty.' The Baron affected hesitation. How he enjoyed watching the hope flare in her innocent hazel eyes. Such unguarded eyes—so easy to make them change. 'I shall spare him. This time. But if I hear so much as a whisper of suspicion against him again, I *will* finish him. We can't afford to support simpletons. 'Tis hard enough finding enough to satisfy my warriors, and they at least earn their keep.' His sword clicked back into its sheath.

'Thank you, Baron,' Beatrice acknowledged briefly, curbing her tongue lest it utter an angry retort, which would only serve to inflame the unpredictable Baron again.

The hall door slammed and bounced open at once. It was Anne. She swirled towards them, her breath clouding the air. Walter scurried out of the Baron's reach under the pretext of closing out the cold. His face had lost its haggard look.

'By Our Lady, 'tis frosty out there!' Anne flung a leather-bound book on the table and smiled at de Brionne.

The Baron returned Anne's smile and Beatrice sucked in her breath. She stared, with dawning intelligence. She had never thought those obsidian eyes were capable of wearing such an expression. They were almost tender. The Norman never looked at her like that. A flash of understanding shocked her rigid. Could it be that Anne and the Baron...that they were lovers?

For those with eyes to see, there had been signs, little hints and glances. They had been right under her nose, but she had not understood their significance. Anne tripping down the gangplank at Pevensey and falling so neatly into de Brionne's arms—she had fallen deliberately. Anne's merry vivacity on the journey to Lindsey, and the rapid change of mood when they had arrived there. Of course Anne had found it difficult to accept the Thegn of Lindsey—for Anne already had a lover in Baron Philip de Brionne!

Beatrice realised her jaw had dropped, and closed her mouth with a snap. Old ideas were shifting, and new ones forming in her mind. If that were true, it went part way to explaining the Baron's hostility towards the Saxons. He did not want Anne to marry their lord any more than Anne did herself. Her brow puckered. There must be more to it than that. There had to be.

Why should the Baron torment her if he loved Anne? A ruse to disguise his true feelings? He could not love Anne, and want Beatrice as well, could he? Beatrice had recognised desire in de Brionne's face when he had kissed her. It was beyond her comprehension that a man should love one woman and desire another.

'I'm to do a small penance for my sins.' Anne was pouting charmingly at the man Beatrice now recognised to be her lover.

De Brionne picked up the psalter Anne had cast on the table and idly turned a page or two.

'What penance is that, Lady Anne?' he enquired with careful courtesy. His formal mode of address gave nothing away.

'I'm to read a few psalms, nothing too testing,' Anne replied indifferently. 'I don't expect I'll bother, though.'

'Anne!' Beatrice was shocked.

'What lovely initial letters.' Anne placed white fingers on de Brionne's and bent her head to look at the volume. 'Baron, do let me see.'

The Baron did not withdraw his hand as he should, and Beatrice observed that his dark eyes rested on Anne's head, not on the illuminated pages of the book.

'Excuse me, I'll see if the wounded men need anything,' Beatrice muttered and rose to her feet.

Neither Anne nor her companion looked up as she left the trestle table and moved across the hall.

'Let me help you, Mistress,' Ella offered, taking a dressing from Beatrice.

'My thanks, Ella.'

'Oh, thank *you*, Mistress Beatrice!' Ella spoke fervently. Tears were sparkling in her eyes.

'Ella?' Beatrice gazed blankly at Ella over the recumbent form of the soldier they tended.

'Thank you for helping Walter. He did not sell the food, Mistress. He's not a thief.'

'What did he do with the food, Ella?' Beatrice wondered.

The maidservant's face was torn with indecision.

'I may be able to help,' Beatrice suggested gently.

'Oh, Mistress Beatrice. 'Twas for the little Saxon girl that he found,' Ella breathed.

'What *little* girl?' Beatrice queried.

Ella shrugged. 'Mistress, I do not know. He found her in the byre, the one hard by the chapel, last evening. He heard crying, went in, and there she was, hiding in the straw. He fetched me. There was blood on her gown, and it were torn. Oh, Mistress Beatrice, I hope we did right to help her. She were that upset, we couldn't not help her. Do you see?'

Beatrice made a decision. 'Come and help me draw clean water, Ella,' she commanded, loud enough for all to hear. 'That well-handle is too stiff for me to turn on my own.'

Ella followed her outside.

The sun shone clear in a pale winter's sky, but its rays were feeble and did not reach her skin. Instead, air sharp as a needle pricked at her cheeks.

Two guards stood posted by the chapel and Beatrice caught herself looking their way, hoping to get a glimpse...but the grey walls reared up solidly before her, there was no peering past them. Resolutely, Beatrice walked to the well. Shivering, the two girls began wrestling with an iron well-handle that numbed fingers to the bone. Even the once muddy earth around the well was rock-hard.

'I didn't want to be overheard,' explained Beatrice.

Ella grunted her understanding and heaved on the handle.

'You saw this girl close to?' Beatrice demanded. 'Was she hurt?'

'Nay, Mistress. Though that's what I thought when I saw her gown. 'Twas as if some beast of a man had...and with her being but a child I was that shocked. But nay, that were the strangest thing. It wasn't her blood. There's not a mark on her.' Ella hesitated, gritting her teeth in her efforts with the well-handle. 'Will you see her?'

'Where is she?'

They cranked the handle round another turn.

'Still in the byre, I should think, unless someone else has found her.' Ella panted, and blew on her hands.

The leather bucket had reached the top of the well-shaft. Small lumps of ice floated in the water. The girls abandoned their fight with the well-handle. Their breath hung in milky clouds above their heads.

'Leave the bucket by the side there,' Beatrice said. 'Show me the girl. Quickly.'

The byre was a small reed-thatched building nestling snugly behind the chapel. Icicles edged the top of the doorway.

'She don't speak our tongue, Mistress Beatrice,' Ella warned.

Inside the byre, it was warm from the combined heat of the animals it sheltered. The beasts stamped and shuffled as they entered, but Beatrice saw no trace of the Saxon girl. They were too late. She must have fled.

Ella marched straight to a pile of hay in a corner and started shovelling it to one side, crooning softly in her native French dialect. ''Tis all right, me lass. Don't be afraid. 'Tis only Ella come to see you're all right.'

There was a little flurry of movement, a whisper of protest, and Beatrice found herself looking down at a small and frightened girl who cowered in the corner with such fear in her eyes that Beatrice winced. Yet there was something about this girl...

'She won't understand our French,' reminded Ella.

A strange lightness had stolen over Beatrice. 'Is your name Hilda?' Beatrice spoke softly in Latin. The girl's wide eyes swivelled from Ella to Beatrice. 'I won't hurt you,' Beatrice persisted. 'Please try and understand. Are you the Hilda that Edmund spoke of?'

At the mention of Edmund's name some of the tension left the small body.

'I'm sure you understand me. Are you Hilda? I want to help you.' Beatrice hunkered down to the child's level and held out her hand in a gesture of friendship.

The girl must have seen about ten or twelve summers. Her clothes were the best quality, though her overdress had been badly torn at the hem, and there was indeed blood on the garment, as Ella had already observed. The child had light brown hair and grey-blue eyes, and it was these that drew Beatrice's attention. They bore a strong resemblance to those of another Saxon, a resemblance that was becoming more and more marked as the terror in them diminished. They were wary now, and Beatrice harboured no more doubts as to the girl's identity.

'You're Hilda!' she exclaimed. 'I know it. You look like him. And I recognise the fabric of your robe. A piece of that cloth was used to bandage Edmund. You used it to stanch his wound in the chapel.'

The Saxon girl scowled back in stubborn silence.

'You saw me in the chapel!' Beatrice realised. ''Twas you whom I heard leave when I was binding him up.

You left the door swinging. You know you can trust me. You saw me help Edmund, didn't you?'

The girl glared at Beatrice, silent and belligerent. All at once her thin shoulders slumped. 'Aye. You helped my brother, Edmund,' the child replied in stilted Latin. 'And for that reason alone I will trust you a little. I have been taught there is not much trust to be found in a Norman.'

The bitterness in Hilda's voice was oddly at variance with her youthful features. But a child grew up fast in this harsh world, or it did not grow up at all.

She stiffened her back, and raised her chin a notch. 'I am Hilda, younger sister of Aiden, Thegn of Lindsey and half-sister to Edmund.' Her voice broke on her dead brother's name.

'What's she saying, Mistress?' Ella demanded. 'Who is she?'

'She's the sister of the Saxon lord my cousin was to have married. The one Baron de Brionne killed yesterday morning.'

Ella sucked in her breath and stared at Hilda with pity in her eyes.

'Hilda, 'tis best that you remain hidden for now,' Beatrice decided. 'Edmund has claimed sanctuary and is safe. But if de Brionne learns you are here, it will give him a lever to use against your brother. Do you understand?'

The girl's eyes grew suspicious. 'You will not bring the Norman Baron here?'

'Nay. I swear it.'

'You will tell my brother I am here. Discreetly, of course,' Hilda commanded.

Beatrice smiled to herself. Hilda of Lindsey worded requests like orders. Already she had regained the easy imperiousness of one who took for granted the respect and deference due her high birth. All nervousness had gone. She was every inch the daughter of a proud and noble house.

'Naturally I will inform your brother as soon as I can,' Beatrice agreed. 'And I will send Ella back with food for you. Come, you'd better get back in this compartment till the times mend.'

Beatrice hustled the girl into her hiding place. She ran back into the yard, with Ella at her heels. Maid and mistress picked up the pail and had staggered halfway across the yard with it, when Anne hailed them from the hall doorway.

'You took long enough filling that,' she commented.

'Have you tried that well-handle, Anne?' Beatrice asked.

Anne lifted her shoulders and gave an idle smile.

'Nay. I thought not. 'Tis rusty and very stiff.' Beatrice rubbed her hands together.

'Come to the fire. Warm yourself,' Anne suggested. 'Ella knows how to finish that job. Don't you, Ella?'

'Aye, my lady.'

Ella heaved the bucket and lurched through the door towards the wounded men. Beatrice made a movement as if to help her, but Anne caught her arm.

'I would talk with you, Beatrice. Come and warm yourself by the fire. You're frozen.' She pushed Beatrice towards the blaze and lowered her voice conspiratorially. 'Why didn't you tell me what you were up to yesterday? I would have helped you if I had known.'

Beatrice turned a blank face on her cousin.

'Oh, Beatrice, don't look like that. You know what I'm referring to.'

'Cousin?'

'The Saxon in the chapel,' Anne hissed over the crackling logs. 'Why didn't you tell me you knew he was there? He's Aiden's bastard brother, isn't he?'

'Don't use such words Anne, 'tis not fitting,' Beatrice protested.

'Oh, Beatrice, you're as pompous as a prelate! I didn't mean it badly——'

'How did you mean it, then?' Beatrice asked, nettled.

'In a literal sense. He *was* born out of wedlock——'

'That makes it better, does it?'

Anne sighed and sat down on a three-legged stool in front of the fire. 'Beatrice, be reasonable. What *has* got into you? He is base-born, after all. The bastard son of the old lord, Thegn Hereward of Lindsey. I know, you see. Hereward was Aiden's father too. Edmund and Aiden were half-brothers. Edmund is the elder, but his

mother was never Hereward's wife. She was married off
to the estate steward soon after Edmund was born.'

Beatrice rubbed her forehead. 'Hilda must be his half-
sister. Aye, that must be right,' she muttered.

'I beg your pardon?' Anne frowned.

'Nothing. How do you know all this, Anne? You never
exchanged more than a word with any Saxon.'

Anne had the grace to blush. ''Tis marked down in
the Latin psalter that Father Ralph lent me for my
penance,' she said. 'The family genealogies are all written
in the front. Look.' Gracefully, Anne rose and collected
the book from the trestle. She pointed.

There it was. Neatly scripted. Beatrice made out
Hereward, the old Thegn, his wife Judith, and their two
children, Aiden and Hilda. There were birth dates by
each name.

There was another date by Hereward's name. Beatrice
assumed it to be the date on which he had died.

'There's a new date to mark down next to Aiden's
name now,' she murmured, before she had time to curb
her wretched tongue.

Edmund's name jumped out of the creamy parchment
at her. It was entered in a different, bolder hand, together
with a date.

'He must be twenty-two,' Anne pointed out unnecess-
arily, for Beatrice had just calculated that for herself.
According to the psalter he was a year older than Aiden.

Beatrice ran a fingertip over Edmund's written name,
only to flush crimson when she noticed Anne's sharp
eyes on her. She shut the book with a crack.

'Why didn't you tell me about your wounded warrior?'
Anne asked, teasingly.

Beatrice glanced round the smoky hall.

'No one can hear,' Anne assured her.

'He's not *my* warrior,' Beatrice stated. 'I did not tell
you because... because I thought you wished all Saxons
to the Devil. I feared you would betray him. I didn't
want the Baron to kill him as he killed the Thegn.'

Anne raised a trembling hand to her brow. 'I did not
wish for Aiden's death,' Anne told her. 'But Philip was
jealous of me—so jealous. He could not help himself.'

Beatrice squeezed her cousin's arm. 'I know that now. At the time I thought him a soulless monster. Murder is no less a mortal sin, of course, but at least I can understand his motives.'

Anne gave a strained laugh. 'Do not deceive yourself about my Baron, Beatrice. He is still a ruthless and ambitious man. He craves power. Do not allow yourself to think otherwise, simply because you know about his relationship with me.'

Beatrice remembered the helpless Saxon youth despatched with such mechanical efficiency, and stared at her cousin. 'How can you...care for him when he's so...' she floundered.

Anne sent her a straight look and shrugged prettily. 'It just happened. I'd been married to Charles de Montreuil for three years when Baron Philip de Brionne came to visit. Charles was Philip's uncle, and his elder by many years. By comparison with my husband, Philip was young and strong. He spoke kindly to me. I was lonely. De Montreuil never gave me any attention. We had nothing in common. All he wanted me for was...' Anne stopped and stared blindly into the flames. 'All he wanted was to beget an heir. I could not give him the heir he so desired. He despised me. Beatrice, I am barren.'

'Oh, Anne.' Beatrice gazed in horrified sympathy at her cousin. There was nothing she could say. Anne's cold, brief description of her married life had sent an icy trickle running down her spine. She sensed there was much that Anne had left unsaid. Her cousin's carefully controlled expression told her that.

'How could you be expected to know?' Anne asked. 'Hiding away in your convent refuge. Oh, Beatrice, I sometimes wish that I could have your innocence and simple faith in the world. But reality has ever been complicated for me. Philip helped me through a terrible time and I have grown used to him. I'm not blind to his faults, I'm learning to live with them. 'Tis not easy, I can assure you.' Anne smiled, and something of her old sparkle kindled in her eyes. 'I can't expect a perfect man, can I?' Anne went on. 'No one can. And certainly not me, with all my sins. I'm vain, greedy, envious, full of lust—

I could go on, but I'm sure I'd shock you. You'd never talk to your sinful cousin again.' Anne's smile grew crooked.

'So that's why you went to confession—because you'd spent the night with the Baron,' Beatrice surmised.

'Nay.' Anne gave another delicate shrug. 'I can't expect forgiveness for a sin that I have every intention of committing again!'

Despite herself, Beatrice found herself responding to Anne's wicked grin.

'Nay, Beatrice, I went to confession because Philip had told me about the Saxon in the chapel. I was curious. Is curiosity a sin? I expect so.' Anne sighed. 'I wanted to see him for myself, and consequently you have before you a shriven maid. I'm absolved of all my sins. Gaze your fill, for you may never see your cousin in such a state of purity again!'

'Anne, can you never be serious?' Beatrice chuckled. Then she sobered. 'Did you see him? Did he look ill? In pain?' she asked.

Anne's eyes were no longer laughing. They were calculating, and Beatrice shivered. There was a ruthless streak in her cousin...

'Do you like him so much?' Anne murmured casually.

Beatrice countered swiftly. 'How could I? 'Tis simply that he was wounded. I've been taught to show concern for the sick.'

'Quite. That pretty toy you're fingering was his, was it not?' Anne probed.

Beatrice dropped the dagger as though it were a hot coal.

'And him a Saxon too,' Anne murmured. 'I expect you'd agree to marry *him* if the King willed it. If unity and peace were at stake. That would be worth sacrificing your future for, wouldn't it, Beatrice?'

Beatrice knew her face was scarlet. She jumped up and twisted away, but Anne's soft taunting voice followed her.

'Life beginning to get complicated, is it, Beatrice? Not quite what it was behind the ordered convent walls?'

Beatrice put her hands on her ears. 'Stop it, Anne! Stop it! 'Tis pointless talking to me like this!'

'Not quite pointless,' de Brionne cut in lazily. He came slowly round the fire and put a hand on Anne's shoulder, but when his hooded eyes saw that Beatrice had watched the gesture he removed his hand.

'How long have you been there?' Beatrice demanded coldly.

'Long enough to hazard a guess that you are not indifferent to the Saxon warrior you have saved. I thought last eve that you were swift to rush to his defence. And there was the little matter of the dagger, too. That gave you away. I see you have it with you still.'

Anne and her lover exchanged glances. Beatrice stiffened, her instinct for danger aroused. They were up to something.

'Raoul!' the Baron shouted.

A burly soldier, who'd been lounging near the threshold, came smartly to attention.

'Sir!'

'Go to the chapel. Inform Father Ralph I am coming over to parley with the Saxon. I have a proposal for him. King William plans to unite this stinking swamp, and I must conform to my sovereign's wishes.' He eyed Beatrice from under heavy lids, and Beatrice felt another icy finger shiver down her back.

The Baron bowed and drew her hand through one arm. Anne attached herself to his other.

'Come, ladies,' de Brionne commanded. ''Tis time to negotiate a betrothal!'

Edmund was seated on a wooden bench, deep in conversation with Father Ralph. The priest looked none the worse for his ordeal, and his open face did not seem to harbour any ill-will towards the man who'd bound him in the night. Edmund looked sombre.

Edmund's head jerked up as Beatrice was pushed into the chapel and his expression lifted. But when he saw that the Baron followed with Anne clinging on his arm, Edmund's face froze. A watchful gleam entered his eyes.

'To what do I owe the honour of this visit?' he enquired. His voice was so cold that Beatrice hardly recognised it.

'I thought we should attempt to negotiate an agreement which would be beneficial to all parties,' de Brionne drawled.

'Aye?' Edmund sounded disbelieving.

'Aye. You wish these lands to remain in Saxon control. And I for my part wish to please my King.'

'The usurper, William, you mean,' Edmund corrected.

'*King* William's right to rule has been proved and his claim upheld. However, I do not propose to discuss the succession here. I was sent to establish a union between our two races, and that is what I intend to do.'

Beatrice felt sick. She wanted to sit down. She realised what the Baron meant to do. Now Aiden was dead, he must mean to marry Anne to Edmund. Anne's face told her nothing. She had been trained to do her duty and no doubt would obey, provided de Brionne was to remain at Lindsey. She drew a shaky breath.

Edmund regarded the two girls, his face as empty as Anne's had been. 'A union,' he murmured. 'If I agree to this, you would guarantee the safety of my people?'

'Assuredly.' The Baron was urbane.

'And they may return to their homes and tend the land as before?'

'But naturally you Saxons must work the lands. You don't expect me to plough them for you, do you? I've brought soldiers with me, not farmers. 'Twas always intended you Saxons should continue to farm the lands.'

The Norman's lips stretched into a wide smile. It was too bright, too easy. Beatrice had been prepared to try and trust the Baron. But that parody of a smile made something click inside, and she knew she'd never trust him. He was without honour. She willed Edmund to look at her, her mind screaming him a warning: Don't trust him. You mustn't trust him.

Edmund did look at her, but only for a second, and no flicker of warmth or recognition was discernible as blue eyes met hazel. Edmund's gaze shifted to Anne. He smiled at Anne.

Beatrice clenched her slender fingers into hard fists. Edmund must not marry Anne! Anne loved Philip! Anne could never love Edmund.

Did Anne find Edmund handsome, too? Beatrice studied his face. The new Thegn was pale. Now he was not smiling, lines of pain slashed across his forehead. Frowning brows and dark lashes accentuated the whiteness of his finely drawn features. Even ill, Beatrice thought him attractive. Not handsome precisely, his nose was too prominent for that, a true Roman nose—but his lips were well-shaped, and his eyes, those deep blue eyes...

The eyes in question encountered hers. He looked amused. Beatrice blushed and hastily focused her attention on her leather shoes, studying them as if her life depended on it.

'I shall act as mediator between you,' Father Ralph announced. 'Ladies, please be seated while we agree the terms.'

Beatrice allowed Anne to lead her to the wooden bench by the west wall.

Pressed at her cousin's side, Beatrice leant back against the stone wall, eyes and ears closed to what was going on about her. The cold seeped through her clothes, chilling her slight frame. She was numb all over.

'You look ill, Beatrice. Are you all right?' Anne shook her arm.

Beatrice forced her eyes open. 'I feel like one of those Saints on the wall painting up there,' she admitted. 'Oh, not saintly, I don't mean that. These Saints are stuck on that wall. They're helpless, passive, and however much they might want to come off the wall and affect what's happening around them, they can't. They never will. I feel like that, Anne, I...'

Anne was no longer listening. She was staring at the Norman Baron, and her face was masked with that empty expression that Beatrice knew her cousin donned when disguising some deep emotion.

There was little difference between Anne's position and her own. Anne had no more control over events in her life than did Beatrice. Anne would not be allowed to marry the man she loved, and neither would Beatrice...

Beatrice caught her breath, dismayed at the turn her thoughts had taken. Her eyes went inexorably to Edmund.

He was scowling at de Brionne, and shaking his head vigorously. A lock of long raven hair had flopped forward and she saw him shove it aside. His speech was rapid and intense.

It's infatuation, nothing more, Beatrice told herself, shattered by the revelation which had flashed into her consciousness. It blinded her to her surroundings. She couldn't be in love with him. She hardly knew him. He was a Saxon Thegn and she was a lowly Norman. Not even of his class. Her cousin was the heiress. She had nothing; no dowry to offer, no lands in Normandy. Beatrice and Edmund were as far apart as the sun and the moon. She mustn't make a fool of herself.

Beatrice shut her eyes. But shutting Edmund from her sight did not succeed in shutting him out of her thoughts.

She could hear his voice, low and gentle.

'Mistress Beatrice!' It sounded like a caress. She kept her eyes firmly closed and tried desperately to think of something else.

'Mistress Beatrice!' His voice was louder now and more insistent. It would not go away.

Beatrice abandoned the futile struggle to banish him from her thoughts. She opened her eyes and found herself gazing directly into those haunting blue eyes.

He held out his hand.

Without thinking, Beatrice placed her hand in his and allowed him to draw her up. She'd forgotten how tall he was. She only came up to his shoulder.

'My thanks.' She smiled and tried unobtrusively to pull her hand away, but he held it fast. She was painfully conscious that he should not be looking at *her* like that when he was about to marry Anne.

'You found my gift, I see,' he whispered, glancing at her waist.

'Gift? Oh, yes. Thank you.' Her cheeks grew warm. 'I've never owned anything half as beautiful.'

De Brionne and her cousin stood close by, together, watching. Beatrice felt her flush deepen. She was confused. Why was Edmund staring at *her*?

Father Ralph coughed. 'Baron de Brionne, a word with you, if you please. And you, Lady Anne.'

Edmund and Beatrice were suddenly isolated with the Saints on the west wall.

'Why the fascination with my tunic?' Edmund asked. 'You're staring at it as though you've never seen it before. 'Tis not particularly remarkable.'

Beatrice raised shy eyes to his and tried to remove her hand from his clasp. He pulled her closer. Her free hand went trembling to his chest, as though to ward him off, but he took hold of that hand too, cradling it within his.

Blue eyes held hers. 'Do not fear me,' Edmund said.

Beatrice caught the query in his voice. 'I don't fear you. I told you that,' she said.

'Then why do you tremble? Is it that you are not in agreement with this marriage?'

Beatrice could not bring herself to speak. She could not tell him that she welcomed the wedding, that would be the blackest lie.

Halted by despair, Beatrice hesitated too long and Edmund's face changed. The signs of concern she had seen were wiped away, and a frozen mask settled over his features. Though he had not moved, she sensed him distance himself, and a cold claw gripped her heart. Edmund dropped her hands as though she were the vilest leper, and rounded on de Brionne. 'Methinks the lady does not like my proposal,' he said, stiffly. 'We cannot therefore come to terms. There can be no union between Saxon and Norman here. I shall resolve this matter another way.'

Anne ran up. 'Beatrice, what are you about? I thought you would be pleased to marry him. You seem to like him. I know he's only a Saxon, but 'tis a better marriage than you could ever hope to make in Normandy.'

Beatrice stared helplessly at Edmund's stiff back, her mind slow to grasp the implications of Anne's words. Then the floor fell away from her feet. A rushing noise filled her ears. 'I don't understand. What do you mean?' she asked stupidly.

Edmund swung round. His face was still unreadable, though a tinge of angry colour now touched his cheekbones. His eyes were like chips of ice.

'Perhaps your convent cousin is choosy, Lady Anne,' de Brionne sneered. 'Perhaps she does not like the idea of marriage with a bastard. You know how strong nuns are on morality. His birth is not good enough for her.'

'No!' Beatrice denied it. She had seen the effect the Baron's jeers had on Edmund. Scorn blazed from his eyes, he was turning away...

'No! You are wrong, Baron! I did not understand. I thought you meant to marry him to Anne. I did not dream he would consider...marrying...me. Believe me!' Beatrice cried.

Edmund's expression froze the marrow in her bones.

Desperately she caught hold of his sleeve, and prayed he would believe her, but he tore himself free. His eyes were filled with the same smouldering hatred she had encountered the first time she had found him in the chapel. The deadly, implacable hatred of Saxon for Norman, of conquered for conqueror, and Beatrice's heart stopped to see him direct it at her. In the face of such loathing, she recoiled.

'Dear Lord, make him believe me.' She whispered a disjointed prayer.

'Get out!' Edmund flared. 'Get out, all of you, before I commit the sin of murder in this holy place.'

'My son, this is not the answer,' Father Ralph said soothingly.

'Out! Out!' Edmund advanced menacingly towards Beatrice. She peered over her shoulder; it seemed she was the last to go. The last to realise Edmund was not to be placated.

'Edmund, please listen——' she began.

'I've heard enough from you,' he blazed. 'The pretty innocent. 'Tis a very convincing act, and with those wide hazel eyes of yours you almost had me fooled. But not quite. I read you now. I'm good enough for a game, but that's as far as it goes. Men have a name for women of your sort.'

Beatrice swallowed and opened her mouth.

Edmund forestalled her, his voice clipped with anger. 'But you would never marry me, would you? My birth, I suppose. My race too. Well, Mistress Beatrice, I apologise for having insulted you with my offer. I shall not raise the subject again.' He paused and gave a twisted smile. 'But then, you play the kissing game so well, methinks I shall insist on a farewell kiss. Our last.'

Her eyes misted.

Edmund's lips swooped down on hers with punishing force. He hurt. Beatrice tried to fend him off. Then she stopped. Perhaps she should respond. Maybe kisses could convince him of her feelings where words would not? The arms she had put up to push him away crept round his neck. She felt him stiffen. She held his head to hers. As her fingers wound into his dark hair the painful onslaught ceased, and startled blue eyes looked a question into hers.

She softened her lips, heard his low moan, and he was kissing her anew. He kissed her gently now, and tenderly, as he had done the previous night. He kissed her eyes, her cheeks, her nose, and then his lips drew back to hers again. Beatrice was melting...

The chapel door slammed in violent interruption. Edmund snatched back his head. For one glorious moment Beatrice thought her kisses had convinced him, but then his face put on that hard and unfathomable mask, and she knew she had failed. Her silent message had been misinterpreted.

She flushed, burningly aware that Edmund had released her while she still had her arms twined round his neck.

'Have you quite finished, Mistress?' he demanded with blistering scorn.

Beatrice dragged her arms away, and averted her face lest he should see the tears prickling in her eyes.

'You still enjoy your sport,' he observed stiffly.

Beatrice swallowed down a sob. Words were beyond her.

'Oh, get you gone,' he said wearily. 'You can go and find another man to amuse you now. This one's not going to play your Norman tricks any longer.'

Beatrice could stem her tears no more. She whirled round and groped blindly into the biting January air.

Edmund followed her with his eyes, until her figure vanished round the side of the chapel. He swore, loudly and comprehensively. White-lipped, he slammed the heavy door so furiously it all but ripped free of its hinges.

Beatrice winced. She'd heard the curses, and though he had spoken in English, which she could not understand, the tone of the words made their meaning quite clear. He was swearing, and he was swearing at her...

Only when she came face to face with the byre where Hilda waited did Beatrice remember her promise to tell Edmund that his sister was safe. But the chapel door had slammed with awful finality. Beatrice wiped her eyes with the sleeve of her gown. She could not go back now. Her attempts to make him understand had been wasted. He had enough pride for an army, and it daunted her.

A large tear rolled down her cheek. She sniffed. If only she had realised sooner. She did want to marry him. But she wanted him to want her, too. She would not have him wed her because his hand had been forced by de Brionne. How could she have explained all that to him with the audience they had had? And then, when he'd driven the others out and they had been left alone, he had closed his ears to her...

Beatrice blinked rapidly. She straightened her shoulders, and strode past the guards, taking the well-beaten track that led away from the Saxon settlement. She was so determined to conquer her anguish that she forgot she wore no mantle, and that to walk abroad so lightly clad on such a morning was sheer madness.

CHAPTER SIX

THE ruts and potholes in the narrow mud track had frozen into hard ridges, making the going difficult. Beatrice was forced to walk alongside the main path. Stiff brown grass crunched underfoot, and iron-cold earth cut through the thin leather of her shoes.

It was some minutes before she was calm enough to notice her surroundings. She was striding briskly down a slight incline and must be on the drovers' path. It wound on down through a wooded area. There was no one else in sight. Alders stood stark and leafless; stripped of their summer foliage, with skeletons exposed, they were grotesque. A wintry sun sparkled on frost-patterned buckthorn and narrow waterways. The harsh cawing of rooks was the only sound.

Or was it? Beatrice peered uneasily over her shoulder. A branch cracked behind her.

'Who's there?' she called in alarm.

The crows cawed in reply; she heard nothing else. The sunlight was reflecting from the surface of the lake she had seen on her way there. She wandered towards it.

It was quiet by the mere. Peaceful. As she walked Beatrice scuffed the tufts of reeds and fen-sedge that grew along the water's edge. A pair of moorhens skulked in the rushes—she caught the flash of their red bills. The water grasses had been harvested recently—she could see where they had been cut. Probably a cottager repairing a leaky roof, for it was no season to undertake major thatching work.

Her eyes skated over the icy flatness of the lake. She wondered how deep it was. Did the Saxons swim there in summer? In midwinter it would be cold enough to kill.

A heron rose heavily from a clump of coppiced willows, and flapped into the air, legs trailing languidly.

Realising she had come farther along the bank than she had intended, Beatrice turned to retrace her steps. In these unsettled times you could not be too careful. She must not forget she was a hated invader here. She shivered, her feet were damp, and she was feeling the cold.

An image of Edmund's face, dark with anger, flashed into her mind. She ground her teeth. She wished now that she had had the courage to tell him clearly what she felt. But it was not all her fault. He had not given her a chance.

She started. There it was again. A slight movement near that swamp-elder. She told herself it must be a bird eating the berries, and then remembered with a sinking feeling that the red fruit was poisonous. A premonition of danger set the hairs on end on the back of her neck.

She quickened her pace, her heart beginning to thump uncomfortably in her breast. She thought of robber bands roaming unchecked the length of the country, of mercenaries out for easy prey, and broke into a run. The air rasped cold down her throat with every breath. She stumbled and slid along the ice-bound ridges of the track.

'Nay, lass. Whither bound in such haste?' a male voice asked.

Beatrice stopped in mid-flight. She had almost reached the edge of the copse, and could see the buildings of the settlement at the top of the rise. The road was blocked by a blond giant. His huge frame was strangely garbed in garish, flowing clothes, that hung about him like un-wound hanks of fresh-dyed wool. Poised to run, Beatrice tipped her head back and stared. He had clear grey eyes. His smile *seemed* reassuring.

'I'll not harm thee, little one.' The giant scanned her tearstained cheeks. 'What ails you, Mistress? Perhaps you saw someone and were frightened?' He posed the question casually, but Beatrice glimpsed tension in the back of his eyes. His voice was deep and rich.

'Who are you?' Beatrice demanded.

'My name is Morcar. I'm a harper, and at your service, Mistress. I come to offer songs and tales for your delight.'

She noticed the harp that was slung over one broad shoulder. 'A minstrel! You're a minstrel!' Beatrice smiled, relieved.

'Aye, a minstrel and much more,' Morcar said mysteriously. ''Tis my role to please. Did you think I was a cut-throat?'

'I...I wasn't sure. I walked out too far on my own. And I thought I heard...but no matter, it must have been you. You did startle me,' she admitted. 'Are you Saxon?'

'For my sins.' He smiled.

'You speak French well, Morcar. Is that common in a Saxon?'

Morcar's laugh matched his frame, it was loud and booming. 'Nay, not common!' He shook his head and grinned. 'But, Mistress, I am not a common man. I have many talents. My harp ensures a good welcome wherever I go, and I have travelled far with it. It opens many doors to me that are closed to others.' He shrugged. 'And Normans pay for their entertainment as well as my own race. I have learned your tongue in my journeyings, Mistress.'

Morcar started up the track towards the stockade, and Beatrice fell into step beside him. She had to take two or three strides to every one of Morcar's.

'I come to see if your people would welcome singing tonight,' he said.

Beatrice smiled up at the giant with his shaggy thatch of yellow hair, and thus she did not observe the crouched figure that broke cover from behind a scraggy shrub and scuttled into the shelter offered by the wood.

'Who's that with you, Mistress?' the lookout challenged suspiciously. The wooden palisade offered little in the way of protection from the wind, and the sentry was frozen to the core.

'This is Morcar. He's a minstrel, come to entertain us,' explained Beatrice.

'A Saxon, by the look of him.' The guard eyed Morcar's vivid clothes and made as if to yell for assistance.

Morcar smiled and clapped the man on the shoulder as though they had met over a pot in a tavern. 'Do you think I'd wear all the colours of the rainbow, if I meant to work harm on you?' He laughed. 'Nay, surely an enemy would be discreet. I've come armed with harp, not sword. I'm no fighter, despite my size.'

'That's a blessing.' The guard smiled with obvious relief. 'I'd not willingly cross swords with a mountain like you.' He waved them through the gate. 'I dare say we'll all be glad of some entertainment. These winter evenings are too long by half. Ho, there! You in the yard! Tell the Baron there's a minstrel at the gate!'

Inside the hall Beatrice hobbled on frozen limbs to the fire. Anne billowed over, fluttering anxiously, but Beatrice brushed aside her concern with a rueful smile. 'I'm all right, Anne. I'll warm up in a minute. 'Tis my own fault for dashing off without my cloak.'

Morcar was accorded a wary welcome. He settled near the blaze, straddling a stool, to tune his harp. Harpers were usually received with open arms, for a skilled minstrel could make tired, cold, homesick men and women forget their miseries. He could transport his listeners to glittering realms where they could all be transformed into heroes and heroines.

But this minstrel was Saxon. The Baron had allowed him into the hall, but so far no one had ventured to join him by the fireside. Unperturbed by his cool reception, Morcar smiled blandly round the room.

Warming through at last, Beatrice watched his gigantic hands as they idly plucked a string or two. It was strange to see how nimble those oversized hands were on the strings of the harp. He wore some fine finger-rings, payment no doubt for the songs he had sung on his travels. A large jewel flashed in the firelight. It was only one of many and, judging from the size and quality of his rings, Morcar was an accomplished player.

'Have you travelled far this day? Would you care for some refreshment?' Beatrice enquired, determining to be polite.

'You could say I've come from another world——' Morcar smiled cryptically '—and I'd not refuse some ale. Thank you, little one.'

Beatrice frowned, puzzled by Morcar's strange remark. She took it to mean that he had walked a great distance.

An assortment of utensils dangled from Morcar's belt. He unclipped his drinking horn and handed it to her. She filled it. It was swiftly drained. She was refilling the vessel when a commotion outside the door drew her attention.

A man cursed. There were sounds of a struggle. A figure was flung across the threshold and landed on all fours on the floor of the hall.

Hilda!

Morcar's hand twitched and some of the ale spilled over the silver rim of his horn and down over his be-ringed fingers. He made no move to wipe up the ale, but stared at the Saxon girl, stock-still.

Beatrice stepped forward. So did the Baron. She found herself facing him across Hilda's small body. The Saxon girl stabbed at the Baron with eyes that glared bitter loathing.

He was unmoved. 'Who in heaven's name are you?' de Brionne demanded coldly. He hauled Hilda to her feet, holding her at arm's length to examine her.

'Be careful, Baron. She's got claws,' the groom who had found her warned. He was rubbing his face. Two long scratches ran down the side of the Norman's cheek and the blood trickled slowly down to his chin.

Hair awry, Hilda stared wildly about the hall. She started visibly when her eyes came to Morcar. Morcar gave an almost imperceptible shake of his head and transferred his gaze at once to the pitcher of ale. He did not glance her way again.

'Who are you?' the Baron bullied, shaking the young girl.

'Her name is Hilda,' Beatrice supplied. 'She is but a child, Baron. Please release her. You can't be afraid she is going to hurt *you*.'

'Beatrice has it aright. This must be Hilda, Aiden of Lindsey's sister——' Anne held out the psalter '—remember her name is marked in this.'

De Brionne grunted and relaxed his grip, baring his yellow teeth in that wolfish grin. Hilda rubbed her arm, her eyes spitting sparks.

'Lady Hilda,' de Brionne drawled. 'Forgive my rough soldier's manners. I had no idea who you were. Wench! Yea, you there, Ella! Some food for the lady. And then, Lady Hilda, perhaps you would care to retire to the upper chamber. I'm sure Lady Anne would not object to your resting there.'

'You mean I am to be a prisoner?' Hilda scowled.

'A prisoner? Whatever gave you that idea? Nay, more of an honoured guest. You look as if you've been short on sleep, Lady Hilda.'

Falsely solicitous, the Baron handed Hilda over to Ella. He gestured two guards over, and indicated that they should keep watch over the Saxon girl.

Seated at the trestle, Hilda glowered into her platter. But she was not stupid and had no intention of starving herself. She broke apart the new loaf Ella gave her, and favoured the Baron with glances so barbed that none doubted it was he she wished torn asunder.

Beatrice intercepted a puzzled frown directed at Morcar. The blond giant remained impassive, and when Hilda had done with her scanty meal she heaved a great sigh and stalked up the stairs.

'Well, Philip, what a stroke of luck! The heiress herself,' Anne crowed.

'Aye. We seem to have Saxon maggots crawling out of the woodwork all over the place today,' de Brionne responded thoughtfully.

Beatrice frowned.

'I wonder if that chit knows where it is. This will require careful handling, I . . .' De Brionne's sharp eyes fell on Beatrice's curious face. 'Beatrice, stop goggling like a witless serf, and do something useful. Go and tell your Saxon lover in the chapel that I shall be visiting him again to reopen negotiations.'

'I have no lover, Baron!' Beatrice declared.

De Brionne's smile would have frozen fire.

'Whatever you say,' he said. 'But do it, will you? Go and tell that half-breed I will be over to parley. But first I must consider . . .' He began to prowl up and down the hall.

Beatrice was dismissed. She hesitated. She did not want to see Edmund yet. Not if he was still seething. The mis-

understanding in the chapel had been ghastly. Beatrice
had assumed he would marry the heiress, Anne. And
Edmund thought Beatrice despised his illegitimate birth.
She could not explain till he had calmed down.

'Get along, Beatrice.' The Baron stopped pacing and
frowned irritably at her.

Smiling somewhat distractedly in the direction of the
minstrel, Beatrice trailed to the door. Her dagger glinted
in the fireglow, and Morcar's thick blond brows snapped
together. Veiling his eyes, the Saxon reached for his horn
of ale.

The chapel was empty.

Edmund had left, and he had covered his tracks. The
cloak Beatrice had given him had vanished, as had the
sword.

And the little space under the altar?

Beatrice snatched back the cloth and peered in.
Nothing, except a solid metal ring set into a stone. She
had not noticed it before, Edmund's body must have
lain across it. She grasped the ring and pulled. Nothing
happened. She put both hands to it and hauled harder,
using all her strength. This time the stone juddered, but
it was too heavy and she could not lift it out. She relaxed
her grip and the slab grated back to its original position.

Feeling oddly dispirited, Beatrice let the ring clank
back. She meandered to the centre of the chapel and
stared blindly at the wooden cross.

He had gone. Edmund of Lindsey had gone. He could
be anywhere, hiding out with rebel Saxons, anywhere.
She might never see him again. What was especially hard
to stomach was that he had gone thinking her a narrow
bigot. She told herself that she had not wanted to see
him, and cursed the hopeless misery that welled up inside
her.

Moments later de Brionne stomped into the chapel.
He pulled up sharply, taking the situation in at a glance.
Beatrice was blank-eyed in the middle of the small nave,
chewing a finger in deep abstraction.

'Where is he?' de Brionne roared, grabbing at his
sword. His swarthy visage was purple with fury.

Beatrice raised sad eyes and shrugged.

'If you've helped him escape,' the Baron thundered, 'you will rue the day you were born!' Sword at the ready, he quartered the chapel. But the target he sought had gone. Unable to vent his spleen, de Brionne raged back to the yard, bellowing loud as a baited bull.

In seconds a pack of mailclad men had overrun the chapel. They scoured every inch of the place. Benches were toppled, wall-hangings ripped. It was only a matter of time before one of the Baron's hounds sniffed out the stone trapdoor. He barked his triumph, and snatched at the iron ring. Reluctantly, the stone scraped out.

The Baron clapped his man on the shoulder, shoved him aside, and peered into the cavity. 'Well done, man,' he approved. Impious booted feet mangled the altar cloth which lay where it had been flung, half wrapped round the toppled cross.

The concealed recess was not large. There was space enough to contain a small box, but nothing more. De Brionne bent and swooped on a tiny object that lay in a corner of the cavity.

Beatrice craned her neck. It was a silver mark. Something clicked neatly into place. Edmund had hidden a casket in her travelling chest. His casket must contain Saxon silver. Obscenities were battering at her ears. She looked at their progenitor.

'Hell and damnation! So this is where that lousy bastard hid it! 'Twas here all the time.' De Brionne swore and rounded on Beatrice so viciously she recoiled. 'I expect you find this amusing,' he snarled dangerously. 'Did you know anything about this?'

Beatrice gulped, wishing she'd not come so close. 'About what, Baron? The silver mark? Or the secret hiding place? I'd not seen either until just now,' she replied truthfully.

The Baron's eyes were black as thunderclouds. Beatrice held her ground and raised her chin a notch, waiting for the storm to break over her head. But, surprisingly, de Brionne merely glowered and slammed out of the chapel.

Mechanically, Beatrice retrieved the cross and set it in its place. The altar cloth was a ruin of crumpled silks. She shook it out. De Brionne's careless feet had damaged the delicate fabric almost beyond repair. She folded the cloth over her arm and trod out after him.

A sorry lookout was sitting at his post, clutching his head in both hands. 'I'm sorry, Baron. He must have come up behind me,' he moaned.

'Fool! Where's your helmet?' de Brionne rapped out, wild with fury. 'Christ! I'm surrounded by fools. Where's that wretched girl? Beatrice, don't you slink off. Tell me what you know about the Saxon's escape. Come on! Now!'

Beatrice bit her lip. 'Baron, he'd already gone when I arrived at the chapel. I know nothing,' she insisted. Her mouth felt dry.

'You expect me to believe you had no hand in this?' snorted de Brionne.

Anger flared up in her breast. It aided her. Beatrice met that coal-black gaze. 'I don't much care what you believe,' she responded flatly. 'I probably would have helped him if he'd asked me to. But he didn't. He escaped without my help.'

Several people, bursting with curiosity, had gathered by the gate. The Saxon giant was among them. Beatrice found herself meeting Morcar's disinterested gaze. He stood casually, but none the less the thought crossed her mind that the minstrel was not as impartial as he would have his Norman hosts believe.

'You are insolent,' de Brionne declared. 'Get to the upper chamber. And you will stay there till we eat tonight. You anger me, and if I have to look at you any more...' His unspoken threat hung in the air, as plain as the misty clouds of his breath.

'So I'm to be incarcerated, too. Very well. Frankly, that is preferable to enduring your company,' Beatrice flung recklessly. It was intolerable. She simmered with a heady combination of fear and rage, aware that the blow of Edmund's departure hurt more than any of the rest. She felt it like a spear-thrust through her vitals.

The Baron champed visibly, face livid. His hands were tight at his side, and Beatrice flinched, fearing he'd strike her. 'Don't get too used to Lady Hilda's company,' he recommended. 'I have plans for that Saxon stray. Plans that will be executed soon.'

His threat followed Beatrice into the hall and rang in her ears all the way up the stairs. Did he mean to kill Edmund's sister? She realised she was biting her nails to the quick, and pulled her hand from her mouth.

This day had given her a formidable enemy. But had she also gained an ally? She twisted her neck and got a glimpse of Morcar. The Saxon giant was back by the fire, tuning his harp. For all that she reckoned him an expert, he had taken a long time over the task. He looked as though his thoughts were miles away. She willed him to look in her direction, but before she could catch his eye a rude hand hit the small of her back and she was shoved into the chamber.

The two girls were isolated in the upper chamber until mid-afternoon. Both were grateful for the respite.

Beatrice occupied herself repairing the damaged altar cloth, conscious of Hilda's speculative gaze resting on her from time to time. At first the Saxon girl looked away when Beatrice attempted conversation, but by the end of the afternoon Beatrice had managed to establish some degree of rapport with Edmund's young sister.

Although Beatrice had not deliberately set out to win the girl's confidence by mending the torn fabric, she had been glad of her impulsive decision to repair it. Who would have thought that a few careful stitches set into a Saxon embroidery would be instrumental in nurturing the fragile blossom of friendship? Hilda remained wary, but Beatrice knew she was winning through.

While she sewed, Beatrice tried to calm her disordered thoughts. The numb misery that she had felt on discovering Edmund's disappearance still gnawed at her. Hilda's presence in the chamber, and sympathy for his half-sister's plight, helped take her mind off her confusion. But fellow feeling, Beatrice discovered, was not enough to remove the hollow feeling from the pit of her stomach.

For her part, Hilda had been relieved when the pretty Norman woman had walked in to share her imprisonment.

In happier times the chamber had belonged to her elder brother, Aiden. Being incarcerated here, under Norman

guard, brought home to the Saxon child how much her
life had changed. The chamber was the same, yet
somehow different. The two Norman ladies' clothes were
strewn about, their travelling chests took up almost all
of the space. Hilda could not see anything that had belonged to her dead brother.

Hilda felt lost and very much alone.

She seated herself on her late brother's bed. Next to
the foreign woman. She glanced furtively at Beatrice
from under her lashes. She could not make her mind up
about the auburn-haired woman sewing placidly at her
side. She seemed kind and sympathetic, and had un-
doubtedly helped Edmund. But she was a Norman. So
Hilda held a part of her aloof, and reserved her
judgement.

Quiet fell over them. Shadows lengthened.

Heavy steps sounded outside the chamber and two
heads swivelled towards the door-curtain.

It was the Baron. He was rubbing his hands together,
and an ugly, gloating smile spread across his face. Thank
God, Beatrice thought, relaxing; his black mood has
gone.

'Good afternoon, ladies.' He bowed with studied
courtesy. Anne entered. She did not look so happy. Her
eyes darted from Hilda to the Baron and back again to
Hilda, and they were brimful of misery.

Beatrice braced herself for some new horror. What
had that fiend devised now?

'Lady Hilda, I have given much thought to the unfortunate situation you now find yourself in,' de Brionne
began, in Latin.

Hilda sniffed.

'I am not wholly unsympathetic to your cause,' he
continued smoothly. 'You are concerned for your people,
and your brother, are you not?'

'You murdered my brother! Treacherous swine!' Hilda
spat, starting up from the bed.

Beatrice laid a restraining hand on the girl's arm. She
knew de Brionne was at his most dangerous in this apparently cool mood. He was acting in a civilised manner,
but Beatrice was not deceived.

'Nay, lady, I refer to your concern about your half-brother, Edmund,' the Baron continued blandly, ignoring Hilda's angry response. 'You do not wish your people to be harmed, or reduced to beggary, do you, Lady Hilda?'

His softly spoken threat hit its target. Hilda subsided.

'I have thought of a way whereby we can unite our two causes and forge a new race, an Anglo-Norman one,' he announced, eyes watchful.

Beatrice erupted. 'You can't! Baron, Hilda is but a child! 'Twould not be fitting!'

'Mistress, stay out of this,' the Norman warned. 'I have had enough of your interference. The King has commanded me to achieve some sort of alliance with these vanquished Saxons. Mark this. It matters little to me *how* I carry out his commands, but carry them out I will. I shall not be crossed. I cannot afford to lose the King's favour.'

'Then you should have considered that before you slaughtered her people!' Beatrice cried, flinging an arm in the direction of Hilda.

Hilda edged nearer Beatrice. 'Please. Explain. I do not understand what you are talking about,' she said.

'Stupid Saxon!' Anne screamed. 'He intends to marry you!'

Hilda went white as whey.

''Tis one way of ensuring good behaviour from that rabble of yours,' de Brionne smirked. 'Your Saxons will not rebel if they know that Aiden of Lindsey's *legitimate* heir is installed as wife to the new Norman overlord!'

Hilda shook his head. 'Nay,' she whispered, and backed till her shoulders hit the wall by the window. She looked desperately young. 'You ... you have it wrong. I'm not necessarily Aiden's heir. I think the Council will support Edmund as Thegn. He's more suitable than I. I ... I ... was ...'

The Baron waved her objection aside. 'I think you will come to realise the advantages of our union, Lady Hilda, and will change your mind. Your people will be safe, no longer inclined to rebel, and the position of Thegn will be filled satisfactorily by ...' de Brionne paused '...myself. Then everyone can get on with learning to live again. Why, I may even pardon that rebel brother of yours. Naturally, his illegitimacy bars him from advancement——'

'Why?' Beatrice demanded. 'Our King is illegitimate, and that has been no bar to *his* advancement.'

'Mistress,' the Baron warned silkily, 'your insolence will yet be your death.' His cold eyes snaked back to the quivering Saxon. 'But I will be merciful, Lady Hilda. If you wed me, I will have your brother exiled. His life would be my wedding gift to you.'

Beatrice subsided, speechless at his gall. Only that morning he had proposed a different marriage in the cause of unity. And now he was putting himself forward as the husband of this child, when all the time he and Anne...

She almost choked. Poor Anne.

Anne was twisting and untwisting the ends of her girdle round her hands with jerky, uneven movements. She would not look at Beatrice.

'You...you would allow Edmund to live?' Hilda asked faintly.

Beatrice could hear the hope in Hilda's voice. The child was weakening. She believed de Brionne's easy lies.

'Hilda! No!' Beatrice cried, revolted by the Baron's plan. 'You're too young. You cannot marry de Brionne.'

Anne's lover placed himself a few inches in front of his prospective bride.

'Oh, she'll grow up quickly enough. I can already see signs of coming beauty,' he declared, smiling into Hilda's rigid face.

Anne let out a strangled sob.

De Brionne's face darkened. 'I won't stand any more arguments from you women. You are none of you in any position to argue. You'll do your duty. I'm dispatching an envoy to the King, and if he agrees my proposal is sound I shall marry the Lady Hilda! Nothing any of you can say will alter my decision.'

Brushing past Anne on his way to the door, he chucked her under the chin. 'Don't scowl, my lady. 'Twill put lines on your beautiful face and mar you. I won't take a lined hag as my mistress,' he finished cruelly and strode from the room.

'How could he use you so, Anne? He's a monster, a beast!' Beatrice cried.

'Nay, Beatrice,' Anne said tonelessly. 'He's just a man. An ambitious man. And one who wants to gain favour with his King.'

'No man, that! He's the Devil incarnate! He has no right to treat you so! I thought he loved you.'

A sad smile hovered on Anne's lips. 'He loves me as well as he is able. 'Tis very strange, Beatrice, but when I was to marry Aiden I did not mind so much. Nor did I mind when Philip put forward a marriage to Edmund as a solution. He did suggest that, but, as you know, Edmund did not want me.' The heart-wrenching smile twisted. 'I've either been married, or been a widow, ever since I've known Philip. It didn't seem to present a problem. But when he suggested *he* was going to marry Hilda...that did...hurt. I think I trust the strength of my own feelings for Philip more than the strength of his for me. I must be jealous! How very vulgar!' Anne made a brave attempt at a laugh, but it sounded more like a sob.

'You *love* that murdering swine?' Hilda asked, temporarily forgetting her hatred for all Normans in her incredulity that anyone could love the worst of them all.

Anne nodded ruefully.

'If it helps you at all, Lady Anne, I do not wish to marry him. But it seems it is not up to me,' Hilda told her with commendable calm.

'This wedding must not take place,' Beatrice announced decisively. 'And we must stop it.'

The two girls stared.

'But...but what can we do? You heard the Baron,' Anne protested.

'There must be a way open to us. There has to be. 'Tis just that we have not seen it,' Beatrice insisted.

For a moment no one spoke. A wintry gust of air blew in through the window, carrying with it the noise of soldiers drilling in the yard. There was so much noise, every last Norman must be present. Beatrice moved to the window. They were a formidable sight. They were finishing, breaking ranks. She saw de Brionne talking to a mounted man. The envoy? The man saluted, and de Brionne sped him on his way with a hard slap on the horse's rump.

'The messenger to King William has left,' Beatrice murmured.

'There is the Saxon treasure hoard,' Anne said thoughtfully.

'What?' Hilda exclaimed.

Anne looked sharply at the Saxon girl. 'You must know about it. 'Tis your inheritance.'

Hilda tossed her head, and sealed her lips.

Anne took Beatrice's arm. 'Apparently, Cousin, there's treasure which belonged to the old Thegn, Hereward of Lindsey. 'Twas mentioned in the prayer book. Philip noticed that someone had written in the margin a reference to the "treasure beyond price" that lay hidden in the chapel.'

'There could be a more spiritual explanation. It could be a reference to the peace of mind, the spiritual solace people find in a chapel,' Beatrice suggested.

'Aye, I thought you'd come up with some pious nonsense,' Anne said scornfully.

'She's right,' Hilda cut in. 'That's what it does mean.'

Beatrice struggled to keep her eyes from shifting to her travelling chest. A shiver ran down her spine. Edmund's casket! She flashed a guilty look at Anne, but Anne had not noticed.

'Nay, Hilda.' Anne would not have it. 'You know full well there *is* treasure. As soon as Philip told me about the hidden recess under the altar, and the silver mark he had found, I knew there was a hoard. It must have been secreted there. How else do you explain Edmund's presence in the chapel? 'Twas a strange hiding place for a wounded man to pick, when it cut off his retreat. Or perhaps you'd have me believe he went there to pray?' She hooted derisively. 'A warrior at prayer when his people were battling for their lives? Nay. Not that one. 'Tis most likely he was hiding Saxon coin. And where is it now, Hilda? Tell me that. Where's that treasure now?'

'I have no idea,' Hilda snapped, and flounced on to the bed.

'Haven't you?' Anne set her mouth. 'What a pity. If you did know its whereabouts, we might be able to persuade Philip to give up this idea of marrying you. We could give him the treasure, and in exchange he'd let you go.'

'Not he,' Beatrice disagreed bluntly. 'He'd still want Hilda. Hilda is the key to any power he may hope to have.'

'Do *you* think he might change his mind if we found the hoard?' Hilda pleaded, fixing hopeful eyes on Anne.

'Do you know where it is?' Anne parried.

Hilda's face dropped. 'Nay. I do not.'

I know where it is, Beatrice thought, keeping a tight rein on her expression. Her mind raced. If she gave Hilda the casket, it might save the child, though she doubted it. Edmund's enemy would end up holding both the treasure and his sister. If Beatrice said nothing, she was condemning Hilda to a lifetime of hell with de Brionne. She rubbed her face. Whatever she chose to do she risked damaging Edmund's cause. There *must* be another answer.

'I have an idea,' she announced. 'We must help Hilda to escape.'

Hilda snorted. 'Mistress Beatrice, you're mad! You've seen the guards de Brionne has posted outside this chamber. The place is bristling with them. What about the sentries, and the lookout? What will we do with them? Weave a magic spell and have them spirited away?'

'Knowing Beatrice, she'll probably pray,' Anne commented drily.

'Anne, do think,' Beatrice pleaded. 'There must be something...'

'I could distract the men in the hall,' Anne began doubtfully.

'Aye!' Hilda's eyes were lit with desperate, eager hope.

'And Beatrice could work on the lookout by the gate...'

Beatrice knew a pang of doubt. 'And how, pray, do I work on the lookout?' she asked.

'You're a woman, aren't you?' Anne smiled
suggestively.

'Anne!'

Her cousin laughed. 'No time for your convent
scruples now, Beatrice. If you want to help Hilda escape,
you'll have to play your part. We have to make absolutely certain that the guards don't suspect what we're
up to.'

'Oh, Mistress Beatrice, please help,' Hilda begged. 'I
cannot marry that soulless swine. My apologies, Lady
Anne, but I cannot like him.'

'You can be as rude as you like,' Anne told her, 'as
long as you don't marry him. Come on, Beatrice, let's
do it now! I'll ask Walter to saddle up Betony, and if
he is asked we can say he must exercise her for you.'

Beatrice had to be sure they had a chance. She took
the sceptic's part. 'Walter will bring Betony into the yard.
He will wait for Hilda and me to appear. I must "distract" the guards. Hilda will leap nimbly on to Betony
and make her escape. Easy. Nothing could possibly go
wrong.'

'Aye, 'twill be simple. A fool could do it,' Anne
declared.

'Only a fool would try it,' Beatrice worried. So much
could go wrong...

'I'm willing. My position could hardly be worse than
it is now.' Hilda smiled, her hostility quite gone. 'Besides,
can you think of a better plan, Mistress Beatrice?'

'Nay,' admitted Beatrice.

Anne grinned. 'Then it is settled! Beatrice, give her
my cloak.' She rummaged in her purse. 'And you had
better take this money, Hilda, you might need it. I'll go
to Walter. Give me a couple of minutes, and then come
out. Agreed?'

Anne vanished before Beatrice had time to nod her
consent.

'The cloak?' Hilda said urgently.

Beatrice pulled her scattered wits together, and deliberately closed her mind to the retribution the Baron
would exact from them for their part in this escapade.
He would probably kill them all...

'Here!' She threw Anne's cloak at Hilda. 'I'm afraid your own clothes were destroyed after the fight the other day.'

'If it were simply a matter of clothes, I'd have no worries,' Hilda said bitterly, and hunched a shoulder at Beatrice. Beatrice heard her suppress a sob.

'I'm truly sorry, Hilda,' she said.

Hilda wiped her face with her sleeve. ''Tis not of your doing. Shall we go?' she asked, eyes over-bright.

Beatrice stayed her with a gesture. 'One moment. I think you had better take this with you.' She drew out her key. When she lifted out the casket, she knew by Hilda's gasp that the child had recognised it at once. She deposited it in Hilda's hands.

'You had it all along! Why didn't you say something?' Hilda demanded.

'I don't think Anne should know. Much as I love her, her loyalties are with de Brionne. She'd be bound to try and get it for him. But if you take it with you, Lady Hilda, you can give it into Edmund's care. Hide it under your cloak.' Beatrice hesitated. 'And . . . and, please, tell Edmund I did not betray its whereabouts to any but you.'

'Oh, bless you, bless you,' Hilda breathed, clutching the casket to her breast.

'Don't thank me, we've yet to get you away——'

A low, sensual laugh floated through the doorway. Anne was already fulfilling her part of the scheme.

Beatrice lifted the tapestry hanging aside, and heard another seductive gurgle and a man's eager response.

It was time to go.

Halfway across the hall a slurred voice challenged, 'And where are you bound, ladies?'

It was the groom with the scratched face. He was very much the worse for several jugs of ale. He lurched aggressively towards them.

Beatrice dug her nails into her palms and summoned her loftiest manner. 'I have permission to escort Lady Hilda to the yard,' she announced. 'We are going to walk. People need exercise as much as horses.' She glared down her nose at the groom and he wavered, rubbed his sore cheek, and crumpled clumsily on to a nearby stool.

Gesturing Hilda through the doorway, Beatrice sailed
out into the dusk.

Her nerves were stretched as tight as a bowstring. Their
mission seemed doomed before they'd even begun. 'This
way, Hilda,' she whispered urgently. 'That drunkard may
yet recall his duty. We must hurry. I pray Walter manages
to get Betony to the gate in time. I'll distract the sentry,
and the rest is up to you. Ride like the wind. Do you
understand?'

Hilda assented.

'So far, so good,' Beatrice murmured on reaching the
gate. Out of the tail of her eye she glimpsed Walter with
Betony. He still had a few yards to cover.

Beatrice eyed the guard boldly. His helmet and nose-
guard hid most of his face, but what she could see was
blue with cold. He looked disgruntled. He was in need
of a shave. 'Good evening,' she smiled, wondering wildly
how on earth one flirted with a man whose expression
was lost behind a metal guard.

'Evening, Mistress,' the man responded, startled. He
focused bleary eyes on the woman in front of him. Lady
Anne's cousin. He had not heard that she dispensed
favours among the men, but then he was not one to miss
chances when they came his way... He straightened to
his full height.

Beatrice swallowed, and wrestled with revulsion. The
man stank. It had sounded easy while they were safely
in the chamber, but now she was confronted with reality
she wasn't sure she could be convincing enough...

She dredged up a dazzling smile. She had used that
smile to good effect once before, and prayed it worked
again.

It did. The guard looked as though he had wagered
for the whole troop's pay—and won.

'Are you on guard *all* night?' Beatrice purred.

'Aye, Mistress, all night.' He stepped forward eagerly,
bringing his stench with him.

Smile nailed ruthlessly in place, Beatrice side-stepped
and evaded him. This put her and Hilda *outside* the
stockade. So far, so good.

The guard grinned. He was not one to be put off by
a little evasive footwork. Not when the pretty lady's lips

smiled such a welcome. A game of cat and mouse was
a fine way to warm the blood.

Beatrice could hear Betony's hoofs clopping on the
iron-hard earth. Not long now.

'You must get very cold and lonely out here.' The
husky throatiness of her voice pleased her. It was perfect;
she sounded almost like Anne. This was easier than she
had thought.

'Aye, my lady. I could do with some warming...' His
leer, and his hot, bold eyes, told her that she had him
completely fooled.

'I shall have to see what I can do about that. Shall
we say...midnight?' she suggested, forcing her lips into
what she hoped was a knowing smile.

The hoof-beats were almost upon them.

'Over here!' Hilda's screech jangled along every nerve.
What was the girl doing? She'd wreck the plan...

Hazel eyes stretched wide. Two horsemen were
pounding up the rise to the palisade. It was impossible
to see them clearly in the blurring twilight, but Hilda
was reacting in the most extraordinary way. She was
running *towards* them, cloak flying, the casket pressed
grimly to her chest.

'Hilda, what are you doing?' Beatrice shrieked.

Walter had halted by the gate, confusion stamped on
his guileless face. He had not been told about this...

Beatrice ran a few yards after the young Saxon girl.
Then she stood, rooted to the spot. What *was* Hilda
doing?

One of the riders called out a harsh command to his
companion. 'Siward, take my sister. I have a score of
my own to settle!'

Hoofs pounded. The horseman was running her down.
His face was pale, and hard as marble. Raven-black hair
streamed out behind him like a banner.

Recognition dawning, Beatrice turned to stone. Her
legs would not move, though the chestnut stallion
pounded directly at her. She knew she would be killed.
No war-horse could swerve now. He had left it too late.
She was conscious of a sensation of surprise—she had
not thought he would kill her. She closed her eyes,

crossing herself, and put herself into the hands of the Almighty. The earth shivered—her eyes snapped open.

The horseman drew level, then, quick as a flash, he struck. He leaned forwards, scooped her into the crook of his arm, and heaved her over the saddle with such a jolt that all the breath was forced from her lungs. He headed his mount down the track and spurred on.

Beatrice fought for breath. It was like being crushed alive. Every hoof-beat was another stone on her ribs. But he had not killed her yet.

Edmund straddled no lumbering Norman war-horse. That was why she still lived. The chestnut was a fine-boned creature, delicate and fleet. His senses had not been blunted to enable him to survive the heat of battle. Able to respond to the most subtle of commands, the stallion had swerved, and its rider had snatched her up.

Edmund groaned, and Beatrice tried to move. But he had her pinned in place with a hard hand in the small of her back. A Norman knight with a high saddle and hampering coat of mail could not have plucked her up like that, could not have held her prisoned across his horse's shoulders...

The blood rushed in her ears, but through it Beatrice heard a girl's voice. It sounded very far off, very shrill.

'Nay! Philip, do not! Have mercy! You may hurt her!'

Beatrice strained for the reply.

'That bitch has betrayed us once too often.' Even distance could not soften de Brionne's grating voice. 'Archers. Take aim, and fire at will!'

'Philip, nay!'

Something feathered past her head, dangerously close. Black patches danced across her vision. White ones dazzled. Another arrow whistled past and quivered in the frost-burned grass.

Beatrice saw no more. Several desperate needs took priority. She gulped for air. The roan's coat scratched her cheek. She was slipping. She tried to cling to the horse-blanket, but her fingers were numb. The world whirled and her head slid lower. There was no slackening of that thundering pace. Any moment now, she would fall. And at that speed, she could not survive. It would be a quick death. Suddenly, the hand on her waist shifted, and she was hauled clear of the ground and the pounding hoofs.

Her lungs were bursting and her brain so scrambled with the juddering that she felt no sense of relief.

The horse reared to a halt. Beatrice was unpinned. She slid from her ignominious position and flopped on to the iron-hard ground, dizzy and gasping for breath, like a beached fish. She was bruised all over.

No sooner had she drawn breath than two booted feet moved into her line of vision. Beatrice managed to lift her head. Edmund gazed down at her, his face grim. 'You really are a whore at heart, aren't you?' he sneered. 'You'd dally with any man. If I hadn't seen you with my own eyes, I might have credited you with some scruples.'

Beatrice opened her mouth, but Edmund cut her off.

'We've no time for arguments,' he said sharply. 'We must follow Hilda and Siward. We'll probably be pursued. I only stopped to shift you. 'Tis difficult for Balder to pace himself with you bouncing across him like a sack of wheat. He's no baggage mule.'

Beatrice bridled and shoved her hair out of her face. 'I take it Balder is your horse?' she retorted.

Edmund nodded.

'My thanks for the consideration!' Beatrice said waspishly. 'But I don't find it much of a way to travel myself!'

Edmund nudged her with the toe of one boot. 'Get up, girl.'

'You can't just carry me off,' Beatrice declared.

Edmund's head was tilted to one side, his eyes watching the track along which they had just pounded. He gave a brittle laugh. 'I just did, though the good Lord only knows why. Do you think you might have any value as a hostage?'

Beatrice scrambled up, still panting, and flung off his hand. She looked around wild-eyed. It was almost dark now, the moon lost behind a cloud. The landscape was bleak and unfriendly. An owl hooted. A shadow flitted across the sky. Nothing else moved.

'There's no one to help you here.' Edmund coolly echoed her thoughts. 'Come on, be sensible, Mistress

Beatrice. If you agree not to struggle, I won't bind you, and you can ride quite comfortably before me.'

Edmund caught hold of her wrist and marched her to his mount. 'Mistress.' He clasped his hands for her and heaved her up on to the stallion's saddle-cloth.

The cloth would not hold her as safely as her own saddle, and he'd be using the stirrups. She would be riding all but bareback. She was afraid, but she would die before she admitted it. Beatrice held herself as straight as she dared and glared at Balder's ears. She felt Edmund climb up behind her.

'Comfortable now, Mistress?' he enquired, sarcastically.

Beatrice turned cautiously to look at him. 'Please, Edmund. Do not do this,' she besought him.

Edmund's eyes moved past her to the path. She was wasting her breath.

She tried changing her tack. 'At least tell me where you are taking me.'

Edmund did not deign to reply. He kicked his mount into a canter which had Beatrice lurching from the saddle. She clutched wildly at the flying chestnut mane, and all but fell. At once a strong arm wrapped round her waist.

'You'll have to force yourself to lean back against me if you want to escape collecting a broken limb,' he muttered in her ear.

Beatrice had to agree. She was no tumbler, that she could ride without stirrups. She eased herself to rest against him, unconsciously accommodating her posture to avoid his damaged shoulder. His body was warm against hers. She could feel his breath on her neck. It *did* feel safer leaning back, with his arms about her. She relaxed.

If only circumstances had been different.

She sighed. The sympathetic, gentle Edmund that had attracted her had gone. A cold stranger had taken his place. He would not listen to her, he believed the worst of her. He was a Saxon and her sworn enemy. A lover no longer. He had made it plain that she was his hostage. Beatrice knew that the Norman Baron would pay no ransom for her. Had it been Anne that Edmund had captured, de Brionne might well have paid up. But there would be no ransom paid for Beatrice, not now. De Brionne suspected her of being in league with this Saxon.

Her eyes stung with a rush of tears. Of no value to anyone, she was mistrusted by both sides.

Hoping to find some warmth in his expression, she twisted her head round to peer at Edmund. He was gazing fixedly ahead, a dark frown bringing his brows together. She wondered what he would do to her when he realised her value as a hostage was negligible.

She shivered. She had heard of bloody Saxon rituals that harked back to pagan times. Would they kill her in revenge for Aiden? She held her breath. She had the dagger he had given her. She could feel it bouncing up and down on her hip as they rode. Why had she not thought to defend herself with it? She freed her breath, realising she could never turn the blade against him. And he must know it too...that was the most shameful thing. He was a warrior. He would not dream of leaving an enemy armed. The fact that he had done so could only mean that he knew she could not use it. She was filled with shame. That she should be so transparent...

The steady rhythm of the cantering stallion lulled her fears. All at once, Edmund pulled up and clapped a hand over her mouth.

Indignantly she made to peel it off. Balder stamped and sidled beneath them.

'Quiet!' he hissed, bringing the stallion under control. 'For God's sake, stop struggling! I think we're being followed. Will you be silent?'

Beatrice nodded, and was released. He needed both hands to hold her and the reins.

'I can't hear anything,' Beatrice whispered, too loudly.

Instantly his hand clamped back on her mouth.

'You may want to betray me, Mistress Beatrice, but I plan on seeing another sunrise,' he hissed in her ear. 'If you're not quiet, I'll have to gag you.'

Then Beatrice heard it. The unmistakable sound of a horse on their trail.

'It sounds as though one man rides alone,' Edmund whispered softly. 'If he were one of my men, he would approach. He must know exactly where we are, and he must be Norman.' Edmund transferred his hand to the reins.

Her mouth free, Beatrice kept her tongue firmly between her teeth. The moon reappeared from behind a cloud and lit Edmund's face. He had turned to listen to whatever tailed them, and his features were etched deeply with lines of exhaustion. She would know that profile anywhere; his patrician nose was unmistakable. His hair hung in wild disorder. She wanted to reach up and brush it from his face. She clenched her fingers into Balder's mane and her nails bit through to her palms. She was a fool. How could she still feel for this Saxon, when he admitted he had captured her to ransom her? He would scorn her concern.

Edmund glanced at her. 'They've stopped, whoever they are. I don't think they are planning to jump us. Not yet awhile,' he muttered in an undertone. He gave her a crooked smile, and something inside her melted. He had been aware of her staring at him.

She lowered her eyes before the question in his, and they fell on a dark patch at his shoulder. 'Edmund!' She reached out to touch it.

'Leave me be.' Brusquely, he pushed her hand aside. Balder broke into a trot.

'B-but,' she protested, 'your wound is bleeding again. You need rest and care.'

Her fingers, sticky with blood, made a grab at the coarse mane. They plunged into a rocking canter.

'I'm well aware 'tis bleeding,' Edmund spoke tightly in her ear. ''Tis one of the reasons I'm in haste to reach a safe haven. It hurts like the devil and I've no intention of passing out to leave myself at the mercy of a Norman! I intend to shake off our shadow first. Hold tight. Come on, Balder, my friend, a little speed now!'

The roan surged forwards through the cheerless night, hoofs ringing loudly on the frost-bound earth. Beatrice set her teeth. It took all her will-power to remain seated. Numbed fingers clung with grim desperation.

She was on a nightmare ride through hell. Dark tree-shapes flashed past them, branches and brambles scratched at face and cloak. Her sense of direction had long flown to the winds. The alien landscape became host to unseen dangers. They grew and multiplied on the fear in her mind. Wolves, robbers, outlaws...

Beatrice was alone in the wilds with a remote stranger. She prayed he might protect her. Then her blood ran cold. Edmund's hand had relaxed its hold on the reins. He was swaying uselessly in the saddle behind her. His breathing sounded like a breeze rustling through dry reeds, and he slumped against her back. Balder, no longer under Edmund's control, slowed to a walk.

Experimentally, Beatrice flexed her fingers. She still had some use in them. Loosing her clutch on Balder's mane, she put one arm behind her and steadied her captor. With the other she picked up the reins that hung slackly on the horse's neck.

Edmund's head lolled against her shoulder-blade. The arm that had earlier been used to hold Beatrice in her place now clung to her for support. His other arm crept feebly round her waist.

'Edmund. You cannot pass out,' Beatrice chided. 'Stay awake a little longer. I will find somewhere to shelter, and then...then you may faint if you have to.'

His answer was no more than an incoherent mumble, but Beatrice took heart from the fact that his arms still circled her waist.

'Edmund! Rouse yourself! This place is unknown to me. Edmund! I need your help. Do you know where we might rest? Are we near shelter?'

Another incoherent mumble.

The wind worried at her face. Beatrice grimaced. It seemed she must find shelter without his help. So much for Edmund fighting off the hordes of the Devil for her!

This desolate spot offered no refuge. The shrieking wind alone stripped flesh from bones. Beatrice nudged Balder's flanks with her heels, and the stallion responded at once. She did not trust herself to urge him to anything faster than a brisk walk. She had to keep them both seated.

Balder plodded placidly into the darkness. And, high on his back, Norman maid and Saxon warrior were huddled together.

Without warning, the stallion jerked his head. He began to resist the guiding pressure on the reins. Beatrice wrestled to hold him, but the beast had the bit between his teeth, and she was outmatched. He veered off the track and dived down a slight incline. Edmund's body was a dead weight behind Beatrice and, in fighting to keep him upright, she was forced to allow the horse his head.

At last Balder stopped. They appeared to be at the bottom of a dry ditch, the banks of which were covered in shrubs. A bush loomed large before them. Beatrice poked the animal in the ribs but, stubborn as a mule, the stallion dug in his hoofs.

'Move, you brainless beast!' She kicked with all her might, but the stallion remained immovable. Recognising defeat, Beatrice capitulated. Behind her Edmund was slipping sideways. At least the wind was less biting down here.

She dismounted, and stood at Edmund's side. He was barely conscious. She reached up her arms. 'Edmund. Help me get you down,' she said, in as commanding a voice as she could muster.

Edmund turned his head in her direction as if wondering who was speaking, but by some mercy he obeyed her. He swung himself off Balder and fell into her arms. She staggered under his weight.

'Well done, Balder,' Edmund mumbled, trying to find his feet. 'Small cave . . . hidden behind bush . . .' His eyes closed and his legs folded. He toppled like a tree, and Beatrice was trapped beneath him.

She lay winded, a protective hand at his shoulder. What had he said—a hidden cave? Hope flaring, she eased herself free.

CHAPTER SEVEN

BENT double behind the prickly bush, Beatrice discovered a cold rockface rearing up to heaven. She frowned. It could not be the side of a hill, for the only rise she had seen near Lindsey was the one the Saxons had built on.

There was a narrow passage behind the bush and Beatrice squeezed along it, holly pricking at hands and face. Her groping hands found a wide crack in the stone. The cave entrance? She did not much like the thought of entering it without a light. Although the moon was full, the holly bush blocked off its light. She forced herself through the gap and found herself in a natural fissure, spacious enough to camp in. Her head banged rock, and she dropped to her knees. Thank God, the earth was dry. Crawling back towards the entrance, Beatrice felt a sharp, stinging sensation sweep up through her robe. Ice. There must be a frozen stream on one side of the cavern.

Leaving the fissure, Beatrice ran to where Edmund lay, sprawled out on the ground. He had not moved since she had left him. A surge of tenderness welled up inside her. She bent to roll him over. He might think badly of her, but for the time being he needed her, and that was a start. She put cold-deadened hands under his shoulders, and, grunting with the strain, began to drag Edmund's inert body towards the shelter of the cavern.

Not a muscle twitched. He lay as still as death, but his heartbeat pumped with steady regularity. There was not much she could do for him till daylight.

Balder whinnied from the gully. Beatrice went back outside.

The stallion stood patiently while she unloaded him. She found a couple of blankets strapped on to his back. Balder's flanks were shining in the moonlight, flecks of

135

sweat streaking his coat. She knew the horse would catch a chill if she did not attend to him. Crisply and neatly, in the minimum of time, she rubbed him down and flung one of the blankets over him. That would have to do. She could not spare the horse more time than that.

Back in the cave, her eyes took time to adjust to the almost total blackness. She fumbled at Edmund's pack, trying to guess at the contents. Some bread, dried meat, a leather water bottle, a knife. Putting these items on a ledge, Beatrice felt for tinder and kindling. She searched in vain. Not even a taper. He must carry these things, everyone did, but she had probably dropped them when she unloaded the horse.

Beatrice shivered and sneezed. She could hear the wind whistling over the ridge. Her head began to throb. If only she could light a fire...

She ran her hands over Edmund's cold form. She put the blanket on the ground and shifted his dead weight on to it. That would prevent the ground-chill reaching him.

She sneezed violently. She felt as though someone had put a heavy iron bar over her eyes. She doubted that she would be able to see even if she had light. It is of no use if I die too, she thought. She unclasped her mantle and tucked it over Edmund's thick fur cloak. She lifted the edge of the cloaks and slid beneath them next to Edmund. The cloaks were very heavy. If she wrapped them both up like a cocoon, it would not be too cold a night.

Delicately, she probed his hurt. His tunic was stiff with blood. It would be awkward to cleanse, but it had stopped bleeding. She could leave it till sun-up with a clear conscience.

Beatrice nestled close, and put an arm about his waist. It was the best way to get them both warm. He need never know, she would waken long before him. Her throat tickled and her head felt muzzy. She needed warmth as much as he did. Vaguely Beatrice wondered why she was justifying herself. She yawned. She smiled to herself. It was working. Slowly but surely, they were warming.

She had never slept with a man before. She wondered what Mother Adèle would have said. Of course, it was all perfectly innocent...

Edmund stirred and flung out an arm. It rested neatly round her shoulders, as if he were embracing her. Beatrice went rigid. Was he awake after all? Edmund turned his head, his cheek resting lightly against her hair, and he sighed. He did not move again, and Beatrice relaxed. She snuggled deeper into his unconscious embrace. He smelt reassuringly of horse and man, exciting, yet comforting. She was safe in his arms.

A few moments later Beatrice was fast asleep.

It was dawn already. Securely enfolded in Edmund's arms, and drowsing in the warmth from his body, Beatrice was content to lie awhile. Gradually, full consciousness returned. He would probably never hold her like this again. It was only because he was insensible. Were he fully alert he would not hold her so tenderly. Edmund's warmth was the one comfort left; her head seemed weighted with lead, the air was a thousand needles stabbing at her lungs. Every bone creaked, every muscle ached. With great reluctance, she tried to lift her head from his shoulder.

His eyes were open. They held a wary, questioning look. He made no move to repulse her, but stared straight into her own startled eyes. Beatrice felt her heart turn over, and knew again that strange fluttering sensation low in her belly.

'At last you're awake,' Edmund sighed.

'I ... I'm sorry,' Beatrice stammered, cheeks glowing. 'I thought you were asleep.'

He grimaced. 'My shoulder, I'm afraid. 'Tis no better. It's plagued me since sunrise.'

She sat up. 'You should have woken me. I could not look at it last evening. There was no light. 'Twas all I could do to keep you ... us warm.' She found she could not meet his eyes.

'I thank you. I did not expect to find you with me when I woke,' he admitted.

'You would have been like to die if I had left you where you fell!' Beatrice cried.

'Aye.' His eyes were hooded. 'Why did you not return to your people?'

'You must have heard de Brionne as we left the settlement?' Beatrice asked.

Edmund gave a short laugh. ''Twas all I could do to snatch you up and still stay mounted,' he confessed. 'I had no ears for de Brionne's encouragements.'

'He named me traitor,' Beatrice told him, watching his face. 'He will not ransom me. He mistrusts me. You've taken me for nothing. You'll get no money for me.' Her face clouded. 'There's nowhere for me to go. I'm suspected by both Norman and Saxon now.'

Edmund's eyes did not flicker. He shrugged, and winced. 'Poor Beatrice,' he mocked softly. 'But I can see at least two ways you could turn this to your advantage.'

'I don't see them. Explain,' Beatrice demanded.

He gave a strained smile. 'For the sake of argument, let us assume that I accept that de Brionne would not pay any ransom for you. You could try winning his favour by turning spy for him. Think, Beatrice, you could stay with me till we reach the Saxon camp. Then all you have to do is return in triumph with details of our position and strength to de Brionne. He'd make you a heroine.'

Beatrice dropped her jaw in disbelief.

'That's one route you could take,' Edmund said. 'And as for the other...' He reached out a long finger and pushed under her chin to close her mouth. His face drained of colour. 'No matter,' he grunted. 'See what you can do with this mess on my shoulder, will you? By the Rood, I'm tired!' He shut his eyes.

Beatrice forced her mind on to the work at hand. Edmund endured her ministrations in silence. Only the lines around his mouth betrayed the pain he suffered. He had a grey look to his skin, his jaw was clenched.

'There. 'Tis done,' she said, at last. 'I'm sorry I hurt you.'

'Many would have hurt me more,' Edmund conceded, with a lopsided grin. 'But I prefer your talents as a bedwarmer.'

Beatrice turned her face away. 'You don't trust me, do you?' she asked, in a small voice.

His derisive laugh was a blow to the heart. 'Trust a Norman? Never!' he declared, with devastating honesty. 'Particularly when she's as beautiful as you. Nay, you Normans operate by some code that has little to do with honour and much to do with self-interest. I, trust you?' She heard his derisive snort. 'Don't waste your time working witchery on me. I won't be charmed.'

'I'll go and see to Balder,' Beatrice announced in a choked voice. A tear ran down her cheek. She dashed it away. She would not let that wretch upset her.

The weather matched her mood, she reflected sourly. Everything was grey. Threatening clouds gloomed overhead. And Edmund's chestnut simply was not there. The unyielding, frozen earth had thrown off the imprint of the stallion's hoofs as though he were an insubstantial spirit, an elf-horse. Beatrice wandered disconsolately to the rise and peered along the path. Not a hoof-print in sight. The wind blew right through her. She shivered. It was truly a place of desolation, and Balder had marooned them in it.

She wanted to wash. The rivulet in the cave wound out of the fissure, under the holly bush, and pooled in the bottom of the gully. The ice was thin and easily broken, the water invitingly clear, but gaspingly cold. She cupped her hands, and drank deeply. She was puzzled to find she could not quench her thirst. The water turned to sand in her throat.

Beatrice straightened, and shook out the green robe. She grimaced down at it in disgust. It would never be the same again. Anne might have a gown for every day, but not one of them had been designed to withstand the treatment this one had received.

She brushed past the holly and poked her head cautiously through the crack. Edmund had fallen asleep. Without the lines of pain, he looked terribly young. Scarcely older than she was, and how pale...

'Edmund,' she whispered, and laid her hand on his forehead. He was cool to the touch. With luck he would not take a fever, though he had suffered enough in the past few days to bring down a man as strong as an ox. She considered him. He was tall and strong, but he was no hefty mountain, like Morcar. Edmund was slender. She remembered the feel of his body in her arms the night before, and her eyes strayed to linger on his parted lips. She could see his white teeth, almost feel the touch of his mouth . . . Beatrice pressed cooling hands to fever-hot cheeks. What was she doing?

Her head felt thick and muzzy. She must still be dis-orientated from that ride. Her throat itched. She was tired, and she must be hungry. Aye, that was what ailed her. She would eat. It was well past the hour for breaking her fast, and she could not take time to be sick now. But the honey cakes from Edmund's pouch lodged in her throat. She could not stomach the thought of the dried meat. She sipped at the water bottle, and resolved to try later.

Edmund dozed.

Beatrice decided to untangle her hair. She unbraided the long coppery strands and began to tug Edmund's comb through them.

'Beatrice!' Edmund mumbled, half-dazed with sleep. He struggled up on one elbow.

The comb fell, forgotten. She was at his side, flask in her hand, hair a bright stream flowing over her shoulders. 'How do you feel?' she asked.

'Thirsty,' Edmund croaked.

She handed him the flask.

'My thanks. I needed that.' His eyes were on her hair.

Beatrice flicked it over her back. Those blue eyes made her hot all over.

'A witch,' Edmund muttered, barely audible. 'Beware the enchanting witch.'

Beatrice put up her hand, partly out of embar-rassment and partly because her nose was itching. 'I had to borrow your comb,' she explained. She sneezed.

'Where's your cloak, woman? You'll catch your death,' he said, exasperated.

'I deemed your need greater.' Beatrice gestured at the cloaks covering his long legs.

'You do me no service if you freeze to death,' he said, bluntly. 'Put your mantle on. I don't want a martyr on my hands.'

Beatrice snatched at her mantle, firing up to hide her hurt. 'Nay, that would be very inconvenient, would it not?' she flared. 'No one to change your bandages. No ransom to swell your coffers——'

'I pity the poor fool who consents to marry you,' Edmund declared, in quelling accents.

'I...I beg your pardon?' Beatrice stared. Her hair had shaken forward. Edmund grinned and let his gaze run insolently over it. Beatrice ground her teeth, and held her tongue.

'The poor man won't stand a chance,' Edmund said. 'Fiery hair and fiery temper. His life won't be his own once he marries you. Why even those hazel eyes of yours spit fire.'

'I do not intend to marry,' Beatrice informed him stiffly. She twisted her hair into a repressive knot at the nape of her neck.

'That won't answer.' Edmund smiled. 'I've seen your true colours, remember?'

'I told you, I'm not for marrying.' Beatrice cast him a harassed look.

'What, never? I'm sure some poor fool would take you. Your case is not that desperate,' he teased.

'I intend...I intend entering a convent. 'Tis what my mother intended. I will carry out her wishes. From what I have seen of the world, I have no desire to be part of it. Greed—ambition—violence. Saxon hating Norman, Norman hating Saxon——'

'Do you hate *all* Saxons?' Edmund asked. He sounded mildly curious.

Beatrice looked away.

'I...nay...that is...I haven't met many,' she temporised.

'Come here, Beatrice,' Edmund commanded, a suspicious light in his eyes.

She shot him a wary glance, but otherwise did not move.

'Beatrice!' He reached out his hand. 'I shall come and get you,' he threatened, pushing the fur cloak aside.

'Nay, lie still, or you will never heal properly. Please, Edmund. Nay, don't do that!' she cried.

He lurched at her with reckless disregard for his well-being, pulled her towards him, and imprisoned her with his body. 'Don't struggle,' he groaned. His face was ashen. 'I'm not going to hurt you. Be still, for the love of God.'

His blue eyes robbed her of all will.

Edmund brushed her cheek lightly with his knuckles and smiled. She felt him touch the nape of her neck. He loosed her hair, and ran an auburn tress through his fingers, as though combing it with his hands.

'Like a burnished cloak,' he murmured, and repeated the movement, making her hair ripple out about her.

Beatrice tried to hide her face.

'Nay.' A gentle touch stayed her.

The strange fluttering sensation that his nearness induced became unbearable. Her limbs felt heavy. She felt she should push him away, but did not. When he took her hand in his and brought it to his lips, his darkened eyes held hers. His cheeks were ashen no more. His fingers laced through hers.

Beatrice gave a little sigh. Her eyes closed. She did not twist her head away when she felt his lips brush hers. His free hand lightly cupped her face. Hers fluttered up, touched his cheek, then retreated to rest on his waist. The pressure on her mouth increased, and suddenly she was clinging, keeping his body tight against hers. One slender, green-clad arm had found its way around his neck.

Edmund lifted his head, eyes smiling down at her. Her eyes were wide and dazed, her hair tumbled about her face like molten copper.

'You see...' he said, kissing her lightly on the lips.

'You do not...' He kissed her cheek.

'Respond as one...' He kissed her neck.

'Who professes she is to enter a convent,' he finished, planting another warm kiss at the top of her gown.

Slowly, he unfastened the ties at the neck of her gown, pressing more gentle kisses on her skin. Beatrice gasped. His touch sent shudders through her body, but it did not feel wrong. Should she permit this? She could not move to stop him. His hand moved to her breast.

'Edmund! No!' she moaned, her mind fighting the weakness of her body. She had lost the ability to think.

Edmund's caress loosed another ripple of delight through her body.

''Tis wrong,' Beatrice said feebly, catching at his hand. 'Do not do this.' She was uncomfortably aware that she was trying to convince herself of this as much as him.

'No?' he asked softly. He met her eyes, his blue ones glowing with undisguised longing. He buried his head in her neck.

Beatrice melted. He could do anything to her and she would make no protest. But afterwards? She knew a sudden thrill of fear. What then? She was his hostage, she must not forget that. Too much hate and horror lay between them.

'Edmund!' She beat at him with her fists.

He mumbled and lifted his head, lips meeting hers with such passion that her toes curled.

'Edmund!' She twisted her head and beat at his shoulder. 'Would you rape me, then, and *prove* your race a pack of barbarians? A breed of bastards?'

He jerked backwards with a moan of pain.

Her heart bumped uncomfortably against her ribs. Panic had made her blind. She had struck his injured shoulder. His face was contorted. He had thought the blow deliberate! Too late Beatrice realised the significance he would read into the words she had hurled so carelessly.

Edmund rolled away, grunting with the pain, and lay on his back. He rubbed his face. The glow in his eyes was utterly quenched.

'Oh, Edmund! Edmund! I'm sorry. I did not mean to strike your wound.' Beatrice put out her hand. She felt horridly cold.

'I had no idea you found me so contemptible,' Edmund ground out.

Beatrice withdrew her hand.

'I had forgotten your scorn for my bastardy overrules all else. I had also forgotten your Norman games. Let me tell you that the games you indulge in are more suited to a whorehouse than a convent,' he spat bitterly.

In the heat of his anger her denial withered unspoken. She risked a tortured glance. His eyes were on her, but he looked away at once. She thought that he sighed.

She searched her mind for something to distract him from his rage. 'Edmund, the stallion's gone,' she announced abruptly.

The dark head jerked back at her. He flinched. 'What! Dear God, why didn't you tell me earlier?'

'I intended to, but first you were asleep and then you…I…we…' She fiddled with the cross at her neck.

His eyes followed her gesture, still frowning. He swore. 'Do you not know the value of such an animal? Did you not think to secure him?'

'Nay,' she admitted. 'I'm sorry. I rubbed him down, and put a blanket on him so he wouldn't catch a chill. And, you might remember, I had you to attend to in the freezing darkness. Next time I'll know to put your horse first,' Beatrice said with heavy sarcasm.

He stared. 'I suppose I should be grateful,' he acknowledged reluctantly.

Beatrice shivered and smothered a sneeze.

His voice softened. 'You are far from well yourself, Beatrice. Don't look so apprehensive, I swear I won't force my advances on you again. Balder may not be lost; there's a chance he's finding his own way home. He's not usually easy to catch, and a thief would have a hard time trying to get hold of him.'

'*I* didn't have much trouble,' Beatrice told him, a hint of pride in her voice.

Edmund glowered at the roof of the cavern. 'See what's in my pack, will you? I'm famished.'

Beatrice rose to spread the fare before him. Honey cakes, cheese, dried meat.

'And fasten your dress,' he growled. 'You've already got a chill. I'm in no position to be caring for a sick woman.'

Beatrice obeyed him.

'Soon it will all be cut off,' Edmund said, irrelevantly. 'What a waste.'

'What?'

'Your hair. When you become a bride of Christ,' he said shortly, and bit savagely into a lump of cheese.

The flint found, Beatrice drove herself outside. God knew their need for fire was great and she must gather what she could in the way of kindling. Edmund had forbidden her to light a fire till dusk, and they had not long to wait now. He had insisted that the smoke from a fire might betray them. He had said he had no intention of making a gift of himself to de Brionne. So, no fire till dark.

But now the sky was darkening fast. Night was almost upon them. Beatrice had had her mind fixed on this moment for some hours. It had stopped her from freezing solid. Keeping a cheerless watch over the weakened Saxon, she had dreamed bright dreams in which their shelter glowed with hot tongues of orange and yellow flame.

She sniffed the twilight air. The weather was going to change. She could smell snow. Threatening clouds moved ponderously overhead, but there was something more...

A sudden sharpening of her senses sent her eyes winging wide and nervous round the gully. She had best hurry. Balancing an unwieldy bundle of sticks, Beatrice scurried back to the cavern. A snowflake floated down. It was chased by another. They were in for a heavy snowfall. Beatrice groaned.

Back at the cave she built a hasty fire. She refilled the waterskin from the pool. Then there was nothing left to do but to sit in the entrance of the cave, staring moodily at the fluttering snowflakes as they transformed holly leaves from darkest green to purest white.

'I wondered when you'd be still,' Edmund commented.

'Oh ... I thought you slept,' Beatrice said, giving him a wary glance. 'I ... I thought it best to get everything ready for the night. I didn't want to be unprepared like last night.'

'Quite,' he agreed, in a dry voice.

Beatrice met his eyes, but his expression was unreadable. 'The snow is settling,' she told him.

Silence. It was not yet dark enough to light the fire.

Beatrice broke the silence. 'Do you think you will be able to travel tomorrow?'

'Are you keen to be ransomed, or just eager to escape my presence?' Edmund countered with uncanny accuracy.

'The snow will make our journey more difficult. Especially now we have no horse. And we don't have much food.'

'I wouldn't have thought a little fasting would daunt a novice like you,' Edmund teased.

Beatrice smiled, glad his temper had cooled. 'I haven't actually committed myself to entering the noviciate,' she admitted. 'I'd planned to return to the convent in Caen after Anne's wedding and make my vows then.'

'So you've not actually taken vows?' he asked.

His tone was light, so why the guarded eyes?

'No. I've made no vows. But I have been committed in my heart for many months now.' The words she had believed to be true came out stiff and stilted, like lies. Beatrice squirmed. The idea of cloistering herself as a nun had turned unexpectedly grim. A penitential imprisonment, now that she...

Edmund was watching the snowflakes. Beatrice wondered what it would be like never again to look into those deep blue eyes, never again to touch his dark hair, never again to hear his voice...the blood pulsed faster in her veins simply at the sight of him. Without him it would be a cold and empty existence. She must love him, for, when he was close by, her whole being flowered.

''Tis dark,' Edmund announced, interrupting her thoughtflow.

'I'll light the fire. 'Twill be an improvement on last night,' Beatrice replied, glad for something to occupy her mind.

She fumbled awkwardly with the flint.

'Here, permit me.' Edmund's breath warmed her ear.

'I didn't hear you move,' she said.

'I'm not crippled,' he grinned.

Beatrice felt her heart lurch. She thrust the tinder into his hands and drew back. He was so handsome when he smiled.

''Tis plain to see you're not used to setting fires,' he mocked without rancour. 'Look, Beatrice, start with the smallest twigs and the dried grasses. And when they're ablaze, gradually feed in larger pieces of brushwood.'

Beatrice watched his hands as he worked. They were well-shaped, with long fingers. Fingers that not so long ago had sent ripples of delight coursing through her...

'Do you see?' he asked. 'Do you think you could manage it better next time?'

'Aye, thank you,' Beatrice acknowledged.

'My pleasure. The good sisters probably didn't think to teach you how to light a fire in a cave in midwinter. You'll have to chastise them when next you see them.' He smiled his devastating smile and Beatrice could not but respond. He lifted a hand to touch her, but then checked himself, and let his hand fall back. 'Come. Time to sleep. You have the blanket, I'll be warm enough with my cloak and the fire. I think it would be best if we slept apart tonight.' He looked at her for agreement.

Beatrice nodded, and avoided his eyes. 'You should have the blanket——'

'No more quarrels, Beatrice, I beg of you,' Edmund said crisply. 'I'll sleep here. In the morning we'll see about finding more congenial surroundings. I shall be fit to travel by then.'

Beatrice wound herself in the cloak and blanket, and lay staring up at the rocky roof. Edmund was only a few feet away, his shape just visible in the firelight. He might as well be in Normandy, she thought. He turned over. *He* could fall asleep at any time. She envied him that. She leaned up on her elbow, but could not see him very clearly. The flickering light showed long dark lashes resting on pale cheeks. His hawk-like nose cast a strange shadow over his features.

A distant howl penetrated the cave. Beatrice stiffened. The sound curdled the blood in her veins. She held her breath and strained her ears. The hairs lifted on the back of her neck. Wolves! But they were far off, surely?

It was late January now. January was the month of the wolves, when hunger drove beasts already wild to a frenzy of killing. She remembered a beggar at the convent gate telling her that wolves had eyes which glowed like

lamps. And if you saw them shining at you through the
night the only thing you could do was pray for a quick
ending. The beggar had said more. He had told her that
you might survive if the wolf had not seen you first.
Aye, that was it. You had to see the beast before it saw
you, for if you did not...

The howling was renewed, a second wolf calling to
the first. This one was closer. Beatrice shuddered.

Hungry wolves attacked people. They were creatures
of the dark. The Devil's own. They hunted in packs and
could rip a man apart. Beatrice glanced at Edmund.
Surely he must wake. That dreadful sound was loud
enough, and near enough, to raise the dead. The wolves
were yowling in unison now. At least a dozen of them.
And getting closer.

Beatrice sprang bolt upright, convinced their shelter
was surrounded by circling fiends with lanterns for eyes.
She shot across the stony ground, tripping over blanket
and cloak in her haste to reach Edmund and safety. She
touched his face. 'Edmund!' His eyes sprang open. She
was shaking all over. 'Edmund, listen to that. There are
wolves outside! Can you hear them?'

'I can only hear your teeth chattering,' he replied,
smiling calmly. 'You're cold.'

Vehemently she shook her head. 'Listen. We're dead
meat.'

The unearthly sound filled the cavern. Beatrice gave
a wail of pure terror and clutched at Edmund's arm.

He sighed and enfolded her trembling body in comforting arms. 'They won't come in here, sweeting. Don't
be afraid. They don't like fire.'

'D-d-don't they?'

'They do not. And if they dared approach, you've got
a strong Saxon warrior who'd protect you with his life.
So stop shaking,' he soothed.

His words might have been meant to reassure her, but
they did more. They sparked off a warm, happy glow
somewhere near her heart.

Gently, Edmund stroked her hair. She had removed
her veil for sleep. His fingers encountered the repressive
braids, and a wry grin twitched at the corners of his

mouth. She was not for putting temptation his way tonight.

Beatrice raised her head from his chest.

'I'm sorry to be so silly,' she apologised.

'Don't be. Do you feel better now?'

A wolf howled. He felt her repress a shudder. 'Aye, but...but can I stay close by you?' she begged, her voice no more than a timid thread of sound.

Edmund tensed. 'I don't want you accusing me of rape,' he warned.

'Nay. Of course I won't. I didn't really think...oh, please, Edmund. I feel so much safer near you,' she pleaded.

'Very well,' he agreed stiffly.

'My thanks. I feel safe with you.'

'Safe with me,' he muttered.

'Edmund, are you angry?'

'Angry? Nay,' he denied, gruffly. 'At least we'll be warmer this way.' He shoved her roughly to one side, and rearranged their coverings. When he had done, he stretched out on his back, and fixed his eyes stolidly on the cavern roof.

Beatrice wriggled nearer to his warmth, her hand brushed his wrist. Edmund jerked his arm away. 'You *are* angry,' she accused, sadly.

'By all that's holy, girl!' he burst out. 'You try my patience!'

'What have I done?'

'I'm no Saint, and to lie here, not touching you——'

The blood curdling chorus rang out. Beatrice sobbed. Her fear of the wolves proved stronger than her fear of Edmund's wrath. She hid her head against his side, and clung like ivy.

'They'll tear us to bits! How will we escape?' she cried, on the edge of hysteria.

'Nay. I've told you. They fear fire and we have a good blaze here.' His arms tightened about her.

'What if the fire goes out in the night?' she worried.

'I'll make certain it doesn't.'

He started to prise her clinging hands from his waist. She whimpered, and gripped harder, half expecting to be repulsed. For a second Edmund seemed to hesitate. Then his touch gentled, he angled his body towards her, and long fingers gently intertwined themselves with hers. He drew her up and pillowed her head on his good shoulder. 'Try to sleep,' he murmured. 'I will protect you.'

Beatrice willed her muscles to relax. If only her head did not throb so. She coughed. She wondered why she felt so hot. It was raw out there.

'You're burning up,' Edmund discovered, fingers on her brow.

Beatrice choked back another cough. ''Tis only a chill,' she croaked and pushed back the covers. 'I'm tired. Why is it so hot?' And why was Edmund covering her up again? Hadn't she just told him she was too hot?

'Beatrice!' Edmund sounded angry. She did not like it when he was angry. 'You must keep covered. The night air will get to your lungs.'

'Nay, I'm too hot,' she moaned, tossing off the blanket.

'You've got a fever. Beatrice, be still. You shouldn't have gone out without your cloak.' Firm hands stilled her restless movements.

'I had to go out,' she mumbled. 'I couldn't face the others.'

'The others?' Edmund queried, puzzled. She must be raving, she slurred her words.

'Anne and her lover,' she got out. 'They told me you were to marry Anne, and yet...' Her voice trailed off into indistinct mutterings.

Edmund heard a rustle outside the cavern and glanced, frowning, at the mouth of the cave. Their unwelcome visitors had not gone. Beatrice had not marked the sound, and that was a blessing. Her mutterings became audible once more. 'Then Morcar came,' she enunciated clearly. 'And I went back with him.'

'Morcar?' Edmund's voice sharpened.

'He's a minstrel,' she said, her voice slurred with sleep.

'Aye. I know.'

'I wonder what his songs are like,' she said with a faint sigh. Her eyelids fluttered and closed.

Edmund settled Beatrice comfortably in his arms and resigned himself to a long night.

Beatrice veered between bouts of high fever and bouts of shivering. One moment she burned up, and flung back the covers, and the next she was like ice and nothing would warm her. She coughed constantly.

She was vaguely conscious of Edmund's presence, warming her when cold, holding her tight and rubbing frozen limbs.

'Don't go.' She clung to his hand. He was angry with her, and was telling her to do something. If only she could understand him, she would obey. 'I don't like you when you're angry,' she told him.

'Beatrice, lie still, you exhaust yourself thrashing about. You may be a good healer, but you are a terrible patient,' he remarked drily.

'Don't leave me,' Beatrice repeated, screwing up her eyes.

If only everything would come clear again. The flickering firelight cast monstrous shapes and patterns on the stone walls. Was it night or day? She did not know. Her eyes would not focus. She could not see him. Her heart banged. He'd left her.

'Edmund!' she wailed.

'I'm here.' A soothing hand stroked her cheek. 'I'll not leave you. Only do lie still. You must rest.'

'Cold. 'Tis so cold,' she shivered.

Edmund's calm voice penetrated the haze of sickness. Gradually soothing her. She shuddered in his arms. He was speaking low, and she could not make any sense of the words. His fingers were locked with hers.

She would remind him when she felt well that she did not speak his foreign tongue. But his voice was gentle, and kind, a healing balm. 'Oh, Edmund, why did we have to be enemies?' she sighed.

He stiffened, and the quiet flow of sound ceased abruptly, but he did not unlace his hand from hers. She was asleep. And a tiny smile hovered on her lips.

Beatrice stirred uneasily in the makeshift bed, aware of an indefinable sense of loss. She coughed, and held down

a groan, her throat was as dry as parchment. She was
alone. Her skin crawled. She sat up. The fire burned,
but Edmund was not in the cave.

Frantic, she looked about. The contents of his pack
were strewn on the ground and a wave of relief washed
through her. He must have fed the fire recently, for it
was piled high with more sticks. He had not left her, but
why had he risked the fire in daylight? For her?

She grasped the waterskin. It was difficult to swallow,
and the liquid seemed to have little effect on her raging
thirst. 'If only Sister Agnes were here,' she murmured
to herself. ''Tis so very, very cold.'

Shivering, she rolled back into the blankets. She did
not want to rise. She could stay wrapped up in here all
day and wish for nothing else. Nothing else? She sighed.
It was far too difficult to get up. The need for sleep was
overwhelming; Beatrice closed her eyes.

She missed Edmund's body next to hers, and his strong
arms around her. He had cared for her. Or had she
dreamed it? Beatrice could not be certain, her head felt
stuffed with clouds that blurred all thought. She recalled
his voice, calm and soothing, murmuring strange words
in her ears. Words that she could not understand, but
which gave comfort, none the less. Surely she would not
dream in a language she herself could not speak? It must
have happened. She had had a fever and Edmund had
been kind.

And what of the wolves? Had she perhaps dreamed
them into existence? Edmund had said he'd protect her
with his life. The afterglow of a remembered pleasure
warmed her. She wriggled deep into the blanket, and
consciousness slid away.

Her head was hammering. She shook it to clear her
fogged brain and regretted it at once as pain stabbed at
her temples. Groping for the waterskin, she realised the
noise had not been in her head, but outside the cavern.
She stumbled to the gap.

There was something out there. Something which
grunted and yelped. Every now and then a flash of colour
moved in the whiteness beyond the holly. Something was
fighting out there, and surely it was not wolves, not in

daylight? Beatrice staggered out into the small clearing, and gaped at what she saw.

Edmund was sitting astride a cowled figure in a ring of trampled and muddied snow in the centre of the ditch. The man pinioned in the slush moved his head from side to side, and groaned.

'Speak up, damn you,' Edmund growled, and pressed a dagger to the man's throat. The hooded man twisted and writhed.

Edmund struck him viciously across the face with the back of his hand. 'Speak, churl!' he commanded tightly. 'Who told you to follow us? I recognise a Norman when I see one. You were at the hall. Did de Brionne send you to spy on us?'

Beatrice could not believe her eyes. Was this brutal Saxon and the tender Edmund who had held her so gently the previous night one and the same? She must have been deceived. He was utterly changed. Outwardly his features were the same. Pale, unshaven face, flowing dark hair, that distinctive nose. But the blue eyes which had softened so tenderly now glittered cold as sapphires. That well-shaped mouth curled back in an ugly snarl. Another cracking blow and the cowled head snapped to one side.

Beatrice stumbled closer. The wretch beneath Edmund moaned piteously. The cowl fell back. Wide, frightened eyes turned on Beatrice in dumb appeal.

Recognition whipped through her. She forced her throat to work. 'Walter!' she choked.

'Speak, slave, or I'll slit your gizzard,' Edmund threatened, pressing on the knife. A drop of blood oozed on to the blade, and formed a red necklace about the Norman's throat.

'Edmund! Don't hurt him, please,' she begged, a hand held to her own raw throat.

'You know this man?' Edmund snapped.

'Aye. If you did see him at the hall, you must know he cannot speak,' Beatrice said. 'What do you gain by torturing him?'

Edmund's eyes narrowed sharply. 'How convenient!' he sneered. 'A spy who cannot speak to his captor! Very useful! Can he write, perhaps?'

Beatrice shook her head.

'Then how, pray, will he relay his findings back to the Baron?' Edmund demanded.

'You know he cannot talk, Edmund. You blood-thirsty barbarian, you're torturing him in revenge for Aiden!' Beatrice accused hotly.

Edmund's nostrils flared. He removed the blade from Walter's throat and turned a white fiend's face on her. He ran a finger along the length of his dagger and smiled coldly. 'Very well, Mistress Beatrice. If he will not speak, perhaps you will in his stead. *You* will tell me why this man has been following us.'

He reached out and caught her by the shoulders.

Out of the corner of her eye, Beatrice saw Walter stand up. Edmund noticed her veiled glance and turned, twisting Beatrice in front of him. His dagger pricked her neck.

Walter held a stout branch poised to strike, but the threat to his mistress disarmed him and he sagged. The cudgel was flung aside. Walter could not incapacitate the Saxon without risk to Beatrice.

Walter was confused. He waited for the Saxon to make the next move. When this Saxon warrior had abducted his mistress, Walter had followed on Betony, determined to see no harm should come to her. Having a head start, he had easily outrun the Baron's men. He had followed Beatrice and Edmund to this cavern, but had been too wary to make his presence known.

Walter knew that Mistress Beatrice had cared for the Saxon in the chapel. He had felt certain no harm would come to her from him. He had seen Beatrice gathering firewood, alone and apparently of her own volition. And during the night he had crept up and had observed the tender way the warrior cradled Beatrice in his arms. He had been reassured.

But now he was not reassured. The Saxon was threatening Mistress Beatrice. He glowered at the warrior.

'So, Beatrice,' Edmund grated in her ear. 'You would conspire to kill me!'

'Nay!' she croaked. 'Walter only seeks to protect me. He's my man! 'Tis no wonder you're a defeated people. You're all wanting in wits!'

Edmund's fist clenched white on the dagger. 'Explain this man's presence here,' he said flatly. 'And you——' he directed his cold, stranger's gaze at Walter '—keep very still, or I shall harm her.'

'Walter came with me from Normandy,' Beatrice informed him. 'Mother Adèle sent him. He's a . . . a sort of manservant. And, Edmund, he cannot speak. Truly he cannot. I'm sure he followed us for my sake, and not at de Brionne's command. Is that not so, Walter?'

Walter assented eagerly.

'He has no reason to like the Baron,' Beatrice added.

'Who has?' Edmund responded.

'De Brionne threatened to cut off Walter's hand. And do you know why?' She put her fingers to the hand at the dagger.

'Nay, but I'm sure you're about to enlighten me.'

'Walter found Hilda hiding out in one of the barns. She was famished. He stole food for her and the Baron found out. Oh, not about her, not at first. Just about the missing food. He accused Walter of stealing, and said he had not enough provisions for the warriors, let alone half-wits.'

'Compassionate as ever,' Edmund murmured.

Beatrice gently pulled at Edmund's wrist. He allowed her her freedom and stood facing her, long legs apart, dagger loose at his side.

'De Brionne accused Walter of selling the food. He was to lose his hand as punishment. 'Twas only later that I found out about your sister. Walter did not betray her. He had a chance to inform the Baron, but he did not do so. Walter has played no part in the conflict between your people and mine. He's nought but a kind man who seeks to repay me for some help I once gave him. His only concern is for my safety.'

Walter smiled.

Edmund searched her face, and jabbed his dagger in its sheath. He swore. 'I must be moon-touched, but I believe you.' He jerked his head at Walter. 'The fellow's clearly besotted,' he said, in Latin. 'I'll play along with you for the time being. Though why I should saddle myself with a silver-tongued maid and a simpleton is beyond me.'

'Walter is not simple! 'Tis just that he cannot speak. There's a difference!' Beatrice defended her man.

'Aye. So you say,' Edmund said carelessly, easing his shoulder. His blue eyes sharpened. 'God's Blood! 'Tis true that I am wanting in wits! Walter could not have followed us on foot...'

Walter looked doubtfully at Beatrice.

Beatrice smiled. 'Take him to Betony, Walter. I don't want either of you to end up hurting each other. We'd better do as Edmund wishes.'

Feeling as though she had been through a mill, Beatrice watched the two men leave the clearing and turned wearily back to the cavern. They would be on their way again shortly. But to where? And what did Edmund intend for her when they got to their destination? Assailed by a hacking cough, Beatrice gritted her teeth. Only God knew the answers to her questions. She prayed He'd let her live to find them out, for at the moment she felt like death.

CHAPTER EIGHT

SHE was installed in solitary state on Betony, while the two men walked on either side. Walter placed himself solicitously at her knee, his brown eyes wide with concern, his hand hovering ready and eager to assist. Not so Edmund. He surged ahead, towing Betony relentlessly in his wake. The Saxon held himself stiffly, and did not glance at her once. None the less, it was on the dark, flowing mane of Edmund's hair that Beatrice fixed her blurring eyes. That black standard fluttered in and out of her vision, along with the rest of the world.

She braced herself to maintain her seat. Her body was a throbbing mass of cramped muscles and tortured limbs. This punishing journey to the rebel encampment was like a bad dream. Beatrice was beginning to feel she had never known anything but pain. All was agony.

The wind lifted the dark pennant of Edmund's hair. It swirled over his cloak, and filled her vision. It eclipsed all else ... There was no light left. She swayed dizzily in her seat.

Walter's semi-articulate cry of alarm brought the raven head snapping round. 'What now?' Edmund demanded.

Beatrice moved her lips, but only a moan came out. She could hardly see. Everything looked hazy. Her throat ached, her head throbbed more with every step they took. She could hear from the tone of his voice that Edmund was angry.

She felt something touch her hand, but could not have said what it was, save that it was warm.

'Hold hard, Beatrice,' Edmund said, his voice gentling.

There was a movement behind her, a creaking of leather, and a sudden rush of warmth. A fur-lined cloak was draped round her failing body and she was pulled back against a lean male form.

157

'My thanks,' Beatrice muttered, gratefully.

'I hope we're not too heavy for your mare,' Edmund's voice passed over her head. 'We won't be going fast, so I think she won't be lamed.' He lapsed into silence. Betony's steady hoof-beats were muffled by the snow that shrouded the earth.

Beatrice lost all sense of time. It felt as though she had been travelling for an eternity within Edmund's encircling arms. They could have been riding thus for days or weeks for aught she knew. She lost all sense of space. Snow-bleached, trackless wastes dazzled her eyes. She was aware of Betony, of Edmund holding her so she would not fall, of feeling sick, but of little else. The snow wavered in her vision like a heaving white ocean. But she was not Anne. She did not suffer seasickness. The white, crested waves were blinding. They hurt her eyes. Great drifts reared gleaming at her. Wall upon wall of snow whipped up by a slashing north wind. Perhaps, after all, she was like Anne. She closed her eyes on the cruel brightness which froze bodies and burned eyes, and trusted Edmund to hold her safe.

Someone was shouting. Beatrice lifted stiff eyelids and shifted in Edmund's hold. The booming voice was male and loud, but she could not for the life of her make any sense of what the man was saying. A knife stabbed in her brain. The pain was a shutter blocking her sight. She pushed it aside and gazed beyond it. She was living a dream. Nothing was real.

The incomprehensible sounds issued from the mouth of a young man of about Edmund's age. His fair hair, like Edmund's, was worn in the long Saxon fashion, but this man was already thinning at the crown—his middle years would see him bald.

Edmund's compatriot was clearly overjoyed to see him. His rosy face was all but cleft in two with a wide, broad smile of welcome. Beatrice registered Edmund's dismounting as a horrid chill on her back, and a feeling that she was estranged and alone. Walter moved at once to stand at a stirrup, but her feeling of isolation did not diminish. Half-blind with exhaustion, Beatrice watched Edmund embrace the possessor of that booming bittern's voice. The man was familiar, but Beatrice could not summon up the energy to remember when she'd last seen him.

Edmund had brought them to a clearing in a flat, marshy area, hacked out of a spindly spinney. The space housed several wooden buildings, hastily cobbled together and mended with worm-ravaged, badly hewn timbers that any carpenter worth his salt would have sold for firewood years ago. Osiers tall and straight as lances pierced the carpet of snow on the skirts of the clearing. Rooks floated overhead like flakes of soot rising from a fire.

The crumbling shacks bore all the signs of dwellings long deserted. It could have been a village for ghosts. But the ill-hewn timber gleamed pale in parts with the mark of the adze. Some had been recently patched. Some were roofless, the thatch rotted through to the roof timbers. Some were being repaired, for Beatrice's failing eyes dropped to a bundle of reeds, cut to size and waiting to be pegged in place. Here was some shelter from the elements.

Edmund had forgotten the two Normans. A group of Saxon men, bristling like hedgehogs with weaponry, emerged silent as wraiths and clustered about him. But this was no dream. The warriors were as solid as the horse beneath her and their silence was of short duration. They clouted Edmund on the back in rough salutation, and directed a hail of questions at him.

From his gestures he appeared to be describing her capture and their subsequent escape. Beatrice picked out her name from Edmund's speech. One man guffawed, and made a crude comment that needed no interpreter and won an appreciative roar of laughter which scattered the rooks from the trees. Cold Saxon eyes impaled her, and she knew they saw her dead already. Fear gnawed at her belly.

Edmund flushed. He mouthed a soft retort, and a sinister hush fell over his audience. Beatrice sat as straight as her aching limbs would allow. This must be the heart of the Saxon resistance. Was Edmund their leader, then, that they should defer to him?

The crashing of a door pointed all heads towards the most solid of the wooden buildings. The tension eased. Beatrice saw two girls coming eagerly towards them. She recognised Hilda's childish form instantly, rushing ahead. The other girl was older. She took her time. She walked with her flaxen head held high and her hips swinging. This Saxon beauty had been the one who had monopolised Edmund at Anne's betrothal feast.

Hilda flung herself joyfully into her brother's arms, talking nineteen to the dozen. She even had a shy smile for Beatrice. And the other girl...? Beatrice drew her head back with a snap, for her eyes encountered a vindictive glare which made the warriors' baleful stares seem benign. Turning her back on Beatrice with studied discourtesy, the girl greeted Edmund. She held herself aloof, and her greeting had none of the childish exuberance exhibited by Hilda. Reading the silent message, Beatrice clenched her jaw. The Saxon girl wanted Beatrice to know that Edmund was hers. The blonde laid her hand on Edmund's arm and kissed him chastely on the cheek, but there was something subtly possessive about the way she did it. Her pale blue eyes swung back to Beatrice, and Beatrice felt suddenly strangled.

Edmund was smiling at the girl. He was pleased to see her...

Finally he remembered Beatrice.

'Can you not dismount?' His voice mocked her weakness. 'Come, my tired Norman, Ingirith will show you where you can rest.'

He waved the possessive girl towards Beatrice and her heart sank. He reached up to help Beatrice down and she was poignantly reminded of the first time she had seen him. Thus he had held up his arms to her, and thus... Beatrice tumbled into his arms, more exhausted this time than she had been on that first fateful day. There were other differences too: this time there was Ingirith beside them, hissing on an indrawn breath and muttering maledictions. Edmund steadied Beatrice. She leant her head briefly on his chest. Then he was pulling away from her and she found herself trailing stiffly across the clearing after Ingirith.

Flinging open the door of a dwelling, Ingirith pushed Beatrice inside.

Beatrice straightened her shoulders and did her best to meet the Saxon woman's murderous gaze with some semblance of dignity. She was cold, she was tired and she was hungry. She had not strength even for tears. She looked about her. There was nowhere to rest. Everything in the hut was covered with a dusting of snow, there was not even a bench to sit upon. She lifted her eyes and she could see the sky through rotten, blackened timbers.

Was this Edmund's idea of Saxon hospitality? Even Baron de Brionne had accorded Edmund the privilege of remaining in the shelter of the chapel. Did he truly mean her to catch her death? If she ever slept here she knew she would not waken in this world.

Ingirith smiled. Complacent as a cat toying with a mouse before the kill. She fingered a silver bangle at her wrist, looked pointedly at her own immaculate gown and then at the damp, bedraggled rags Beatrice clutched about her slight form.

Beatrice smiled experimentally at her Saxon hostess. Perhaps she was imagining the hostility. Perhaps Ingirith would respond to friendship—Hilda was Saxon, and Hilda had had a smile for her after all . . .

'If you could find me another cloak, I would be grateful,' Beatrice ventured.

Ingirith lowered her brows. She spat in the snow at Beatrice's feet.

Ingirith was not to be won over. Defeated, Beatrice shut her eyes. A cough rose up to choke her and she turned aside till it was done. The spasm left her throat raw, and her eyes full of tears. She had to blink before she realised that Ingirith had gone.

Beatrice sagged against the warped, half-rotten door and rattled the latch. It would not lift. It had been wedged from the outside, and short of climbing the walls to go through the worm-eaten roof timbers, Beatrice was a prisoner.

*   *   *

'In here! Sweet Jesu, who put you in here? Did Ingirith do this?' The owner of the clipped and furious voice was pulling at her shoulder.

Beatrice moaned. She wanted to sleep, to sleep. That way the cold wouldn't hurt so. Oblivion could claim her and the numbing frost would leave her bones forever.

She was lifted against a warm chest, carried. Every step jarred her bruised brain against her skull. She thought her head would burst. She moved it feebly from side to side and tried to open her eyes.

She became aware of a musky male scent that was pleasantly familiar. The arms about her were strong, safe arms. They would not hurt her. Beatrice let out her breath and let her pounding head rest against that warm chest. Under her breath she murmured a name.

She was deposited on something soft. 'Beatrice, wake up!' She knew that commanding voice now—Edmund's. He was shaking her so mercilessly her teeth rattled. 'Later you'll have time to sleep, but not yet.' His tone changed. 'Hilda, fetch Aelflaeda. Mistress Beatrice needs a hot tisane at the least. Hurry!' He was unfastening her girdle and peeling off her clothes. They had grown heavy with damp and stuck to her skin.

'Sleep, must sleep,' Beatrice groaned.

'Soon,' Edmund sounded soothing now. Was it really Edmund? She hoisted leaden eyelids. It was Edmund. He was stripping her. Her hands fluttered in feeble self-defence.

Edmund touched her face softly with the back of his fingers in a gesture of reassurance. 'Be still, I would have you dry and in warm clothes.'

She was naked. He flung a cloth over her and rubbed her briskly. There was nothing of the lover in his manner; indeed, he reminded her of Sister Agnes with a recalcitrant patient. Beatrice submitted to his ministrations. A prickling in her veins told her she was thawing out, and sensation crept slowly back into her blood-starved limbs.

She was able to take stock of her surroundings. She was lying on a truckle bed in a small chamber, amid a pile of furs. A fire crackled and spat. She'd been re-clothed in an amber-coloured gown. It looked new. The cloth was woollen, finely woven and soft. Edmund's fur-lined cloak warmed her feet.

He was striding to the door.

'Thank you,' she whispered, and flinched. Her lips were split and sore.

Edmund checked mid-stride, small lines creasing his brow. 'I'll send our healer to see you. Hilda must have been sidetracked.' The door clicked shut.

Beatrice was not alone for long. She had barely time to appreciate the warmth of the small chamber when Ingirith burst in. The Saxon's face glowed with angry colour. She loosed a torrent of words at the bewildered Norman on the bed.

Beatrice gazed at her blankly. ''Tis no good. I cannot understand you,' she admitted.

Ingirith's blue eyes narrowed. She pounced on the discarded green robe, and extracted the jewelled dagger. She waved it in the air.

Another flood of English invective filled her ears. Ingirith repeated one word over and over.

Beatrice frowned.

Ingirith jerked the blade free of its sheath, and waved it at Beatrice, every look a threat.

'He gave it to me,' Beatrice said. She tried to smile. 'Be careful, you could hurt...' She read murder in Ingirith's eyes and recoiled. Ingirith's fist clenched tighter on the jewelled shaft.

Struggling to move out of range, Beatrice tangled in the covers. She sprawled heavily over the side of the bed, and knocked the breath from her body. Her hands flew to fend off the blow, and she braced herself.

Nothing happened. Surprised, she looked up.

Edmund had returned. He had hold of Ingirith's wrist. The dagger clattered hollowly on the boards.

Ingirith pouted, smiled at Edmund and muttered something in a low, husky voice. Beatrice winced, stabbed with jealousy if not cold steel. The wretched girl could even sulk beautifully.

There was a movement at the door. Hilda stood there, open-mouthed, an old crone of a woman at her side. The crone watched the scene before her with avid, bright eyes. Ingirith stormed past them and the old woman loosed a delighted cackle.

'Beatrice, keep this close to hand,' Edmund recommended, handing back her dagger and resettling her under the furs.

Beatrice curled her fingers round the jewelled hilt. If only he would smile like that more often... 'What did she say? I can't speak your tongue,' she reminded him.

Hilda piped up. 'Most of it wasn't worth hearing. She seemed to think you had stolen my brother's knife and she was accusing you of theft. Edmund told her it was his gift to you.'

Edmund rubbed his injured shoulder and grimaced. Instantly Beatrice sat up. 'Your hurt needs attention,' she said.

'Nay! You need care more than I.' He indicated the old woman. 'This is Aelflaeda. She is wise in the art of healing. If you could but speak the same language, I think you would find much to talk about.' He flicked her cheek, and smiled. 'I'll leave you in her tender care. There are matters which demand my attention.'

Beatrice let her eyes follow him out of the chamber. Aelflaeda cackled softly, and Beatrice felt her colour rise. She pretended to examine her nails. Aelflaeda's berry-bright eyes saw all too much...

A withered hand touched Beatrice's head. Aelflaeda began her examination. She peered into Beatrice's eyes, opened her mouth, felt her throat, under her arms. And all the time the old woman muttered. She placed a pot of water on the fire and flung dried herbs therein, and still she mumbled, like a nun mouthing prayers.

'What does she say?' Beatrice asked Hilda.

Hilda sat down on the edge of the bed. 'Some healing charms to make the coughing sickness leave you,' she explained.

'Oh. I thought 'twas a prayer.'

Hilda gave a strange smile. 'Not our Aelflaeda. She's no Christian. She clings to the old ways.'

Beatrice stared incredulously at Aelflaeda's back as she hunched over her brew. 'You mean she's a pagan?' she exclaimed. 'I thought the Saxons were all Christian.'

'Most are. I am, and so is my brother. But no one is sure about Aelflaeda.' Hilda shrugged. 'Her charms cannot do much harm; she's been healing our people for years. No one would dream of telling her to stop her chanting. She believes 'tis a part of the cure. She's a good woman. *She* is not baying for your blood like most of our people.'

Beatrice looked sharply at Hilda.

Hilda nodded. 'Aye. 'Tis vengeance they're after. Ingirith is not the only one who objects to your presence here. You must tread carefully.'

'Oh, God,' Beatrice groaned.

Hilda put her hand on her shoulder. 'Don't worry. I will stand by you. I am doubly in your debt.'

'Doubly?'

'Aye, you helped me escape, and you cared for Edmund,' Hilda said. 'When his horse came back without him, I feared the worst. I thought him dead. Without you, he would have been.'

'That day you escaped, Hilda, I had no idea that Edmund and his friend...' Beatrice paused.

'Siward,' Hilda supplied.

'I had no idea that Edmund and Siward were planning an attack.'

Hilda grinned. 'They weren't. They were assessing de Brionne's strength. Siward told me they could not believe their luck when they saw us standing by the gate. They took a chance and made a run for us. If it hadn't been for your help, I wouldn't have been in the right place at the right time. And one of them might have been killed trying to free me. That is a great debt I owe you, Beatrice. *And* you gave me the casket. You can definitely count on me as your other supporter.'

'*Other* supporter?' Beatrice queried.

'Edmund, of course. They want him as their leader. He's speaking for you now. 'Tis not easy for him, for he's not used to being unpopular. But, if his ambitions are to be realised, he'll have to learn he cannot please everyone.'

'He wants me as a hostage,' Beatrice confessed miserably.

'A hostage?' Hilda looked thoughtful, but did not disagree.

Aelflaeda bustled up with a mug of steaming liquid. She was still muttering. Her bright eyes roved over every inch of her patient. The old woman smiled. Her teeth were black and broken. Delving into the grimy recesses of her gown, Aelflaeda brought out a small glass pot, stoppered with a cork. She thrust it into Beatrice's hands and gabbled at her.

''Tis a salve,' Hilda translated. ''Twill aid your breathing. Rub it on your chest, or on a piece of cloth and hold it to your face.'

Beatrice sniffed warily at the contents of the pot. Her expression cleared. 'I know this!' she cried. 'We make this at the infirmary. It works well. Please thank her for me, Hilda.'

Aelflaeda smiled her gappy smile and hobbled from the chamber.

Edmund was standing over the bed, watching her. Beatrice yawned, winced, and probed her sore lips. A dark scowl marred Edmund's features, but when she glanced up his face lightened. Beatrice felt her stomach flutter.

'Oh! I'm sorry, was I asleep?' she apologised.

His eyes were warm. 'I asked Aelflaeda to put a soporific in the tisane,' he admitted. 'She always maintains that sleep is the greatest healer, and I'm inclined to agree with her.'

He had changed his clothes. His hair was damp from washing. A handsome stranger with a beautiful smile.

Suddenly unable to meet his eyes, Beatrice fussed with the furs and blankets on the pallet. The leather thongs of the pallet creaked and Edmund was perched in the space lately vacated by Hilda. 'You look much better,' he said, his eyes wandering slowly over her face. Frowning faintly, he placed a long finger on her cracked lips.

She knew her colour was rising. 'I feel better,' Beatrice whispered, and began twisting one of her plaits round and round in her hand.

Edmund sighed and removed his finger. He stared into the fire, pale and very still.

'What is it?' she asked. She wished she dared touch him.

He faced her. 'What am I to do with you?'

Beatrice took a frost-bitten lip between her teeth, and shook her head.

'I've been elected in my brother's stead. My men are crying for blood-money——'

'What's blood-money?' Beatrice broke in, her heart heavy as lead.

Edmund was shaking his head. 'According to Saxon law every man has a value. We call it his *wergild*. A Thegn's *wergild* is higher than a warrior's. A warrior's is higher than a peasant's. And when a man is killed it is the duty of his kindred to extract the man's *wergild* from his killer.'

'And . . . and if they do not?'

'Failure to extract *wergild* means a grievous loss of honour to the kinsmen. It is unthinkable to a Saxon that the *wergild* should not be paid.'

'It . . . it sounds like another name for revenge,' Beatrice stammered. She felt sick. Aiden had been killed. Aiden was their Thegn. What *wergild* would be demanded for his death?

'Saxons call it compensation. And my men are demanding immediate settlement for Aiden's death.'

Hilda had warned her. 'They mean me, in revenge for Aiden!' She clutched Edmund's arm.

Edmund got clumsily to his feet.

'I'll not let them,' he muttered, avoiding her eyes. 'But 'twill not be easy. 'Tis an old idea that has had its day. The coming of you Normans will change many Saxon traditions.' He swung back to Beatrice, and his voice hardened. 'You must help me if you wish to live. You must do exactly as I ask.'

Beatrice nodded.

'Wear your dagger at all times,' he advised. 'Trust no one here, except Hilda and Aelflaeda. Do not leave the encampment. Is that clear?'

'Aye, perfectly. Am I to be kept prisoner here indefinitely?' she asked.

Edmund looked startled. 'You're no prisoner. 'Tis for your own safety that I confine you here,' he corrected her.

'And then you would ransom me? Sell me back to de Brionne? What is to become of me later? I am a traitor to my own people because of you. Your people revile me because of my Norman blood. They want me dead. And you, you would sell me back to the Baron for a few paltry coins to fill your coffers!' Her voice rose. 'Do you know how de Brionne deals with traitors? I do. I know. I've seen it and I——'

Edmund towered over her, and grabbed her shoulders. 'Stop this, Beatrice! You're hysterical!'

Beatrice laughed shrilly, all reason fled. 'I have a right to be. Who wouldn't be hysterical in my position? If I want to be hysterical you're not going to stop me. The whole——'

Her tirade was smothered by his lips. He kissed her hard and ruthlessly, dropping his tall body on to the bed. He kissed her with a new, fierce passion that she'd not yet seen in him. She could not fight it, and lay limp in his arms until he had done. When he raised his head she could taste blood on her lips.

His eyes were dark, his breathing uneven, as though he'd been running. 'That stopped you,' he grinned.

'I like it better when you're gentle,' Beatrice admitted, fingering her bruised mouth. And as soon as she'd uttered those foolish words she regretted it. It sounded like an invitation.

Edmund ran his finger down her cheek and smiled that rare and beautiful smile which melted her insides.

'I know you do,' he said softly. 'Those hazel eyes tell me more than you know yourself. Come, I'll salute you gently now. I was only brutal to stop your hysterics.'

This overt statement of intent unnerved her, and when he bent his head again his mouth met only the side of her face. Undaunted, he nibbled her earlobe, and a shiver of delight coursed down her body. His lips were warm on her neck, they nuzzled her throat, her cheeks. He must be able to feel her trembling...

She reached for his face, and an arm slid unbidden round his neck. Their lips joined.

It was a long kiss. Beatrice had not known a kiss could rob one of all will. She wanted it to last forever. She was not sure whether she should have responded so freely, but she could no more have checked herself than fly. Her trembling fingers explored his lean cheek, traced the contours of his face. She liked the feel of his hair, his long, raven-black hair. It smelled of rosemary from its washing. She ran her fingers through it, and Edmund's arms tightened on her.

A guilty voice at the back of her mind kept telling her it was wrong to feel like this. The voice reminded her that Edmund had already likened her to a whore. She was only giving him more fuel for insults. But she did not heed that nagging voice. She slid her hands down Edmund's broad shoulders and linked them firmly at the base of his spine. She was holding him as tightly as he held her.

Silver armbands jangled and Edmund's hand slid to cup a rounded breast. Beatrice gasped. She ached with wanting. His other hand kept her tight against him, and she realised with a *frisson* of fear that she wanted to explore his body, too. Suddenly out of her depth, she pushed at his chest.

'What's the matter?' he asked huskily.

'I ... I can't. We ... we mustn't,' Beatrice gasped.

They were lying close on the narrow bed. Edmund smiled and nibbled her ear. 'Why not? 'Tis good to kiss with you. You like it. Admit it,' he teased, and watched colour flow into her cheeks.

'Aye. I do, but 'tis wrong,' she insisted.

'Wrong? What on earth can be wrong about our kissing like this? No one is being forced. We both gain pleasure ... ah. I remember. Your mother's plans for the convent. You must accept that your destiny does not lie in a nunnery, Beatrice.'

He bent his head to her neck, and sent fresh ripples of pleasure shivering through her body. Beatrice had to tense herself to prevent her lips seeking his. She could drown in those deep blue eyes ...

'You make a wanton of me,' Beatrice said. 'Only common women enjoy——'

'What?' He drew back, startled.

'My mother told me. 'Tis not ladylike to find pleasure in...carnal matters. Only men and harlots...' Beatrice halted, too embarrassed to continue.

Edmund sighed and leaned up on one elbow. His hand found hers and he wrapped his fingers round it. 'Explain it to me,' he prompted.

'There's nothing to explain. Common women may marry where they choose. But not women in my class. If marriage is to be our portion we must marry according to the dictates of duty. We have to honour only our husbands. We cannot take lovers. I was destined for the convent. I should not be kissing you. In any case, my mother assured me carnal love was revolting. She said she couldn't imagine any well-bred lady enjoying...love.'

Edmund stared incredulously at her, a hint of amusement in his eyes. 'And you believe this? Aye, I see from your face you do.' He pushed himself up to a sitting position and tossed his disordered hair back from his face.

Beatrice never knew what he would have said next, for the door of the chamber crashed open and what looked like the entire Saxon resistance crowded in. Slowly, Edmund climbed to his feet. His back was very straight, his head high.

In a voice Beatrice had never heard, he barked a question at his troop. The exchange that then took place was vehement and, to Beatrice, incomprehensible. Once or twice Edmund spoke her name. Each time a dark and thickly bearded hulk of a man spat on the ground. Ingirith had matched that gesture.

Beatrice felt her heart skip a beat. They were baying for her blood. Most were driven by fury, and they had their swords out. A few appeared more temperate—they merely fingered their weapons and eyed their fellows as though waiting for a lead. None would meet her gaze.

Siward, the man who had snatched Hilda from Lindsey, and greeted Edmund so gladly, pushed past them. Siward too held his sword at the ready, but he met her eyes with open curiosity. She held her breath. It seemed that one of them at least was not measuring her for a winding sheet. Indeed, Siward's eyes, blue like

Edmund's, softened. He smiled. Perhaps Hilda had been speaking to him on her behalf.

Beatrice swung shaky feet to the floor, and stood up. She would not die without a struggle. Her nose lifted. Her head swam. The bearded hulk was bawling at Edmund, veins standing thick and dark on his neck. Would Edmund fight his own men for her? Surely not. He was their commander. He could not afford division within his ranks. Loyalty was all. The Saxon cause came first.

The apoplectic warrior shoved past Edmund, and seized Beatrice by the arm. The point of his sword pricked her breast.

Edmund did not move. He spoke. Quietly and succinctly, but what he said transfixed the company. Someone gasped.

Beatrice felt her legs go weak at the knees, and had to put all her concentration into staying upright. She must not fall. She must not disgrace her race.

The Saxon's cavernous mouth gaped open. He had thick lips which hung slack with amazement. Beatrice staggered. Edmund's arm went round her waist.

Puzzled, she searched his face. What had he said? She could not read his face, but whatever he had said had disarmed his compatriots. They looked stunned, dumbfounded.

Again, Siward was the exception. He inclined his head at Beatrice. Edmund dropped a soft question into the gruesome hush.

Purple in the face, the aggressive Saxon champed slack jaws together, sheathed his weapon and stomped out. The other invaders of the small chamber followed his lead and the room emptied. Siward only remained. Only when the last of the troop had gone did Edmund's ally put away his sword and breathe a long sigh.

'My thanks, friend, for your support,' Edmund smiled, speaking in Latin so Beatrice understood.

'I'm glad I was not needed. I confess I would be loath to fight with our own men,' Siward answered. His Latin was heavily accented, less fluent than Edmund's.

'My congratulations, my lady,' he said, and quitted the chamber.

Beatrice caught Edmund's guilty glance. 'What was all that about? And what did he mean by congratulating me?' she demanded.

Edmund led her to the bed. He had lost his deathly pallor and was quite flushed. 'They came for their revenge,' he said, evasively. 'Sit down, Beatrice.'

She remained on her feet. 'What was it you said that prevented them from carrying out their desires?' A ghastly suspicion took root at the back of her mind.

Edmund flashed her a grin. 'I told them there was no point in killing you in revenge for our Thegn, Aiden, because your value was less than Aiden's. I told them that if they wanted proper compensation for their murdered lord, a lady with no estate and no real title was a poor substitute.'

'Thank you very much.' Beatrice glared at him. 'A poor substitute indeed! I thank you!' Edmund's eyes gleamed. 'I do not think it amusing, Edmund,' she finished crossly.

'Neither did they, my sweet. They still would have had their vengeance. I was forced to...' His colour deepened.

'Aye?' Beatrice prompted. 'You were forced to...what, Edmund?'

'I would not have wished it this way,' Edmund rubbed his hand round the back of his neck.

'For pity's sake—tell me.' Her hand flew part way towards him, but he made no move to take it. She let it fall.

Edmund muttered inaudibly at his boots.

'I beg your pardon?'

A muscle moved in his cheek. 'Hell and damnation!' he swore. 'I told them I was to marry you.'

Beatrice caught her breath, stunned into silence

Edmund looked at her uneasily. 'I'm sorry the idea is so abhorrent,' he said quickly. 'But it must be better to be alive and married, even to me, than spitted on a Saxon sword.'

He seemed to be appealing to her. But Beatrice did not trust herself to speak. If only she could believe what she saw in his eyes...

Edmund shrugged carelessly. 'I'm accounted no bad match. I've inherited lands of my own from my father.

And given Hilda's youth and inclinations, my claim to be Thegn of Lindsey stands a good chance of gaining support. I might even persuade your King to ratify my title in exchange for my warriors' oath of fealty. That would be one way of ending this pointless bloodshed.' He paused.

Was he waiting for her agreement? 'Marriage to me would strengthen your claim, would it not?' Beatrice asked flatly.

'It might,' Edmund admitted. 'But, believe me, I had not that thought in mind when I decided to wed you.'

'Decided to wed me?' Beatrice said bitterly. 'You've just admitted it was forced on you. Am I meant to be pleased with such a graceless proposal? You were forced to it! I thank you for your gracious offer.' She lifted her skirts and gave him a mocking curtsy. ''Tis all very convenient, is it not?' Beatrice continued, longing for him to contradict her. 'I agree you've just saved my life. But why? I'm merely another weapon in the battle for your father's lands. And pray, what about your sister Hilda? Surely she has a prior claim? *She* was born in wedlock. Where does Hilda figure in all your plans? In the bottom of the deepest well?'

Edmund clenched his teeth. 'Always you insult me,' he exploded. 'You'll never forget my bastardy, will you? And for you to imply that I would harm my sister——'

'Nay, I spoke but in anger,' Beatrice backed down at once. 'But you have to admit your claim——'

'Christ, woman! This is no time for caveats and complexities.' His skin was stretched across his cheekbones like bleached parchment. He fumbled in the pouch at his belt. 'Here, put this on, if it does not offend your flesh to touch it. 'Twill serve to remind those bloodthirsty warriors of mine not to harm you.'

He grasped her hand and thrust a ring clumsily on to her wedding finger. 'And remember 'tis wise to pretend you like the idea. My men will tolerate your presence, just, if you do. We've had enough of your haughty Norman airs. Remember, Beatrice, your life depends on it.' And throwing her a murderous glare, he slammed from the room.

Beatrice took a pace after him, then stopped. There was no advantage in talking to him till his temper had cooled. She flopped down on the narrow bed, and looked at her hand. Her fingers burned from his touch, and the ring felt heavy. It was a gold ring, simple in design with a plain unadorned shank. Set into it was a polished sapphire of great size and beauty. Beatrice's eyes grew round. It must be worth a king's ransom.

She was to have been ransomed—she grimaced at the thought. But if Edmund was to be believed it seemed that fate had other plans in store for her. Did he truly mean to marry her? Or would she still be ransomed? She twisted the ring from her finger to examine it more closely. There was an inscription on the inside. She sighed; it was in English and she could not decipher it. She would ask Hilda what it said.

Carefully Beatrice replaced the ring. She did not know what to think. Edmund had carried her from Lindsey, intending her to be a hostage. He had no real desire to marry her—that was something he had been forced into to save the life of a prisoner who was worth more alive. The few kisses they'd shared meant nothing. She was no longer that naïve. Look how de Brionne had handled her... and he loved her cousin, Anne.

Edmund *was* protecting her, but that was not his prime consideration. She was the key that might unlock the door to his beloved Lindsey.

If only he *were* marrying her, and from choice. How happy she would be. 'I love him, but...oh!' she addressed her frustration to the crackling fire.

She wished she had checked her angry pride. She wished they had not quarrelled. Edmund did not love her, and she had only alienated him. She would try and make amends. She had enough love for them both. And no matter what Edmund thought of her he had shown her kindness. She would act out the part he had assigned to her, and maybe in time...

Beatrice heaved Edmund's fur-lined cloak around her. She would go and ask Hilda's help. She would make a start at learning his language.

Beatrice squared her slender shoulders and lifted the latch.

Outside a chill wind shrieked round ramshackle buildings and byres, and whipped the door from her hands. Beatrice drew Edmund's cloak tighter round her body, relishing the luxury of fur.

A group of Saxon warriors had gathered at one edge of the clearing. Some were sharpening long-handled axes and others their long swords, honing bright blades to murderous points. Siward was among them, engaged in combat practice with the dark, bearded hulk who had lately threatened her.

Even the training looked perilous. Beatrice observed them from her standpoint by the hut. Siward twisted in and out of reach of his opponent's relentless flashing blade, as fluid as a snake. The dark Saxon wielded his sword with the steady rhythm of a reaper, yet one slip could see Siward maimed for life. Suddenly Siward noticed Beatrice. He raised his hand and all movement ceased. He smiled across the yard at her, saluted. Diffidently, Beatrice acknowledged his greeting. The hulk also inclined his head, but even at that distance Beatrice could see how reluctance hobbled the man's movements.

She turned and walked slowly away. Her back prickled under the combined and hostile regard of all those Saxon warriors. Their hostility had not yet dissipated, she could almost feel a dagger-thrust between her shoulder-blades...

The rooks were squabbling in their lofty rookery. She craned her neck to see them. It made no difference to the birds whether the clearing was populated by Normans or Saxons. They had territorial fights of their own to settle.

The snow crunched underfoot, and the amber gown was already drenched at the hem. She walked till she had put a hut between herself and the Saxons, but her skin still crawled as though they spied on her. Affecting unconcern, Beatrice squinted up at the rooks' untidy nests. Her shoes were leaking. She hauled up damp skirts, she would go and find Hilda...

She halted. A woman was standing, alone by the wooden buildings, watching her. She was too tall to be Hilda. The wind caught at the woman's cloak, and snatched the hood from her head. Bright yellow hair shone in the sunlight. Ingirith! Beatrice put a smile on her face, but did not expect a response. Ingirith shrugged herself deep into her hood and held her ground, unsmiling.

Beatrice grimaced. If Ingirith was determined to be unfriendly, so be it.

Suddenly, all was movement and noise. A menacing mailcoated figure, with a steel mask where his face should have been, leapt out of the brush at her.

Beatrice started to run towards Ingirith. 'Ingirith!' she screamed. 'Help me!' Her voice rang shrill across the snow-shrouded ground.

Ingirith was still as a statue, and just as responsive.

'Muzzle the bitch! Keep her quiet!'

Beatrice thought she would die. The harsh voice was Norman. It could only be one of de Brionne's scouts. They had come looking for her, after all. Someone thrust a rough cloth over her head. She fought to keep it from suffocating her, flailing out in blind terror. Her heart was pumping cold dread through her veins. Was Ingirith fetching help?

'Bind her later—no time to stop,' said another Norman voice. 'Hurry! Get her to the boat!'

Beatrice renewed her struggles. She was rewarded with a ringing blow at her temple.

'Ingirith,' she gasped. But it was no use, her voice was muffled by sackcloth and was unintelligible. Even if Ingirith could understand her, the girl had made it plain she would never help her. 'Ingirith——'

Another brain-bruising blow from a mailcoated fist, and Beatrice bit her tongue. Rough hands lifted her. She was carried, bundled into something. There was the scrunch of splintering ice, a hollow wooden clank, the sounds of water. A boat? The world rocked. A boat. They must be on one of the waterways. She tried to listen. She heard the squeal of a water rail. There was a scrape, followed by a plopping, splashing noise. Scrape, splash, scrape, splash. She must be in a punt. She groaned. Edmund would think she'd gone willingly. He would think she had betrayed him.

'Mistress Beatrice?' Someone thumped her on the back.

'Mmm?' she groaned. She knew that voice, but the choking sacking muddied the sound and she could not place him. The man smelt rankly of sweat.

'De Brionne has some questions for you, Mistress. We're taking you home.'

'Home?' Beatrice mumbled as best she could. Whom did that voice belong to? She coughed. There was not enough air in this sackcloth. She would suffocate...

'To Lindsey. Aye. And we have unfinished business, you and I.'

That sounded like a threat. But Beatrice felt too ill to consider it. De Brionne's scouts lapsed into silence. The boat rocked, but it was no cradle to lull her to sleep. The bottom of the punt was hard, and cold. The sacking sawed at her skin. It rasped over the bruises where she had been struck. Her feet were unwieldy blocks of ice that no longer belonged to her. She suspected her shoes had been lost, for the wind whistled through her hose and played over nerveless toes.

The boat tilted. Her lungs were desperate for air. She was falling into a swirling vortex of flashing lights and disembodied voices that babbled about her, rising and falling like waves. And like the waves they had no meaning.

Then there was silence. And the voices began again. Only this time they had meaning. But when Beatrice had made sense of them she wished she had remained in ignorance.

'Dump her here. That'll do. I'll guard her. You go and tell de Brionne. But...Hugh?'

'Aye, Robert?'

'Give me half an hour...alone with her, before you inform the Baron. Understand?'

Beatrice heard the distinct chinking of coins changing hands. She tried to rouse herself. She could hear a bolt being rammed home. Someone was locking a door. She subsided; it was too painful to move. Besides, the sound seemed so far off it could have no relevance to her. She shook her head. The hood itched like the plague.

'Let's be seeing you!'

Blessed relief! The smothering sackcloth was whipped away. She blinked and scrubbed at her face. A Norman soldier leered down at her.

She had been cast on a dirt floor, still wearing Edmund's cloak. The light dazzled; she screwed up her eyes, and regarded the man crouched on his haunches beside her. She froze to her marrow. She knew him, all right. He was the guard at the gate. The one she had flirted with on the day of Hilda's escape.

'I'm glad you've decided to keep our rendezvous after all, Mistress.' He stretched thick lips into a smile.

Beatrice all but gagged. She should have known—that smell...

'Night's drawing on fast, Mistress.' He brought his face close to hers. 'I know how you like to comfort lonely guardsmen in the dark hours. You shouldn't have run off with that Saxon upstart before we had time to get to know each other. I've been looking forward to renewing our acquaintance.'

Her mouth went dry. She could see the open pores on his cheeks. Beatrice edged away, clutching the fur-trimmed edges of the cloak tight about her, as though it could save her. Cold sweat trickled down her back.

'Now, don't you go all coy on me. I know the truth,' he leered.

'The t-truth?' Beatrice stuttered, while her brain sought for some escape. She backed away. He moved in. She backed—and hit a wall-beam.

His eyes glittered greedily. He licked his lips. She knew there was no help for her...

'We all know about you.' The guard had her cornered. 'You're not too choosy. A Norman wench who gives favours to the Saxon enemy is nought but a harlot. And if you'll accept scum like that, you'll be honoured by my attentions.'

Beatrice found her voice. 'Nay! Nay! You mistake the matter.'

'Treacherous whore!' Ugly, insensitive hands reached for her. She could see the calluses on his fingers.

'The Baron will not permit you——'

'The Baron, not permit me,' he brayed. 'Don't make me laugh. He won't know till it's too late. And why should he be concerned for a faithless whore? You're mine for a space. I found you. I'll soften you up, ready for interrogation. And, who knows, maybe our Baron will honour you too before we're done...'

CHAPTER NINE

'COME, Mistress.' Her gaoler leered. 'Now you can fulfil those pretty promises you made earlier.'

'Never! I wouldn't touch you if you were the last man on earth!' Beatrice cried. 'You smell like a cesspit! Keep away!'

But it was no use. Grasping hands mauled her, greedy lips latched on to hers. His teeth were rotten, like those of a man of fourscore years. The bile rose in her throat. Choked with revulsion, she began to cough. The man's hold slackened. The spasm became intense, it scraped her throat and lungs. She welcomed this pain, for her gaoler was forced to delay his pleasures. Better the scalding agony in her chest than the torture of his touch.

A quick glance at the Norman warned her the spasm could not be prolonged forever. He suspected trickery. She had never seen less pity on a man's face. He did not look human. Dirty nails dug deep, hands gripped. He would give no quarter. A pleading white face and piteous eyes only spurred this man to greater cruelty. A clumsy hand kneaded her breast.

I must faint, Beatrice thought. Sweet Lord, grant me the mercy of oblivion. I cannot suffer this.

For a moment she believed her supplication had been heeded. The chamber tilted, a black fog rose up. But the Lord was not listening, it seemed. As she was shoved to the ground, her head cracked against the plastered wall. She was stunned. The hand that had lately bruised her breast was scrabbling at her skirts, pulling them up over her thighs, but she was unable to move. A broken nail scratched her legs—she did not even flinch. The guard's foul, panting breaths offended her nostrils. The dingy prison cell revolved slowly about her, just as Normandy had done on a distant day that suddenly, incongruously,

180

came back to her. She had been dancing round a maypole in an apple orchard...

The guard heaved himself on to Beatrice.

'You grunt like the pig you are,' Beatrice managed.

Her arms were pinned above her head. The guard thrust a stocky leg between hers. He was strong. Beatrice cried out, resisting him with what little strength she had left.

Her gaoler dealt her a neck-snapping blow across her jaw. ''Tis no use calling on that name for help, Mistress. There are no Saxons here now. 'Twould take a potent spell indeed to make that bastard hear you.' He fumbled with the ties of his trousers.

Logic told Beatrice resistance was useless. Here was an animal who only understood violence, and she was angering him. If she resisted he would probably kill her. She knew quiet submission was the safest course.

But she could not lie still. The hand that crawled over her body made her flesh shrink. It tore at her gown. It gripped her chin. Rage ripped through her. Beatrice kicked out. She would die if he kissed her again. Her hands were immobilsed, but she had teeth. She snapped, and bit, and kicked. He would not take her easily...

Suddenly full daylight streamed into the hut. An icy draught whooshed over the couple wrestling in the dirt. The door crashed shut and the chamber dimmed.

'Curse you!' Her assailant swore, scowling over his shoulder. 'Can't you let me have my turn in peace?'

Bright as a jay, Morcar swayed unsteadily into the room, each hand holding a wineskin. The Saxon giant peered at them, his expression bleary. He shrugged, unconcerned, and took a swig from one of his wineskins.

'Don't let me cramp your shtyle,' he said, slurring the words. He slumped back against the wall, and closed bloodshot eyes. He hiccuped and opened one eye to peer at the Norman guard. 'Jusht looking for somewhere to sit down. No need for you to shtop your fun.' The blond head lolled.

The Norman eased his thickset body off Beatrice. Morcar blinked at him through the wine-haze. 'As you're here, you can let me have a drink,' the guard said. He winked at Morcar. 'Then when I've finished you can take your turn.'

Beatrice pulled her skirts down over her legs. Her hands did not function very well. The amber material was soiled and torn. Another ruined gown, this one finer than any she had ever had, and now it too was wrecked. Surprisingly, she heard herself give a bitter laugh.

She dragged her scattered wits together. Surely the minstrel would not sit there watching while... while...

Morcar had handed the Norman the other wineskin. One apiece now. Two drunks, and she on her own...

The Minstrel's grey eyes locked on hers. They *seemed* perfectly clear. Beatrice caught her breath. Her heart thumped, and it came to her. Morcar was no more drunk than she was. And there was more... there was something about his manner. He evoked a vivid memory of the nuns in the chapel about to chant—waiting for their note. Morcar was waiting for something...

The minstrel glanced speculatively at the sapphire ring, his brow creased. The only sound was her gaoler's gulping at the wineskin. The man staggered. A grubby sleeve protruded from under his mailshirt, and he wiped his mouth with it.

'Good shtuff, our Norman wine.' The Norman grinned. 'Far shtronger than washy Shaxon ale, my friend. Thash all froth. Thish really... ish... good... shtrong... shtuff.' His eyes glazed.

The Norman sounded as though he had downed a barrel, not one small wineskin. Eyes lighting with hope, Beatrice waited. The man staggered. Ungainly as a fatted swine, he thumped down and wallowed on the filthy floor, nursing his head in his hands.

'Keep... an... eye... on... her, will you?' he mumbled. He stretched his jaws wide in a yawn which displayed his rotting teeth in all their hideous glory. He flopped over on to his side and began to snore.

Beatrice stared, and felt her lips smiling. 'What was in that?' she demanded.

The minstrel came towards her. 'Something to dull his ardour, and his memory,' Morcar answered.

The minstrel's smile *looked* reassuring enough. She let him take her hand and watched him stare at her ring.

'You accepted this willingly?' he asked.

'I...er...' Beatrice floundered, and withdrew her hand.

'Do you wish to marry him?' Morcar pressed.

It was no use pretending she did not know whom he was talking about. Her shoulders slumped. 'Aye,' Beatrice sighed. 'I do.'

Morcar echoed her sigh. 'Then I am glad I stopped this...animal. 'Twas worth the risk to our cause. I saw them bring you in, my lady.'

'I...I've no title,' Beatrice corrected him.

'You're my lord's lady,' Morcar said simply. ''Tis all I need to know. I did not believe the evidence of my eyes,' he went on. 'It astounds me that a man of any race—even your harsh Norman one—could subject a woman to this...indignity. I could not be sure who it was he had beneath the sacking, but the Lindsey ring was in full view.' Morcar grinned. ''Tis not one you can miss. I realised I would have to help you whoever you were. And now I see you are the young lady who welcomed me at the copse, and I am glad.'

The Lord had sent her a saviour, but he had picked a strange one. 'You're a Saxon spy!' she realised.

'Hush! Never say so.' But Morcar bowed his shaggy mane in acknowledgment.

Her mind reeled. She opened her mouth and shut it again.

'I was sent to rescue our new lord,' Morcar told her.

'I did wonder, but why did de Brionne not suspect you?' Beatrice asked.

'My conspicuous bulk and appearance shield me. No one fails to notice me, but people will never suspect the most obvious man. De Brionne would look for subtlety in a Saxon spy. I came to help my lord, but he did not need my help. Then I thought his sister did, and so——'

'You stayed.'

'Aye, and I know what you——'

The measured tramp of mailclad feet approaching the prison hut stopped further confidences. Beatrice felt her blood run cold. She moved to Morcar's side, and clutched at his tunic.

'The Baron,' she whispered, eyes dilated with fear.

'Nay, lady.' Morcar disengaged himself. Gone was the friendly giant. A blond sot slid drunkenly down the wattle walls and landed in a heap next to the sleeping gaoler. He looked like a vast bundle of unsorted linen. 'My lady.' Bright eyes peeped out from the garish cloths. 'There's no need for me to ask you to act as though fear has driven the wits from your skull—you're as pale as a ghost! But please disarrange your clothing, you don't look nearly ravished enough.'

Silently, Beatrice did as she was bidden. Thank heaven she did not have to face the Baron alone.

Skirts and hair mussed, she was sprawling in a shadowed corner when de Brionne stalked in. She dragged herself up and faced him.

'He's left some spirit in you, then,' the Baron remarked, securing the door. 'I can see from your eyes that your ordeal with my man has not completely cowed you.'

The Baron's gaze raked her, taking in her bruised face, disarranged hair, and bare legs where her gown was torn.

'I was only just informed of your presence, Mistress,' he said. 'Otherwise I would have spared you this.'

Beatrice drew the ragged edges of her skirt together, and lifted her head. 'Would you?' she asked, with biting scorn. 'Would you really?'

The Baron's lips curled, and Beatrice understood that he had not known what the guard was attempting, but she also knew that he did not care, one way or the other.

'You were scratched a little, I see.' The Baron purred. He oozed false solicitude. 'And look at your poor face. I am so sorry, Mistress.'

Beatrice clenched her fists. 'You dishonour your family, your country and your King,' she spat. 'How much further into the slime will you sink? You revolt me.'

She saw him direct a dark frown at the slumbering minstrel. 'And don't pretend you didn't send him to complete my humiliation,' Beatrice added hastily. 'I know better. You're a filthy, stinking, verminous reptile!'

'Oh, Beatrice!' Diverted, the Baron swung back to her. 'Not *two* of them. Believe me, I had no idea.' He laughed. 'But had I thought of it...'

'And they're drunk,' Beatrice put in for good measure.

'Tsk. Tsk. Did you not like it?' De Brionne caught hold of a dishevelled braid and twisted it around his fist. He jerked and tears of pain sprang to her eyes, but she made no sound. The Baron gave another turn, and a gasp escaped her. He gave a grisly smile. 'Well? Answer me!'

'What do you think?' Beatrice hissed.

The pressure on her scalp eased.

'Now, Mistress,' de Brionne said, pleasantly. 'I shall ask you a few questions. If you answer me correctly, I shall not hurt you. But if you refuse to answer...' Winding her hair, he wrung another moan from her. 'You understand?'

'Aye, I understand. You stoop to torture. Mind you don't grow so bent you'll never stand upright again.'

'I'm glad, Mistress, that your recent ordeal has not dulled your wits,' he drawled. 'Tell me, did the Saxon chit give the casket to her brother?'

Beatrice looked into the face of her cousin's lover, and hesitated. Tearing pain seared her scalp. But she could answer this truthfully, without harm to anyone. 'I do not know,' she replied. ''Tis likely she did, but I do not know.'

'She had it when you helped her escape. She was seen holding it. What happened to it?' Another turn.

Agonised, Beatrice felt her knees buckle, and her hand shot to his mailed wrist. 'Please, Baron, don't. I don't know.'

Another false smile. The pain intensified. 'Lying whore,' he whispered, soft as a lover. 'Let's try again. Where did they put the casket? Come, Mistress. Believe me, I'd avoid damaging you if I could.'

'Now who's the liar?' Beatrice gasped out.

De Brionne sniggered, and shook his head. 'What would Anne say? She'd never forgive me.' His eyes and his words did not march the same route. She would have no hair soon...

'I don't know. Truly, I don't,' she bit out, holding on to her tormentor for support. 'The Saxons trust me no more than you do!'

'I say you lie!' De Brionne released her braid, but her relief was short-lived, for he merely transferred his grip to her wrist, and planted pain there instead of on her scalp. He regarded the sapphire ring.

'Look at this. A pretty trinket from your Saxon lover. It proves you false.' His eyes were black as death. 'You've chosen well, it seems. Your lover is generous with his gifts. Where's the dagger? Lost it in the water? How very sad. Don't whinge to me that the Saxons don't trust you. I will not believe it.'

''Tis the truth,' she protested. 'They do not trust me.'

De Brionne's lips thinned. 'If you could see yourself! Two of my scouts find you prancing freely about a rebel camp, flaunting your new possessions. You have a fur-lined cloak fit for a princess, a new gown, a sapphire ring... I'd not have recognised our little convent novice if it hadn't been for that blaze of hair.' The Baron rubbed his chin. 'I should have realised a real novice would never have let her hair grow, whatever its colour. You never had the slightest intention of returning to the convent, did you? You came with Lady Anne with one thing in mind—trapping yourself a rich husband. You're very clever, you played the role of devoted cousin to the hilt.' He began easing his sword from its scabbard.

Morcar shifted and mumbled.

Beatrice tensed. She did not want bloodshed if it could be avoided. 'N-no,' she cried at the bright bundle of rags. 'No!'

Morcar subsided.

'Eh?' De Brionne glowered down at her.

'I-I mean...you're wrong, I did mean to return to Caen.'

The Baron's mocking laugh rang round the rafters. 'You could have done better than that verminous beggar,' he said. 'You should have confessed your ambition to me, Mistress, before turning traitor. I would have ac-commodated you. I can be generous, too, when I choose. There was no need for you to crawl to a Saxon for the treasures you crave.'

'You're so warped I wonder that you ever see straight.' Beatrice was almost at the end of her tether. Yet, if she could, she would wriggle out of this with both her skin and Morcar's intact. 'The Saxons believe me to be a Norman spy,' she said, truthfully. 'They want me dead.'

De Brionne snorted and stared at the ring.

'Not one of them at the camp would trust me.' And that, she thought sadly, was no lie either.

'Do you deny that you helped the Thegn's rightful heir to escape?'

'No. I did get Lady Hilda to the gate,' Beatrice admitted. Her wits were clearing, and she steeled herself to meet those dead eyes. If she could but delay the Baron's interrogation till later, there might be some hope that she and Morcar...

'I had no thought in my mind of going with her,' Beatrice declared. 'I knew nothing about the horsemen. We had planned only that Lady Hilda should escape on my mare.'

'We?' the Baron queried gently.

'I-I mean Hilda and I.' Beatrice tried to retrieve her slip. She would not buy her safety at the cost of Anne's.

'And you gave the Saxon chit the casket?' De Brionne's fingers tightened.

Beatrice nodded.

'Where is it now?' he barked, so loudly that she started. 'At that camp? Answer me, girl, or you'll rue the day you were born, and what has happened to you so far will seem tame by comparison.'

Beatrice swallowed.

Morcar moved restlessly, muttering as if in drunken altercation. The Baron barely spared him a glance. 'You do not answer me, Beatrice, but you'll learn. I'll leave you now. You'll get nothing to drink, nothing to eat. We'll see if hunger or thirst loosens your tongue.'

Beatrice hung her head so the Baron would not see her eyes blaze with triumph. She had bought some time, at least.

De Brionne hammered on the door. 'Open up,' he bawled. Light streamed through the door. 'No food or drink for this one. I'll visit her when I get back.' The bolts scraped home.

Morcar uncurled and put his ear to the door.

'You're ready to leave?' he asked.

'Leave?' Beatrice echoed. 'You've thought of a way?'

'Aye. I don't rate your chances if you stay,' Morcar said, with the ghost of a smile.

Beatrice stared blankly at the minstrel. He was right. She had not betrayed anyone, yet here she was...

'It matters not where I am,' Beatrice said dully. Facing the Baron had drained her of all her strength. 'Everyone believes the worst of me, Norman and Saxon both.' Her head drooped.

'I don't.'

'Do you not?' With an effort she rallied, and eyed the snoring Norman in the dirt. Her countryman. She sighed. There were too many obstacles to overcome. It would never come right. 'I thank you, but——'

'You think of my lord,' Morcar said.

The bright head shot up. 'Aye.'

'Edmund does not think badly of you. I know this.'

'No.' She could not believe it. 'How do you know? You haven't spoken to him for days. How can you possibly know what Edmund thinks?'

Morcar put a large finger on the sapphire. 'You carry that ring. That tells me much of his trust in you. Our new Thegn would not have given you that lightly.'

''Tis not as it seems.' The minstrel dwarfed her. But a softness in his eyes encouraged confidences. 'Edmund took me to the camp and your people were screaming for revenge. I was to be the scapegoat. *Wergild*, I think they called it.'

Morcar nodded.

'My life was to be forfeit. Your warriors broke into the room where I was resting, and they would have killed me there and then. Edmund saved me. He lied to them. He told them he was to marry me, and thus diverted their anger.'

'He must indeed value you highly.' Morcar grinned. 'Can you read our tongue?'

'Not one word. Neither can I speak it.'

'Give me your ring,' the minstrel commanded.

Beatrice placed it in his broad palm. Her hand felt naked without it.

'I've heard how...' Morcar trailed off and squinted at the inscription. 'Aye! Here it is! So it is true.'

'What? What does it say?' Beatrice demanded.

The minstrel's eyes crinkled when he smiled. He passed back the ring, and watched her slip it on her finger.

'My lord does trust you,' Morcar insisted. 'He would never have given you that ring otherwise.'

'You sound very sure. I wish I shared your faith.'

'Believe in the ring,' Morcar advised.

'Help me. Tell me what it says!'

'Nay. 'Tis not my place. Here, my lady, some wine will strengthen you for what lies ahead. Drink. 'Tis untainted, I assure you.'

'He thinks I hold his bastardy against him,' Beatrice confessed, raising the wineskin to her lips.

'And do you?'

'What?' Beatrice frowned. She was tired. She ached all over. Now the immediate danger was over she could not think.

'Hold Edmund's illegitimate status against him?'

'Nay, of course not. I never did, even when I did not know him. And how could I now, now that I know him?' The wine was warming her stomach.

'You can tell him that when you see him. He could use real loyalty and affection. The old Thegn would never admit how much his firstborn son meant to him. He feared 'twould hurt his lady, Judith, and his legitimate son.'

'But his natural mother? Surely she loved Edmund?' Beatrice probed.

'She'd have died rather than admit it. She nursed a bitter hurt, and Edmund was too like his sire. Edith never truly forgave Hereward for deserting her and marrying Lady Judith. As Thegn, Hereward could not marry Edith. He did love her, but she was too low-born to be his wife. Her father was a foreigner—a Dane. Hereward had been betrothed to the Lady Judith by his father because Lindsey needed Lady Judith's dowry. A pauper's love-match was out of the question.' Morcar relieved Beatrice of the wineskin and milked it of the last drops. 'Bah, 'tis finished,' he announced with regret, and tossed it into a corner.

'So Edmund's own mother rejected——'

'He'll not want pity,' Morcar said incisively. 'And Edith did not dislike him. 'Twas just that she found his

presence hurtful. He was a constant reminder of what
she had lost to Lady Judith.'

The guard rolled over and grunted.

Morcar's eyes narrowed. 'My lady, we must act swiftly,
before this man awakens,' he said, urgently. 'Do you
trust me?'

'Aye.'

'I'm going to leave you here. I won't be long. If he
comes round before I return, you'll have to hit the hog
with that broken pail. Do you think you can manage
that?'

Remembering how the man had terrorised her, Beatrice
did not hesitate. She nodded.

Morcar smiled. He assumed the legless gait of a man
well soused, and battered at the door. It was opened a
little and the Saxon directed a string of sot's impotent
curses through the crack. There was a roar of appreciative laughter from the guards outside, the door was
thrown open, and the minstrel staggered out into the
compound and fell sprawling. It was a faultless per-
formance from a professional entertainer. It nearly
fooled Beatrice, let alone the sentries.

Shrinking back from her gaolers' goggling eyes,
Beatrice waited till they had sealed her in. Then she
dragged the pail within easy reach and settled down to
wait for the minstrel's return, her eyes never leaving the
unconscious Norman.

Morcar could only have been gone a few minutes, but
to Beatrice it seemed like hours. As his blond bulk pushed
through the door, relief washed over Beatrice like a spring
tide. Someone followed him, someone who was shrouded
from head to toe in a rich, heavy cloak that Beatrice
knew at once.

'Anne!' Beatrice dropped the handle of the bucket and
flung herself at her cousin.

'Oh, Beatrice.' Anne's voice was muffled by the folds
of her hood. 'I'm so sorry. This is——' Anne shuddered. 'Dear God, what have they done to you? Your
face——'

'Don't worry, Anne. There are no bones broken.
Bruises soon fade, I'm sure they look worse than they
are.'

Anne flung back her hood. Beatrice almost gasped. The eyes that stared out were hollow and haunted. Anne's sparkle had quite gone. She looked as though she had been on the rack.

'I'm certain Philip knows I was involved in Lady Hilda's escape,' Anne blurted. 'It may be cowardly of me, Beatrice, but I haven't had the courage to admit it. I'm terrified of what he'll do to me. He's changed. I'm so sorry, Beatrice, I know he is taking out his anger on you. Please forgive me.' She offered her hand, tentatively. It was shaking.

Beatrice felt her heart twist. Where was Anne's careless confidence now? She smiled gently, and pressed her cousin's hand. 'There's nothing for me to forgive. I don't believe he does suspect your involvement—there was one moment when I thought I'd unwittingly betrayed you but it passed. There's no need for him to find out. I won't tell him,' she assured her.

'But, Beatrice, I can't bear to think of you in here,' Anne wailed.

Morcar stepped forward. 'You can help get her out of this dismal pit,' he said.

Anne brightened. 'Can I?'

'Aye. We can get her away, but only if you are prepared to defy the Baron.'

Anne's face collapsed. 'Oh,' she said. Her shoulders slumped.

Morcar would not meet Anne's eyes. ''Tis simple,' he said bracingly. 'You and your cousin must exchange clothes, and my lady will leave in your stead. The guards will assume Lady Anne has finished visiting her treacherous cousin. They would not challenge her.'

'Nay!' Beatrice objected. 'I cannot leave Anne to face the Baron. He's capable of anything.'

'I'm sure he wouldn't harm *me*——' Anne began.

But Beatrice heard the doubt in her voice. 'Nay, Anne. I won't take my freedom if it means implicating you. But there is something...' She hesitated.

Anne grasped her arm. 'What is it? Is there another way?' The hand still trembled.

'We...we could bind you up,' Beatrice suggested. 'Tight enough to look as though we'd overpowered you.

De Brionne could not blame you then. Of course, it will mean that Morcar cannot remain here any more, for they'll know he helped me.'

A slow grin dawned on Morcar's face. He bowed. 'My lady, I would be honoured to escort you,' he declared.

Beatrice waited for Anne's response. It was her cousin who would be running most of the risk. It was for her to decide.

'Very well,' Anne announced abruptly. 'But you'll have to gag me too. Or they'll want to know why I didn't screech my head off.' She cast a harried glance at the door, unfastened the brooch which secured her cloak, and handed it to Beatrice.

'You're certain, Anne?' Beatrice asked.

'Aye, aye. Hurry up, Beatrice. This at least I can do,' Anne answered. She looked more like the old Anne Beatrice knew and loved. She was cool again, more controlled. 'Minstrel, face the wall, will you? I'm not stripping for your pleasure,' she added, drily.

But Anne was still a shadow of her former self. The Lady Anne de Vidâmes would never have changed with such frenzied haste. She had to prise Edmund's cloak from Beatrice's fingers.

'Mine is just as fine,' Anne remarked.

The old Lady Anne would never have noticed her cousin's regret at parting with the garment, either.

'Thank you, Anne. I know that. 'Twas the donor I was thinking of,' Beatrice admitted.

'We're doing our best to ensure you'll see him again.' Anne flashed her a grin. 'He seems generous, your barbarian.'

Morcar produced a length of twine. 'We'll bind you now, my lady. If you would lie down? I'll not tie you too hard, I swear it.'

'You'd better not leave it too loose, either,' Anne commented, obeying him. She pulled at her bonds. 'I could get out of that. He'll be suspicious if it's too loose.'

Morcar wrenched at the twine.

Anne let out a strangled gasp. 'Oh! That's better.'

Morcar picked up a scrap of material. 'Hold your head still, my lady,' he said.

Anne blanched. 'Oh, God! That filthy rag isn't going in my mouth, is it?'

'I'm afraid it is. If I gag you with silk, it won't fool anyone.' Morcar smiled.

'Very well. Get on with it.' Anne sighed, resigned. 'Nay! Hold! Hold a moment! There's something I must tell Beatrice.'

'My lady, please hurry,' Morcar urged.

'Beatrice, do you recall the Baron sending an envoy to King William?'

'Aye. He wanted permission to marry Lady Hilda.'

'He didn't only want approval for the marriage,' Anne said. 'He presented the King with a series of charges against your barbarian.'

'What!'

Beatrice and Morcar exchanged glances.

'If we don't leave now we may never be away,' the minstrel warned.

'What did the King say?' Beatrice demanded, staying Morcar's arm from applying the gag.

'Edmund of Lindsey has been outlawed,' Anne informed them. 'Anyone who helps him will be considered outside the law. You will be a criminal, Beatrice, if you go to him.'

Dazed, Beatrice stared at Anne. 'I must go,' she said.

Morcar tied the gag round Anne and scooped up a handful of sooty dirt. Anne's eyes widened when she realised the minstrel's intentions.

'Nay, Lady Anne,' Morcar admonished. 'Don't turn your head. 'Tis only a speck of dust to add a touch of colour to the tale you must tell.' His large hand plucked at Anne's braids, disordering her hair. 'You were altogether too tidy. Now you look to have been mishandled.'

Beatrice bit her lips. Anne's flawless skin was as grimy as any peasant's, her clothes all mired. The irony of it appalled her. It would have been funny, if it were not so desperate. That Anne, who took so much pride in her appearance, was prepared to submit to this...

'I'll warrant you would have preferred a more ladylike role,' Beatrice said. 'But I thank you, cousin, with all my heart.'

'Come, my lady, we must go.' Morcar hustled Beatrice to the door.

Beatrice hung back. A lump had formed in her throat. 'Farewell, Anne, and my thanks. I will never forget this.'

Anne rolled her eyes and jerked her head dismissively at the door. Beatrice observed the tears forming in Anne's brown eyes, and knew her cousin was wondering if they would ever see each other again. She bent to hug her.

Morcar tugged insistently at her sleeve. 'My lady...'

Beatrice pulled the hood of Anne's mantle over her head. It was imperative she hid her hair. Every Norman in the compound knew that Lady Anne's glossy tresses were brown. It only needed one bright lock to stray from the hood and they would all be lost. Head well down, Beatrice took in a fortifying breath. The lady Anne would precede the Saxon minstrel. And so must she.

The three sentries outside the prison-hut looked up from the game of fivestones which occupied the greater part of their minds, and winked knowingly at one another. Lady Anne's bowed head indicated deep hurt. The lady was much upset at the sight of her cousin being housed in such conditions. And no wonder. No doubt the minstrel would attempt to console her.

Ah! They were to take a ride. Probably Lady Anne hoped an hour or two in the saddle would take her mind off her cousin's cruel confinement.

'Better inform the Baron where his lady's gone,' suggested a guard, reluctant to leave the game.

'Aye, he may want her followed,' agreed one of his companions. He did not budge, either.

'Don't he trust his own lady, then?' another asked, blowing on his fingers.

'Baron don't trust no one, not even his own shadow, I shouldn't wonder. But there's no hurry. They'll be easy enough to follow, what with the tracks they'll be making in this snow.'

'That's true. In any case, the Baron's not here. He's smoking Saxons from their lair. We've plenty time to finish our round. There! Beat that if you can!' he challenged exultantly.

The riders were forgotten. Three heads, engrossed and greedy to win, bent over the game.

CHAPTER TEN

NOON the following day. During the night a brisk wind had swept the sky clear of snowclouds. The sun shone down from a vault of clearest blue, but there was a snap in the air.

Morcar and Beatrice stood at the market cross in the middle of the fenland village which had offered them food and shelter. Morcar, who was obviously well known to the villagers, had, by some mysterious means, acquired another harp. It was St Paul's Day, and to mark that festival a fair was being held around the raised stone cross. Morcar intended to play his harp.

Wagons and handcarts had gathered from surrounding districts. The place teemed with activity. Any fair was an excuse to break the monotony of the daily round, and one held in midwinter was especially welcome.

Beatrice watched the motley groups of people thronging the different stalls and booths. There was a festive atmosphere. Despite the cold, or perhaps because of it, people were determined to enjoy themselves. There were acrobats, jugglers and dancing bears. There was a noisy cockfight—Beatrice averted her head from that, but not before she had caught a glimpse of broken feathers and blood crimsoning the snow. A shiver ran down her back. In all that gaiety, the red splashes of blood were an omen of doom.

She pulled herself together. 'Where will your friend be? The one who knows where Edmund will have taken his men?' Beatrice whispered in case any should wonder at hearing her native accents.

Morcar climbed up the steps around the cross, and scanned the crowd. His height gave him an advantage.

'No sign of her yet,' he replied. He swung the harp down from his shoulder and, brushing slush from the stone steps, settled down to play.

'Aren't you going to look for her?' Beatrice urged. 'You won't find her if you stay there.'

Morcar's eyes twinkled. 'Have faith, lady. There are many of us fighting Lindsey's cause. We all have our own ways of making contact.' He indicated his harp. 'I use my stock in trade. I have a particular song which my friend will recognise.'

'Oh.'

'If she's here, she'll come. 'Tis a signal she'll not forget. And 'tis one a minstrel can use without rousing suspicion,' Morcar pointed out. He ran his fingers across the strings in a trickling cascade of sound.

'What if de Brionne's men see you?' Beatrice worried.

'There is none here,' Morcar replied absently, concentrating on the harp. A discordant note brought a frown to his face. He shook his head, tried again and the sound rang clear and pure.

'I think I'd like to wander round the booths while you play,' Beatrice announced, feeling she had become a distraction. 'You won't move from here, will you, Morcar? I want to be able to find you later.'

'I'll rest here,' Morcar reassured her. His eyes met hers. 'Have you any money, my lady?'

Dull colour stained her cheeks.

'I thought not.' He tossed her his purse.

It felt heavy. 'But...but...I don't need all this,' Beatrice protested.

Morcar shook his head deprecatingly. 'Nay, lady. Pride's a terrible sin. Edmund will repay me, if that eases your mind.'

Beatrice could not take his purse. She extracted a couple of coins for herself and smiled, placing the purse beside him on the step. 'I will not take more in case we get separated. Then what would you do without money?' she said firmly.

'Do? Why, I'd earn more, my lady.' He touched the strings, and rippling melody filled the air. 'I'll be here if you should need me.'

Beatrice pushed into the crowd.

No sooner had she left Morcar's side than she began to question the wisdom of having left him. The people pushed and pressed all about her. Their speech was harsh and unfamiliar. How stupid she was! These peasants were all Saxon. Not only was there no chance of making herself understood, for they could not speak Latin, let alone Norman French, but they'd probably turn on her if they discovered she was Norman. The premonition of foreboding was back again. She could not shake it off.

She could no longer hear the reassuring twang of Morcar's harp. The faces about Beatrice seemed grotesque. Dirty and unkempt, the men for the most part were unshaven. They frightened her. Her ears were filled with the guttural, foreign sounds of peasant English. She managed to smile at one man who jostled her elbow, but there was no answering response in his eyes. Only the mean and furtive suspicion of a man for whom life was one long, hard battle.

Her stomach had turned to water. She must find Morcar again. If she was silent, and did not speak, then these Saxons would not harm her. She told herself that the faces about her were not really malevolent. She told herself that they had no means of knowing she was a hated invader. She was just another girl enjoying the entertainment.

She twisted the sapphire ring round and round her finger with her thumb. A pockmarked face leered down at her. Beatrice shrank into herself, and tried not to breathe. It was as though they knew, as though the crowd had sniffed her out as being different. Somehow they knew she was not one of them. She must not say a word. Rather they thought her dumb than find out she was Norman.

An olive-skinned hand reached out from the crowd and seized her arm. Beatrice found herself looking into the swarthy face of a girl of about her own age. The girl smiled. One of her front teeth had been broken, but her smile was warm, and her teeth were white.

The girl tugged insistently on her arm. Beatrice was glad to follow, and in a moment she found herself on the skirts of the crowd, breathing easily.

She regarded her companion with open curiosity.

The girl had long black hair which hung in a thick cloak about her shoulders. Her dress was strange. Like Morcar's, it comprised many multicoloured layers of fabric. But it was the girl's mantle which drew the eye. The cloak was a patchwork of many different materials, but so cunningly designed that, as the girl moved, Beatrice caught glimpses of various shapes: a horse, a moon, a star. All the shapes whirled and danced about her companion as though they were part of some pagan ritual and the girl was the high priestess.

Cold fingers clutched round her heart. Indeed, the girl must command unseen forces, for she had cut her way through the dense throng as easily as a red-hot poker would carve its way through snow.

The girl spoke first. 'Your future lord and ring-giver——'

Beatrice gasped. The girl spoke Norman French! 'Edmund? You know of him? Where is he?' she demanded.

The girl smiled a secretive smile. 'Before he comes into his own, he must die and lose his name. He bears the wolf's head even now,' she chanted in a singsong voice.

'What do you mean?' Beatrice snapped, staring in consternation, as an unpleasant prickling sensation spread over the back of her neck. She snatched at the fantastic mantle, suddenly afraid the strange maid was an apparition who would melt away like a morning mist. 'You cannot mean Edmund of Lindsey! He's not going to die! Who are you, that you dare make such a prophecy? Only God can do that.' Her voice cracked.

'God is different things to different people,' the girl observed cryptically in lilting tones. 'I speak of a bastard Thegn with sky-tinted eyes. The ring-giver.' A brown

finger fluttered over Beatrice's ring, barely touching it.
She smiled.

'How dare you rhyme of death and still smile?'
Beatrice burst out. 'Where is he? I'll take none of your
prophecies, but I swear you know where he is.'

The girl's eyes came nearer, dark and very intense.
'You will see him once, before he dies,' the girl whispered. 'He is close, even now.' The shining eyes travelled
on past Beatrice to the heart of the fair.

Beatrice followed her lead, glancing uneasily over her
shoulder, half expecting Edmund to materialise and come
striding up to her. She sighed. Of course he was not there.
And suddenly nor was the girl. Somehow she had freed
her garment from Beatrice's grasp. Beatrice saw the vivid
splash of her clothes melt into the throng. She took a
couple of steps after her, but the crowd, which had parted
to admit the girl, closed ranks and formed an impen-
etrable wall. A woman on the edge of the crush made
a hurried, nervous gesture.

Beatrice recognised the sign for warding off the evil
eye. She sympathised with the superstitious dread on the
woman's face. She felt it herself. Her own fingers itched
to make that sign.

I will not let a madwoman's riddles upset me, she decided. Far better to consider the strange girl a lunatic
than to believe her words. For if she were to believe
them . . .

She shivered. Beatrice steered her thoughts firmly in
another direction. She would watch the jugglers. Then
she would find Morcar.

A man was at her elbow, smiling. He was selling hot
sweet chestnuts. Mindful not to speak, Beatrice held out
a coin in exchange for a handful of the chestnuts. The
man asked her a question. Beatrice made her eyes blank
and gave him a vacuous smile. The chestnut-seller's eyes
softened. He patted her kindly on the arm. Her ruse was
working. The vendor believed her simple. If he believed
it, then others might. He gave her some change and continued on his way.

Munching the warm chestnuts, Beatrice moved through the crowd with growing confidence. As long as she remained silent and smiled her fool's smile, she was safe. She remembered how kind the nuns had been to a simpleton who had turned up begging at La Trinité. Mother Adèle had made it plain that to be cruel to such an unfortunate would be to invite great misfortune. She hoped the Saxons shared Mother Adèle's views—it looked as though they did.

Some children were playing a noisy game with hoops. Others were swinging from the Giant's Stride. A long rope was suspended from a leafless oak tree, and half a dozen children clung to it like the last leaves of autumn. The winner would be the one who held on the longest. Beatrice kept her vapid smile in place and watched as all but two of the children fell, shrieking loudly, into the cushiony snow. Cheered by their fellows, the two remaining contestants clung like leeches. At length one gave a wail of anguish, and let go of the rope. The victor swung back and forth in solitary triumph, grinning at the world, then his reddened hands gave up the struggle, and he too landed in an inglorious sprawl in the snow.

There were pedlars, with baskets of ribbons and trinkets, leather-workers selling beautiful purses and belts. There were tinkers and beggars, and vintners offering steaming measures of mulled wine and ale. It seemed that all of England had come to the fair.

A rising hubbub caught her attention. Beatrice noticed a young girl stumbling blindfold through the press, her hands stretched out in front of her, feeling her way. Beatrice watched her. The girl was not distressed, her lips curved into a wide smile. This must be another game. Everyone was avoiding the girl's outstretched arms. They called out to attract the girl's attention, and leapt laughingly out of the way as she groped towards them. Beatrice grinned. She had played this game at home, years before her father had died and her mother had brought her to the convent. It was Blind Man's Buff.

Too late, Beatrice realised that the girl was stumbling straight at her. She leapt to one side, but the girl heard her move and was quicker. Beatrice was caught. The crowd roared and shouted. The girl bobbed a deep and inexpert curtsy and removed the blindfold.

Giggling, she offered Beatrice the blindfold. Beatrice backed away. The girl repeated her gesture. There was no way out. If Beatrice protested it would betray her Norman blood. She nodded and submitted to the blindfold being wound round her eyes. She was whirled round and released.

Disorientated and dizzy, Beatrice could hear the crowd hooting encouragements at her. There was someone by her left hand—no, her right—no, behind her. She spun on her heels, surely she sensed someone on her right?

Suddenly there were no more shouts and cries to guide her. It was as though the Saxons had been struck dumb *en masse*. There was only the thudding of her heart, and her feet crunching in the snow. The ground was uneven here. Beatrice caught her foot and tripped. Strong arms steadied her. Her hands closed round them and the crowd roared. They had their next victim!

Still blindfolded, Beatrice hesitated. Voices came at her from all directions, demanding no doubt that she play her part and give her forfeit. But what was she to do? She could not understand them. She shook her head and reached for the blindfold. A moment more and her secret would be out. Would they kill her when they realised they had an interloper in their midst?

A warm hand covered hers and firmly removed it from the blindfold. Fingers entwined with hers in a familiar gesture which set her heart thudding faster and sent bright colour rushing to her cheeks. Edmund had held her hand like this...

A light pressure under her chin tilted back her head. Warm lips brushed hers. She did not pull away. Vaguely she heard the raucous cries of the crowd, but these sounds faded to nothing. All of her consciousness was centred upon the hand that held hers, so gently, and the lips moving over hers. Her bones began to melt, like snow when the thaw comes. She found herself responding, unsure which of them was the captive and which the captor.

Her eyes were still closed, her lips welcoming those of her mysterious captive, when the blindfold was snatched from her head. Reluctantly she opened eyes that shone bright as stars. The outside world rushed back at her.

'Edmund,' she whispered, clinging to his hand.

Eyes that were the colour of the summer sky glared down at her.

'Are you mad?' Edmund stormed, shoving an unsteady hand through his hair. 'Whatever possessed you to join in this game? If I hadn't seen you, Lord knows what would have happened. If they had found out you couldn't speak English... They're smiling now, but their mood can change like lightning. They would tear you limb from limb given half a chance.'

He broke off as the girl who had caught Beatrice came to stand before him. The young woman pointed at the forgotten blindfold. She was urging him to take his turn in the game.

Beatrice took the cloth and secured it round Edmund's eyes. The relief shone from her eyes. She could not hide it. She stood to one side, and laced her hands tightly together to stop herself hanging on Edmund's arm.

The girl spun Edmund round and pushed him into the crowd.

Beatrice had eyes for no one but him. He was still the hue of tallow, but he moved with the light and agile grace of a cat. He was recovering.

He wore a pale blue tunic and his silver armbands, and he looked like a barbarian prince. Weaving and bobbing in and out of the crowd, he had several chances to grab a victim, but always turned away at the last moment. It looked as though he was deliberately prolonging the game. Or could he be searching for a particular person?

Whatever the cause of the near misses, they guaranteed Edmund's popularity with his audience. Each time his hands closed on the empty air, the multitude howled itself to a fever. In and out of the mill he ducked, his face alight with laughter.

A young woman stepped out of the mass and placed herself directly in Edmund's path. Beatrice stiffened. She knew that flaxen hair. It belonged to Ingirith.

Beatrice shrank back, hoping to avoid the girl's unsympathetic eyes. She needn't have worried, for Ingirith's whole attention was centred on Edmund. The Saxon stood waiting for Edmund to catch her. She looked serene, confident. Beatrice wanted to spit in her face. Edmund reached out. The mob clamoured. Ingirith walked into his arms.

Disgusted, Beatrice turned away. A voice bawled out the nature of the forfeit. Beatrice gritted her teeth. She knew what it would be. Someone whooped. She had to look, she had to...

Edmund had put up a hand to examine the face of his captive. At the sight of those sensitive fingers running over Ingirith's smug face, Beatrice screwed her eyes shut. When she opened them again, things had, if anything, got worse. Edmund's beautiful mouth curved upwards, he pulled Ingirith firmly into his arms, and kissed her with dramatic thoroughness. At last he made to release her, but Ingirith's slim hand lifted. Gracefully the Saxon caught hold of Edmund's head, and held him to her for another of those comprehensive kisses. The audience loved every minute.

And Edmund did not object.

Beatrice felt as though someone had kicked out her insides. Edmund whipped off the blindfold and fastened it round Ingirith, for her to take her turn. And still he smiled.

By the time he reached Beatrice, he had wiped the smile from his face.

'My thanks for my rescue,' Beatrice offered through clenched teeth, not looking at him.

Edmund gripped her upper arm and marched her through the crush. She managed to steal a glance from under her lashes. His profile was stern and unyielding.

'Ouch! You're hurting,' Beatrice complained. 'What are you doing? Where do you think you are dragging me to now?'

Edmund grunted. He towed her to the fringe of the crowd.

'Edmund, you're hurting,' she repeated.

He freed her. Beatrice rubbed her arm and her hazel eyes flashed.

'That hasn't hurt you half as much as they——' Edmund jerked his head at the massed Saxons '—would have done, if they'd found you out,' he fumed.

'I-I don't understand,' Beatrice faltered.

'Exactly,' he said drily. 'Listen, woman. When you caught me the crowd were shouting at you to kiss your captive. How the hell did you think you'd understand them? You would have removed the blindfold and spoiled their game. If I had not seen you——'

'Oh,' Beatrice said in a small voice. 'So that's why you kissed me like that—to avert suspicion.'

He looked keenly at her. 'You sound disappointed, Beatrice. Surely you didn't think I kissed you for the joy of finding you?'

Beatrice squirmed. 'N-nay. I don't suppose you would. 'Twas only the game. You kissed Ingirith too,' Beatrice said, keeping her voice carefully neutral. She did not want to sound like a nagging, jealous shrew. She stared out over the flat unreclaimed marshland, she looked at the pale sky, at a straggle of geese flying across it—anywhere but at him. She did not want him to read the pain in her eyes, a burning, envious pain. It seared her heart.

An awkward silence dropped over them. Watching the rustling reed-beds, Beatrice struggled to bury her feelings. 'You look very fine in your new tunic,' she commented. An inane remark, but surely an uncontentious one?

He was scowling abstractedly at some long, waving grasses. 'What? Oh, aye.' He glanced wryly down at his silver-edged tunic. His lips twisted. 'Aye, I'm happily betrothed, am I not? I have to dress the part. Even if my bride chooses to run off with de Brionne's scouts and betray my people.' He glowered down at her.

Beatrice was suddenly swamped with heady fury. How could he? Trembling with rage, she tugged at the sapphire ring. This finely dressed Saxon would insult her no longer! He was her enemy. He would never trust her. He would barter her for a handful of gold and not even blink. The ring clung to her finger.

'You don't have to marry me, Edmund,' she declared, all but dislocating her finger. 'I'm sure that Ingirith will be pleased to oblige.'

'I'll release you,' Edmund said, in a cold, hard voice. 'There was no need for you to betray the location of our camp to de Brionne to escape marriage to me. I thought you understood. I was marrying you to protect you. If you had told me how abhorrent the idea was I would have released you freely. Not immediately, 'tis true, for it was necessary that my people believed our betrothal genuine. I would not have forced an unwilling maid into marriage, even if she was Norman.' He spat out the last word with blistering scorn.

Beatrice looked at his mouth. It was hard to believe he had kissed her so tenderly. She searched his face for the smallest hint of warmth, but his handsome features were set like granite, his deep blue eyes cold as glass. She would waver no more. She wrenched at the ring.

'Oh, why won't this thing come off?' she cried, tears prickling behind her eyes.

The muscle in Edmund's jaw twitched.

The ring came free. Beatrice held it out. Edmund made no move to take it back.

'I did not betray you to the Baron,' Beatrice declared huskily. She must tell him even if he would never believe her. She thrust the ring under his nose. His blue eyes looked past the ring, and into hers. They burned with cold fire, like the stone in the ring. He was so still. And his face gave nothing away.

'You left the guesthouse and went to meet his scouts,' Edmund accused.

'Nay! I went out to...to...try and find Hilda. I thought she would help me with your language. I wanted to learn. I wanted to know what's inscribed in this ring.'

Edmund flushed, and she saw him clench his jaw.

Beatrice read his silence as disbelief. 'I see now how foolish I have been,' she said. 'You were right, there can be no alliance between us. I am Norman and you will never forget that. You have told me often enough that none of us can be trusted. I thought that I would be able to win your trust. I see now how wrong I was. What a dolt I am. Once a pig-headed Saxon mind has been made up, it never changes. So I give you back your sapphire ring. I would not marry a man who cannot trust me, for without trust there can never be...love.'

To her horror, Beatrice felt a tear spill over and run down her cheek. She twisted away and stared blindly towards the waving reeds. She felt his fingers brush her cheek, the merest ghost of a touch, but it was enough. She raised brimming eyes to his. Edmund reached and took the solitary teardrop on to his forefinger. He curled his finger into his palm as though he would hold on to her tear forever.

'Ingirith told me you had gone willingly,' he offered slowly.

'Ingirith!' Beatrice cried. She had been strangely moved by his gesture with her teardrop and was determined he should not exploit her weakness. 'Your jealous lover! She would tell you anything if it set you against me!'

'Ingirith is not my lover. She never has been my lover,' Edmund said with conviction.

'It certainly didn't look that way a few minutes ago!' Beatrice was astounded at the bitterness in her voice. What was happening to her? She scarcely knew herself.

'You wouldn't be jealous, of course?' Edmund's lips twitched.

'Never!' she gritted.

His eyes held hers. Beatrice had never looked more alive, more desirable. A young girl alone, surrounded by foreigners but spitting in the face of fate, her spirit shone out bright as a flame. Arm bracelets jangled as Edmund's hand rose to her cheek, in a featherlight caress.

Her stomach fluttered. She swallowed.

'Never?' he questioned, very low. His free hand caught hers and he pulled her up against him.

The sapphire ring dropped into the snow.

'That's why your hazel eyes are begging me to kiss you. And when I touch your cheek and pull you close, thus——' he suited the action to the words '—you do not protest.'

Beatrice tried, half-heartedly, to pull away.

Edmund gave a laugh and turned her face back to his. He did not have to use force. 'And when I kiss your pretty lips...' Again he acted out his murmured words.

Beatrice dissolved, shamelessly. She abandoned herself. He felt so good. Wrapped in his arms, and lost in his kiss, she felt all the horrors might never have happened. She felt healed, whole. His hair was soft under her fingertips. His mouth was warm and gentle. She wanted to feel him, all of him, next to her. She wanted to lie with him. She wanted to love him. She wanted him to love her... Shocked, she drew back. She was breathless and her eyes stretched wide.

Edmund's sky-bright eyes teased and danced. 'Now, my lady Beatrice, 'tis time you taught your eyes and your body to speak the same language your mouth does. They betray you. I understand how much you hate me.' He grinned.

Beatrice hid her face in his shoulder. She pressed one hand to her cheeks to try and cool them. The other was wrapped round Edmund's neck. Conceited, arrogant Saxon! He thought to charm her with a single smile, did he? And not a word of love?

'That means nothing,' she said, pulling her hand from his neck. 'You said yourself that I am a whore. 'Tis but a game. A passing pleasure.' She tossed her head, and instantly regretted her foolish pride, for the laughter went out of his eyes.

'So you did betray us to de Brionne,' he gritted, through tight lips.

'No! 'Twas one of his scouting parties! They found me by chance and took me by force! Edmund, I——'

His eyes scorched her, raging blue fire, his face was white with rage. 'He dressed you in fine silks, I see. Our Saxon rags were not good enough for you. My ring too base, no doubt.' His nostrils flared. 'Aye, I see you clearly now. You are a whore. Such innocent, lying eyes! Such an air of virginity!' He sketched a bow. 'Your talents are doubtless the result of years of practice at William's ducal court in Normandy. I salute your success.'

Beatrice could not believe it. He was walking back into the crowd. She reached out a hand as though to snatch him back.

'Edmund!' she cried, starting after him. But what about the ring? He had forgotten it. She could not leave it lying in the mud and snow to be trampled upon. She was afraid to move from the spot, in case it was lost forever. She wanted to run after him, to explain that her pride had been talking...

Torn, Beatrice raised her voice. 'Edmund! Come back! Your ring. 'Tis of great value,' she choked.

'Keep it,' he shot back coldly. 'I would not give it to any other now it has been yours. Keep it as a reminder of how you fooled an ignorant Saxon. Farewell.' He bowed stiffly, with chilling formality, and shouldered his way back into the throng.

Nailed to the place where the sapphire ring had fallen, Beatrice drew a shuddering breath. Her eyes followed his tall form. Her throat closed up. She sniffed. She would find the ring, and then she would go after him.

Beatrice bent and began to scrabble in the slush their feet had made of the snow.

Where was it? She picked something up and glanced at it. A pebble. She threw it aside. Heedless of the dirt she was grinding into the hem of her gown, Beatrice fished miserably through the stinging snow. Then she paused, staring at the tracks they had made, as if they could tell her where the ring lay. Tears welled. She gulped, scrubbed at her eyes with the back of her hand and blinked.

Two sets of footprints, one large, one small, were stamped clearly into the snow. She ran her fingers over the larger of the prints. The two sets met, toe to toe. They must have made these when they had kissed.

Ruthlessly, Beatrice plunged her hands in as far as her wrists, destroying the footprints. Nothing. Nothing but snow. So cold it burned. Her desperation increased. The ring *must* be near here...

'Here is what you seek.'

Beatrice recognised that lyrical voice at once. A brown hand was outstretched, pink palm uppermost. And nestling safely in her palm—the sapphire ring.

Relief flooded through her as Beatrice looked directly into the sharp brown eyes. The girl smiled, revealing her broken tooth. For an instant, a young Aelflaeda stood before her.

'Oh, I thank you!' Beatrice cried fervently. She took the ring and slipped it back on to her finger. 'Who are you?' she wondered.

'Do not grieve,' the lilting voice rang out. 'Your lord is now dead to the world. But he will be forgiven and will rise anew.'

'What——'

'You are not of the Old Faith. But I know your faith tells of resurrection and rebirth. I am correct, no?'

'Must you always speak in riddles?' Beatrice demanded. 'Riddles that have the ring of blasphemy. I cannot understand you.'

'I speak no blasphemy. You will understand in time. I speak to cheer you.' The girl flicked Beatrice's tear-stained face, and Beatrice flinched.

The dark girl lifted her shoulders. 'Your ring-giver will throw off the wolf's head and be an outlaw no longer. *Then* will be your time. Your destiny is to march with his. So it has been ordained.'

'Wolf's head? Outlaw?' Beatrice erupted. 'What are these riddles? Speak plainly.' Anne had said something about outlaws...

'The herald will tell all. Listen, but do not be seen,' the girl warned, utterly unaffected by the anger of the Norman girl.

Suddenly a cry went up, and a large troop of horsemen was upon them, approaching the market cross. Hoofs pounded, chain-mail clinked, steel helmets gleamed, and flags fluttered.

Baron Philip de Brionne was at their head. He straddled his brutish black war-horse, the one the grooms dared not handle. It seemed as clumsy and inelegant as a bull after Balder's fine, delicate lines.

Beatrice did not need the girl to tell her twice. Clutching Anne's cloak tightly about her face, she hurtled into the welcome anonymity of the crowd. Joy had drained out of them like water from a sieve. Sullen faces turned to where the horsemen reined in at the carved cross.

There were uneasy mutterings, low rumbles like those preceding thunder, but Beatrice knew they were not directed at her. She was safe in the crowd. Strange, that it should be so welcoming now, when earlier she had felt like an outcast.

Icy fingers crawled over the back of her neck. Her premonition had returned to haunt her, and it was twice as strong as it had been before. The air cut her lungs.

Baron Philip de Brionne barked a command. A fanfare trumpeted out. Then there was silence.

De Brionne conjured an impressive scroll into his hand. It was hung about with red seals. He started to read from it. He spoke in clipped tones, in his native French, and declared that the King had given him complete control of the lands and rights formerly associated with the Thegn of Lindsey. He told the blank-faced peasants that they owed their allegiance to him, and him alone.

A hundred hostile eyes pierced their new overlord. If looks were lances, Beatrice thought, the Baron's armour would not save him. He would have a thousand wounds.

'Edmund, the self-styled heir to Lindsey,' the Baron continued, and Beatrice sharpened her ears, 'has been declared an outlaw, by order of King William. Henceforth his head shall bear the price of a wolf's. He may be killed without fear of reprisal. Indeed, if any man does kill him, he must come to me, and I will give that man the reward for slaying a wolf.

'Further, if any man or woman should help this so-called Edmund of Lindsey, in any way, either by feeding him, or clothing him, or harbouring him from justice, then that man or woman will also be declared criminal and will be dealt with accordingly.'

Her blood ran cold. Beatrice scanned the crowd.

The Baron gestured at a herald, handed him the document, and the man began to translate the Baron's words into English. Like wind in the reeds on the nearby fens, his words caused a rustling and stirring to spread through the crowd.

Frantic, Beatrice cast her eyes about. Where was Edmund? Was he still here? Would the Baron see him?

The herald still read from de Brionne's scroll.

Some in the multitude gasped, while others shuffled and shook their heads. They began to mutter. And every man, woman and child turned a face of loathing on the mounted and mail-covered figure of their newly appointed lord.

The mutterings grew louder. De Brionne glowered at his people. A snowball bolted through the air and hit the shining black war-horse squarely on the rump. The brute sidled and tossed his head—his eyes rolled white and thick veins stood out like cords in his neck. Foam dribbled from his bit.

Someone called out. Beatrice gasped. De Brionne's harsh features formed a mask of pure evil. He spurred his horse directly into the densest part of the throng. Packed as tightly as salted herrings, the people could not leap out of the way. Some were too old, some too young and some infirm. The Baron took no accounting. He raised his horse's switch and began to lay about him.

The crop whistled. Someone began to wail, a long, thin, keening sound. The Baron's horse-soldiers exchanged uneasy glances. Hands hovered over sword-hilts.

'You'll learn to obey me——' de Brionne's crop
cracked '—if I have to beat obedience into your thick
skulls one by one.' The switch slashed down, the war-
horse ploughed on, and the people could not escape.

Somcone was going to get killed—they would fall and
be trampled upon, Beatrice realised. Her horrified gaze
fell on a young child, a little girl of about five years of
age. She stood directly in the path of the Baron's war-
horse. It was the girl who wailed, her mouth seeming to
fill her face. The child was too absorbed in her terror
to take even one step to save herself. A young woman,
who could only be the child's mother, reached out desperate arms through the wall of people, but sheer
numbers held her back. She would never reach the girl
in time.

The Baron spurred on.

Beatrice could not get to the doomed child either. She
was too far away. Stabbed through with impotent horror,
she could only watch, wide-eyed, as de Brionne urged
his horse towards the crying child. He was going to ride
right over that small girl.

The face of the child's mother was as white as chalk.
Beatrice would never forget the expression on it as long
as she lived. She closed her eyes and heard the Baron's
switch whistling, again and again and again.

Suddenly, the whistling ceased. A deathly hush gripped
them all. What was happening?

Beatrice did not want to see that mother's face again.
She half opened her eyes. The woman was smiling!
Beatrice stared. Joy had replaced terror, and tears of
relief streamed down the woman's face. The woman
opened her arms and received her child from the hands
of the man who had plucked her from beneath the flailing
hoofs of de Brionne's war-horse. Beatrice felt the
woman's joy as though it were her own—she looked at
the man who had saved the little girl.

He wore a fine blue tunic, edged with silver braid.
Raven-dark hair was swept back from his head. Blue
eyes blazed a challenge at the mail-clad Norman astride

the lumbering war-horse. Beatrice would have known that profile anywhere.

'No!' She choked down a scream. She elbowed her way through the knot of people in front of her.

Edmund's slender hands rested casually on his hips, his legs braced apart as though he expected a blow at any moment. The sight of that slim blue-clad figure quietly facing de Brionne in all his armour tugged at her heart. Beatrice pushed towards them.

De Brionne would kill Edmund without compunction. Edmund had not reached for his sword. And even if he had, on foot and dressed only in blue worsted, what match was he for the heavily armoured Baron?

De Brionne's lips lifted in gloating triumph. His mail flashed in the sunlight as he gestured two of his soldiers forward to take Edmund. 'You wouldn't be so foolish as to draw your sword, would you?' the Norman purred.

Edmund said nothing, but his eyes were very eloquent.

De Brionne drew his head back, and took a sharp breath. 'Someone might get hurt,' he warned, with an edge to his voice. 'One of the innocents, for example. They might get trampled in the rush to arrest you. 'Tis very obliging of you to come forward to give yourself up,' de Brionne sneered.

The guards were almost upon Edmund. Beatrice knew what would happen if they seized him. She was not going to allow it to happen. Not while she breathed. She hurled herself bodily at the nearer of the guards, catching him unawares. They both toppled to the ground.

'Run! Edmund, run *now*!' she shrieked.

Edmund was staring at her like a man in a daze, an arrested expression in his eyes, his face confused and suddenly vulnerable.

'Run,' Beatrice repeated urgently. 'Run!'

The woman whose child Edmund had saved did not know the words Beatrice was shouting. But she understood her meaning. The fine lady who lay tangled and muddied on the ground, struggling frantically with the Norman guard, meant to help her lord escape. Clutching her daughter to her breast, the woman murmured to the man at her side. Several stalwart Saxons moved, and a protective wall of flesh and blood surrounded Edmund.

Panting, Beatrice sat up and shoved her veil out of her face. She felt as though she had been rolling in the midden.

The people surged, picking Edmund up. He was being carried away, by a human wall of peasants. His face strained towards her. It was difficult to interpret the look that he sent her, but it seemed to Beatrice to contain that same blend of agonised and hopeless longing that she felt. Perhaps *now* he would believe in her. Perhaps *now* he would trust her...

Shakily Beatrice staggered upright.

De Brionne's sin-black eyes bored into her. 'Well, well, well, Mistress Beatrice.' He spoke quietly, through clenched teeth, and emphasised each word. 'You have made a fool of me once too often. You will live to regret this day.'

'Never! I will never regret what I have done,' Beatrice defied him bravely, but the slow slamming of her heart proclaimed her fear.

'Traitor!' de Brionne accused.

'If 'tis treachery to side with a man who would risk his own life for that of a child, against one who would kill in cold blood, then, aye, I am a traitor. And proud to be one!' Beatrice declared with more defiance than wisdom.

The Baron's hand tightened on his crop. He was almost beside himself with rage. And for Beatrice to defy him, determined even in defeat, was more than he could stomach. There she was, a drab of a girl, with the veil slipping off that improbable hair, covered in mud, *still daring to cross him*. He would bring her low if it was the last thing he did.

Beatrice steeled herself. A searing pain slashed across her cheek. Her involuntary cry of pain was drowned by the onlookers' sympathetic gasps. Shaking, her fingers explored her cheek—already a weal raised her skin.

'A taste of things to come,' the Norman warned.

'Beat me all you like,' Beatrice challenged him, 'but I would do it again.'

De Brionne's face set. 'Guard! Mistress Beatrice is returning to the hall. Bind her. You heard her. She has admitted her guilt before witnesses. She is unrepentant.'

The subdued murmurings were growing louder.

The Baron scowled. 'I'll not have rebellion on my hands,' he muttered. 'I'll not have this mob make a martyr of you.' His saddle creaked as he faced the crowd. 'This woman has conspired with the outlaw, Edmund of Lindsey, to help him escape from justice,' he declared. 'We are all witnesses. The law must be upheld. This woman will be put on trial for treason. The trial will be held at dawn tomorrow. I would not sully your Feast Day by trying her now.'

Beatrice snorted. The true cause of the delay was that de Brionne dared not risk a riot. Someone wrenched her arms behind her and she felt rope scorch her wrists.

Leaderless, the mob bubbled and seethed. They looked blankly to the herald for his translation.

The herald hesitated.

The Baron waved a mailed fist at him, and the man stumbled into speech. Golden spurs flashed, the black stallion surged forwards. Mud churned and splattered Beatrice. Something cut into her waist. They had tied a rope about her, and she was hauled behind de Brionne like a calf going to market. She knew she too was bound for the butcher's slab. De Brionne's men-at-arms closed ranks about her.

Her cheek burned where the crop had struck her. She was cold, wet and muddy, but she did not care. Her heart was light as air. Edmund remained free. This day was not to be his last. The dark girl's prophecy had come true, in part. Edmund now bore the wolf's head, as the Saxons said of outlaws. But he would not die. She had seen to that. He had been cast out from society, but he would live.

A ripple of sound floated over her head. Morcar's harp! Twisting her head, Beatrice found him. His blond hair shone like a hilltop beacon over the heads of the throng. He was staring at her as though willing her to read a secret message in his eyes. Beatrice frowned, puzzled. The rope jerked and she staggered.

'Watch your feet, wench!' de Brionne snarled over his shoulder. 'That's better. You'd better start praying to your favourite Saint.'

De Brionne had not seen Morcar. Beatrice risked another glance in that direction. Her eyes widened. Walter was at the harper's side, trying to shoulder the giant towards her. De Brionne must not see them, she must engage his attention...

'You recommend prayer? You?' Beatrice said, incredulously.

'Aye. I've decided that your trial shall be a trial by ordeal. So much more...entertaining for everyone, do you not agree?' de Brionne drawled.

'You godless viper, you make a mockery of justice,' Beatrice declared. She was beginning to feel the cold now. Her valour was deserting her.

'Tsk. Tsk. I thought a woman of the Church would long for just such a trial. It gives God a chance to ensure that the truth is revealed.'

'You don't believe that,' Beatrice said flatly.

The Baron's steel helmet tipped back when he laughed. ''Tis an accepted method of trial,' he countered.

Beatrice tried to keep her head up. ''Tis superstitious nonsense. You believe in it no more than I,' she declared.

'I don't need to believe it. To be seen to believe is enough,' de Brionne sneered. 'These Saxon sheepheads will believe anything I tell them.'

The wind must have changed; it must be coming from the north. Her head was shrinking with cold. Her tongue felt stiff. 'You can't do this——'

'I assure you I can.'

Her feet skated on mud. 'Which? Which ordeal do you have in mind?' she got out.

The Baron pretended to consider. 'Let me think. There's ordeal by fire, ordeal by iron, ordeal by water. So many to choose from.'

'Women never undergo trial by water,' Beatrice said, too quickly. She hoped he hadn't noticed.

De Brionne lifted his lips from his yellow teeth. 'So you admit that ordeal is an accepted method of trial?'

'I admit only that it is used. Not that it is acceptable,' Beatrice responded, forcing one foot in front of the other.

De Brionne looked straight at her, with eyes as sharp as darts, and pounced. 'You're rather swift to insist you shouldn't undergo trial by water,' he commented. 'Why is that? Are you afraid of water, Beatrice? Do you not like the look of the lake? Can you not swim?'

Beatrice matched him, glare for glare. She attempted a shrug. ''Tis the truth. Women do not submit to trial by water.'

De Brionne's brows lowered. 'You will,' he stated with dreadful finality. 'You will.'

'Nay!' The rope at her waist was as merciless as de Brionne. It bit into her skin.

'If the water drags you down and you sink, you will be declared innocent. And if you float you are guilty. The water rejects the guilty, of course. It throws them up and will not hold them. 'Tis fitting that you should be tried by water. This wet wasteland holds little else.'

Beatrice suppressed a sob. 'So, if I'm found innocent, I drown. And if not, you put me to death.'

'I see you've understood. 'Twill be held at noon tomorrow.' He laughed. 'We'll have to break the ice on the lake.'

A mud-clot hit Beatrice in the eye and she winced.

'Pray hard, Mistress Beatrice, pray hard. I hope you believe in miracles!'

CHAPTER ELEVEN

THE court was a small one—a single trestle had been set up at the edge of the lake. De Brionne, Father Ralph and Anne sat in the places of honour. Anne's eyes were red and puffed with weeping. Half a dozen guards flanked Beatrice, who was led before them, bound, cloakless, and as hungry and ill-kempt as a beggar. A scribe perched on the edge of a stool, and sharpened his quill as though it were a weapon.

Beatrice lifted her eyes to the pale orb of the sun. It shed no more heat than the moon.

'My lord——' Father Ralph blurted, wringing his hands together.

'Priest?' acknowledged the Baron.

'I know this method of trial is often used...but...but I cannot agree with it.'

De Brionne smiled thinly. He drummed blunt fingers on the board. 'If you are not prepared to do your duty, Priest, pray say so. I will find another cleric. There are doubtless many who would be happy to take your place. And your living,' he added significantly.

'Oh! N-nay, Baron. I-I will stay,' stammered Father Ralph, easily routed. He glanced unhappily at Beatrice, and shook his head. There was nothing he could do. If he refused to sanction the trial he would be replaced. And he knew the sort of man the Baron would recommend in his stead. He must stay and pray he could do something to alleviate the girl's suffering.

'Read the charges, Father,' de Brionne ordered.

Anne clutched a mailed sleeve. 'Please, Baron, unbind my cousin,' she begged. 'What harm can she do with those guards breathing down her neck?'

De Brionne heaved a sigh. He wanted this business over as quickly as possible. He could not risk a riot. The

King had not yet approved his seizing of power, despite the elaborate lies he had spun for the crowd at the fair. If he proved able to keep the peace, King William would surely grant *him* the lands. After that, come what may, but till then...

He looked coldly at the fingers on his arm.

Hastily Anne withdrew her hand. 'Please, Philip——'

'Very well.' De Brionne nodded at his men. 'But I'll stand no more interference from you. Your cousin has assisted the rebels' cause more than once. She will be punished. My ears ring with your wailing and I will hear no more of it. Priest, read the charges.' He twitched a document from the scribe's fingers and thrust it at Father Ralph.

Beatrice massaged her wrists. De Brionne would never forgive her for depriving him of Edmund. He was as set on revenge as were the Saxon warriors. A curious sense of inevitability came over her. It numbed her senses.

Father Ralph began to read aloud. 'Beatrice Giffard, you are accused of treason towards the Norman State.' Beatrice lifted her chin. 'You are to be tried by ordeal on this day, the Twenty-Sixth of January in the First Year of the Reign of King William. The charges are fourfold.

'Firstly, that you did give aid to the outlaw known as Edmund of Lindsey, after that same Edmund of Lindsey did perpetrate an affray causing severe and regrettable loss of life. You did on this occasion render assistance to this outlaw, to the detriment of our Norman peace-keeping soldiers, a number of whom were injured.'

'That's a foul lie!' Beatrice gasped at the blatant falsehood. 'Edmund did not cause the fight! 'Twas you, you barefaced——'

'Silence!' De Brionne's fist struck the table with such force that the scribe's ink-horn bounced in its stand. 'The accused will remain silent while the charges are being read.'

'Secondly,' Father Ralph went on, 'you did conspire with the Saxon, Lady Hilda, then in the custody of Baron

Philip de Brionne, and engineered her escape. You did also give into the hands of the said Lady Hilda sufficient monies from our own treasury to enable the rebel forces to purchase weapons and thus prolong their resistance to the rightful rule of our sovereign, King William, established by trial of arms. Further, you did abscond with the aforementioned outlaw, the so-called Edmund of Lindsey, and did betray to him information regarding Norman fortifications and troop numbers.' The priest paused and glanced uncomfortably at Beatrice.

'Philip, I *must* speak!' Anne sprang to her feet.

'Nay! Cousin, do not,' Beatrice besought her. ''Tis of no use. The outcome has already been decided.'

Anne placed herself squarely before her lover. She went down on one knee in the frozen mud.

'Anne! Nay!'

Anne clasped her hands together at her breasts. 'Baron, do not be angry. 'Twas my fault Beatrice helped Hilda. I could not bear for you to wed that Saxon child. I asked her to help. She did so for me. And she did not run off with the Saxon. He abducted her.'

Beatrice groaned. Now Anne would be called to account...

'And just how do you know all this?' de Brionne asked, dangerously quiet.

'Anne, no more!'

But Anne was set on self-destruction. She looked de Brionne straight in the eye, and finished in a rush. 'I know because I helped her plan Hilda's escape. But we...we didn't know Edmund was out there.'

'You expect me to believe that the Saxon's appearance was coincidental?' the Baron roared. 'Nay, my lady. But to find that *you* have colluded with rebels...?'

Anne quailed visibly.

'Baron, do not believe her!' Beatrice intervened. 'My cousin is lying to try and save me. Forgive her, 'tis only her love for me that makes her speak so.'

'So you admit to plotting Lady Hilda's escape, do you, Mistress Beatrice? And to giving her the treasure casket?' asked de Brionne silkily.

'Aye! On both counts, aye. But the casket was Saxon, not Norman.'

'Spoils of war,' the Norman said abruptly. 'That casket was booty. Spoils of war, my dear, become the property of the victor. Scribe! Have you written down this woman's confession to the second charge?'

The scribe gave a sycophantic nod.

'Beatrice…' Anne climbed to her feet. Her pretty face was pinched with cold and ugly with fear.

'I'm a dead woman, Anne,' Beatrice told her. 'Can't you see it? There's no point in both of us dying. Remember, you're not the stuff martyrs are made of.' She attempted a smile, but knew it was a poor one. Her mouth was dry.

'You're a fool, Beatrice! Noble, but a fool! If you expect me to be able to sit and watch while you…you…' Anne's voice wobbled.

'Begone, then!' de Brionne suggested harshly. 'We can proceed without you.'

'Farewell, cousin,' Beatrice said steadily. 'You'd best go. He's impatient to be done and, frankly, so am I.'

Anne sobbed, stepped forwards and dropped an icy kiss on her cousin's lips. Then she whirled, and, picking up her skirts, ran wailing but without a backward glance up the slope towards the hall.

Beatrice felt her eyes mist over. Lady Anne de Vidâmes was wont to walk slowly, and with dignity. But the figure she was watching stumbled and scrabbled up the hill like a madwoman outrunning the hounds of hell.

A distant church bell tolled. It all seemed unreal. She was on trial for her life.

'The third charge, Priest.' De Brionne poked a mailed elbow at Father Ralph.

'The third charge is that you did collude with a Saxon spy, Morcar, and with his aid did drug and overpower a guard in the conduct of his duty.' Father Ralph licked his lips and gulped. 'And the fourth is that you, Mistress Beatrice, did impede the course of justice by causing a diversion which prevented the arrest of the outlaw

Edmund of Lindsey. There are witnesses to this last charge, Mistress,' the priest said, apologetically.

'How plead you to *these* charges?' de Brionne yawned, his eyes flickering in the direction of the lake.

'What is the point? I am already condemned.'

The Baron shrugged. 'You have recorded that I gave her the opportunity to speak?' he demanded of the scribe.

'Aye, Baron.'

De Brionne kicked back his stool. 'We will proceed with the ordeal. To the lake!'

'B-baron, I know you are not a religious man. You do not believe in this method of judgement,' Father Ralph faltered. 'I fear you are blaspheming. My son, if you seek merely to torture this poor girl, your eternal soul is in danger.'

'This "poor girl" is a self-admitted traitor!' de Brionne declared. 'She does not merit such concern.' He lowered his voice. 'I would hate to think she caused your downfall, too, Priest.'

'Baron, if you are set on this course, I too must beg leave to depart.'

'No stomach for it?' de Brionne jeered, curling his thin lips. 'Very well. Go and calm Lady Anne; I won't stand for any more dirges from her. If she's not amenable by the time I get back she'll regret it.'

Father Ralph turned to Beatrice and formed a shaky cross over her head. 'Bless you, my child. And may the good Lord forgive us *all* for our part in this day's work.' He cast a speaking glance over the handful of guards and backed away.

The guards' eyes were empty—expressionless pits. Two of them took Beatrice by the arms and half lifted, half dragged her to the water's edge.

Her dulled senses jerked awake. She could hear the far-off church bell pealing the angelus and, nearer, the rooks cawing in the copse. But the sounds closest to her were the chink of mail and the dull swishing of her ruined robe as it dragged round her knees. Her breath formed clouds which mingled with those of her judges. She no-

ticed the broken rushes fringing the lake. A duck, startled
by their approach, waddled along on the dark, icy skin
of the mere. It slipped, picked itself up and skated to
the cover offered by the swamp elders about a leafless
alder.

Beatrice drew a steadying breath. The air was fresh
and cool. She wondered why she had never appreciated
the joy of breathing until the moment it was about to
be taken from her.

Then it was very quiet. The rooks had fallen silent.
The only sound was that chiming bell. Beatrice waited
for the Baron to order the ice to be broken. She peered
at the frosted surface of the mere. She'd not last long
in these temperatures. It did not matter that she could
not swim. The shock would probably kill her. How deep
was it? Was it bottomless? Queer, that she should feel
so calm...

She lifted her head, and tilted it to one side. She
frowned. What was that new tinkling noise? And why
had the guards not broken the ice? What were they
waiting for?

Her captors' eyes were not on her. Confused, she followed their gaze. Half a dozen wretched figures were
dragging themselves towards them. Beggars, perhaps?

The figures moved with a stiff, ungainly gait. They all
wore long, filthy brown robes which hung in tatters
around their lumpish bodies. One was exceptionally tall,
and probably male, but it was impossible to tell either
sex or age, for their features were completely concealed
by voluminous cowls.

Beatrice felt her stomach heave and wrinkled her nostrils. Those garments hadn't seen water in years. It was
only the dirt that held them together.

The leader rang his handbell. 'Unclean! Unclean!' he
rasped. A bubble of hysterical laughter rose up in her
throat. The disreputable band moved inexorably towards
the knot of Normans by the lake.

'Lepers, by the Rood!' exclaimed one of the guards.
He crossed himself and started backing up the hill.

'Hold, I say!' the Baron commanded, but he too took a cautious pace backwards.

Beatrice had never before seen the Baron disconcerted. In other circumstances she might have appreciated the sight, but not today. Not on her last day on earth. She wanted to live. The desire to live was overwhelming. It gripped her so strongly that she almost cried aloud.

The lepers' leader brought his hideous crew closer.

'K-keep back,' the guard restraining Beatrice stammered on a rising note. His nerve cracked, he loosed her arm and hared off out of danger.

Beatrice giggled stupidly. 'They cannot hear you. They've probably lost their ears.'

The leper leader pressed on, making no sign that he'd marked either the guard or Beatrice.

Beatrice dug in her heels. Her hazel eyes were dilated with horror. The abominable stench sent her hand to her nose.

Another guard's nerve broke. He marched stiffly towards de Brionne. Beatrice stood alone.

'Stay with her, you idiot!' the Baron ground out, boiling.

Beatrice bit her lip. A desperate idea was taking hold of her mind...

'Not I, Baron,' the man apologised. 'I'd rather face a month in solitary than a lifetime's dose of leprosy.'

De Brionne seethed, but he did not dare approach her either. She was too close to the lepers.

Beatrice forced herself to look at the leper with the handbell. She cleared her throat. 'Take me with you,' she whispered hoarsely. 'Take me with you *now*.'

The leper shot her a swift, furtive glance, as though afraid to meet her eyes. Perhaps lepers never accustomed themselves to seeing revulsion on the faces of their fellow men. Perhaps this one had adopted that shooting glance so as to avoid seeing people turn away in disgust. Beatrice steeled herself. She would not betray her disgust. But the leper's face turned towards her for only a fraction of a second. She glimpsed no more than a face that was obscured by months of muck and grime.

The lepers clustered around her. Their bodies were twisted and grotesque, the smell of putrefaction smothering.

'Take me with you,' Beatrice repeated urgently. 'I am dead if they——' she indicated the impotent Normans '—have their way. The water would kill me. I'd rather go with you and have some small chance at life than stay here and die for sure.' She made her lips form a smile.

'We are the living dead,' the leper replied. His voice betrayed his gender, and was surprisingly pleasant. 'There is no cure for our infection. We are reviled and cursed by all. Outcasts. If you come with us you may never more seek society.'

'Are you out of your mind, woman?' de Brionne bawled.

'Nay. I want to live!' Beatrice cried. The blood pounded in her temples, the numbness left her veins. 'You dare not approach these lepers. I will go with them, and you shall not stop me. You shall *not* rob me of my life.'

'You won't be able to go to your Saxon lover,' the Baron announced. His thin lips twisted. 'He won't want the plague you'll carry if you touch those devils! You may as well be dead!'

'I embrace them willingly.' Giving herself no time for thought, Beatrice flung her arms around the leper leader in a dramatic enactment of her words. A foul stench filled her nostrils, but she didn't flinch. She felt a heavily bandaged stump rest momentarily on her arm and tried not to think what lay beneath the dirt-streaked wrappings.

'I can come with you?' she asked, wriggling away from the contamination of his touch as soon as she was able. She was sure she could feel the infection working on her skin; it tingled where she'd touched him.

The tall leper let out a loud guffaw of raucous male laughter. She glanced sharply at him, but he hung his head and, cloaked by that filthy cowl, she could see nothing of his face.

The leper with the handbell inclined his head. 'Come with us,' he agreed, and rang his bell again. 'Unclean! Unclean!'

One of his feet was heavily swathed in bandages. Had he lost some toes? All of his toes? A fit of trembling shook through Beatrice and she realised that his fate would become hers. She had embraced the living dead.

One of de Brionne's men nocked an arrow. 'Baron, shall I?' he asked.

De Brionne clenched his jaw. Then he smiled. 'Nay. Let her go. She's a dead woman, anyway. Let her die the slow way.'

It was not the miracle she had prayed for, but it was better than no miracle at all. Stumbling as though their disease had already hobbled her, Beatrice went with them. It was the extreme cold which caused her eyes to water. She was not weeping. She was not.

Beatrice awoke very, very slowly, yawning and groaning. She was stiff all over.

'Beatrice, do you feel rested now?' a voice asked softly. It was Edmund's.

Beatrice shot upright, her eyes blank with horror. She was lying in a one-roomed wooden house in a crude box-bed. Edmund sat on a stool beside the bed, smiling at her.

Beatrice put up her hands. 'Don't touch me!' she shrieked, remembering who had brought her to this damned, dead village. She must not infect Edmund.

He directed an enquiring look at her. 'What? May I not help the maid who gave me freedom at the cost of her own?' His blue eyes teased her.

Arming herself to resist his easy charm, Beatrice averted her head. 'I am unclean, Edmund. I-I have been contaminated.' She halted, uncertain how to proceed.

'I know,' Edmund said, and grinned.

She wished he would not look at her like that. 'You don't understand. I escaped de Brionne in the company of a band of lepers. Lepers, Edmund. I—touched them.'

She waved her arm. 'They put me in here. This is one of their huts.' She picked up the edge of her blanket. 'This is theirs. They gave it to me. I must surely be infected. You must not touch me. You must get away from here.'

'Must I?' Edmund asked softly. He leaned towards her, ignoring her strangled cry. 'What if I were to say that I did not care if you were to embrace a thousand lepers?'

Beatrice stared incredulously at him. 'You don't mean that,' she whispered.

He held out his hand.

She batted it away. 'Edmund, don't!'

'You've touched me now,' he laughed.

Beatrice met his teasing blue eyes, a dawning suspicion in her own. Why was he not worried? He smelt strongly of soap. His skin had a freshly scrubbed look about it, his hair shone...

'Edmund——'

But before she could voice her suspicion, his hand was back, tugging at her shoulder. It pulled her to his chest. Beatrice went into his arms on a trembling sigh of relief. She listened to the steady beat of his heart. He was so warm.

'I never thought to be in your arms again,' she confessed shyly.

'Did you not?' His arms tightened round her. His chin rested on the top of her head.

Beatrice pulled back and frowned at him. 'How could you mislead me for so long?' she demanded. 'I was in torment. I thought——'

'I'm sorry, Beatrice,' he apologised. 'We had so little time. When de Brionne took you at the fair, my people held me back. I could do nothing.'

'I saw,' Beatrice said softly. 'They love you.'

Edmund flushed, and pushed his hair back. 'I am English.' He shrugged. ''Tis no more than that.'

Beatrice knew better than to argue. 'What happened then?'

'You have Walter to thank. He went after you,' Edmund informed her. 'He overheard de Brionne planning your ordeal. He's a clever man, that Walter of yours. He managed to make me understand, and——'

'You, taking notice of a Norman?' Beatrice asked, incredulous.

Edmund avoided her eyes. ''Twas so unlikely that a Norman should return unarmed to a Saxon and demand help that I believed him. Morcar added his pleas to Walter's.' Edmund raised a dark brow. 'You have made a conquest there. 'Twas Morcar's bright idea to disguise ourselves as lepers.'

'He must have been the tall one!' Beatrice realised. 'The one who laughed.'

'Aye. For all his skill at deception, 'tis ironic that he should be the one who almost gave us away. He found it amusing that you should choose to embrace me.' Edmund gave her a rueful grin. 'He said that that proved the measure of your love, that you could recognise me through all my filth and rags!'

Beatrice hoped her face was blank. 'But I didn't recognise you,' she said bluntly.

The light went out of Edmund's eyes. 'I know.'

Beatrice caught her breath. She wanted to rekindle that light. 'I am grateful to you for saving me,' she blurted awkwardly.

Edmund stood up. 'I did but return the compliment,' he said, suddenly cool. 'You risked your life for mine at the fair. Why did you do it, Beatrice?' He swung round at her.

'I could not see you die!' Beatrice exploded, jumping to her feet. 'Sweet Jesu! What do you think of me?'

'You're a Norman. And for a Norman to risk her life for an illegitimate Saxon——'

'You fool!' Her voice was sharp. 'I care not which side of the blanket you were born! I never have. 'Tis you who have presumed as much. I know well enough 'tis the quality of the man that matters, not his birth. Being born in wedlock is no guarantee of anything. Look at de Brionne!'

Edmund took a step towards her. His eyes were fastened on the sapphire ring. 'Then you would not in principle object to marrying someone born out of wedlock?'

Beatrice must have imagined the pleading tone in his voice, for when he raised his eyes to her hazel ones they were hard as blue ice. They quelled a frank answer.

'Nay, not in principle,' she said evasively.

Edmund placed a light hand under her chin and turned her face so that it was illumined by a shaft of light from a gap in the roof. 'They hurt you badly,' he observed. A gentle finger traced along the angry red weal. 'They have bruised your beauty.'

''Tis a little painful, but not that bad,' Beatrice lied.

His eyes were on her lips. 'I am afraid to hurt you,' he muttered, and dipped his head in the briefest of kisses.

She swayed towards him, limbs already turning to water, but Edmund held her at arm's length. He released her. If only his eyes had softened . . .

'I'm sorry this accommodation is not what you are used to,' he announced, glancing critically around the dingy room.

Beatrice frowned. ''Tis well enough,' she replied, watching him closely. She had to clench her fists to stop her hands reaching out to him.

He was staring at a gap in the bottom of a wall, where chickens had scratched out a door for themselves. 'You could return to your cousin now you know you are not tainted,' he suggested stiffly.

Beatrice averted her head. A cold ache settled round her heart. He was rejecting her. Her hazel eyes brimmed with tears. 'What? H-how could I? Under Norman law my life is forfeit.' Pride squared her shoulders, and she dashed away the too-betraying tears. 'But if I am un-welcome here I shall remove myself.'

Edmund gave her arm a gentle shake. 'Nay,' he said. 'I did not mean to imply you are not welcome. You are, most welcome. But you must stay here of your own free will. If you do not wish to stay with us, I will escort you wherever you wish to go.'

Beatrice kicked the edge of the box-bed with her toes. 'There is nowhere else I can go.'

'You had plans once for the cloistered life,' Edmund reminded her. Beatrice darted a glance from under her lashes. His face was set. 'Have you given them up?' he asked.

Beatrice stared at him. 'Aye.' She gave a bitter laugh. ''Twas ever my mother's scheme. Never mine. I must find my own way now.'

Edmund let out a breath. A small smile played about his mouth. ''Tis well,' he mumbled. He reached for the door-latch. 'Beatrice, can you trust me for a little while?'

Beatrice put her heart in her eyes. 'Aye.'

He was halfway through the door. He stopped and came back to her. Oddly hesitant, he picked up her hand and stared at the ring. 'I'm glad you still wear it,' he admitted.

Beatrice watched his downbent head. Her throat ached.

Edmund turned her hand and placed a warm kiss in her palm. The tingling sensation ran all the way up her arm. He lifted his eyes. 'This ring has never been given save in the spirit for which it was made,' he whispered, so low that Beatrice could scarcely hear him.

Beatrice opened her mouth to beg an explanation, but Edmund spun on his heel and was at the door before the words were more than half formed.

'I must go,' he said briskly, his shadow darkening the chamber. 'De Brionne has driven us from bad to worse, and I would put an end to this skulking on our own lands. There is a Council meeting, and I must attend it.'

Beatrice curled her fingers over the kiss in her palm.

And Edmund's shadow was gone.

That evening Beatrice was roused by a clatter of hoofs. She stuck her head through the door of the wooden hut. A handful of torches revealed Edmund and Hilda, both mounted, and riding away. Siward was with them. Beatrice hauled her skirts free of the slush and dashed after them.

'Edmund? What's happening? Where are you going?' she demanded.

Edmund wheeled Balder about. Beatrice heard him swear. She winced and skidded to a halt. A large be-ringed hand fell on her shoulders, anchoring her where she stood.

'Let him go easy, my lady,' Morcar advised. ''Tis for the best.'

Edmund and Morcar exchanged glances. The hand on her shoulder felt like a lead weight. Balder tossed his head and sidled away from Morcar's flaring torch.

'Edmund?' Beatrice swallowed.

'Morcar has his instructions,' Edmund said. His lips curved into a smile, but it seemed to Beatrice to be a poor imitation of the smile she loved. He lifted a gloved hand and blew her a casual kiss. ''Till we meet again, Beatrice.' His heel skimmed Balder's shining flanks, and Balder sprang into the darkness.

The weight lifted from her shoulder.

'Morcar? Where has he gone?'

Morcar gave her a direct look. 'My lady, I cannot say. We must both be patient. Come back inside, 'tis warmer there. I'm to keep you safe, not see you catch your death.'

The days passed uneasily. Morcar was steadfast in his refusal to tell Beatrice where Edmund had gone. All he would say was that he had promised to guard her. Rather wildly, Beatrice wondered whether Morcar was guarding her from his countrymen or her own.

Walter appeared, and took it upon himself to care for her needs. He kept a warm fire going for her. He snared a mallard and roasted it for her. He stuffed rags in the cracks in the wall, and kept out the shrieking wind. He mended the roof, and swept the snow from the door.

Beatrice found Walter's silent presence comforting. She had plenty of time and no interruptions. She could try and untangle the mess in her mind.

She thought about Edmund.

In one sense, Beatrice was glad that Edmund did not return immediately. Events had moved so quickly that her mind had not had time to catch up with them. She felt strangely out of step with the world, and needed to sort it all out. Edmund had asked her to trust him. And she did, she trusted him as well as any. But what trust did he have in her, that he should skulk off without so much as a word? Where had he gone? What was he doing? If he trusted her, surely he would have confided in her?

Two long weeks passed. Her bruises faded. Then, one day, when the snow was as crisp and white as a newly washed fleece, Beatrice heard the jingling of harness and the muffled stamping of horse's hoofs, and knew at once the waiting was over.

She went to the door of her hut, looked out and the bottom dropped out of her world. Edmund was astride his chestnut roan *amid a score of Norman horse-soldiers*. Hilda rode alongside him, wearing what looked like a grey sack instead of her gown. Siward's horse had been hemmed in by two Norman knights.

Beatrice knew she blenched. Edmund looked haggard. His face was grey with fatigue, his clothes crumpled and travel-stained. His hand eased his wounded shoulder. He'd ridden too far, too soon. And now he was a prisoner.

Beatrice whirled. Where was Morcar? Where were the Saxon warriors? She could not believe that they should abandon Edmund so lightly.

Before she could utter a word, a middle-aged man dismounted from a charger more awesome than de Brionne's, and addressed her in French. 'You must be the Lady Beatrice,' he said, removing his helmet.

Beatrice could only gape and nod. The Norman had cropped grey hair, and his armour all looked new. This was no raw recruit, though; he bore himself so proudly that he must be the knights' commander. The man kissed Beatrice clumsily on both cheeks. It flashed through her mind that he was unused to the company of women.

'I recognise you from Edmund of Lindsey's description,' the grizzled man told her. 'But had he not described you, I think I still would have known you, for you are very like your mother.'

'I—I don't understand,' Beatrice stuttered, anxiously pleating her gown into little folds. 'Who are you? Have you arrested Edmund? You won't kill him, will you?'

'Peace, wench, peace,' the grizzled man growled. 'I am Geoffrey de Vidâmes——'

'The Comte de Vidâmes!' exclaimed Beatrice, her brow clearing. This man was the uncle she had never met, and father to Lady Anne.

'The same.' The Comte bowed. 'Lord Edmund has not been arrested; he——'

'Thank God!' Beatrice breathed, and her eyes flew to Edmund's. His gaze was bright, but guarded. With a start she noticed that he still had his sword. So did Siward. Panic had blinded her; she should have realised . . .

'Lindsey has given his oath of fealty to the King,' Geoffrey de Vidâmes said. 'He is now the King's loyal servant.'

Edmund swung down from Balder. 'You've been to plead with the King!' Beatrice cried.

'I could not tell you where he had gone,' Morcar muttered in her ear. 'He made me promise not to tell you, in case it should not go well with him.'

Beatrice allowed relief to creep into her expression. She felt it too strongly to hide it. 'The Comte called you *Lord* Edmund?' she probed.

Edmund had his arm draped around his sister. 'My sister's wish has been granted.' He smiled. 'She has signed her inheritance over to me. In return for my oath of fealty and that of my men, King William has decreed that I shall now hold the title of my father. I am now the rightful Thegn of Lindsey.'

The Comte nodded. 'Just so, just so,' he agreed.

Beatrice indicated the mounted soldiers. 'Then why have you brought all these knights with you, my uncle? They are yours, aren't they? What are they here for?'

'Questions, questions, questions,' grumbled the Comte. 'You women are all the same. Damned curiosity

never satisfied. They *are* my men. and I am to accompany my Lord of Lindsey to his home to acquaint
Baron Philip de Brionne with the King's wishes.'

'Oh, no! There will be more fighting,' Beatrice protested, her eyes flying to Edmund.

'Not if I can help it,' Edmund declared flatly. 'There
have been enough good men lost in this conflict.' He
flexed his shoulder and grimaced wryly. ''Tis time to
heal the wounds and start afresh. Your Norman blood
should unite with ours.'

'Quite right, my boy. Quite right,' the Comte approved. 'I can see why William was so taken with you.
We need reasonable Saxon men like you to fight with
us, not against us. Your Lindsey militia will be a valuable
asset. Every man has his part.' He caught Beatrice's eye.
'And every woman,' he added. This last phrase was
spoken with less conviction than the rest, as if the Comte
had his doubts about it.

Beatrice bit back a smile. She would not insult her
new-found uncle by appearing to mock at his gruff,
soldierly manners. But she could not let his comment
pass.

'Oh. We women have our part to play, do we, Uncle?'
she asked sweetly. 'And pray tell me, what is mine to
be?'

Edmund groaned, and buried a disgusted face in
Balder's mane.

The Comte patted her on the cheek and waded blithely
into the quagmire. 'Your part is simple, my dear. You
will wed this Saxon Thegn and give him children. You
are the King's gift to the new and loyal Thegn of Lindsey.'

Beatrice choked. All amusement fled. Her face was
stiff with embarrassment. She could not look at Edmund,
and thus missed the step he took towards her. She stared
unhappily at the ground.

'What, girl! Are you not pleased?' the Comte snapped
irritably. 'Say so now, for the King has charged me to
ensure that you are a willing bride. Why the King doesn't
command you to wed and have done, I'll never know.
Maybe 'tis because you come from the Abbaye aux

Dames. 'Twas endowed by his wife, and perhaps he would not deprive it of an incumbent.'

The Comte might have been adept with a sword, but he had no understanding of women. His bluff features radiated resentment at the indignity that the King had forced upon him—the indignity of having to consult a woman. He was dead to all finer feelings.

'Well?' the Comte prompted gruffly.

Beatrice shrivelled up inside. Not in front of all these people, she thought.

'Speak up, niece. Are you content to do the King's will in this matter?'

'Aye,' Beatrice whispered to her shoes.

'Eh?'

'Aye!' Hazel eyes spat sparks. 'I am content.' Beatrice braced herself and glanced at Edmund. He offered her his hand, but his smile was strained and forced. There were shadows under his eyes.

Formally, Beatrice put her fingers on Edmund's. His felt like icicles.

Her uncle heaved a noisy sigh of relief. 'Good girl!' He beamed. The King would not regret having sent Geoffrey de Vidâmes on his business.

Suddenly the Comte noticed what a comely little wench his niece was. And she was sensible, too—at least, as far as could be expected in a woman. He clouted Beatrice on the shoulders so hard that she staggered. Edmund slipped a strong arm round her and pulled her close.

'I knew you wouldn't disgrace the family,' the Comte declared with avuncular pride. 'Bred to duty, eh?' He winked at Edmund. 'She'll breed well, my boy. No need to worry on that score. Fine warriors, I'll be bound. And——'

'Aye, I'm sure,' Edmund cut in brusquely. 'Come on, Vidâmes, some food. We have no wine to offer you, I fear. Not till we reach Lindsey.'

Beatrice shut her eyes to close out the sight of her uncle's coarse face and Edmund's rigid one. She'd never felt more mortified. She wished the earth could swallow her up. She realised she had Edmund's hand in a death-grip and relaxed her hold. But his fingers tightened on hers, and she felt his thumb stroke the back of her hand in a soothing, sympathetic gesture that somehow managed to take her away from the staring folk around them and ease her discomfiture. As the troop broke up and led away the horses, Beatrice leaned towards Edmund till they stood thigh to thigh. She pointed her nose at the sky and ignored her uncle's grinning men-at-arms. She even managed to smile.

CHAPTER TWELVE

GEOFFREY DE VIDÂMES had made the one concession of his life to womankind. Now he insisted that Beatrice should be put back in her proper place. Over refreshments it was agreed that the Comte de Vidâmes and the Thegn of Lindsey could ride on to meet de Brionne, but Beatrice must stay back with the Saxon womenfolk, and could follow only when all was resolved.

It did not take long. Beatrice hardly had time to wonder how her cousin was, and what her uncle had planned for de Brionne, when Morcar came galloping up the track amid a flurry of snow. He had Betony on a leading rein.

'Come, my lady.' Morcar flung his huge bulk from the saddle. 'You are expected. And you too, Lady Hilda.'

'Already?' Beatrice grabbed her cloak. 'What about de Brionne? I can't see him surrendering peacefully.'

Morcar grinned. 'It seems your Norman King has other plans for him.' He led Betony to a handy barrel that was used as a mounting-block, and Beatrice climbed into the saddle. 'He's being sent north. They're a stubborn breed up there, and apparently they're refusing to bow to the inevitable. De Brionne is being sent to help them see wisdom.'

'I pity them,' Beatrice said.

'Aye,' agreed Morcar soberly. 'I can think of few worse fates than having de Brionne set over you. Come, my ladies, we're to hurry.'

It was strange to see the settlement at Lindsey again. There was the little stone chapel, the hall and . . .

'Anne! Anne!' Beatrice exclaimed, catching sight of her cousin emerging from the hall.

'God's teeth! 'Tis Beatrice!' Anne picked up heavily embroidered skirts and sailed over. 'I thought never to see you again. Where in heaven's name have you been?' She looked well.

Beatrice dismounted, and made as if to embrace her cousin, but Anne drew back sharply. 'Anne?' Beatrice frowned.

Anne shrugged prettily, her eyes were dancing. 'Ah, Beatrice, reassure me. There was some talk of lepers, and I am attached to all of my fingers...'

Beatrice grinned. Anne grinned back. 'At least your barbarian keeps you well robed.' Anne grimaced in Hilda's direction. 'Look at what Hilda's come back with. Don't tell me the poor girl's been to Court in *that*.'

Beatrice smiled at Hilda. She had to admit that Hilda's gown left much to be desired.

''Tis not a gown,' Hilda explained, clambering from her pony. ''Tis the habit of a novice.'

Beatrice stared, for the first time seeing the ornate silver cross Hilda now wore.

'Aye. I'll be joining my mother at the Priory.' Hilda smiled.

Anne shook her head. 'Convents,' she said with a shudder. 'They're the same the world over. I don't know how they do it. They must weave them from pig bristles. And as for the colour...' Anne broke off and blushed. 'I'm sorry, Hilda, but I'd earmark that stuff for burning, not wear it!'

Beatrice laughed aloud. 'Oh, Anne! I'm glad you're yourself again. Do you never stop thinking about clothes?'

'Hardly ever,' Anne admitted wryly. ''Tis better than worrying.' She linked one arm with Beatrice, offered the Saxon girl the other, and drew them both towards the shelter of the hall. Her expression became earnest. 'Beatrice, my father is here.'

'I know, Anne.'

'De Brionne's being sent to the north, and I'm to accompany my father to Court.'

Beatrice searched her cousin's face. 'Do you mind?'

Anne pushed at the hall door and waved Beatrice through first. 'The fire's built high for you,' she said evasively. 'Are you thirsty? Edmund will be here soon; he——'

'Anne! Answer me! Do you mind?' Beatrice caught Anne's arm and forced her cousin to meet her eyes.

'I—I—oh, Beatrice, I don't know. I'm not sorry to go to Court, if that's what you mean.'

'And de Brionne? What of him?' Beatrice pressed.

Anne's head drooped. 'He no longer holds my affections,' she admitted quietly. 'How could he, after what he tried to do to you? He changed, Beatrice. The man who was so kind to me in Normandy no longer exists. I wonder now if he ever did. Maybe I created him out of my need.' Anne looked at Beatrice. 'I mourn for what I have lost, but sometimes I wonder whether I mourn for a dream. Let him go up north. I care not. I'll go to Court, and I'll have silks and satins and——'

Beatrice pressed Anne's arm. 'Oh, Anne——'

'I'll love it,' Anne declared fiercely. 'I will, just you see.'

The hall door flew open. Geoffrey de Vidâmes and Edmund of Lindsey stalked through it.

Beatrice felt her heart lurch. Edmund looked better. His face no longer had that ashen pallor. He was wearing his blue tunic and hose. His sword swung at his hip and a new dagger was stuck into his belt. He seemed taller and stronger and rather remote.

'My lady.' Edmund took her hand, and kissed it, and did not release it.

'We'll have the wedding now,' Comte Geoffrey announced, without preamble.

'N-now?' Beatrice stammered. Edmund's fingers stiffened on hers.

'Aye. My daughter and I are leaving at first light, and I'll see this matter through before we go,' said the Comte.

'How touching,' grated a cynical voice.

'De Brionne!' Beatrice gasped, suddenly cold. She felt Edmund's hand slide warm and reassuring round her waist.

'My lady.' De Brionne acknowledged her with an insolent bow. 'I hear congratulations are in order. You have done well, have you not? Quite a step up for you.'

'De Brionne!' Edmund warned.

'Tsk, tsk, tsk. Still the hothead, my lord?' de Brionne needled. 'Try to remember you're not a rebel now. You put your lands at risk——'

'Enough!' barked Comte Geoffrey. 'De Brionne, you exceed yourself. You've been warned. Now, for this wedding——'

'My lord,' Edmund put in stiffly, 'I would not have my lady rushed.'

De Brionne let out a snort. 'The King has given her to you, man,' the Baron said. 'She's yours for the taking!'

'Nevertheless, I would speak with her privately,' Edmund declared coolly.

Comte Geoffrey's eyes were round with a mixture of astonishment and impatience. 'Let me give you some advice, my boy,' he said, drawing Edmund aside.

Beatrice saw Edmund shoot her a glance of pure despair. He flung off the Comte's arm. 'Nay, my lord, I will have my way on this,' he insisted, darkening with anger.

Comte Geoffrey's face hardened. He snatched at his sword. Edmund's hand mirrored the Comte's.

'Uncle!' Beatrice burst out. ''Tis as I have said. I am content. Let the wedding take place.'

Edmund made a gesture towards her. 'Beatrice? You're certain this is what you want?'

Beatrice went over to him, and peeled his long fingers from the hilt of his sword. 'Quite certain,' she said, and smiled into his eyes.

She was married. She, Beatrice Giffard, was wife of Edmund, Thegn of Lindsey.

Beatrice sat on the wooden stool in the upper chamber she had shared with Anne, and fixed her eyes on the tapestry door-curtain. She chewed her lips. She was waiting for Edmund, for her husband. Sounds of revelry still drifted up from the hall. At least his Saxon warriors were not so set against her that they could not celebrate the wedding of their lord.

Beatrice shifted on the hard stool. Several butterflies fluttered and danced inside her. Why was he taking so long? She glanced at the candle-clock jammed on its pricket by the bed. It was well past midnight. Jumping up, she flung back the window shutter and looked out.

A giant hand had snuffed out the stars. The moon was out, too. There was nothing to see but darkness. Nothing out there to distract her, to stop her worrying...

Beatrice had been glad of Anne's company at the wedding ceremony and feast afterwards. It was not that Edmund had mistreated her. On the contrary, he had been most polite, most attentive. But his blue eyes had been cold—she'd not even seen a flicker of that warm, teasing light. He was remote, detached, very much the lord of his people, and Beatrice began to wonder if she, like Anne, had been deluding herself.

She slammed the shutter and dropped the wooden bolt in place. She eyed the bed. Perhaps if she pleased him he would learn to love her? A sigh escaped her. There was no doubt that an attraction flared between them. But Beatrice had little idea of what was expected of her. She remembered the strictures she had read about the duties of a wife. It was not ladylike to enjoy what went on between husband and wife. Only whores enjoyed *that*. It was her duty to produce an heir for Edmund. That was why he had wed her.

Beatrice perched on the edge of the stool, and twisted her hands together. He had wed her because the King had given her to him. She scowled. Damn the King for making her part of his terms. She did not want to be forced on anyone. Now if Edmund had *chosen* her... if he had truly wanted her...

Beatrice heard a light footstep from the gallery outside. Her throat went dry, and she gulped. She had begun to think that he had changed his mind about sleeping with her, and had gone elsewhere. He'd led her up here from the feast hours ago, or so it seemed. He had murmured something about fetching some wine. And he'd been so long about it that she'd thought...

Edmund ducked through the curtain, holding a drinking horn in each hand. His eyes glittered in the torchlight.

'Here. Drink this. I mulled it myself,' he said.

'My thanks,' Beatrice replied faintly, avoiding his fingers as she took the vessel from him. Her whole body was tight as an overstrung lyre. She sipped at her drink, and lowered her eyes.

'Don't you like it?' Edmund asked, dropping to his knees before the stool, so that their faces were level.

'What?' She started.

Long fingers touched her cup. 'The wine. Did I mix it to your liking?' His fingers strayed on to hers. They felt warm. Hers were cold.

'Thank you, my lord. I do like it. It reminds me of the drink that Anne brought me on St Agnes' Eve.'

Edmund gave a soft laugh. 'You called me Edmund before we were wed. Why so formal now?'

'I-I'm nervous,' she admitted, white teeth worrying her lips.

His eyes were very penetrating. Edmund lifted a hand and brushed her cheek, light as thistledown. He sighed, let his hand fall and stood up, moving abruptly into the shadows.

'I will do nothing you do not wish,' he said harshly out of the gloom. 'I do not frighten women, and I'm not going to start with my own wife.' He yawned and stretched. 'Let's to bed. You are safe with me. You told me that once, remember?'

'I remember,' Beatrice answered softly.

Edmund walked round the bed and sat down, easing his finely embroidered wedding tunic over his head. He kept his back to Beatrice and began to unwind the thongs binding his trousers, unaware of her scrutiny. The flickering light gleamed on well-muscled arms and back. She looked at the white bandage which crossed over his right shoulder. The last time she had seen him without his tunic he had been helpless in her arms in the sanctuary of the chapel. Despite that bandage, he did not look so helpless now.

The butterflies were back in her stomach. She found it hard to breathe. Her fingers itched to touch him. She wanted to feel the slender strength of his body under her hands. She wanted to kiss him and to tell him that she loved him. She wanted him to hold her. She wanted to hear him say that he loved her, too.

She remembered his wound. She set her wine aside. 'Edmund?'

'Aye.'

'When was your wound looked at?'

He continued his unwinding. 'Yesterday...the day before...I cannot rightly remember.'

'Let me see it.' Beatrice said.

''Tis well enough.'

'That may be,' Beatrice answered steadily, and climbed on to the bed, 'but I would see for myself.'

Edmund sent her a sharp look. He put his hands behind his neck and obediently stretched out his long length on the covers.

'Do your worst,' he grinned.

Her heart beating like a drum, Beatrice gently drew the wrappings aside. She could feel Edmund's gaze burning into her. He flustered her. 'Thank God these rags are cleaner than your leper's ones,' she said, to cover her discomfiture.

Edmund was watching her lips. His eyes lifted. They were very dark. They seemed to smoulder.

'Well?' he demanded huskily. 'Will I live?'

Beatrice nodded. 'Aye,' she managed. ''Tis healing cleanly.' All thumbs, she replaced the bandage. She turned to roll off the bed.

'Beatrice, stay.' Edmund caught at her arm.

She froze. He hand slid down her arm and he curled his fingers round hers. Her stomach tightened.

'Won't you tell me what the matter is?' he asked.

'M-matter?'

'Aye. Do you regret marrying me, after all?'

'N-nay. I've told you already——'

Edmund expelled a breath. 'I know, and before so many witnesses. Believe me, Beatrice, I would have had it otherwise, but circumstances——'

'I know.' Beatrice looked away. ''Tis not that.'

Edmund reached to cup her chin with his hand and brought her face back. 'What, then?'

'I—I did not want to be the King's gift.'

Edmund stared. His hand dropped. 'I see,' he said in a cold, hard voice.

'Nay, you misunderstand,' Beatrice blurted. 'Allow me my pride, too.'

'Pride?' Edmund frowned.

'I wanted—hoped that you would want me, too. I did not want the King to make me a condition of your regaining your father's lands.'

Edmund's brow cleared. 'Is that all?'

Beatrice gave a strained laugh. 'All? 'Tis no small thing in my mind.'

He took her chin again, and made her meet his gaze.

'Beatrice, I went to the King...for you,' he said simply.

'What?'

'You heard. I went to the King for you.'

'You went for your lands—for your people and your lands.'

Edmund shook his head. 'Not entirely. I also went for you,' he whispered, very low, and his fingers were at the back of her neck, caressing, warming...

'B-but Edmund, I don't understand.'

Edmund smiled. 'Neither do I,' he admitted wryly. 'Our races were at war, my people driven from their lands, and all I could think about was a little maid with bright hazel eyes.' He paused. 'The King would have had me wed with Anne.'

'Anne is an heiress,' Beatrice told him.

'I know.'

'I have nothing.'

'*You* are all I want. God's Blood, woman! I paid your King good Saxon gold to get you. My father's treasure.'

'You mean you bought me?' Beatrice cried in disgust.

Edmund ran his hands through his hair. 'Dear God! Must you twist *everything* I say? Your King is little more than a mercenary. Gold speaks to him in a way that little else can. The gold I gave him bought me freedom of choice. As his liege-man I could not wed without his approval. The gold did not buy you, it gave me leave to ask you for your hand.'

He grasped her by the shoulders and his eyes burned with a fierce light. He shook her. 'Beatrice, I will be denied no longer. I want you so much. And you are my wife...'

A flush scorched her cheeks. Beatrice swallowed. 'You have made a poor bargain, I fear. I should have brought you something. I have no lands, no dowry.'

'Be quiet,' Edmund ordered, and reached for the circlet which kept her filmy veil in place.

'Wh-what are you doing?' she stuttered.

A light kiss fell on her lips. The look in Edmund's eyes made her protestations dissolve along with her bones. 'I need you, Beatrice,' he told her. 'No more words. 'Tis time I showed you what I feel. Your wedding veil, beautiful though it is, has no place in our bed.' Deft fingers moved on her hair, and veil and circlet were cast to the floor.

'Edmund, 'twill be crumpled,' Beatrice said feebly.

He grinned. 'I care not. Now your hair.'

He pulled her plait over her shoulder. His face was very close to hers. He was concentrating on untying the ribbons. Beatrice let her eyes wander over his face, noting the way his hair grew back from his temples, the long line of his nose, the curve of his mouth. He was right, the words could wait. After all, what matter that he had not said he loved her? He was her husband, and she loved him...

His fingers fumbled at the silken bows.

'Let me,' she said, catching his hand.

The ribbons followed the veil to the floor. He loosed her hair with unsteady fingers and spread it about her shoulders.

Edmund paused, a question in his eyes, and Beatrice opened her arms to him. 'You're shaking, too,' he said, softly, and gathered her close.

'Aye.' Shyly, Beatrice ran her hand over his naked shoulder. She felt his muscles flex and tense. She cleared her throat. 'Edmund?'

'Mmm?' He pressed his lips to her neck.

'I'm not sure I feel safe with you any more,' she confessed, her hand straying through his dark hair. The skin on his neck was soft and warm. She liked the feel of it beneath her fingers.

His mouth lifted from her neck. His breathing had become ragged. 'Do you want to feel safe?' he asked.

Beatrice smiled. She could not trust her voice, so she shook her head.

'Thank God for that.' His voice was rough. He buried his head in the mass of her hair and inhaled its fragrance. 'Lavender,' he murmured.

He rolled on to his back and pulled her down so that she fell half across him. One of her legs tangled, deliciously excitingly, with his. He smiled. His eyes glowed in the flaring yellow light. 'Kiss me, Beatrice,' he commanded.

Gently, Beatrice touched a lean cheek. Her hair flowed, red tongues of fire, over his chest and white bandage. Shyly she dipped her head. Their lips met, clung for a moment, and when she would have lifted away Edmund held her head in place and would not free her.

The kiss went wild. Her lips softened, parted for him. Gold fire ran along her veins. He'd set her alight. Every inch of her tingled where she touched him. His mouth moved under hers, warm and tender. She pressed closer. She could feel the warmth of his chest through her gown and it made her breasts ache. Even the leg that was still half over him tingled too. Beatrice groaned and, soft and malleable as melting wax, she sagged against him.

Edmund ran a hand lightly down the length of her body. A *frisson* of delight rippled through her.

'How do you do that?' she gasped.

He tilted his head and smiled his heart-stopping smile.
'Natural charm.' A wicked light gleamed in his eyes.
'Many's the maid who...'

'Why, you conceited ass!' Beatrice pulled back and
raised a clenched fist.

Edmund deflected the blow. 'Careful, love,' he reminded her. 'I'm not quite mended.'

Beatrice stared aghast at the snowy bandage.
'Oh ... I'm sorry——'

'So you should be. 'Tis a terrible thing to strike a
wounded man,' he declared, shaking his tousled head.
His expression changed. It tugged at her heart, disarmed
her. He shifted in the bed, and put a strong arm round
her waist. 'Come here, woman.'

Hazel eyes fixed wide on his, Beatrice moved into his
arms. Edmund's long fingers stroked every inch of her
face, then moved down to her neck, leaving a trail of
fire. He kissed her mouth. He groaned, and his hand
continued its gentle exploration, moving to her shoulders,
her breasts.

Beatrice tried to keep her breathing even, but could
not. She tried to stop herself from clinging to him like
a drowning woman, but that, too, was impossible. Her
arms looped round his neck. Her fingers dived into his
raven locks; they clung to him, ran over his back. She
was suffocated, drowning in a sea of longing. She had
never realised how much desire was like hunger.

Then Edmund's dark head was at her breast, kissing
her through her gown. Faint with longing, Beatrice held
him close. Her arms did not seem to belong to her any
more. Edmund lifted his head. He smiled again, that
rare, heart-stopping smile.

Beatrice did not protest when his fingers found the
fastenings of her gown. She could not have spoken if
she'd tried. As if in a dream she watched her gown float
through the air and land on the discarded veil and
ribbons.

Edmund's sharply indrawn breath woke her to reality,
and she realised with a shock that his eyes were on her
naked body. Her hands became her own again, and she

snatched a blanket over her. She burned from head to toe.

Edmund put warm hands on hers. 'You are so beautiful, Beatrice. Let me look on you.' He bent to bury his face in the hair which swirled at her neck, his lips seeking the skin beneath. He brushed hands and covering aside. He raised his head. Beatrice gave an inarticulate murmur and tried to hide her flushed face. But he would not have it. Long fingers kept her head towards him. 'Look at me, my love,' he said.

His eyes were dark with desire, full of undisguised longing. They were irresistible.

A slender hand came up and her fingers brushed shyly across his mouth. 'Edmund,' she whispered.

He planted a kiss in the palm of her hand, and sought her lips. Beatrice gasped. The kiss heated every fibre of her being. Her fingers wound into his hair and she felt him tugging impatiently at his remaining clothing. She couldn't breathe. She shut her eyes and buried her head in his neck.

He was naked. She could feel him, all of him, next to her. She could feel his legs, lithe and well-muscled, could tell how much he desired her. Her stomach tightened. She went rigid with apprehension.

Edmund prised himself free. 'Beatrice?'

She gave an inarticulate murmur. When it was done, she'd be able to talk again, but not till then.

She heard a sigh and felt Edmund cover them both with the furs.

'Beatrice? You are a liar,' he accused.

Beatrice opened her eyes.

His expression was tender. He cupped her face with his hands. 'You said you did not fear me——'

'I don't.'

'Then why have you turned to wood in my arms? Relax. I will be gentle,' he promised. 'Beatrice, please...help me make this good for you.' Blue eyes smiled deep into hers.

'I love you, Edmund.' She went, unhesitating, into his embrace. She felt Edmund's long body move over hers, heard his low groan of desire.

'Oh, my sweet, sweet girl,' he muttered in her ear. His legs nudged hers apart. Edmund raised himself over her. He was so far away. She wanted him close. She caught at his waist.

'I'll be gentle, and you'll see——' he said, lowering his hips between her thighs '—next time...next time...it will not hurt at all...'

They were watching each other's faces as he entered her. Beatrice saw the yearning in his eyes, the flare of passion, barely held down. She winced at the burning sensation low in her belly. It felt strange to have him inside her. But that was all.

Edmund waited so that her body had time to accustom itself to him. Her hazel eyes were wide and startled, filled with surprise, not pain. She kissed his shoulder and smiled at him. He wanted to move...

He found her lips. They were soft and welcoming. One of her arms was round his neck, the other tight about his waist.

Edmund moved.

The torch had gone out. One last candle flickered low in the wall sconce by the bed. Beatrice sighed, nestled safe in strong arms. 'I didn't know it would be like that,' she admitted sleepily.

'Mmm?'

'Wonderful. Like magic. Did you find it so?' Hazel eyes scanned his face, his dark ruffled hair.

'Mmm.' Edmund kissed her brow, his arms tightened on her and a smile curved the finely chiselled lips. His eyes were closed.

'Edmund?'

'Mmm?'

'There's something missing,' she murmured softly. ''Tis not enough.'

He gave no sign that he'd heard her. Beatrice took a deep breath and raised her voice. 'Edmund, when—when you abducted me—would you really have ransomed me?'

He lifted his eyelids, suddenly fully awake. 'What? What did you say?' he demanded sharply.

'Would—would you have ransomed me?'

'Nay,' Edmund said, a smile hovering at the edge of his mouth. ''Twas never my intention to ransom you. You know that.'

'Do I?' she persisted. 'Edmund, why did you carry me off?'

Edmund rubbed his face. His fingers sought for her sapphire ring. He wiggled it and grinned at her. 'I could not resist your beauty,' he said flippantly. 'You have this to prove it.'

Beatrice sat up, tossed her hair back over her shoulders, and pulled the ring from her finger. 'Tell me what it says.'

'For the love of God, Beatrice. Let us sleep now,' he groaned.

But Beatrice glimpsed that wicked light in his eyes. 'Tell me,' she insisted.

Edmund's lips twitched. He took the ring from her and made as if to peer at the inscription. 'Alas! The light is so poor, I cannot make it out.'

'Edmund...'

He heaved an exaggerated sigh. ''Tis simple enough. It says "To my beloved".'

Her heart began to sing. She kissed his chest.

''Tis one of two,' Edmund went on. 'My father had them made. One—this one—he gave to my mother. The other was fashioned with garnets. He gave that one to his wife.'

'But—but——' Beatrice objected '—sapphires have greater value than garnets.'

'Ah. You mean 'tis a strange thing to give the cheaper ring to a wife?' Edmund said.

'Aye.'

'My father loved my mother. He would have married her if he could. But a marriage had been arranged with the Lady Judith. It had to be honoured.'

'Was there an inscription inside Lady Judith's ring?' Beatrice wondered.

'Aye. ''To my betrothed'',' he informed her.

'You have both rings?' Beatrice asked.

'I do.'

Beatrice sighed happily. 'And you gave me this one.'

Edmund nodded. His blue eyes were very warm. 'Aye. At last you begin to comprehend. Put it on again, my love, or you'll lose it in the bedclothes.'

'You...you *do* love me,' Beatrice stammered, and her eyes shone.

'Aye,' Edmund agreed softly. 'I did from the first.'

'Truly?'

He laughed and nodded. 'Though why I should fall for a Norman...' His voice deepened, his lips sought hers.

Beatrice ran her hand down his back, delighting in the shudder of desire she loosed through his body. She was weak again, weak with longing.

'Barbarian,' she murmured lovingly against his mouth, and pulled him close.

DESPERADO – Helen Conrad   £2.75

In this fast-paced and compelling novel, jewel thief and embezzler, Michael Drayton, has a five thousand dollar price on his head. With Jessie MacAllister after the reward and hot on his trail, the Desperado turns on his devasting charm, leaving her with one key dilemma... how to turn him in!

ONCE AND FOR ALWAYS
Stella Cameron   £2.99

The magic and beauty of Wales and the picturesque fishing village, Tenby, form the backdrop to Stella Cameron's latest poignant novel. Caitlin McBride's past reads like a fairytale, and returning to Tenby seems to offer the only escape from a dead marriage and hellish family life. But would the spell still exist – and would she find the love she had once left behind?

Published: DECEMBER 1989

W●RLDWIDE

Available from Boots, Martins,
John Menzies, W.H. Smith, Woolworths
and other paperback stockists.

2 NEW TITLES FOR JANUARY 1990

Mariah *by Sandra Canfield is the first novel in a sensational quartet of sisters in search of love… Mariah's sensual and provocative behaviour contrasts enigmatically with her innocent and naive appearance… Only the maverick preacher can recognise her true character and show her the way to independence and true love.*

£2.99

Faye is determined to make a success of the farm she has inherited – but she hadn't accounted for the bitter battle with neighbour, Seth Carradine, who was after the land himself. In desperation she turns to him for help, and an interesting bargain is struck. **Kentucky Woman** by Casey Douglas, best-selling author of Season of Enchantment. **£2.99**

W●RLDWIDE

TASTY FOOD COMPETITION!

How would you like a years supply of Mills & Boon Romances ABSOLUTELY FREE? Well, you can win them! All you have to do is complete the word puzzle below and send it in to us by March. 31st. 1990. The first 5 correct entries picked out of the bag after that date will win **a years supply of Mills & Boon Romances** (*ten books every month - worth £162*) What could be easier?

```
H O L L A N D A I S E R
E Y E G G O W H A O H A
R S E E C L A I R U C T
B T K K A E T S I F I A
E E T I S M A L C F U T
U R C M T L H E E L Q O
G S I U T F O N O E D U
N H L S O T O N E F M I
I S R S O M A C W A A L
R I A E E T I R J A E L
E F G L L P T O T V R E
M O U S S E E O D O C P
```

CLAM	HOLLANDAISE	OYSTERS	SPICE
COD	JAM	PRAWN	STEAK
CREAM	LEEK	QUICHE	TART
ECLAIR	LEMON	RATATOUILLE	
EGG	MELON	RICE	
FISH	MERINGUE	RISOTTO	**PLEASE TURN**
GARLIC	MOUSSE	SALT	**OVER FOR**
HERB	MUSSELS	SOUFFLE	**DETAILS**
			ON HOW
			TO ENTER

HOW TO ENTER

All the words listed overleaf, below the word puzzle, are hidden in the grid. You can find them by reading the letters forward, backwards, up or down, or diagonally. When you find a word, circle it or put a line through it, the remaining letters (which you can read from left to right, from the top of the puzzle through to the bottom) will ask a romantic question.

After you have filled in all the words, don't forget to fill in your name and address in the space provided and pop this page in an envelope (you don't need a stamp) and post it today. Hurry - competition ends March 31st 1990.

Mills & Boon Competition,
FREEPOST,
P.O. Box 236,
Croydon,
Surrey. CR9 9EL

Only one entry per household

Hidden Question _____

_____

Name _____

Address _____

_____

_____

_____ Postcode _____

You may be mailed with other offers as a result of this application.

COMP 8